nickelodeon

GARFIELD

Full Course

BY JIM DAVIS

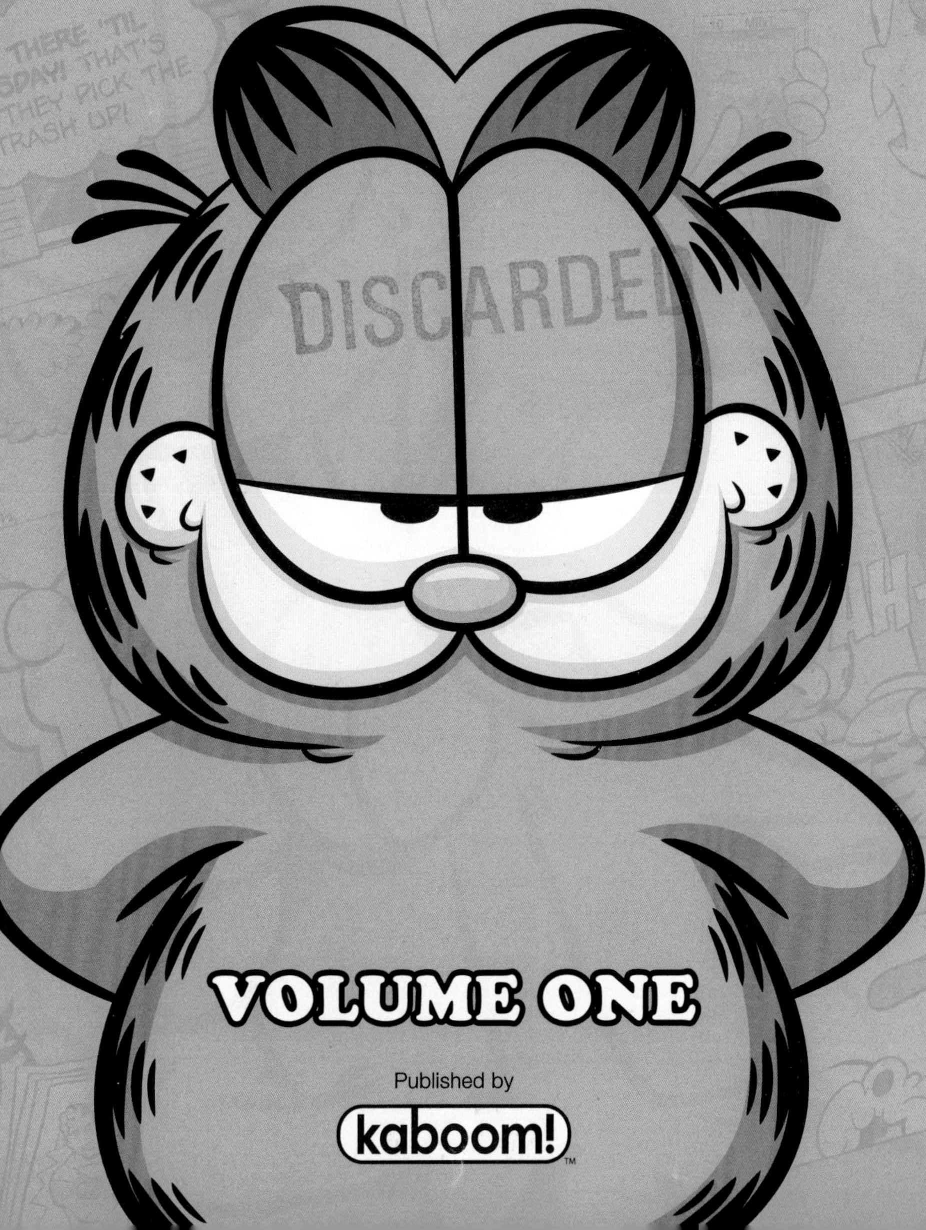

VOLUME ONE

Published by
kaboom!

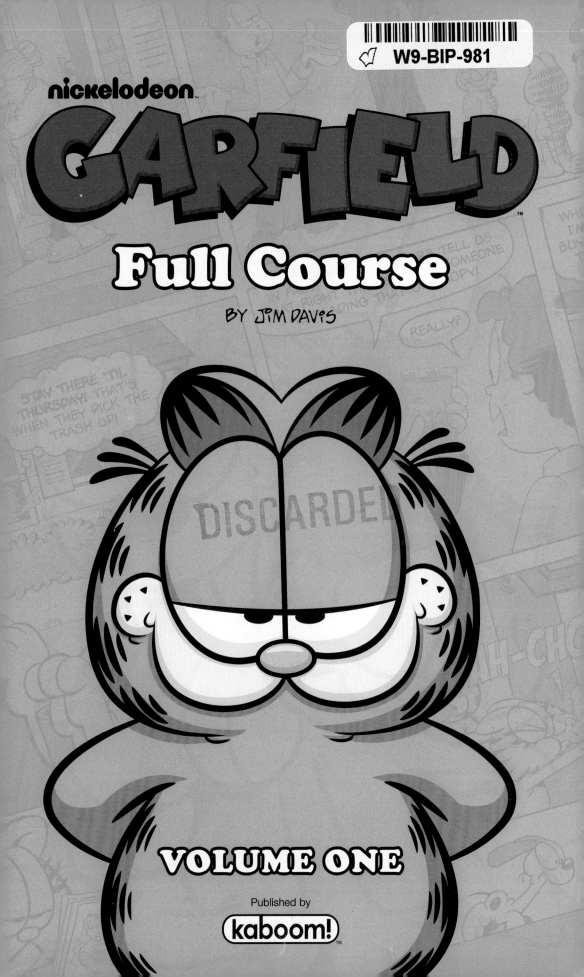

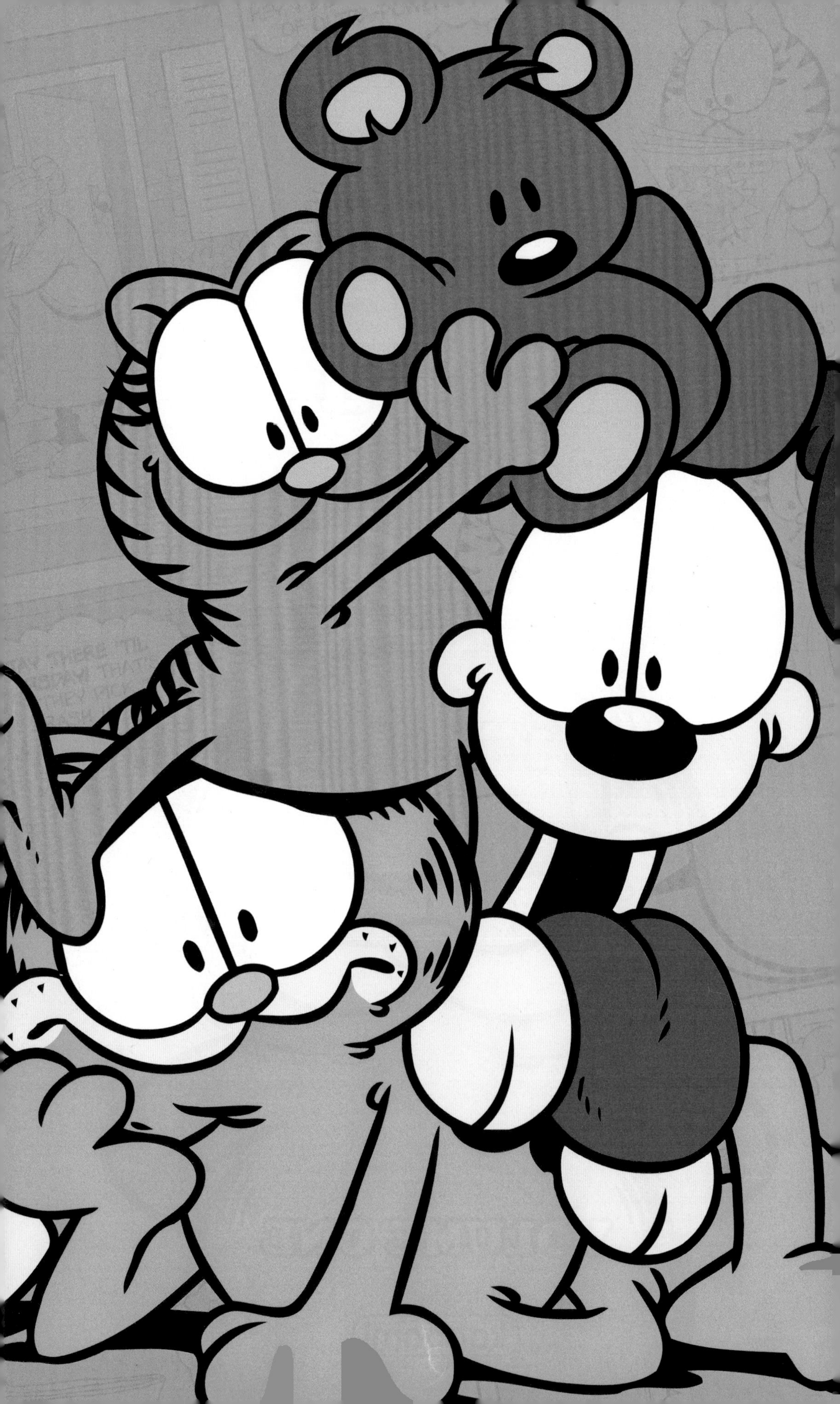

Created by

JIM DAVIS

Written by

MARK EVANIER
SCOTT NICKEL

Art by

GARY BARKER
DAN DAVIS
MIKE DeCARLO
ANDY HIRSCH
MARK & STEPHANIE HEIKE

Colors by

BRADEN LAMB
LISA MOORE

Letters by

STEVE WANDS

Cover Design by

MARIE KRUPINA

Original Series Assistant Editor
CHRIS ROSA

Original Series Editor
MATT GAGNON

Collection Editor
SHANTEL LaROCQUE

Collection Designer
ARMANDO ELIZONDO

Special Thanks to Scott Nickel, David Reddick, and the entire Paws, Inc. team, and Jeff Whitman, Micol Hiatt, and Claire Posner-Greco at Paramount.

Ross Richie Chairman & Founder
Jen Harned CFO
Matt Gagnon Editor-in-Chief
Filip Sablik President, Publishing & Marketing
Stephen Christy President, Development
Adam Yoelin Senior Vice President, Film
Lance Kreiter Vice President, Licensing & Merchandising
Bryce Carlson Vice President, Editorial & Creative Strategy
Josh Hayes Vice President, Sales
Eric Harburn Executive Editor
Ryan Matsunaga Director, Marketing
Stephanie Lazarski Director, Operations
Mette Norkjaer Director, Development
Elyse Strandberg Manager, Finance
Michelle Ankley Manager, Production Design
Cheryl Parker Manager, Human Resources
Rosalind Morehead Manager, Retail Sales

kaboom!   **nickelodeon**™

GARFIELD: FULL COURSE Volume One. November 2023. Published by KaBOOM!, a division of Boom Entertainment, Inc. ©2023 by Paws, Inc. All Rights Reserved. "GARFIELD" and the GARFIELD characters are trademarks of Paws, Inc. Nickelodeon is a trademark of Viacom International Inc. Based on the Garfield® characters created by Jim Davis. Originally published in single magazine form as GARFIELD No. 1-8. ™ & © 2012 Boom Entertainment, Inc. and PAWS, INCORPORATED. All rights reserved. KaBOOM!™ and the KaBOOM! logo are trademarks of Boom Entertainment, Inc., registered in various countries and categories. All characters, events, and institutions depicted herein are fictional. Any similarity between any of the names, characters, persons, events, and/or institutions in this publication to actual names, characters, and persons, whether living or dead, events, and/or institutions is unintended and purely coincidental. KaBOOM! does not read or accept unsolicited submissions of ideas, stories, or artwork.

BOOM! Studios, 6920 Melrose Avenue, Los Angeles, CA 90038-3306. Printed in Canada. First Printing.

ISBN: 978-1-60886-128-6, eISBN: 978-1-93986-750-6

45th Anniversary Edition ISBN 978-1-60886-129-3

FOREWORD

It's incredible to see that after all this time, Garfield continues to be a big, fat, and hairy deal! It's been 45 years since my first *Garfield* comic was published and fans are still in love with him—sassy cattitude and all. I suspect that the fact that there's a little Garfield in each of us has helped to capture hearts around the world. However this cat-next-door has impacted your life, it's been an honor to be part of this global phenomenon. As we celebrate this anniversary with the release of KaBOOM!'s earliest *Garfield* comic stories, may your Mondays be moody, your naps be long, and your lasagna large!

JIM DAVIS

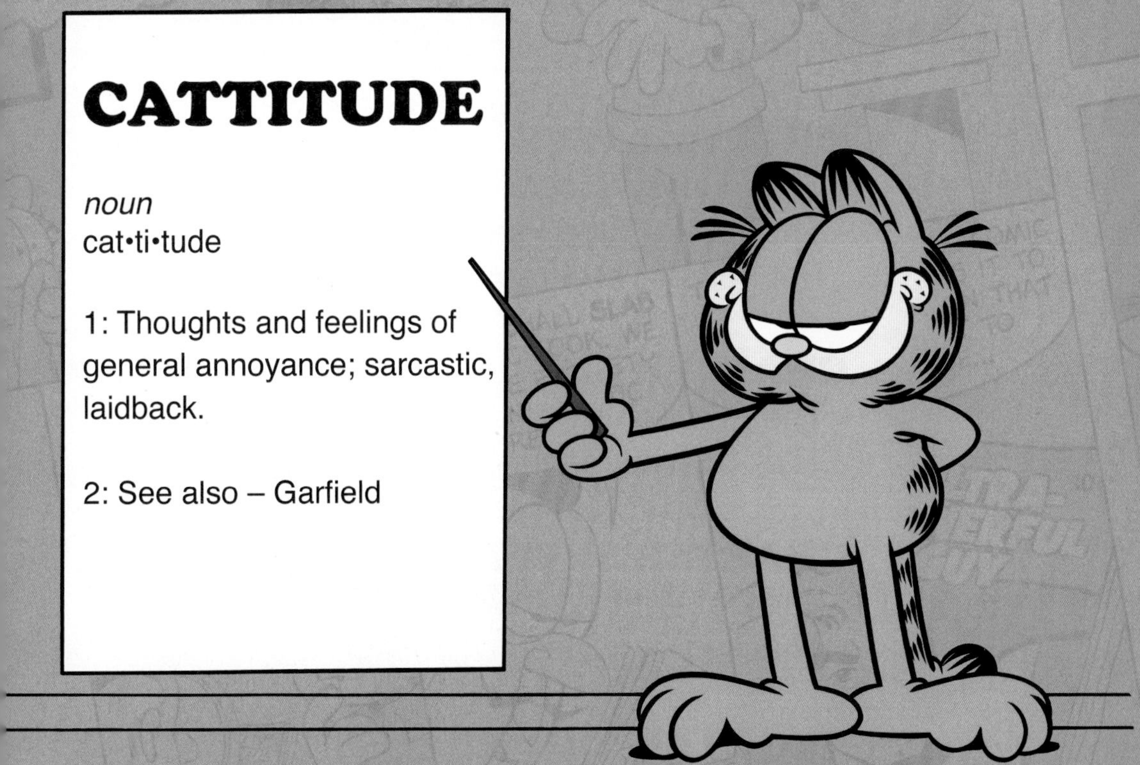

CATTITUDE

noun
cat·ti·tude

1: Thoughts and feelings of general annoyance; sarcastic, laidback.

2: See also – Garfield

TABLE OF **CONTENTS**

CHAPTER ONE

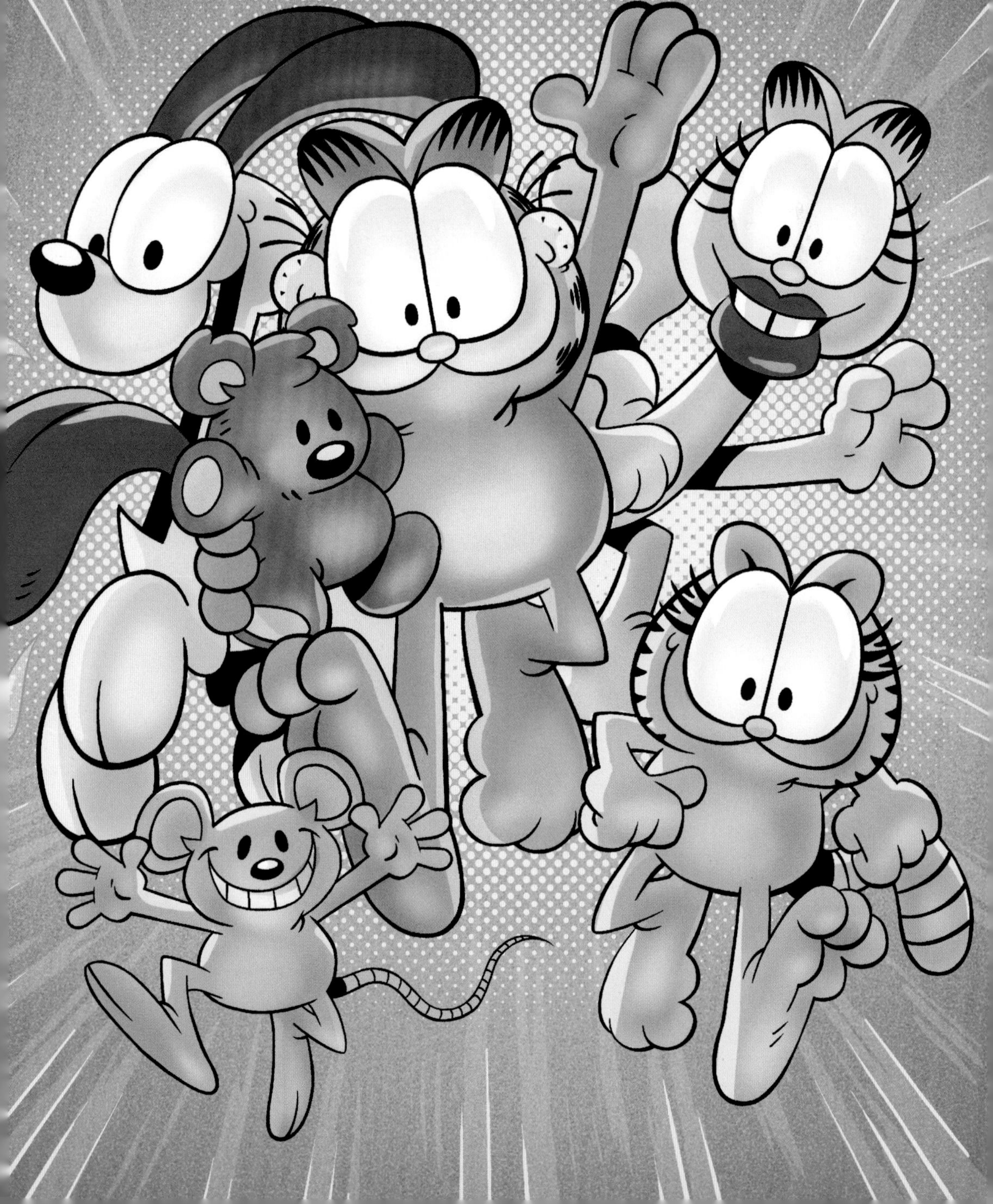

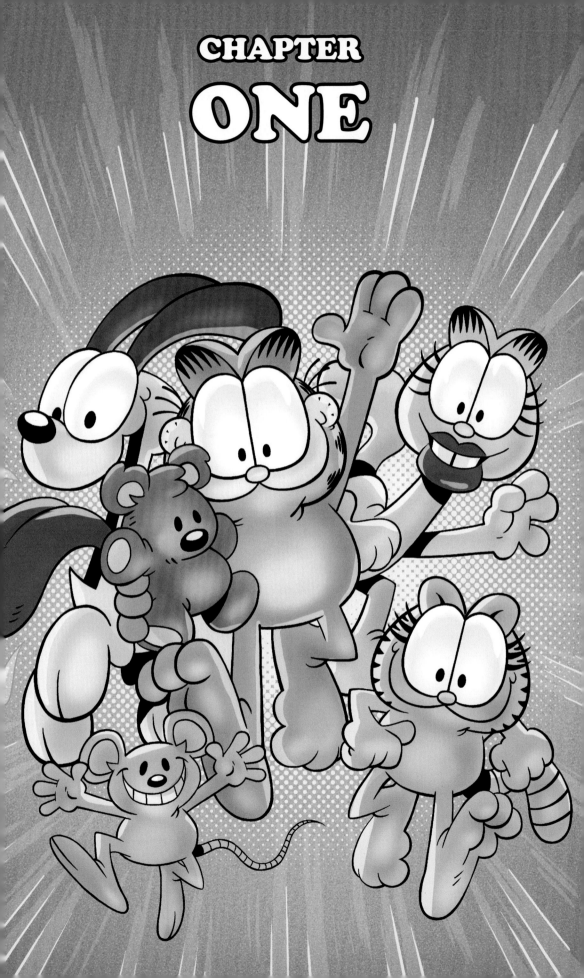

COLLECTORS CLASSIC
BIG MOUSE MEAL

Written by
MARK EVANIER

Art by
GARY BARKER

Colors by
BRADEN LAMB

Chapter Break Art by
GARY BARKER
WITH BRADEN LAMB

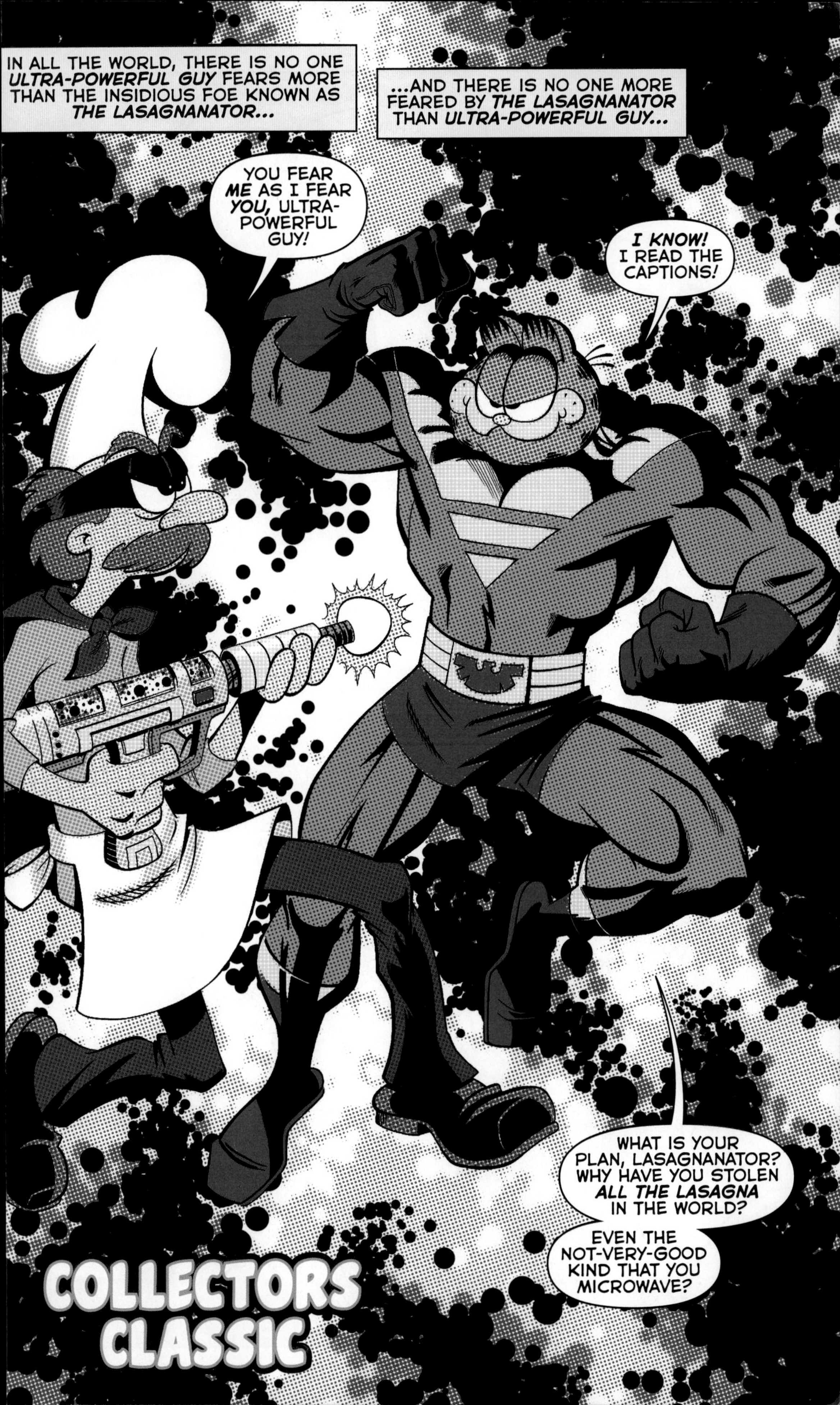
IN ALL THE WORLD, THERE IS NO ONE ULTRA-POWERFUL GUY FEARS MORE THAN THE INSIDIOUS FOE KNOWN AS THE LASAGNANATOR...
...AND THERE IS NO ONE MORE FEARED BY THE LASAGNANATOR THAN ULTRA-POWERFUL GUY...
YOU FEAR ME AS I FEAR YOU, ULTRA-POWERFUL GUY!
I KNOW! I READ THE CAPTIONS!
WHAT IS YOUR PLAN, LASAGNANATOR? WHY HAVE YOU STOLEN ALL THE LASAGNA IN THE WORLD?
EVEN THE NOT-VERY-GOOD KIND THAT YOU MICROWAVE?
COLLECTORS CLASSIC

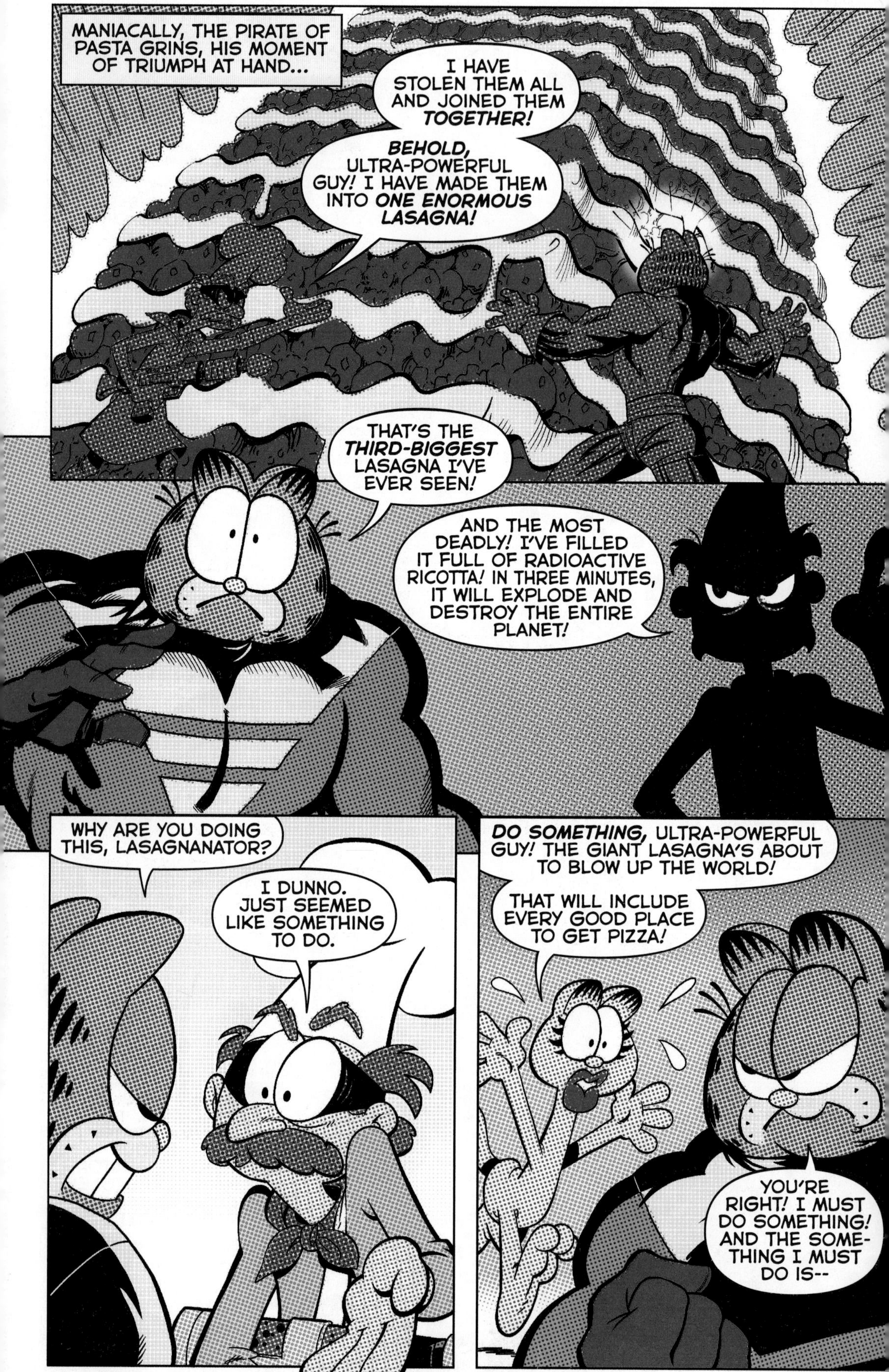
MANIACALLY, THE PIRATE OF PASTA GRINS, HIS MOMENT OF TRIUMPH AT HAND...
I HAVE STOLEN THEM ALL AND JOINED THEM TOGETHER!
BEHOLD, ULTRA-POWERFUL GUY! I HAVE MADE THEM INTO ONE ENORMOUS LASAGNA!
THAT'S THE THIRD-BIGGEST LASAGNA I'VE EVER SEEN!
AND THE MOST DEADLY! I'VE FILLED IT FULL OF RADIOACTIVE RICOTTA! IN THREE MINUTES, IT WILL EXPLODE AND DESTROY THE ENTIRE PLANET!
WHY ARE YOU DOING THIS, LASAGNANATOR?
I DUNNO. JUST SEEMED LIKE SOMETHING TO DO.
DO SOMETHING, ULTRA-POWERFUL GUY! THE GIANT LASAGNA'S ABOUT TO BLOW UP THE WORLD!
THAT WILL INCLUDE EVERY GOOD PLACE TO GET PIZZA!
YOU'RE RIGHT! I MUST DO SOMETHING! AND THE SOMETHING I MUST DO IS--

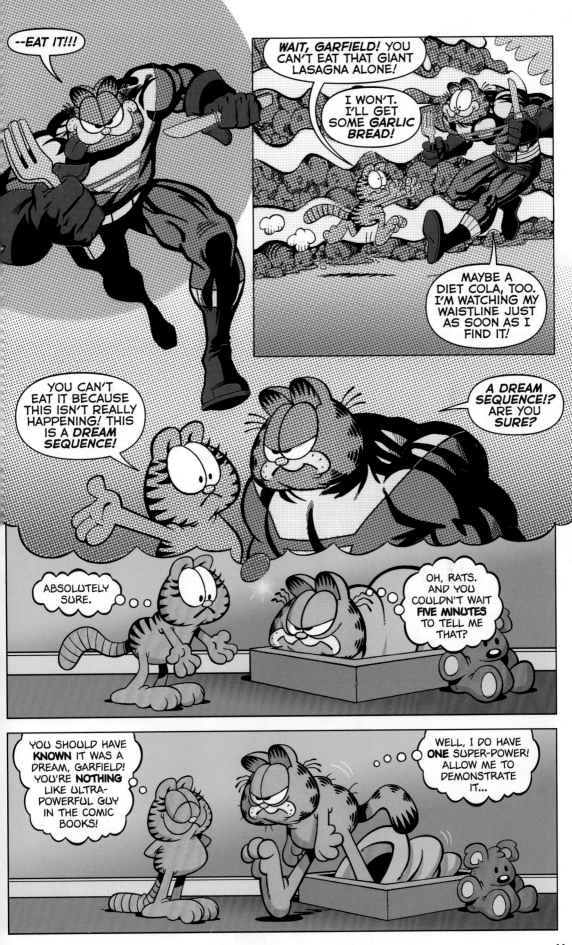

--EAT IT!!!

WAIT, GARFIELD! YOU CAN'T EAT THAT GIANT LASAGNA ALONE!

I WON'T. I'LL GET SOME GARLIC BREAD!

MAYBE A DIET COLA, TOO. I'M WATCHING MY WAISTLINE JUST AS SOON AS I FIND IT!

YOU CAN'T EAT IT BECAUSE THIS ISN'T REALLY HAPPENING! THIS IS A DREAM SEQUENCE!

A DREAM SEQUENCE!? ARE YOU SURE?

ABSOLUTELY SURE.

OH, RATS. AND YOU COULDN'T WAIT FIVE MINUTES TO TELL ME THAT?

YOU SHOULD HAVE KNOWN IT WAS A DREAM, GARFIELD! YOU'RE NOTHING LIKE ULTRA-POWERFUL GUY IN THE COMIC BOOKS!

WELL, I DO HAVE ONE SUPER-POWER! ALLOW ME TO DEMONSTRATE IT...

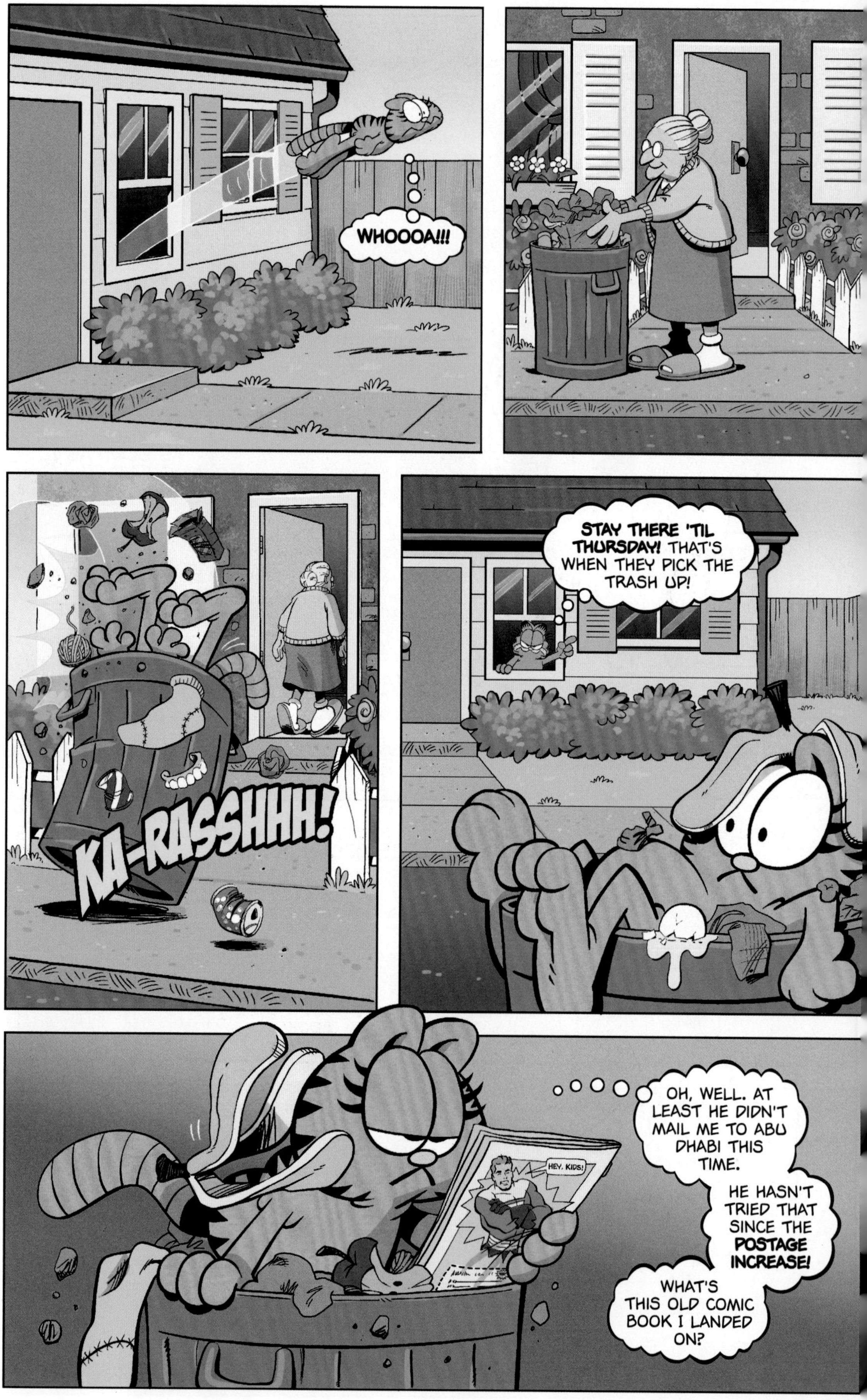
WHOOOA!!!
KA-RASSHHH!
STAY THERE 'TIL THURSDAY! THAT'S WHEN THEY PICK THE TRASH UP!
OH, WELL. AT LEAST HE DIDN'T MAIL ME TO ABU DHABI THIS TIME.
HE HASN'T TRIED THAT SINCE THE POSTAGE INCREASE!
WHAT'S THIS OLD COMIC BOOK I LANDED ON?
HEY, KIDS!

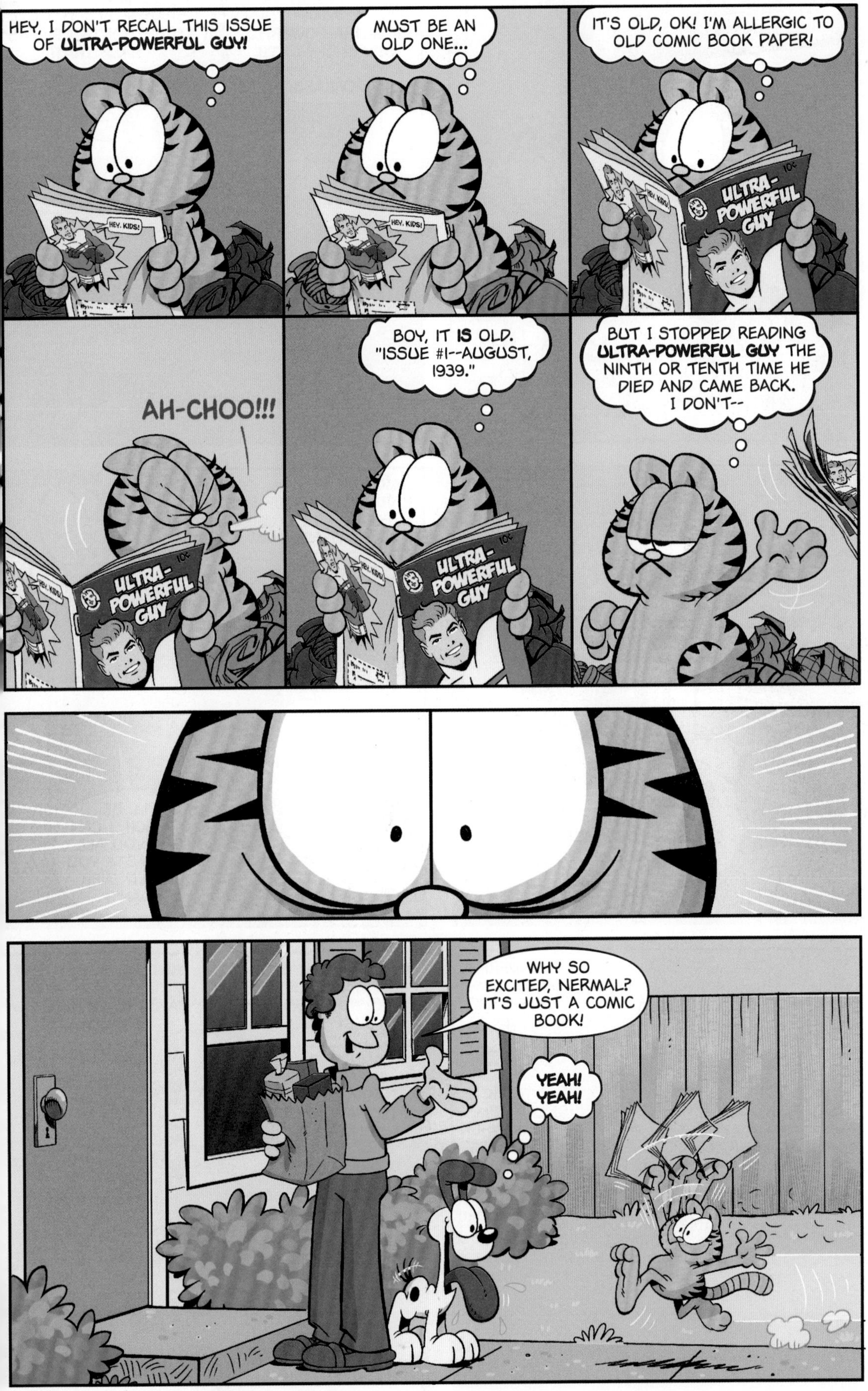

HEY, I DON'T RECALL THIS ISSUE OF ULTRA-POWERFUL GUY!
HEY, KIDS!
MUST BE AN OLD ONE...
IT'S OLD, OK! I'M ALLERGIC TO OLD COMIC BOOK PAPER!
ULTRA-POWERFUL GUY
10¢
AH-CHOO!!!
BOY, IT IS OLD. "ISSUE #1--AUGUST, 1939."
BUT I STOPPED READING ULTRA-POWERFUL GUY THE NINTH OR TENTH TIME HE DIED AND CAME BACK. I DON'T--
WHY SO EXCITED, NERMAL? IT'S JUST A COMIC BOOK!
YEAH! YEAH!

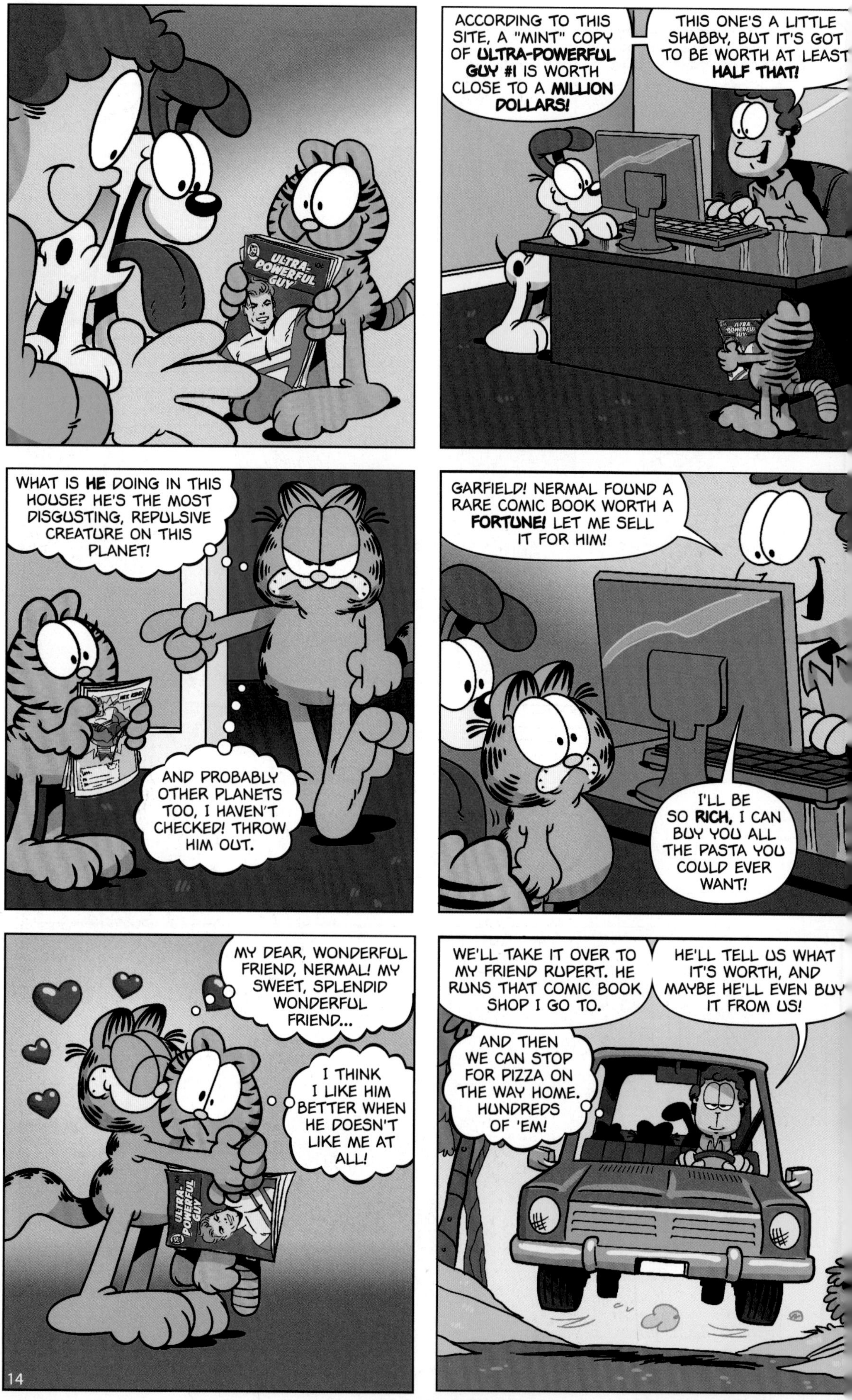
ACCORDING TO THIS SITE, A "MINT" COPY OF ULTRA-POWERFUL GUY #1 IS WORTH CLOSE TO A MILLION DOLLARS!
THIS ONE'S A LITTLE SHABBY, BUT IT'S GOT TO BE WORTH AT LEAST HALF THAT!
WHAT IS HE DOING IN THIS HOUSE? HE'S THE MOST DISGUSTING, REPULSIVE CREATURE ON THIS PLANET!
AND PROBABLY OTHER PLANETS TOO, I HAVEN'T CHECKED! THROW HIM OUT.
GARFIELD! NERMAL FOUND A RARE COMIC BOOK WORTH A FORTUNE! LET ME SELL IT FOR HIM!
I'LL BE SO RICH, I CAN BUY YOU ALL THE PASTA YOU COULD EVER WANT!
MY DEAR, WONDERFUL FRIEND, NERMAL! MY SWEET, SPLENDID WONDERFUL FRIEND...
I THINK I LIKE HIM BETTER WHEN HE DOESN'T LIKE ME AT ALL!
WE'LL TAKE IT OVER TO MY FRIEND RUPERT. HE RUNS THAT COMIC BOOK SHOP I GO TO.
HE'LL TELL US WHAT IT'S WORTH, AND MAYBE HE'LL EVEN BUY IT FROM US!
AND THEN WE CAN STOP FOR PIZZA ON THE WAY HOME. HUNDREDS OF 'EM!

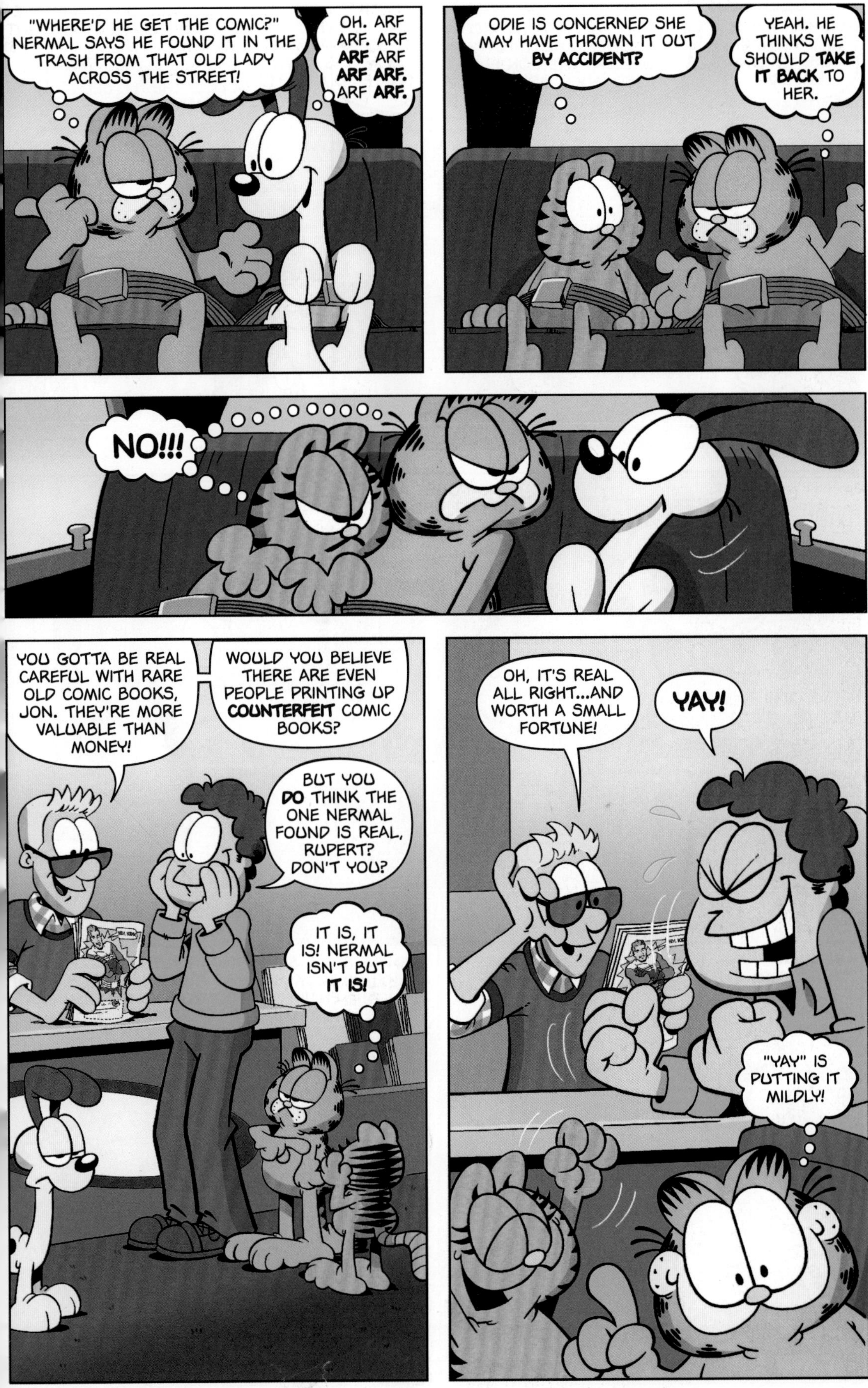
"WHERE'D HE GET THE COMIC?" NERMAL SAYS HE FOUND IT IN THE TRASH FROM THAT OLD LADY ACROSS THE STREET!
OH. ARF ARF. ARF ARF ARF ARF ARF. ARF ARF.
ODIE IS CONCERNED SHE MAY HAVE THROWN IT OUT BY ACCIDENT?
YEAH. HE THINKS WE SHOULD TAKE IT BACK TO HER.
NO!!!
YOU GOTTA BE REAL CAREFUL WITH RARE OLD COMIC BOOKS, JON. THEY'RE MORE VALUABLE THAN MONEY!
WOULD YOU BELIEVE THERE ARE EVEN PEOPLE PRINTING UP COUNTERFEIT COMIC BOOKS?
BUT YOU DO THINK THE ONE NERMAL FOUND IS REAL, RUPERT? DON'T YOU?
IT IS, IT IS! NERMAL ISN'T BUT IT IS!
OH, IT'S REAL ALL RIGHT...AND WORTH A SMALL FORTUNE!
YAY!
"YAY" IS PUTTING IT MILDLY!

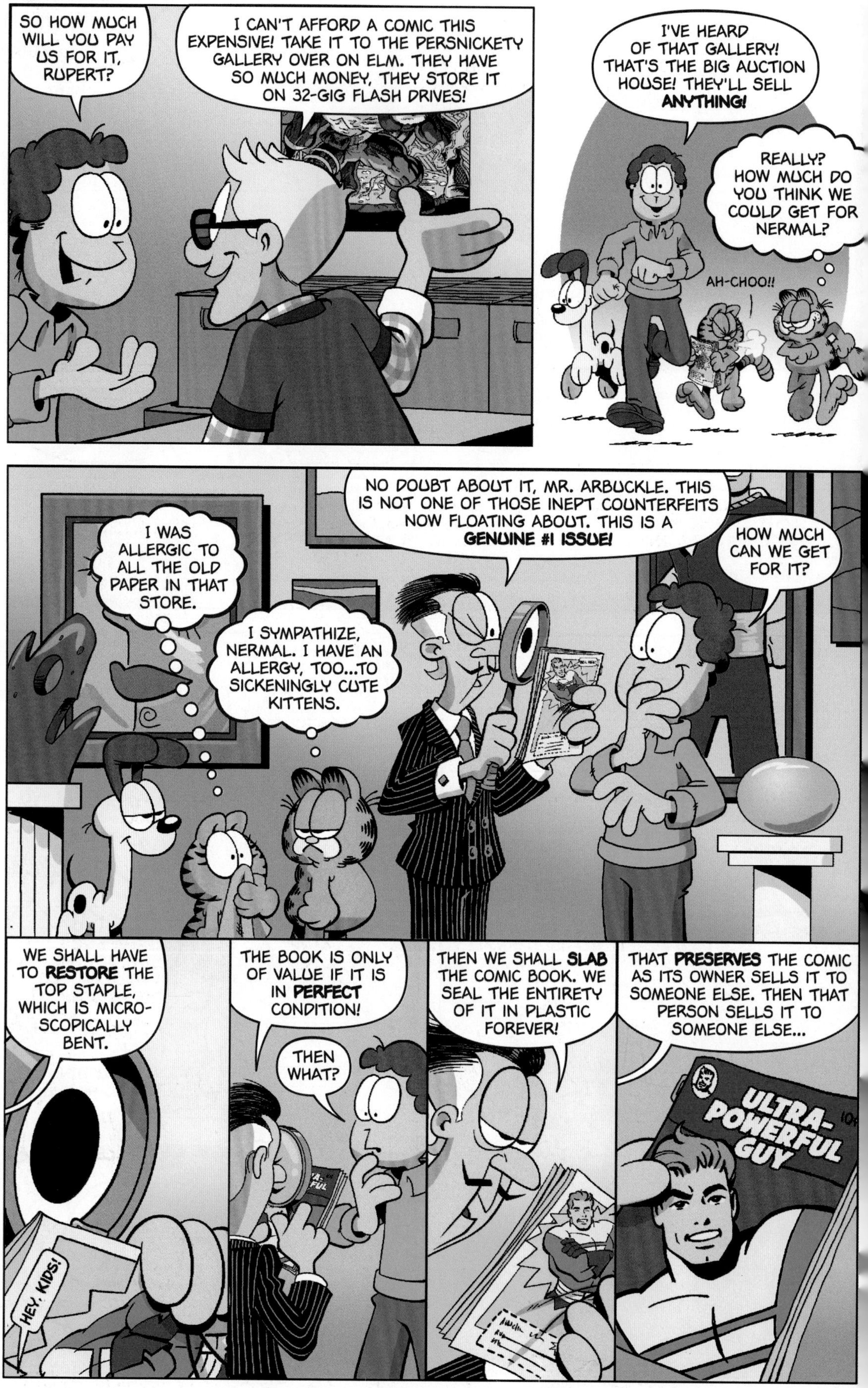
SO HOW MUCH WILL YOU PAY US FOR IT, RUPERT?
I CAN'T AFFORD A COMIC THIS EXPENSIVE! TAKE IT TO THE PERSNICKETY GALLERY OVER ON ELM. THEY HAVE SO MUCH MONEY, THEY STORE IT ON 32-GIG FLASH DRIVES!
I'VE HEARD OF THAT GALLERY! THAT'S THE BIG AUCTION HOUSE! THEY'LL SELL **ANYTHING!**
REALLY? HOW MUCH DO YOU THINK WE COULD GET FOR NERMAL?
AH-CHOO!!
NO DOUBT ABOUT IT, MR. ARBUCKLE. THIS IS NOT ONE OF THOSE INEPT COUNTERFEITS NOW FLOATING ABOUT. THIS IS A **GENUINE #1 ISSUE!**
HOW MUCH CAN WE GET FOR IT?
I WAS ALLERGIC TO ALL THE OLD PAPER IN THAT STORE.
I SYMPATHIZE, NERMAL. I HAVE AN ALLERGY, TOO...TO SICKENINGLY CUTE KITTENS.
WE SHALL HAVE TO **RESTORE** THE TOP STAPLE, WHICH IS MICRO-SCOPICALLY BENT.
HEY, KIDS!
THE BOOK IS ONLY OF VALUE IF IT IS IN **PERFECT** CONDITION!
THEN WHAT?
THEN WE SHALL **SLAB** THE COMIC BOOK. WE SEAL THE ENTIRETY OF IT IN PLASTIC FOREVER!
THAT **PRESERVES** THE COMIC AS ITS OWNER SELLS IT TO SOMEONE ELSE. THEN THAT PERSON SELLS IT TO SOMEONE ELSE...
ULTRA-POWERFUL GUY

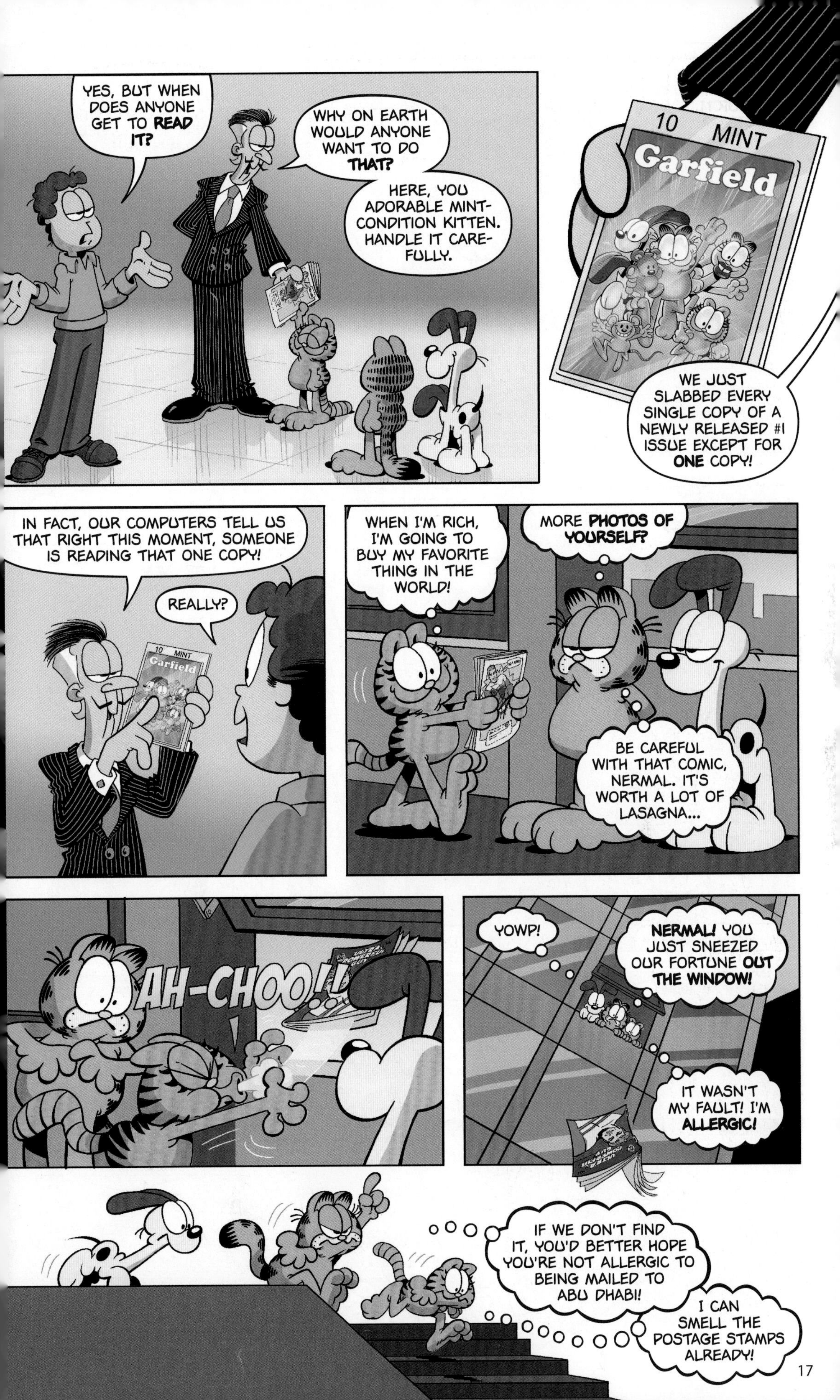

YES, BUT WHEN DOES ANYONE GET TO READ IT?
WHY ON EARTH WOULD ANYONE WANT TO DO THAT?
HERE, YOU ADORABLE MINT-CONDITION KITTEN. HANDLE IT CARE-FULLY.
10 MINT
Garfield
WE JUST SLABBED EVERY SINGLE COPY OF A NEWLY RELEASED #1 ISSUE EXCEPT FOR ONE COPY!
IN FACT, OUR COMPUTERS TELL US THAT RIGHT THIS MOMENT, SOMEONE IS READING THAT ONE COPY!
REALLY?
WHEN I'M RICH, I'M GOING TO BUY MY FAVORITE THING IN THE WORLD!
MORE PHOTOS OF YOURSELF?
BE CAREFUL WITH THAT COMIC, NERMAL. IT'S WORTH A LOT OF LASAGNA...
AH-CHOO!!
YOWP!
NERMAL! YOU JUST SNEEZED OUR FORTUNE OUT THE WINDOW!
IT WASN'T MY FAULT! I'M ALLERGIC!
IF WE DON'T FIND IT, YOU'D BETTER HOPE YOU'RE NOT ALLERGIC TO BEING MAILED TO ABU DHABI!
I CAN SMELL THE POSTAGE STAMPS ALREADY!

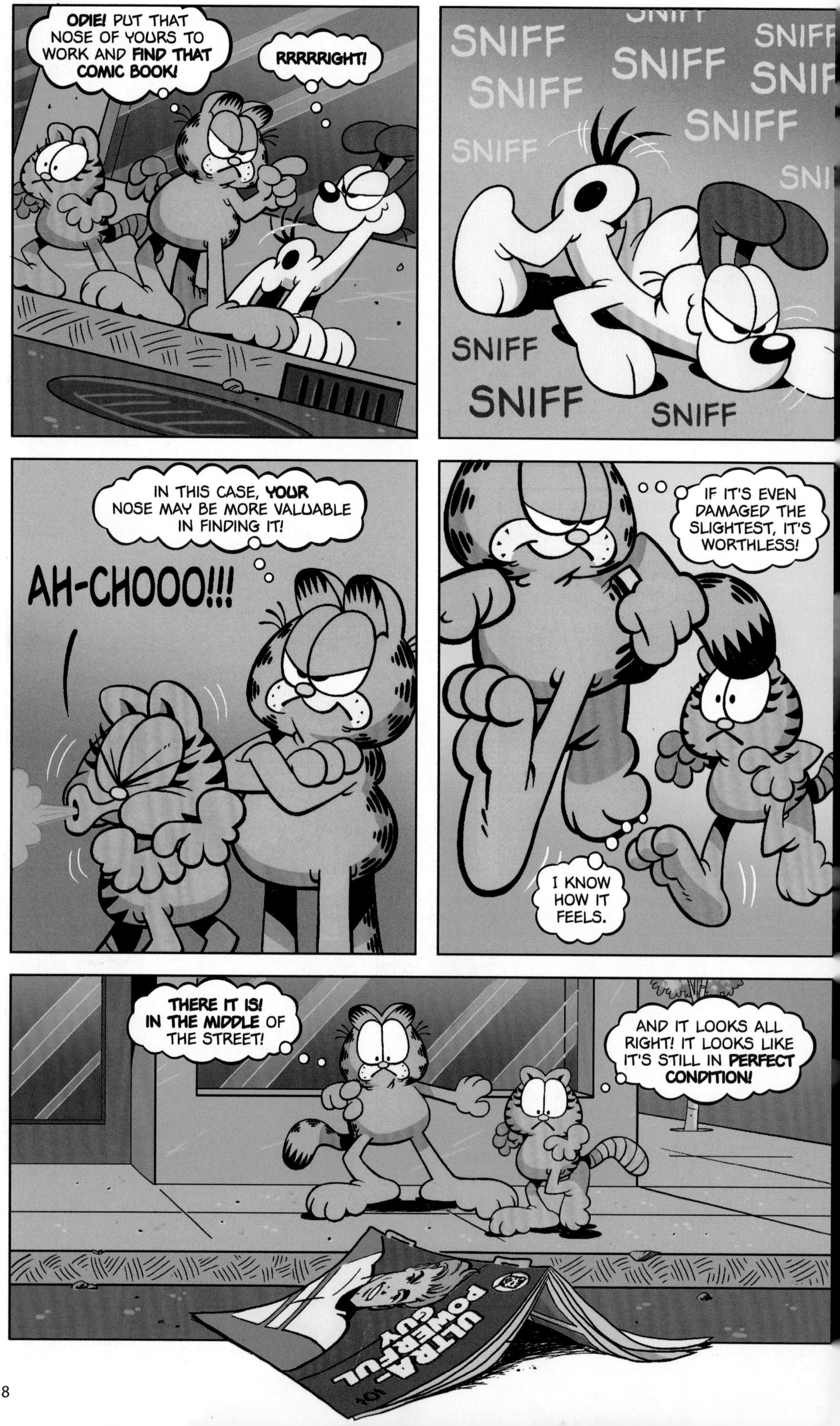
ODIE! PUT THAT NOSE OF YOURS TO WORK AND FIND THAT COMIC BOOK!
RRRRRIGHT!
SNIFF SNIFF SNIFF SNIFF SNIFF SNIFF SNIFF
SNIFF SNIFF SNIFF
IN THIS CASE, YOUR NOSE MAY BE MORE VALUABLE IN FINDING IT!
AH-CHOOO!!!
IF IT'S EVEN DAMAGED THE SLIGHTEST, IT'S WORTHLESS!
I KNOW HOW IT FEELS.
THERE IT IS! IN THE MIDDLE OF THE STREET!
AND IT LOOKS ALL RIGHT! IT LOOKS LIKE IT'S STILL IN PERFECT CONDITION!
ULTRA-POWERFUL GUY

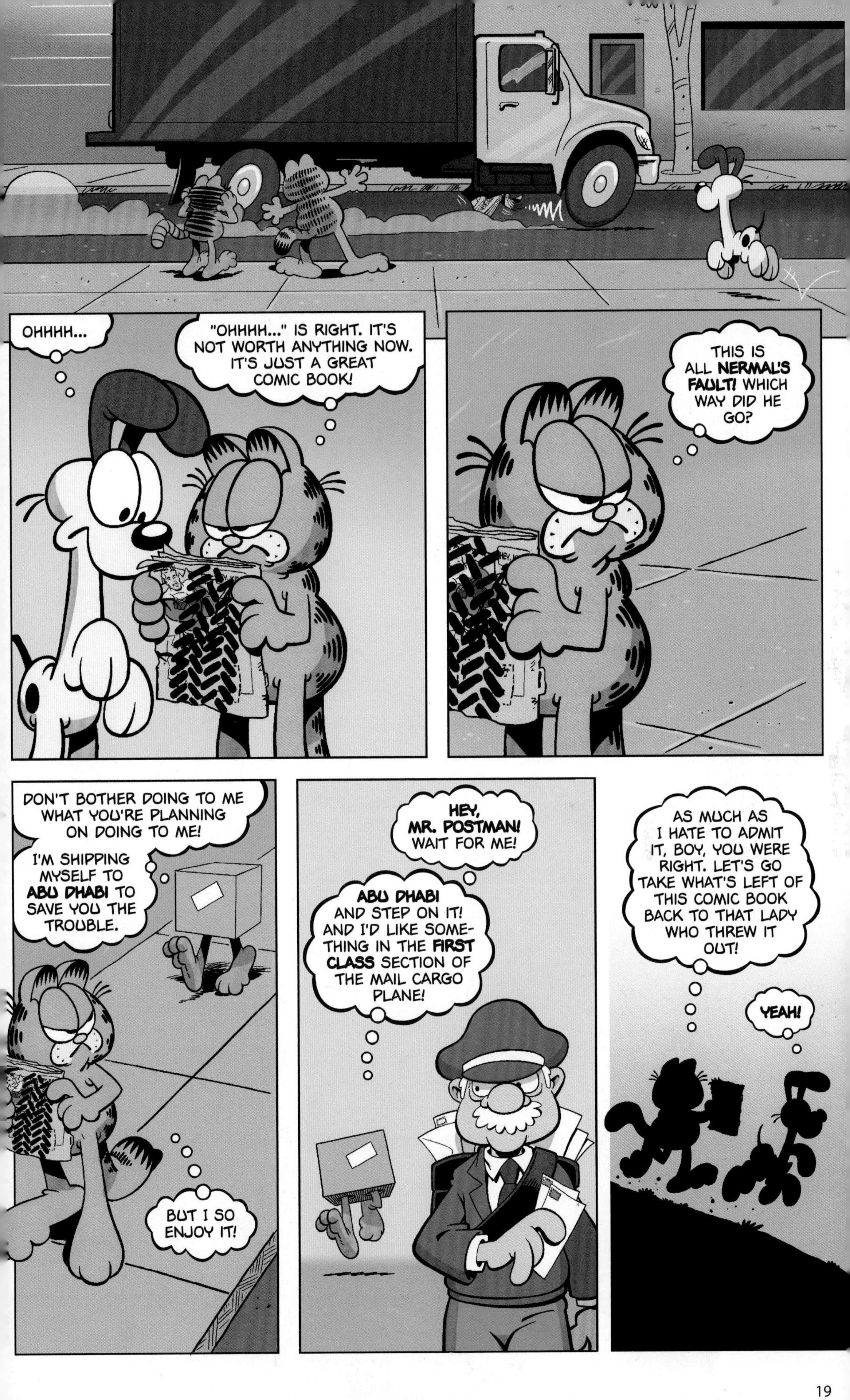
OHHHH...
"OHHHH..." IS RIGHT. IT'S NOT WORTH ANYTHING NOW. IT'S JUST A GREAT COMIC BOOK!
THIS IS ALL **NERMAL'S FAULT!** WHICH WAY DID HE GO?
DON'T BOTHER DOING TO ME WHAT YOU'RE PLANNING ON DOING TO ME!
I'M SHIPPING MYSELF TO **ABU DHABI** TO SAVE YOU THE TROUBLE.
BUT I SO ENJOY IT!
HEY, MR. POSTMAN! WAIT FOR ME!
ABU DHABI AND STEP ON IT! AND I'D LIKE SOMETHING IN THE **FIRST CLASS** SECTION OF THE MAIL CARGO PLANE!
AS MUCH AS I HATE TO ADMIT IT, BOY, YOU WERE RIGHT. LET'S GO TAKE WHAT'S LEFT OF THIS COMIC BOOK BACK TO THAT LADY WHO THREW IT OUT!
YEAH!

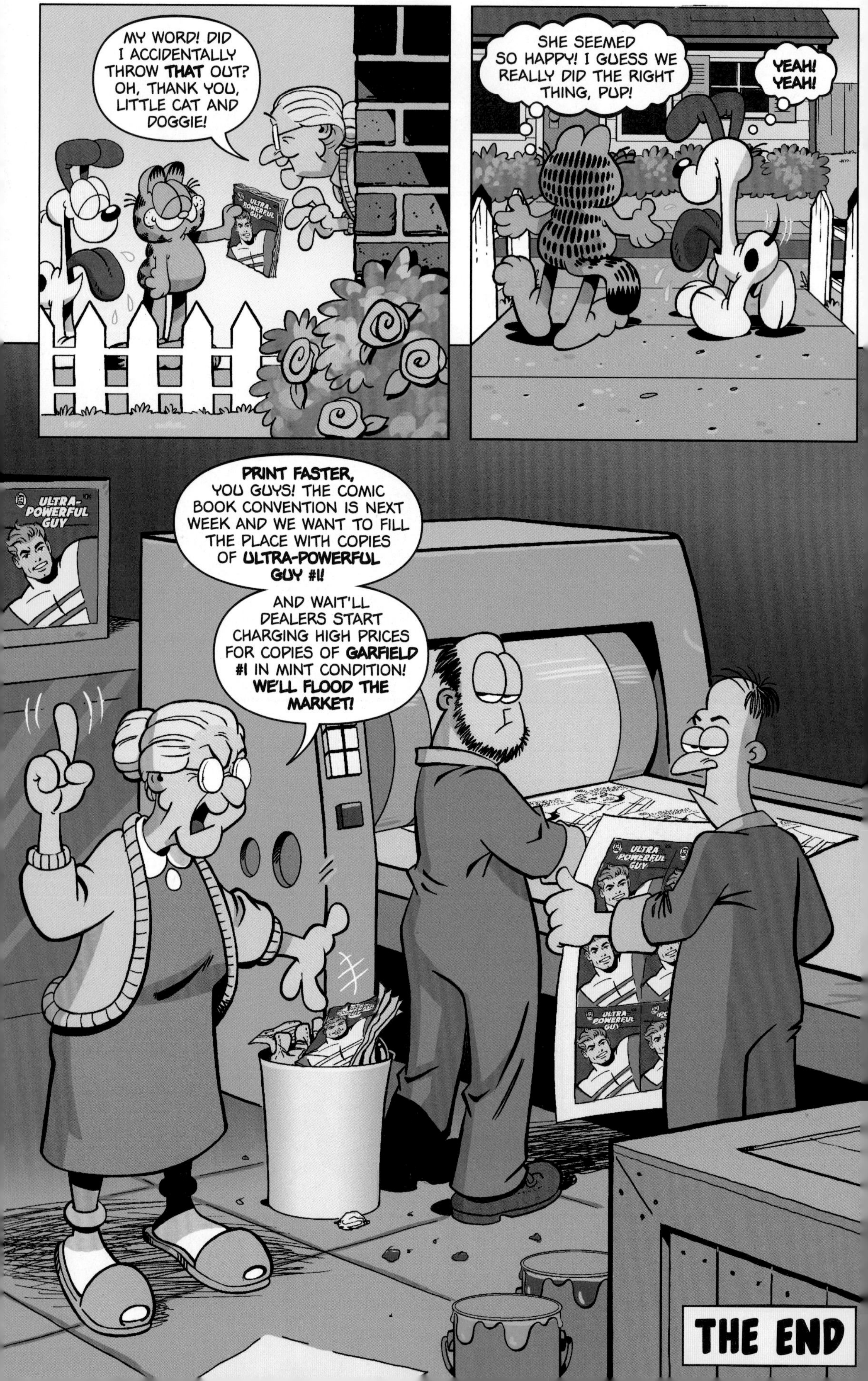
MY WORD! DID I ACCIDENTALLY THROW THAT OUT? OH, THANK YOU, LITTLE CAT AND DOGGIE!
ULTRA-POWERFUL GUY
SHE SEEMED SO HAPPY! I GUESS WE REALLY DID THE RIGHT THING, PUP!
YEAH! YEAH!
ULTRA-POWERFUL GUY
PRINT FASTER, YOU GUYS! THE COMIC BOOK CONVENTION IS NEXT WEEK AND WE WANT TO FILL THE PLACE WITH COPIES OF ULTRA-POWERFUL GUY #1!
AND WAIT'LL DEALERS START CHARGING HIGH PRICES FOR COPIES OF GARFIELD #1 IN MINT CONDITION! WE'LL FLOOD THE MARKET!
ULTRA-POWERFUL GUY
ULTRA-POWERFUL GUY
THE END

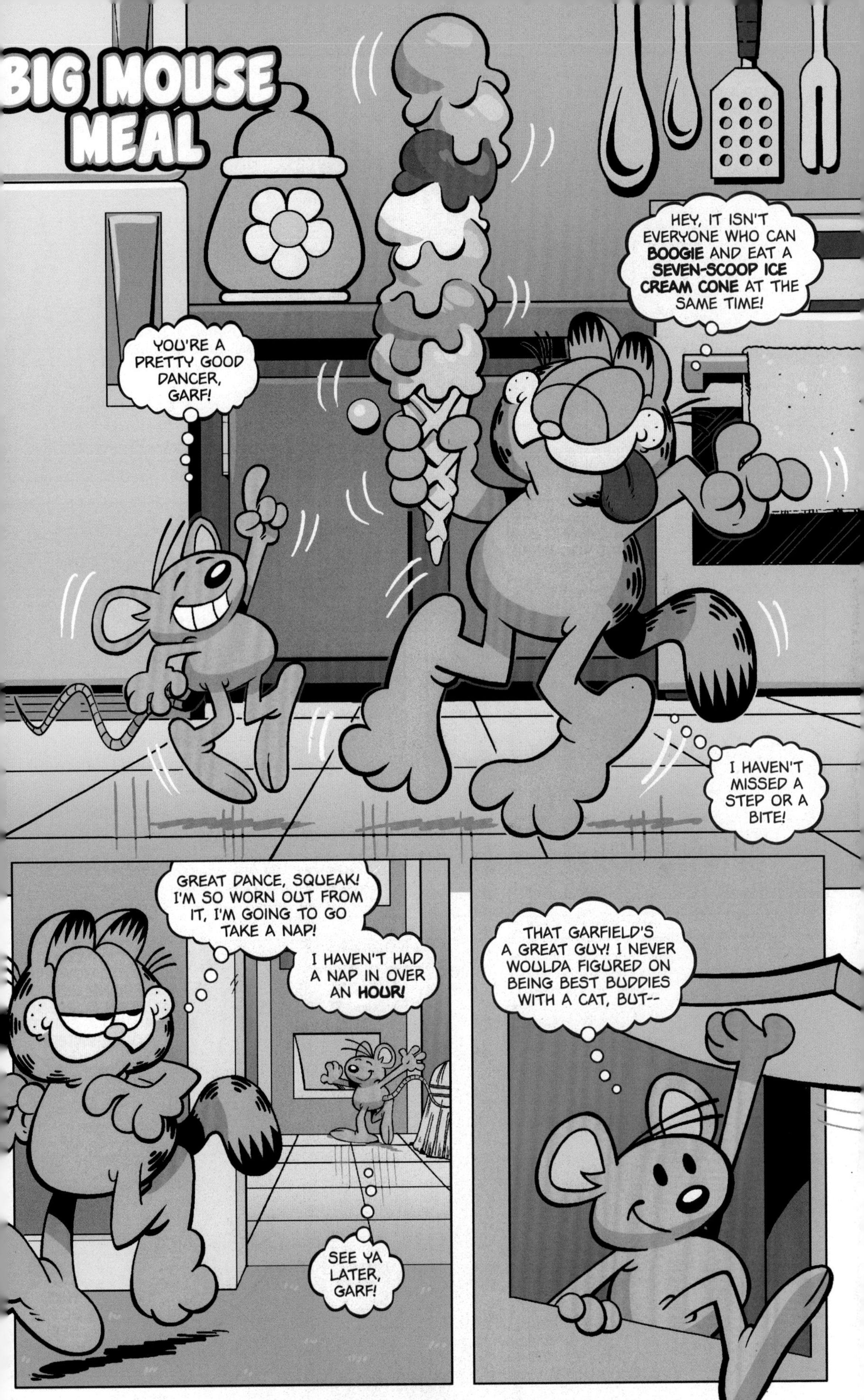
BIG MOUSE MEAL
YOU'RE A PRETTY GOOD DANCER, GARF!
HEY, IT ISN'T EVERYONE WHO CAN **BOOGIE** AND EAT A **SEVEN-SCOOP ICE CREAM CONE** AT THE SAME TIME!
I HAVEN'T MISSED A STEP OR A BITE!
GREAT DANCE, SQUEAK! I'M SO WORN OUT FROM IT, I'M GOING TO GO TAKE A NAP!
I HAVEN'T HAD A NAP IN OVER AN **HOUR!**
SEE YA LATER, GARF!
THAT GARFIELD'S A GREAT GUY! I NEVER WOULDA FIGURED ON BEING BEST BUDDIES WITH A CAT, BUT--

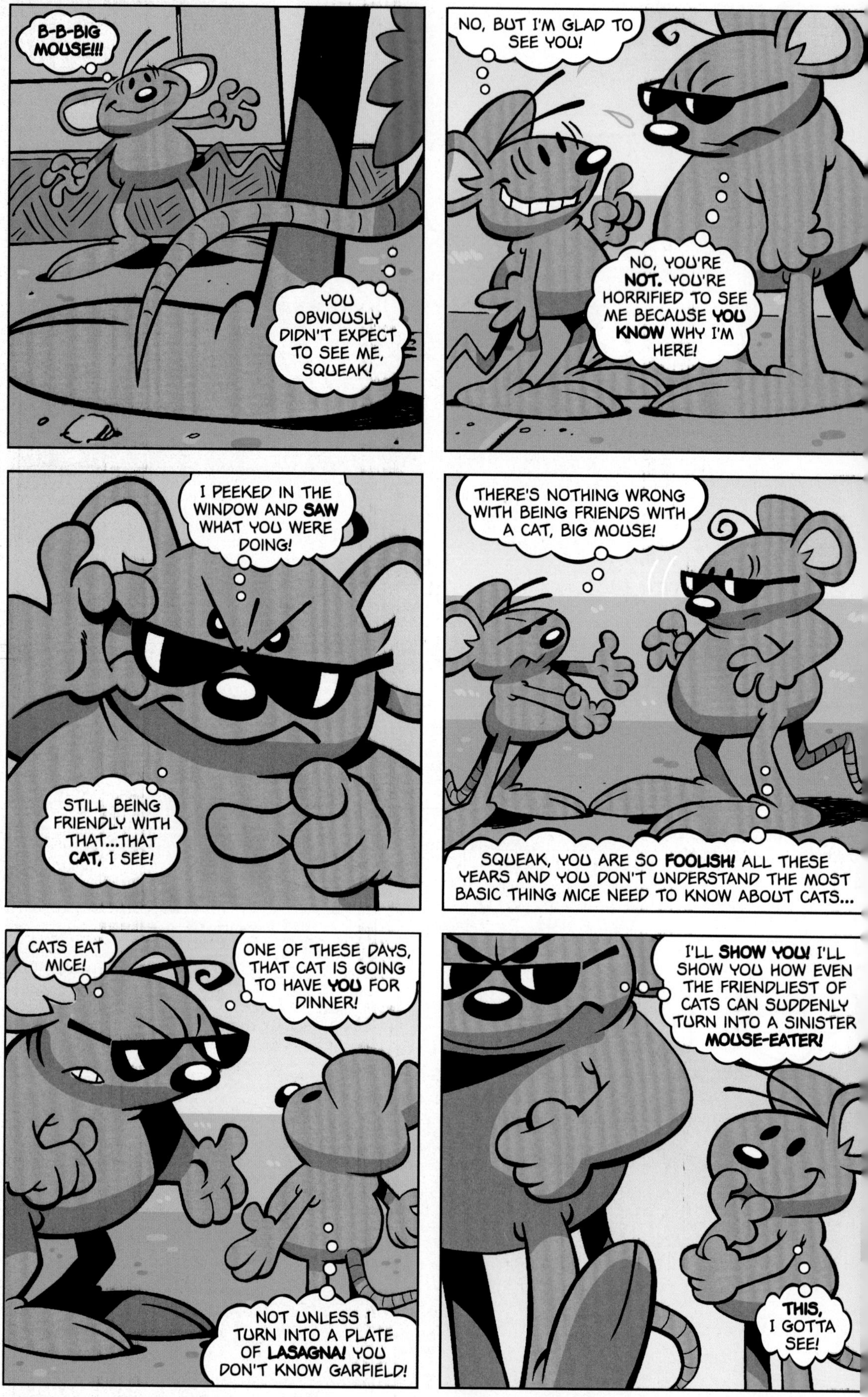
B-B-BIG MOUSE!!!
YOU OBVIOUSLY DIDN'T EXPECT TO SEE ME, SQUEAK!
NO, BUT I'M GLAD TO SEE YOU!
NO, YOU'RE NOT. YOU'RE HORRIFIED TO SEE ME BECAUSE YOU KNOW WHY I'M HERE!
I PEEKED IN THE WINDOW AND SAW WHAT YOU WERE DOING!
STILL BEING FRIENDLY WITH THAT...THAT CAT, I SEE!
THERE'S NOTHING WRONG WITH BEING FRIENDS WITH A CAT, BIG MOUSE!
SQUEAK, YOU ARE SO FOOLISH! ALL THESE YEARS AND YOU DON'T UNDERSTAND THE MOST BASIC THING MICE NEED TO KNOW ABOUT CATS...
CATS EAT MICE!
ONE OF THESE DAYS, THAT CAT IS GOING TO HAVE YOU FOR DINNER!
NOT UNLESS I TURN INTO A PLATE OF LASAGNA! YOU DON'T KNOW GARFIELD!
I'LL SHOW YOU! I'LL SHOW YOU HOW EVEN THE FRIENDLIEST OF CATS CAN SUDDENLY TURN INTO A SINISTER MOUSE-EATER!
THIS, I GOTTA SEE!

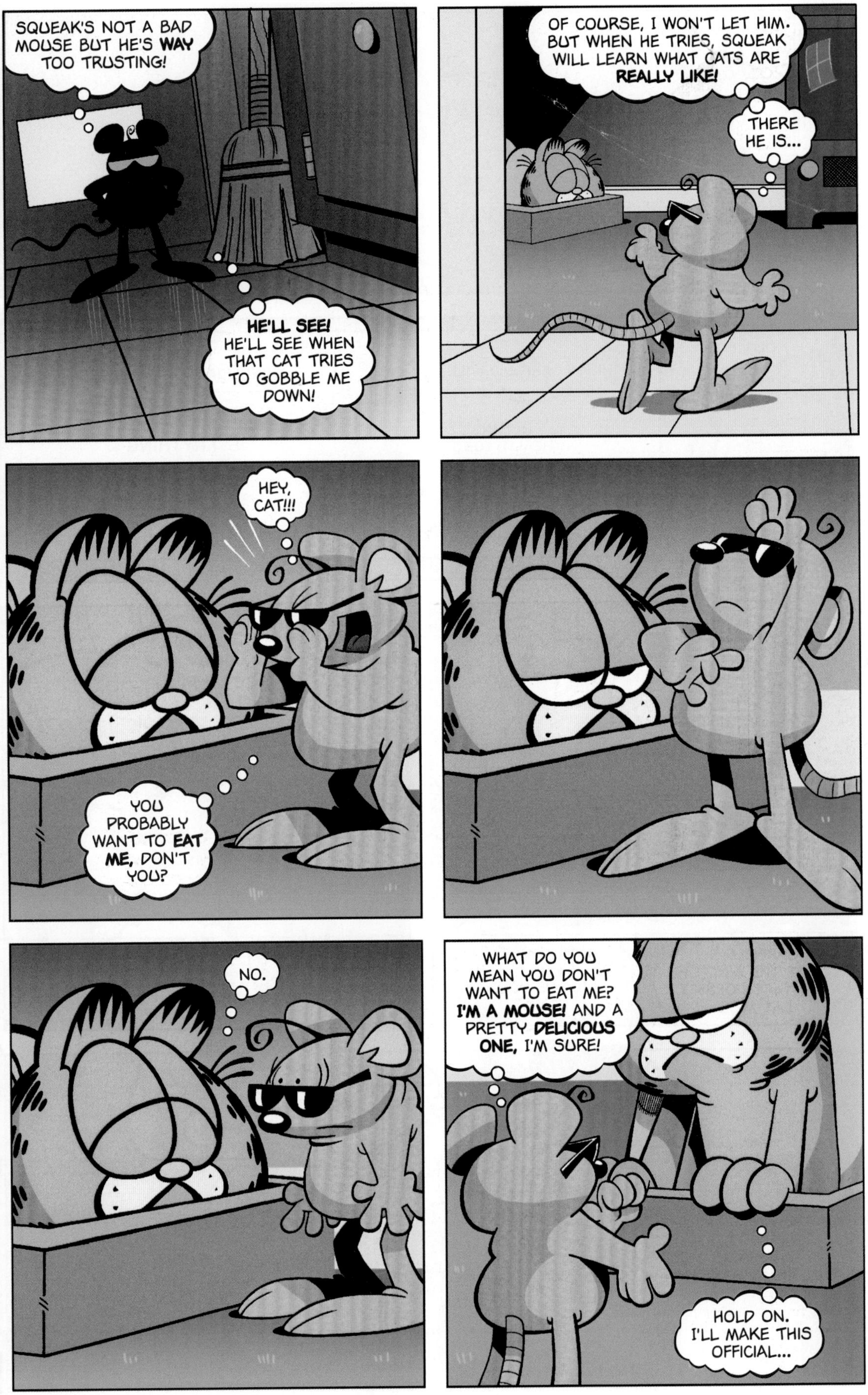
SQUEAK'S NOT A BAD MOUSE BUT HE'S **WAY** TOO TRUSTING!
HE'LL SEE! HE'LL SEE WHEN THAT CAT TRIES TO GOBBLE ME DOWN!
OF COURSE, I WON'T LET HIM. BUT WHEN HE TRIES, SQUEAK WILL LEARN WHAT CATS ARE **REALLY LIKE!**
THERE HE IS...
HEY, CAT!!!
YOU PROBABLY WANT TO **EAT ME,** DON'T YOU?
NO.
WHAT DO YOU MEAN YOU DON'T WANT TO EAT ME? **I'M A MOUSE!** AND A PRETTY **DELICIOUS ONE,** I'M SURE!
HOLD ON. I'LL MAKE THIS OFFICIAL...

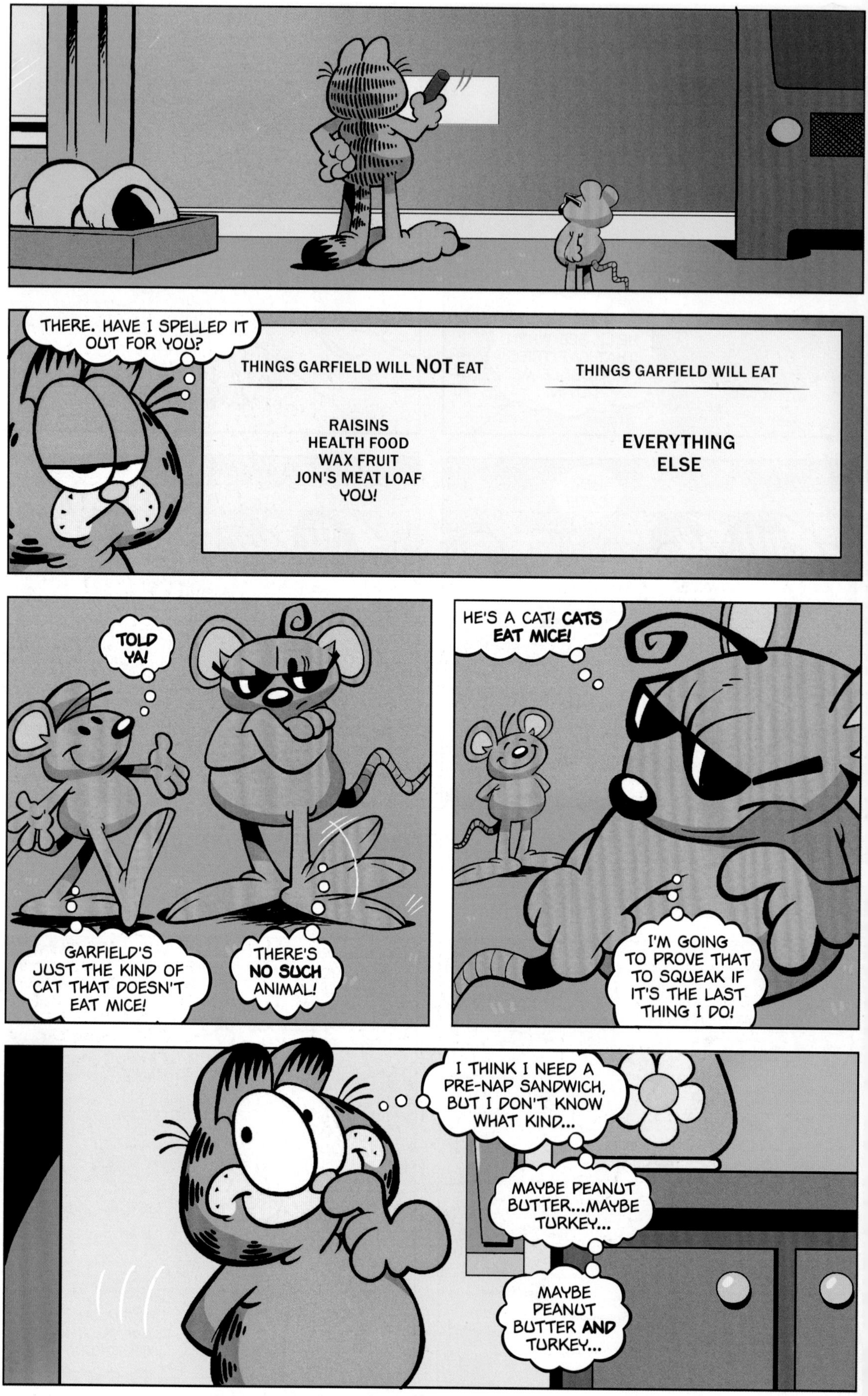
THERE. HAVE I SPELLED IT OUT FOR YOU?
THINGS GARFIELD WILL NOT EAT
RAISINS
HEALTH FOOD
WAX FRUIT
JON'S MEAT LOAF
YOU!
THINGS GARFIELD WILL EAT
EVERYTHING ELSE
TOLD YA!
GARFIELD'S JUST THE KIND OF CAT THAT DOESN'T EAT MICE!
THERE'S NO SUCH ANIMAL!
HE'S A CAT! CATS EAT MICE!
I'M GOING TO PROVE THAT TO SQUEAK IF IT'S THE LAST THING I DO!
I THINK I NEED A PRE-NAP SANDWICH, BUT I DON'T KNOW WHAT KIND...
MAYBE PEANUT BUTTER...MAYBE TURKEY...
MAYBE PEANUT BUTTER AND TURKEY...

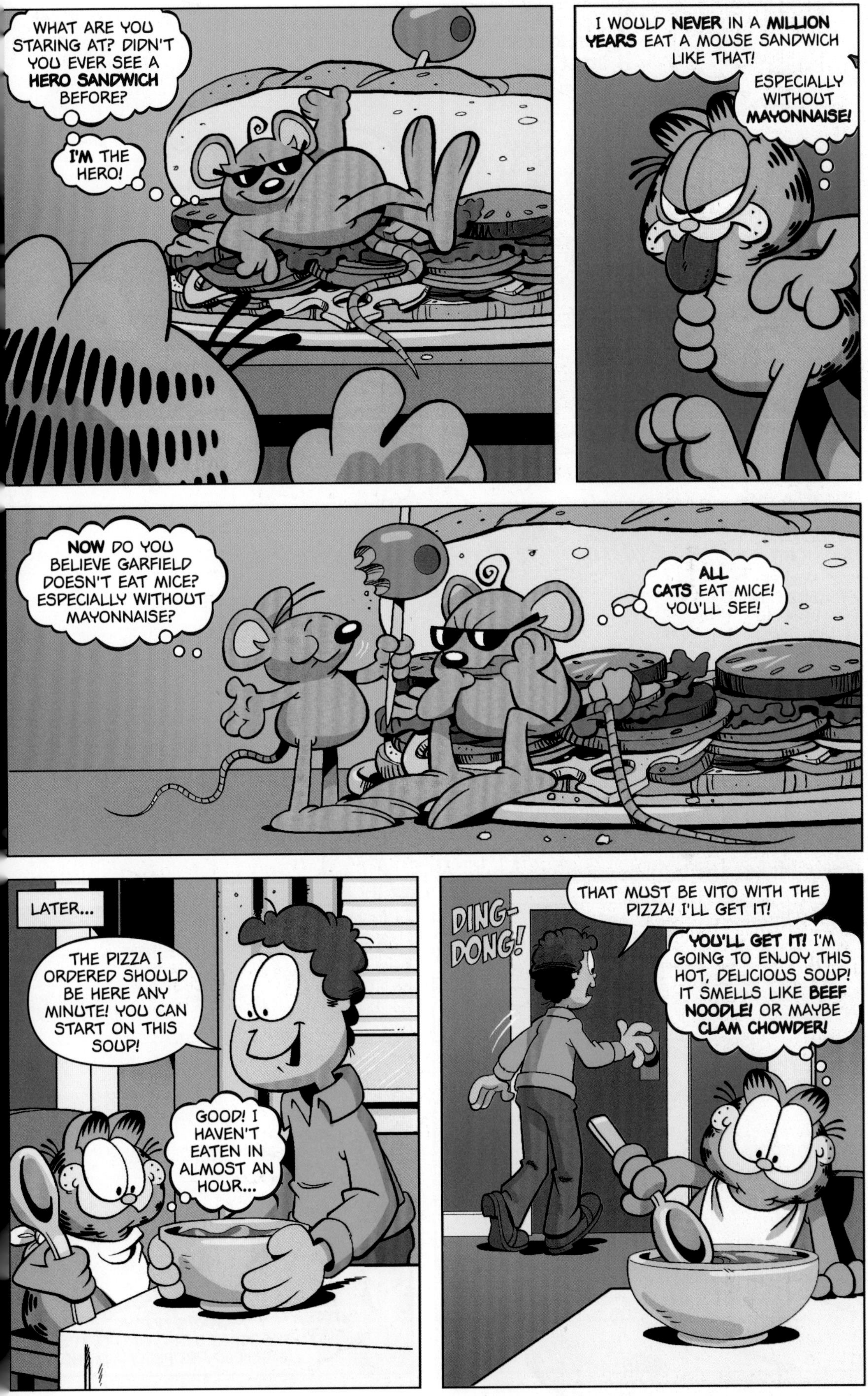
WHAT ARE YOU STARING AT? DIDN'T YOU EVER SEE A **HERO SANDWICH** BEFORE?
I'M THE HERO!
I WOULD **NEVER** IN A **MILLION YEARS** EAT A MOUSE SANDWICH LIKE THAT!
ESPECIALLY WITHOUT **MAYONNAISE!**
NOW DO YOU BELIEVE GARFIELD DOESN'T EAT MICE? ESPECIALLY WITHOUT MAYONNAISE?
ALL CATS EAT MICE! YOU'LL SEE!
LATER...
THE PIZZA I ORDERED SHOULD BE HERE ANY MINUTE! YOU CAN START ON THIS SOUP!
GOOD! I HAVEN'T EATEN IN ALMOST AN HOUR...
DING-DONG!
THAT MUST BE VITO WITH THE PIZZA! I'LL GET IT!
YOU'LL GET IT! I'M GOING TO ENJOY THIS HOT, DELICIOUS SOUP! IT SMELLS LIKE **BEEF NOODLE!** OR MAYBE **CLAM CHOWDER!**

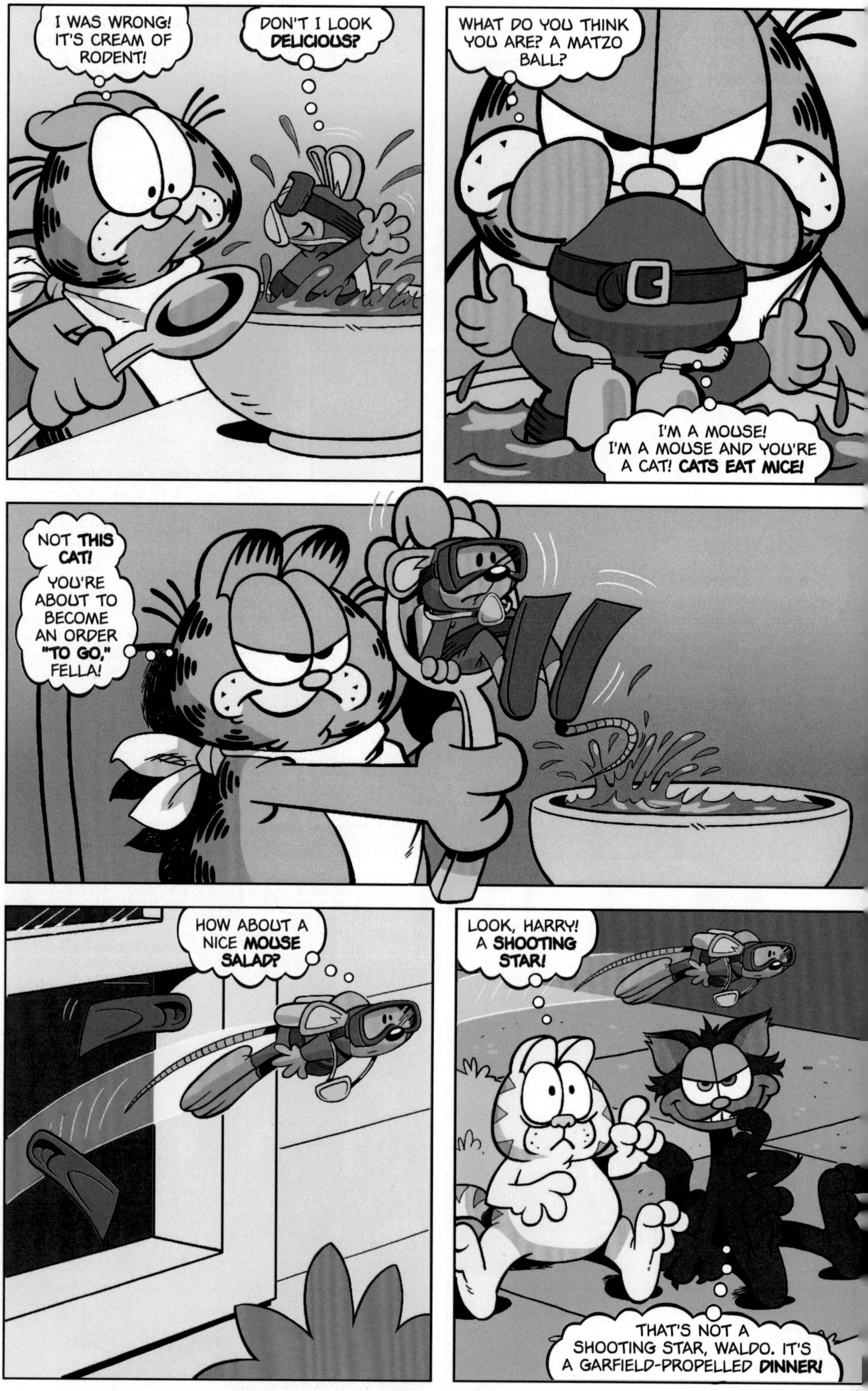

I WAS WRONG! IT'S CREAM OF RODENT!
DON'T I LOOK **DELICIOUS?**
WHAT DO YOU THINK YOU ARE? A MATZO BALL?
I'M A MOUSE! I'M A MOUSE AND YOU'RE A CAT! **CATS EAT MICE!**
NOT **THIS CAT!**
YOU'RE ABOUT TO BECOME AN ORDER **"TO GO,"** FELLA!
HOW ABOUT A NICE **MOUSE SALAD?**
LOOK, HARRY! A **SHOOTING STAR!**
THAT'S NOT A SHOOTING STAR, WALDO. IT'S A GARFIELD-PROPELLED **DINNER!**

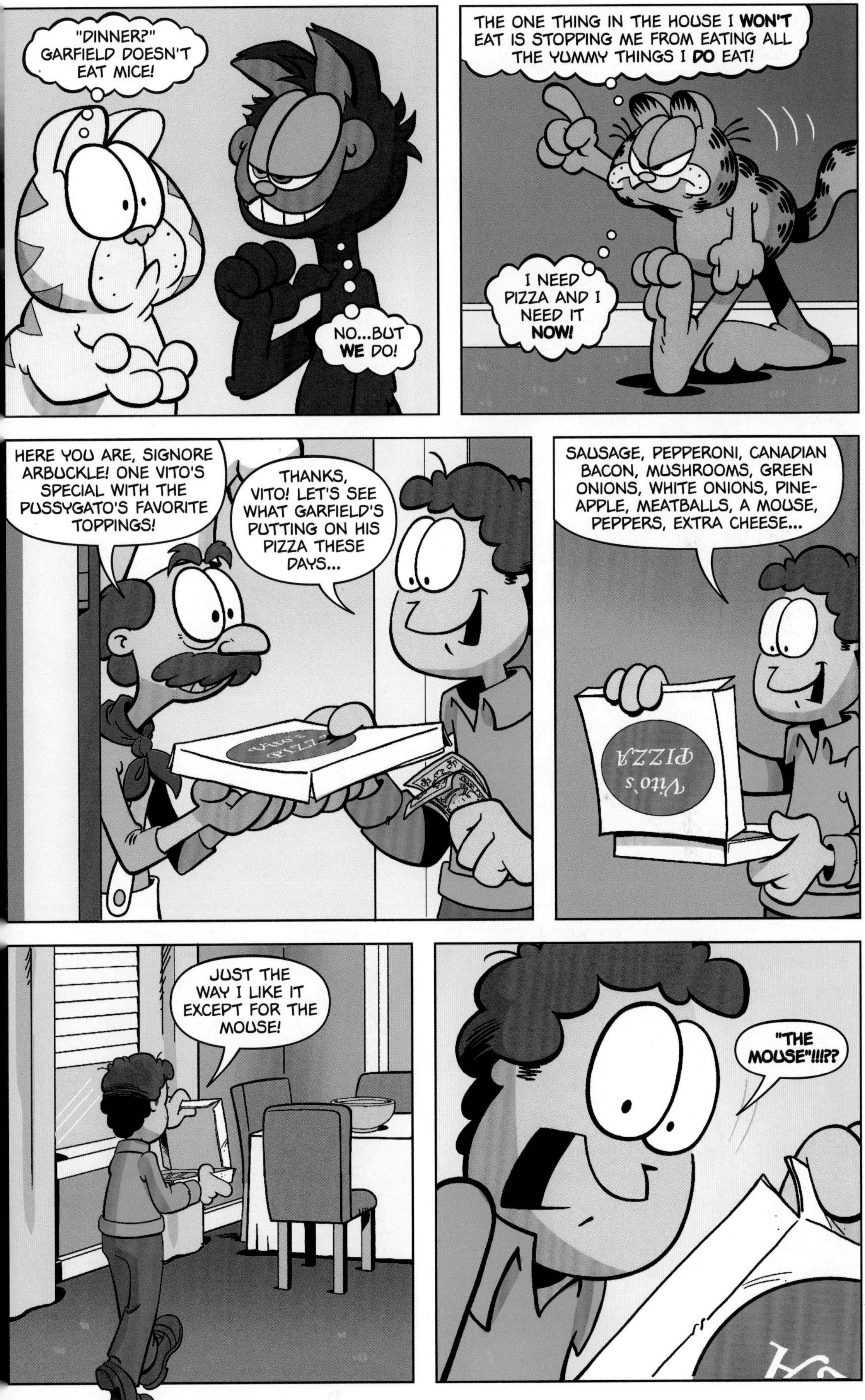
"DINNER?" GARFIELD DOESN'T EAT MICE!
NO...BUT **WE** DO!
THE ONE THING IN THE HOUSE I **WON'T** EAT IS STOPPING ME FROM EATING ALL THE YUMMY THINGS I **DO** EAT!
I NEED PIZZA AND I NEED IT **NOW!**
HERE YOU ARE, SIGNORE ARBUCKLE! ONE VITO'S SPECIAL WITH THE PUSSYGATO'S FAVORITE TOPPINGS!
THANKS, VITO! LET'S SEE WHAT GARFIELD'S PUTTING ON HIS PIZZA THESE DAYS...
SAUSAGE, PEPPERONI, CANADIAN BACON, MUSHROOMS, GREEN ONIONS, WHITE ONIONS, PINE-APPLE, MEATBALLS, A MOUSE, PEPPERS, EXTRA CHEESE...
JUST THE WAY I LIKE IT EXCEPT FOR THE MOUSE!
"THE MOUSE"!!!??

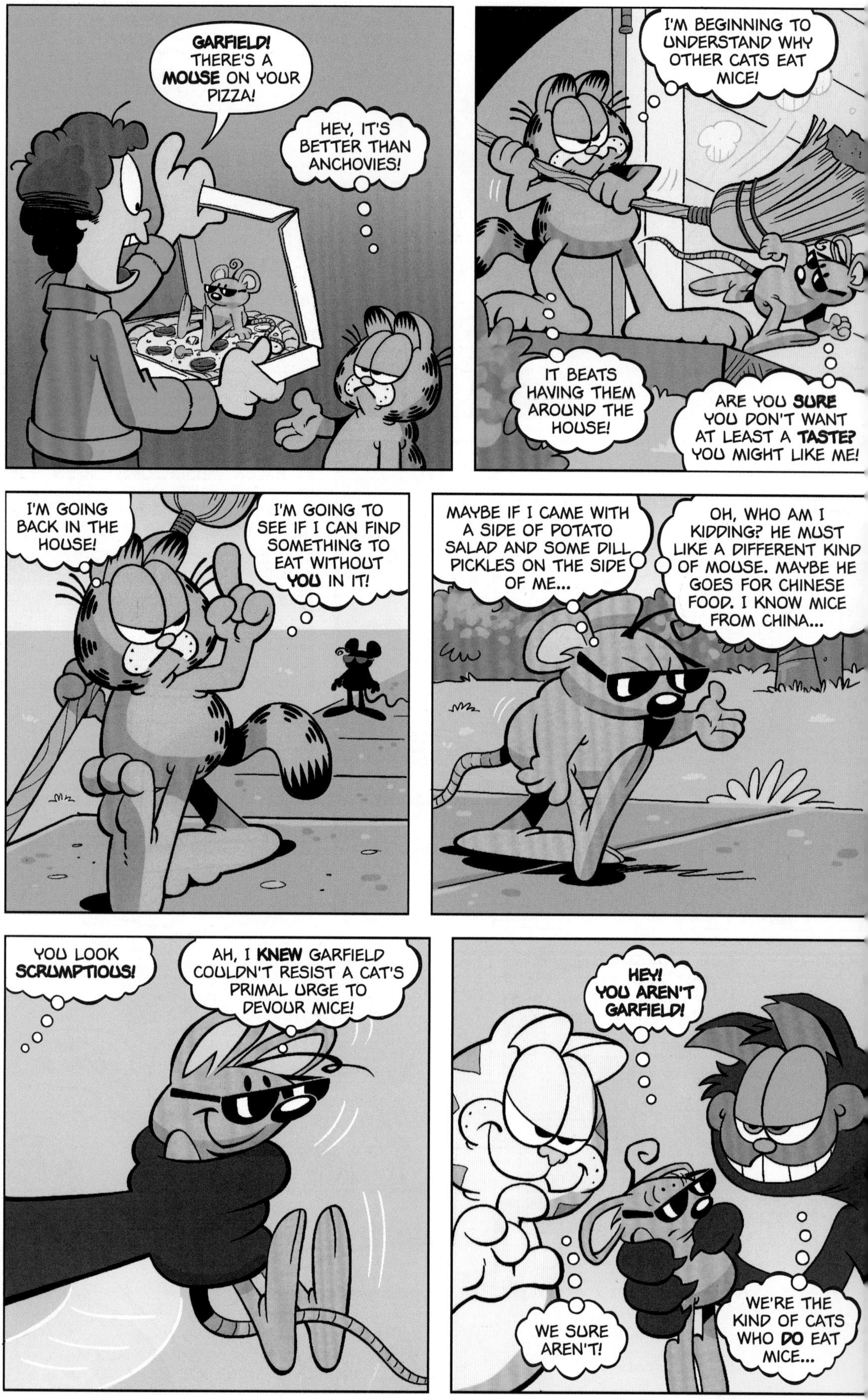
GARFIELD! THERE'S A MOUSE ON YOUR PIZZA!
HEY, IT'S BETTER THAN ANCHOVIES!
I'M BEGINNING TO UNDERSTAND WHY OTHER CATS EAT MICE!
IT BEATS HAVING THEM AROUND THE HOUSE!
ARE YOU SURE YOU DON'T WANT AT LEAST A TASTE? YOU MIGHT LIKE ME!
I'M GOING BACK IN THE HOUSE!
I'M GOING TO SEE IF I CAN FIND SOMETHING TO EAT WITHOUT YOU IN IT!
MAYBE IF I CAME WITH A SIDE OF POTATO SALAD AND SOME DILL PICKLES ON THE SIDE OF ME...
OH, WHO AM I KIDDING? HE MUST LIKE A DIFFERENT KIND OF MOUSE. MAYBE HE GOES FOR CHINESE FOOD. I KNOW MICE FROM CHINA...
YOU LOOK SCRUMPTIOUS!
AH, I KNEW GARFIELD COULDN'T RESIST A CAT'S PRIMAL URGE TO DEVOUR MICE!
HEY! YOU AREN'T GARFIELD!
WE SURE AREN'T!
WE'RE THE KIND OF CATS WHO DO EAT MICE...

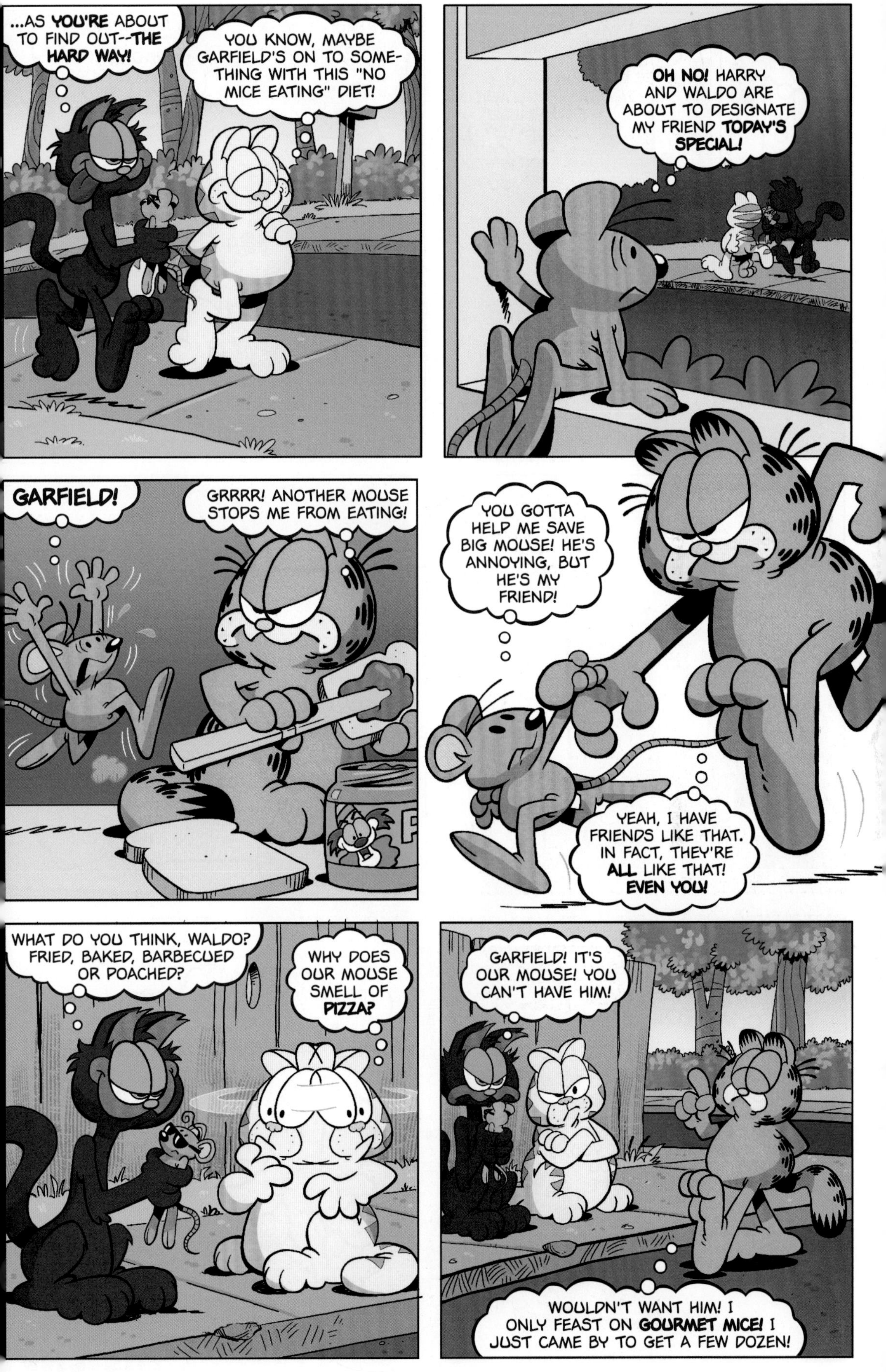

...AS YOU'RE ABOUT TO FIND OUT--THE HARD WAY!
YOU KNOW, MAYBE GARFIELD'S ON TO SOMETHING WITH THIS "NO MICE EATING" DIET!
OH NO! HARRY AND WALDO ARE ABOUT TO DESIGNATE MY FRIEND TODAY'S SPECIAL!
GARFIELD!
GRRRR! ANOTHER MOUSE STOPS ME FROM EATING!
YOU GOTTA HELP ME SAVE BIG MOUSE! HE'S ANNOYING, BUT HE'S MY FRIEND!
YEAH, I HAVE FRIENDS LIKE THAT. IN FACT, THEY'RE ALL LIKE THAT! EVEN YOU!
WHAT DO YOU THINK, WALDO? FRIED, BAKED, BARBECUED OR POACHED?
WHY DOES OUR MOUSE SMELL OF PIZZA?
GARFIELD! IT'S OUR MOUSE! YOU CAN'T HAVE HIM!
WOULDN'T WANT HIM! I ONLY FEAST ON GOURMET MICE! I JUST CAME BY TO GET A FEW DOZEN!

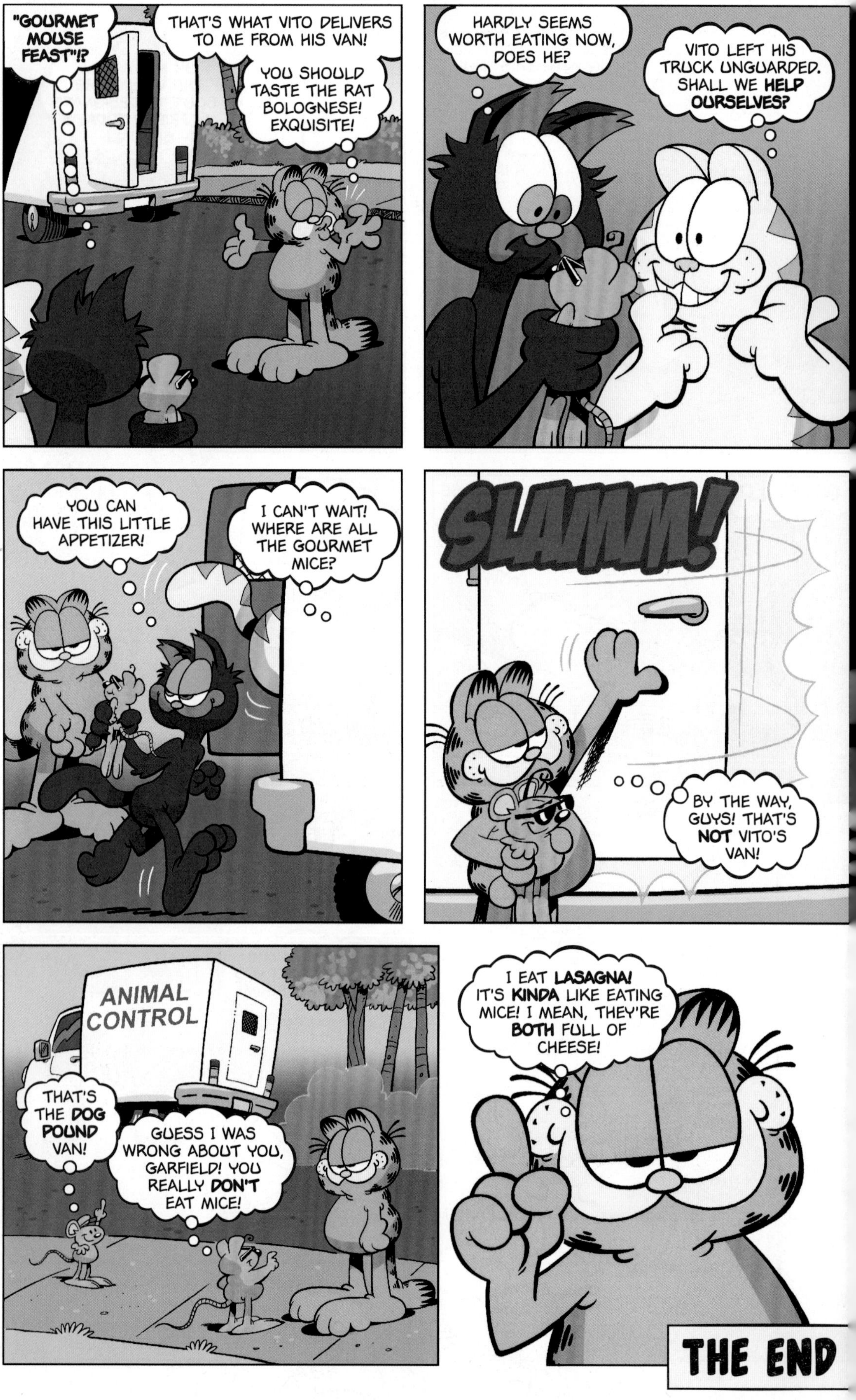

"GOURMET MOUSE FEAST"!?
THAT'S WHAT VITO DELIVERS TO ME FROM HIS VAN!
YOU SHOULD TASTE THE RAT BOLOGNESE! EXQUISITE!
HARDLY SEEMS WORTH EATING NOW, DOES HE?
VITO LEFT HIS TRUCK UNGUARDED. SHALL WE HELP OURSELVES?
YOU CAN HAVE THIS LITTLE APPETIZER!
I CAN'T WAIT! WHERE ARE ALL THE GOURMET MICE?
SLAMM!
BY THE WAY, GUYS! THAT'S NOT VITO'S VAN!
ANIMAL CONTROL
THAT'S THE DOG POUND VAN!
GUESS I WAS WRONG ABOUT YOU, GARFIELD! YOU REALLY DON'T EAT MICE!
I EAT LASAGNA! IT'S KINDA LIKE EATING MICE! I MEAN, THEY'RE BOTH FULL OF CHEESE!
THE END

CHAPTER TWO

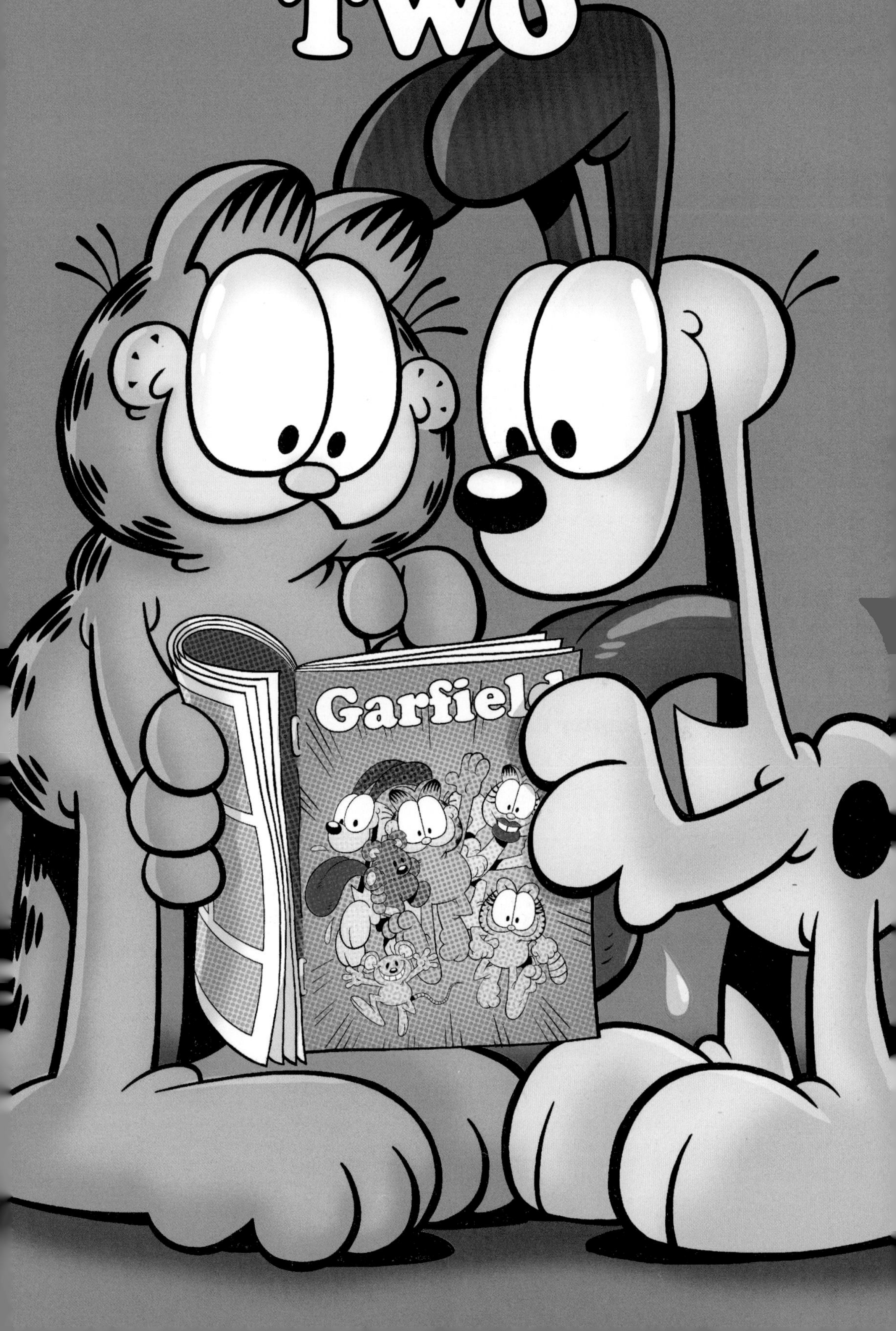
Garfield

STICKING POINT
DOWN FOR
THE COUNT

Written by
MARK EVANIER

Art by
GARY BARKER
AND DAN DAVIS

Colors by
LISA MOORE

Chapter Break Art by
GARY BARKER
WITH BRADEN LAMB

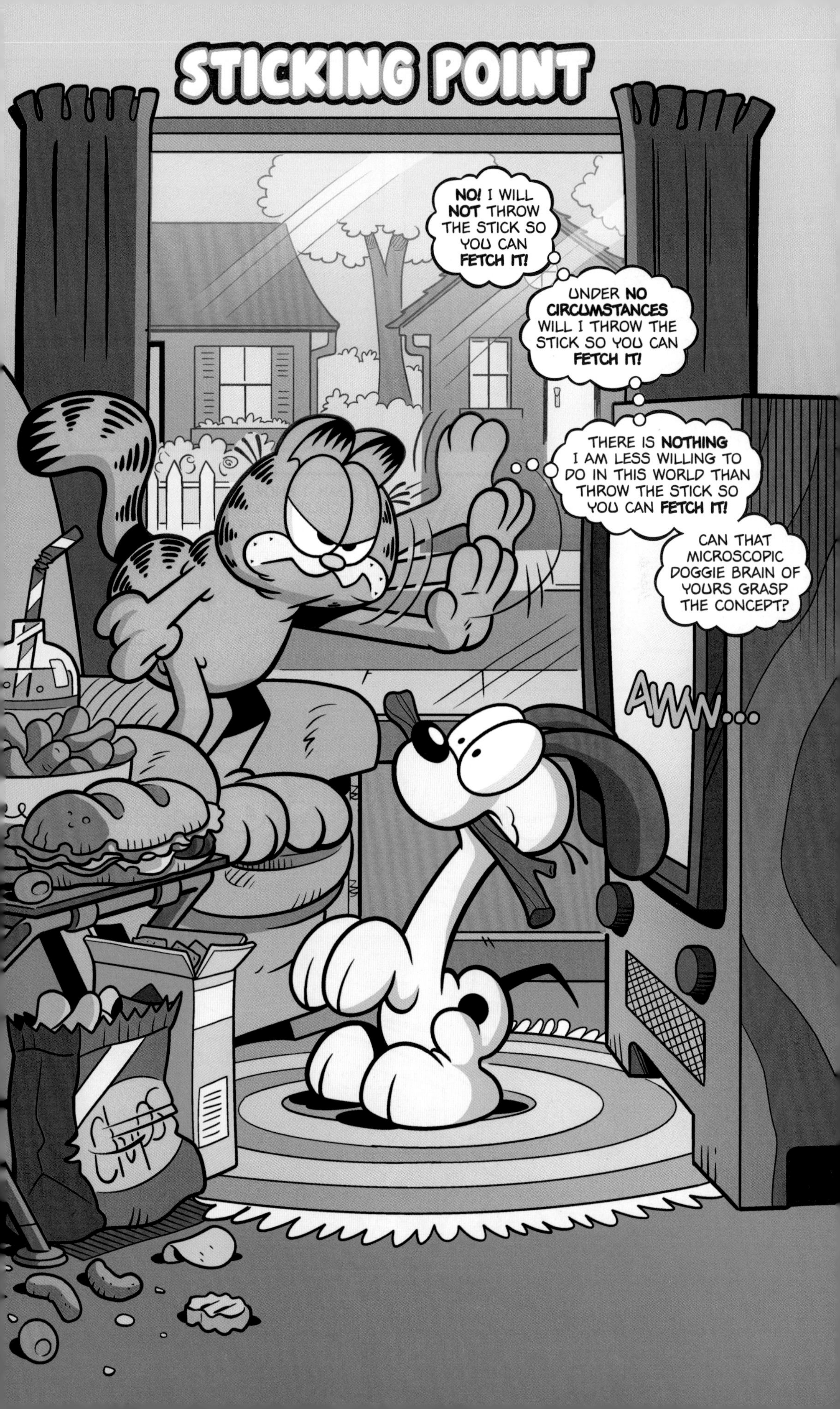
STICKING POINT
NO! I WILL NOT THROW THE STICK SO YOU CAN FETCH IT!
UNDER NO CIRCUMSTANCES WILL I THROW THE STICK SO YOU CAN FETCH IT!
THERE IS NOTHING I AM LESS WILLING TO DO IN THIS WORLD THAN THROW THE STICK SO YOU CAN FETCH IT!
CAN THAT MICROSCOPIC DOGGIE BRAIN OF YOURS GRASP THE CONCEPT?
AWW...
Chips

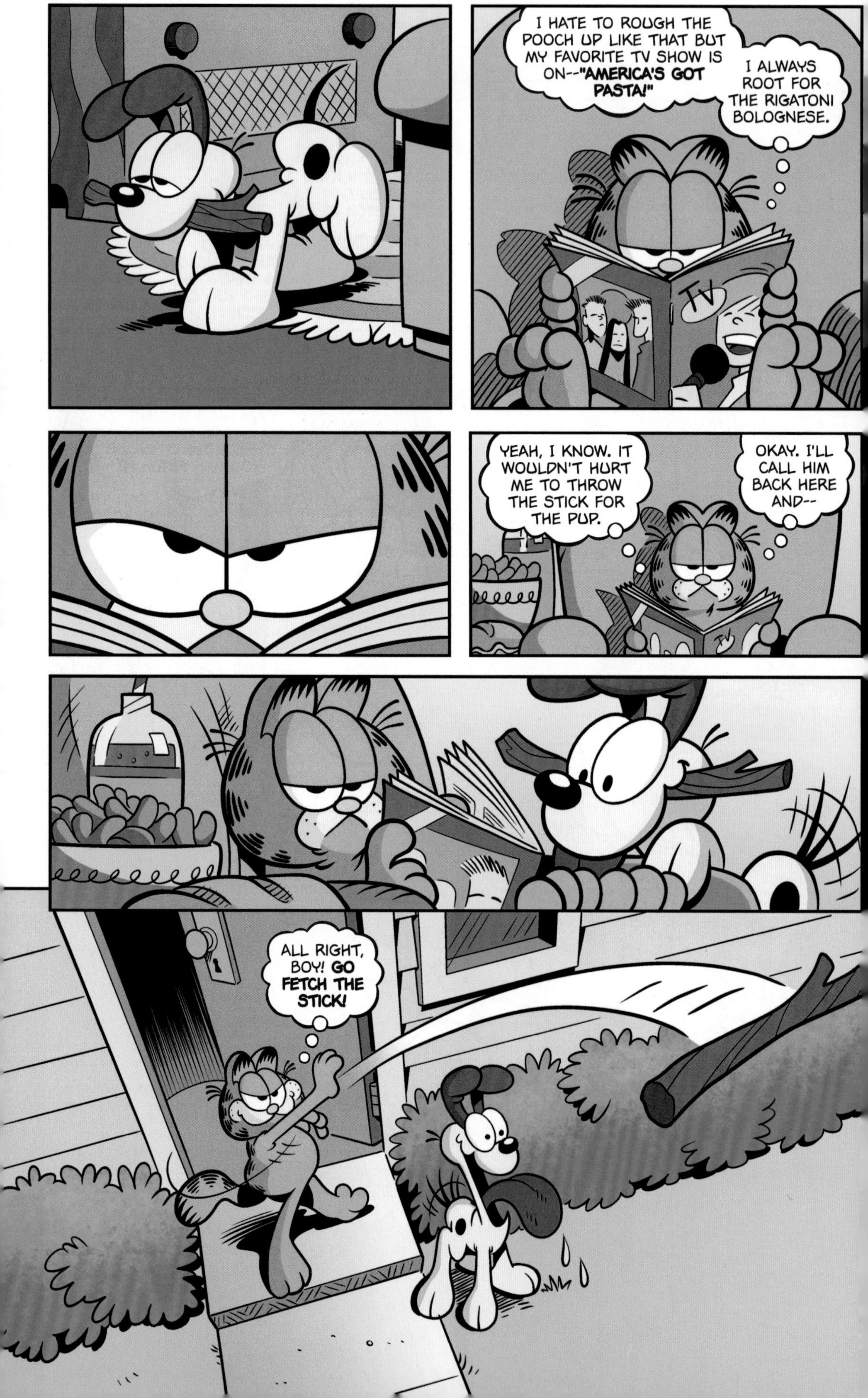

I HATE TO ROUGH THE POOCH UP LIKE THAT BUT MY FAVORITE TV SHOW IS ON--"AMERICA'S GOT PASTA!"
I ALWAYS ROOT FOR THE RIGATONI BOLOGNESE.
TV
YEAH, I KNOW. IT WOULDN'T HURT ME TO THROW THE STICK FOR THE PUP.
OKAY. I'LL CALL HIM BACK HERE AND--
ALL RIGHT, BOY! GO FETCH THE STICK!

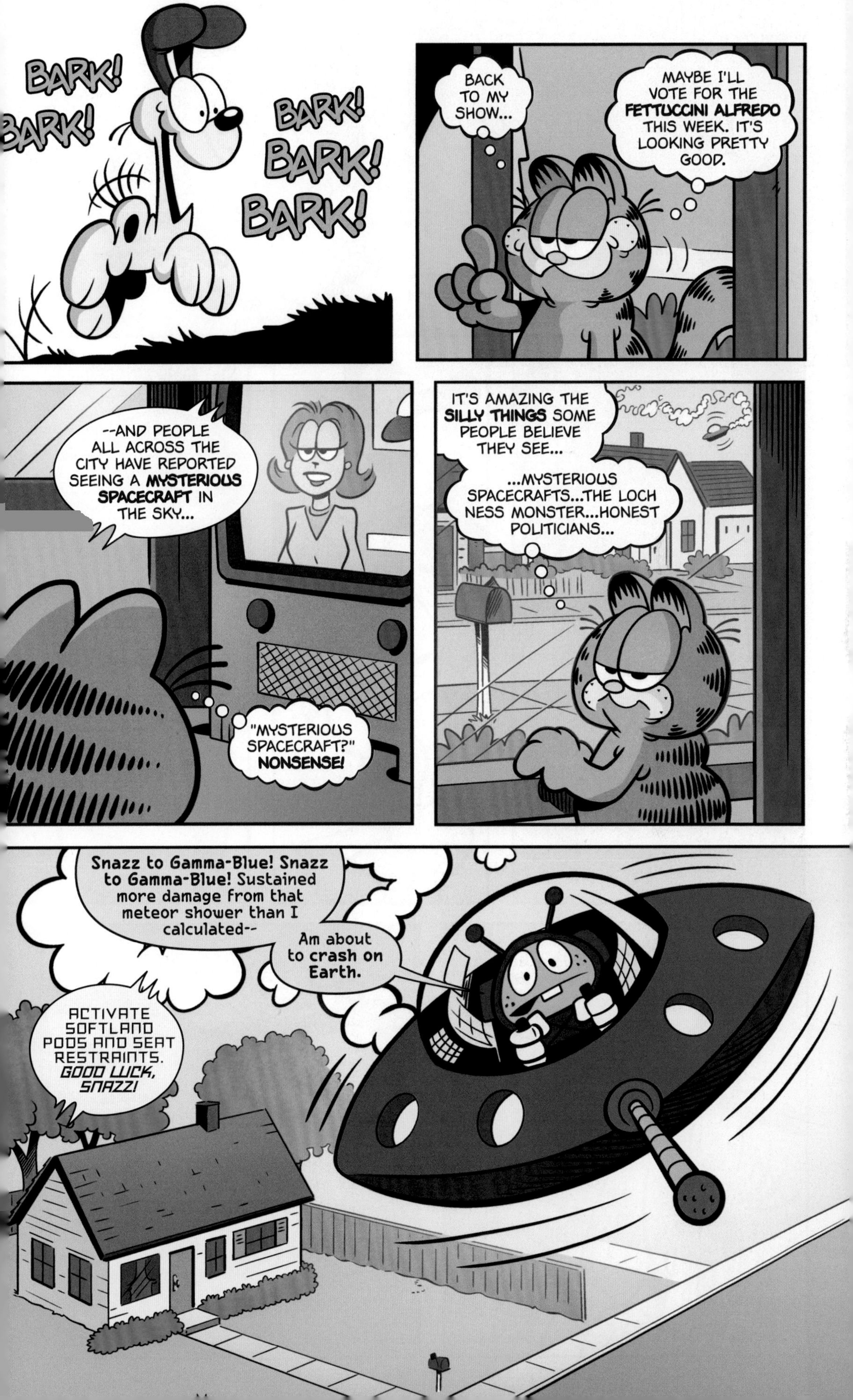
BARK! BARK! BARK! BARK! BARK!
BACK TO MY SHOW...
MAYBE I'LL VOTE FOR THE FETTUCCINI ALFREDO THIS WEEK. IT'S LOOKING PRETTY GOOD.
--AND PEOPLE ALL ACROSS THE CITY HAVE REPORTED SEEING A MYSTERIOUS SPACECRAFT IN THE SKY...
"MYSTERIOUS SPACECRAFT?" NONSENSE!
IT'S AMAZING THE SILLY THINGS SOME PEOPLE BELIEVE THEY SEE...
...MYSTERIOUS SPACECRAFTS...THE LOCH NESS MONSTER...HONEST POLITICIANS...
Snazz to Gamma-Blue! Snazz to Gamma-Blue! Sustained more damage from that meteor shower than I calculated--
Am about to crash on Earth.
ACTIVATE SOFTLAND PODS AND SEAT RESTRAINTS. GOOD LUCK, SNAZZ!

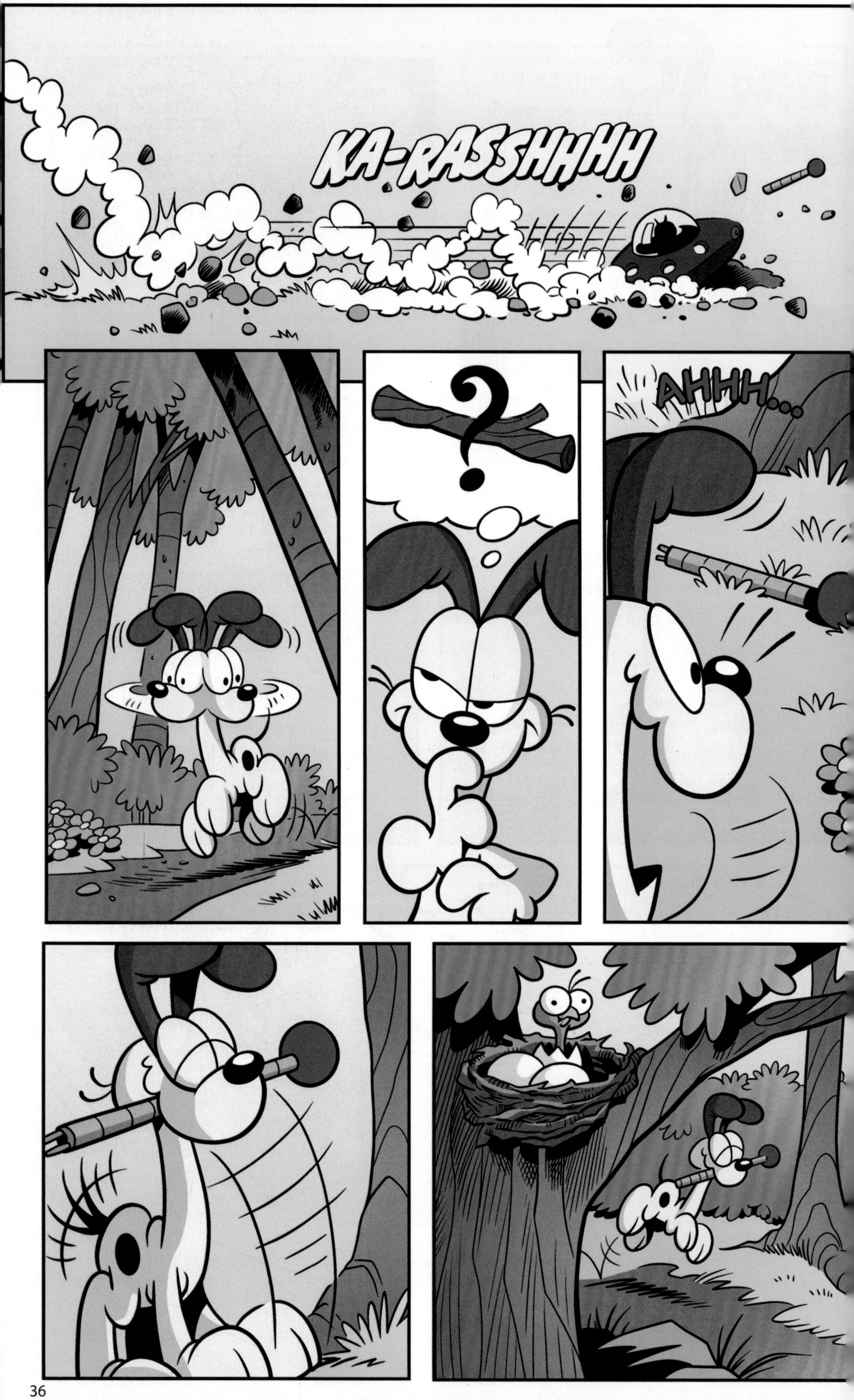
KA-RASSHHHH
?
AHHH...

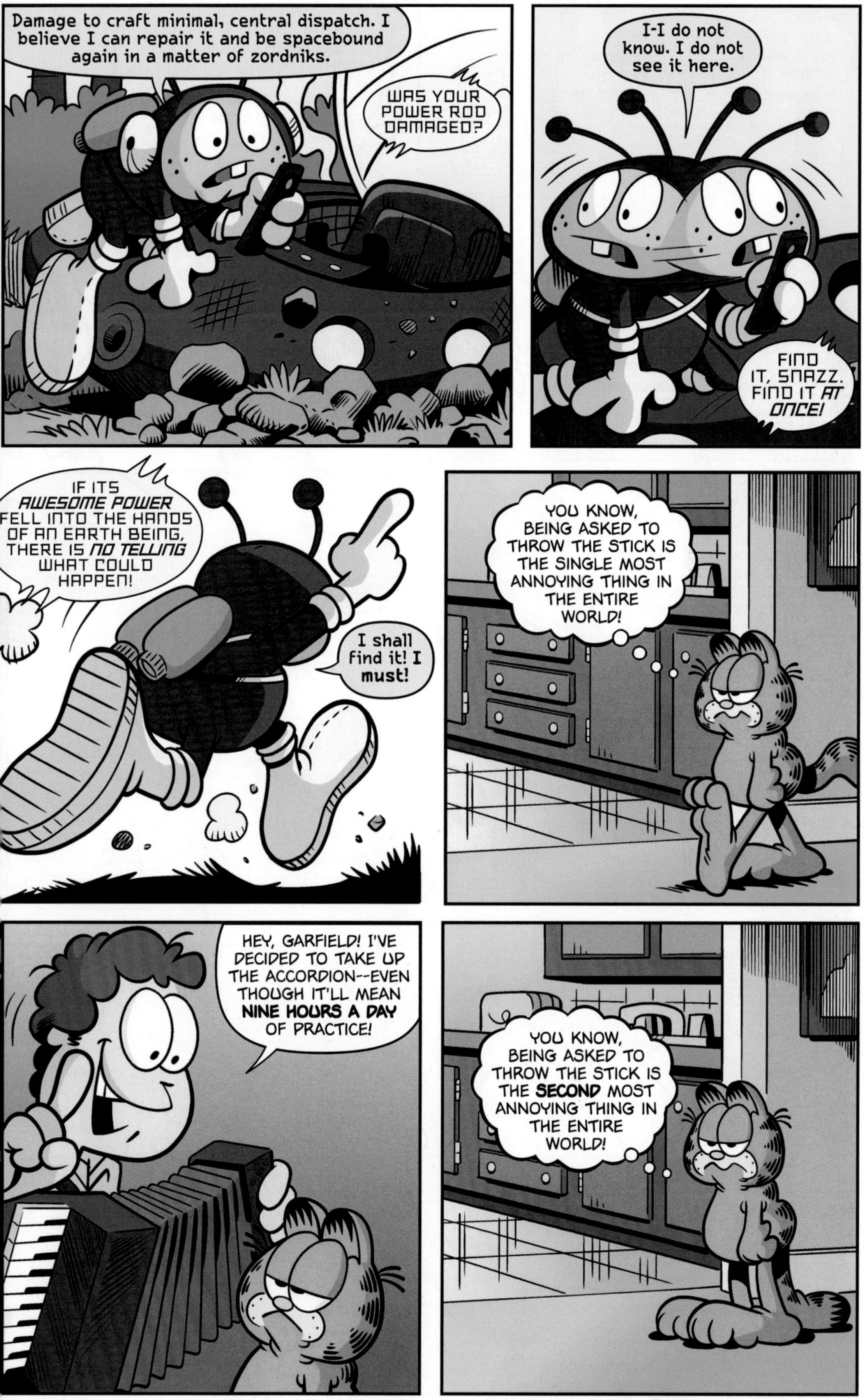
Damage to craft minimal, central dispatch. I believe I can repair it and be spacebound again in a matter of zordniks.
WAS YOUR POWER ROD DAMAGED?
I-I do not know. I do not see it here.
FIND IT, SNAZZ. FIND IT AT ONCE!
IF ITS AWESOME POWER FELL INTO THE HANDS OF AN EARTH BEING, THERE IS NO TELLING WHAT COULD HAPPEN!
I shall find it! I must!
YOU KNOW, BEING ASKED TO THROW THE STICK IS THE SINGLE MOST ANNOYING THING IN THE ENTIRE WORLD!
HEY, GARFIELD! I'VE DECIDED TO TAKE UP THE ACCORDION--EVEN THOUGH IT'LL MEAN NINE HOURS A DAY OF PRACTICE!
YOU KNOW, BEING ASKED TO THROW THE STICK IS THE SECOND MOST ANNOYING THING IN THE ENTIRE WORLD!

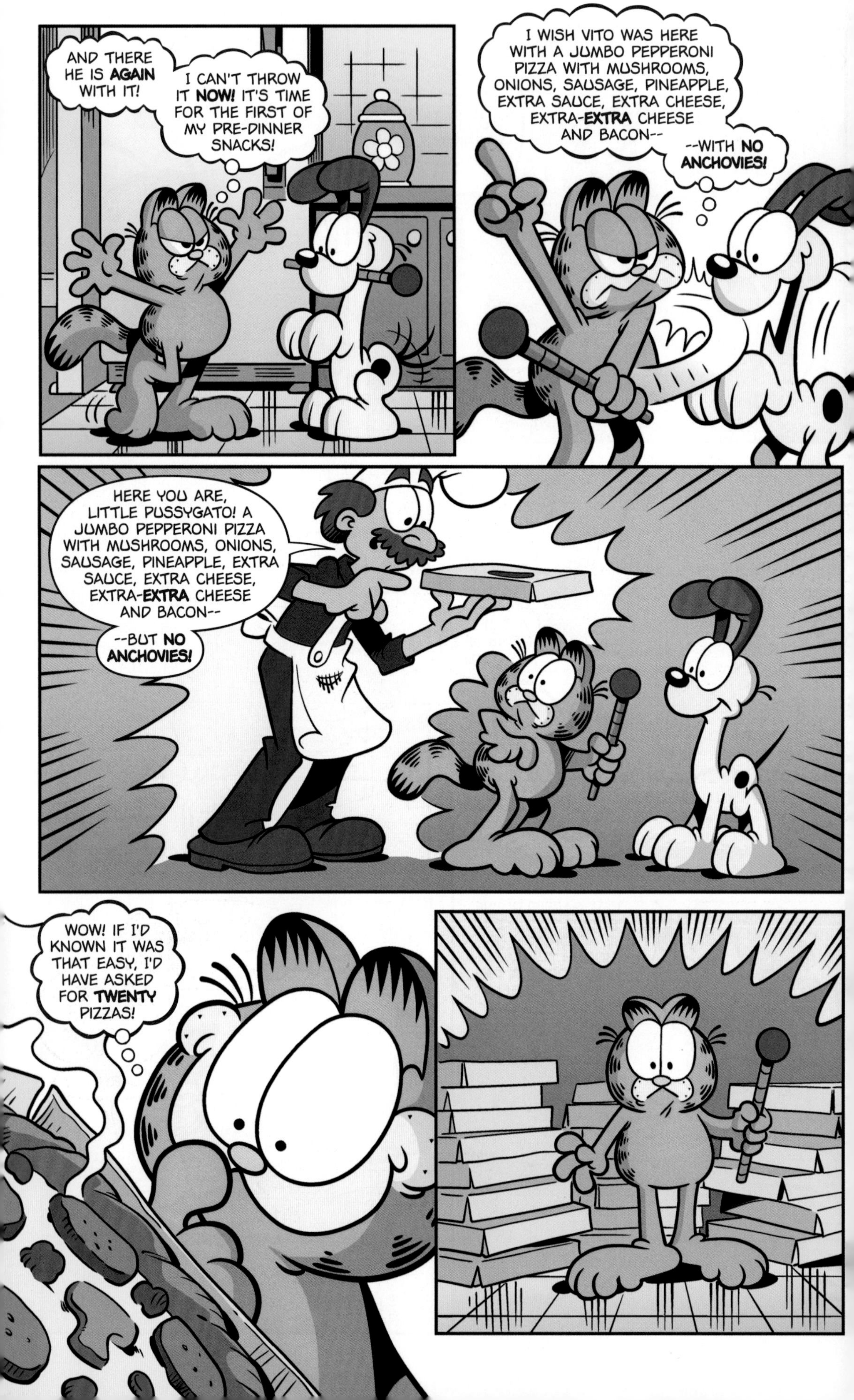

AND THERE HE IS **AGAIN** WITH IT!
I CAN'T THROW IT **NOW!** IT'S TIME FOR THE FIRST OF MY PRE-DINNER SNACKS!
I WISH VITO WAS HERE WITH A JUMBO PEPPERONI PIZZA WITH MUSHROOMS, ONIONS, SAUSAGE, PINEAPPLE, EXTRA SAUCE, EXTRA CHEESE, EXTRA-**EXTRA** CHEESE AND BACON--
--WITH **NO ANCHOVIES!**
HERE YOU ARE, LITTLE PUSSYGATO! A JUMBO PEPPERONI PIZZA WITH MUSHROOMS, ONIONS, SAUSAGE, PINEAPPLE, EXTRA SAUCE, EXTRA CHEESE, EXTRA-**EXTRA** CHEESE AND BACON--
--BUT **NO ANCHOVIES!**
WOW! IF I'D KNOWN IT WAS THAT EASY, I'D HAVE ASKED FOR **TWENTY** PIZZAS!

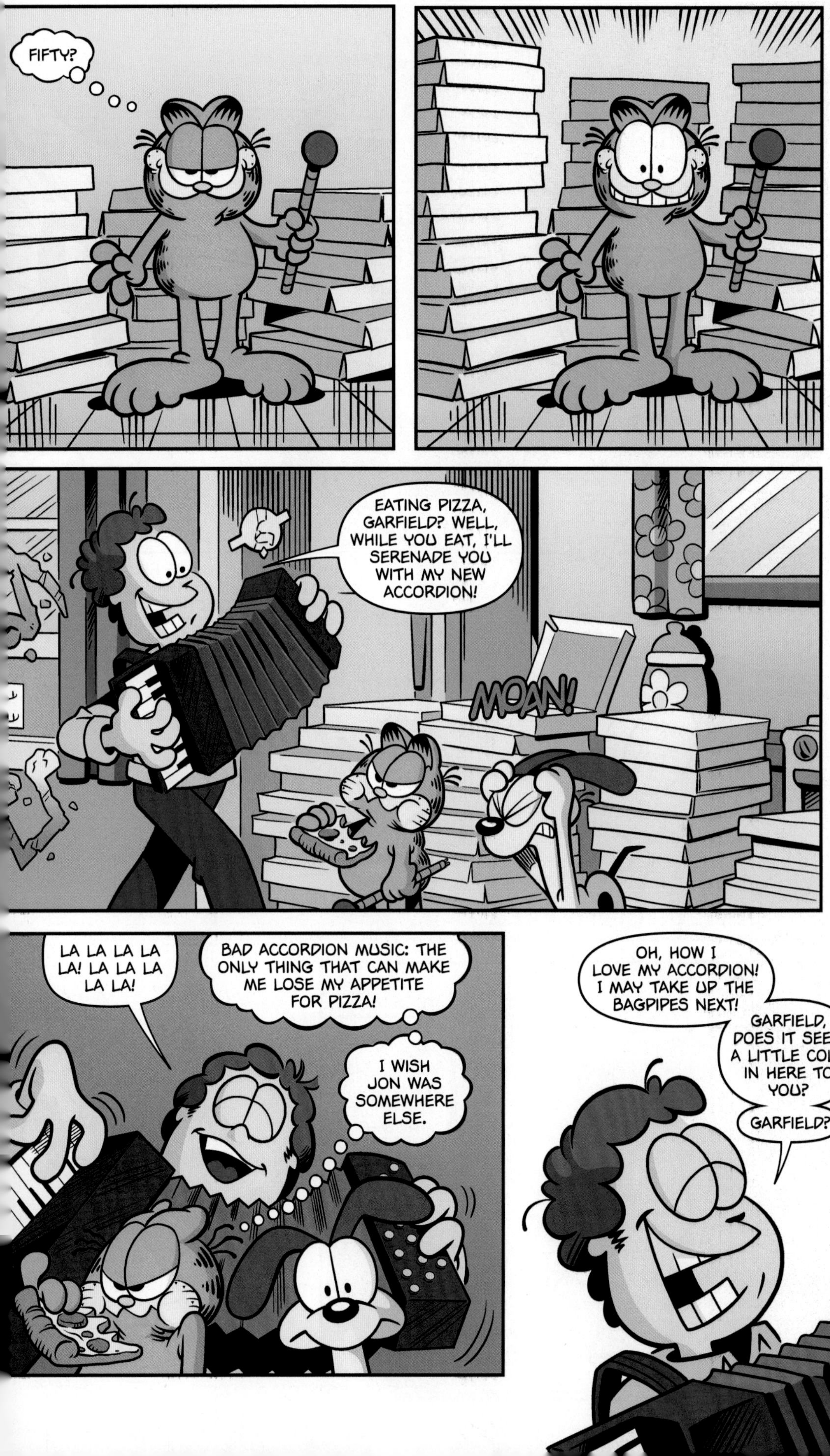

FIFTY?
EATING PIZZA, GARFIELD? WELL, WHILE YOU EAT, I'LL SERENADE YOU WITH MY NEW ACCORDION!
MOAN!
LA LA LA LA LA! LA LA LA LA LA!
BAD ACCORDION MUSIC: THE ONLY THING THAT CAN MAKE ME LOSE MY APPETITE FOR PIZZA!
I WISH JON WAS SOMEWHERE ELSE.
OH, HOW I LOVE MY ACCORDION! I MAY TAKE UP THE BAGPIPES NEXT!
GARFIELD, DOES IT SEEM A LITTLE COLD IN HERE TO YOU?
GARFIELD?

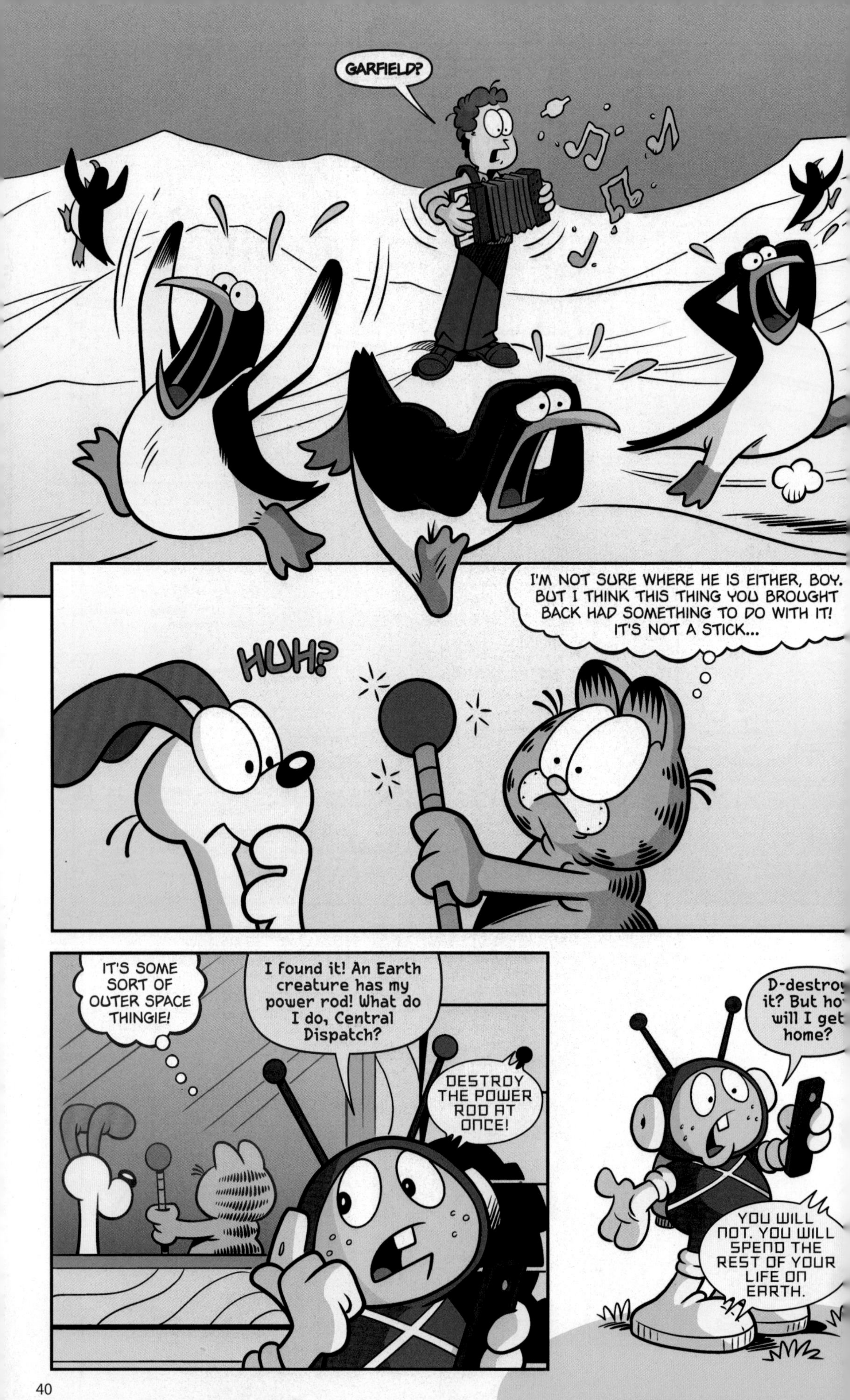
GARFIELD?
I'M NOT SURE WHERE HE IS EITHER, BOY. BUT I THINK THIS THING YOU BROUGHT BACK HAD SOMETHING TO DO WITH IT! IT'S NOT A STICK...
HUH?
IT'S SOME SORT OF OUTER SPACE THINGIE!
I found it! An Earth creature has my power rod! What do I do, Central Dispatch?
DESTROY THE POWER ROD AT ONCE!
D-destroy it? But how will I get home?
YOU WILL NOT. YOU WILL SPEND THE REST OF YOUR LIFE ON EARTH.

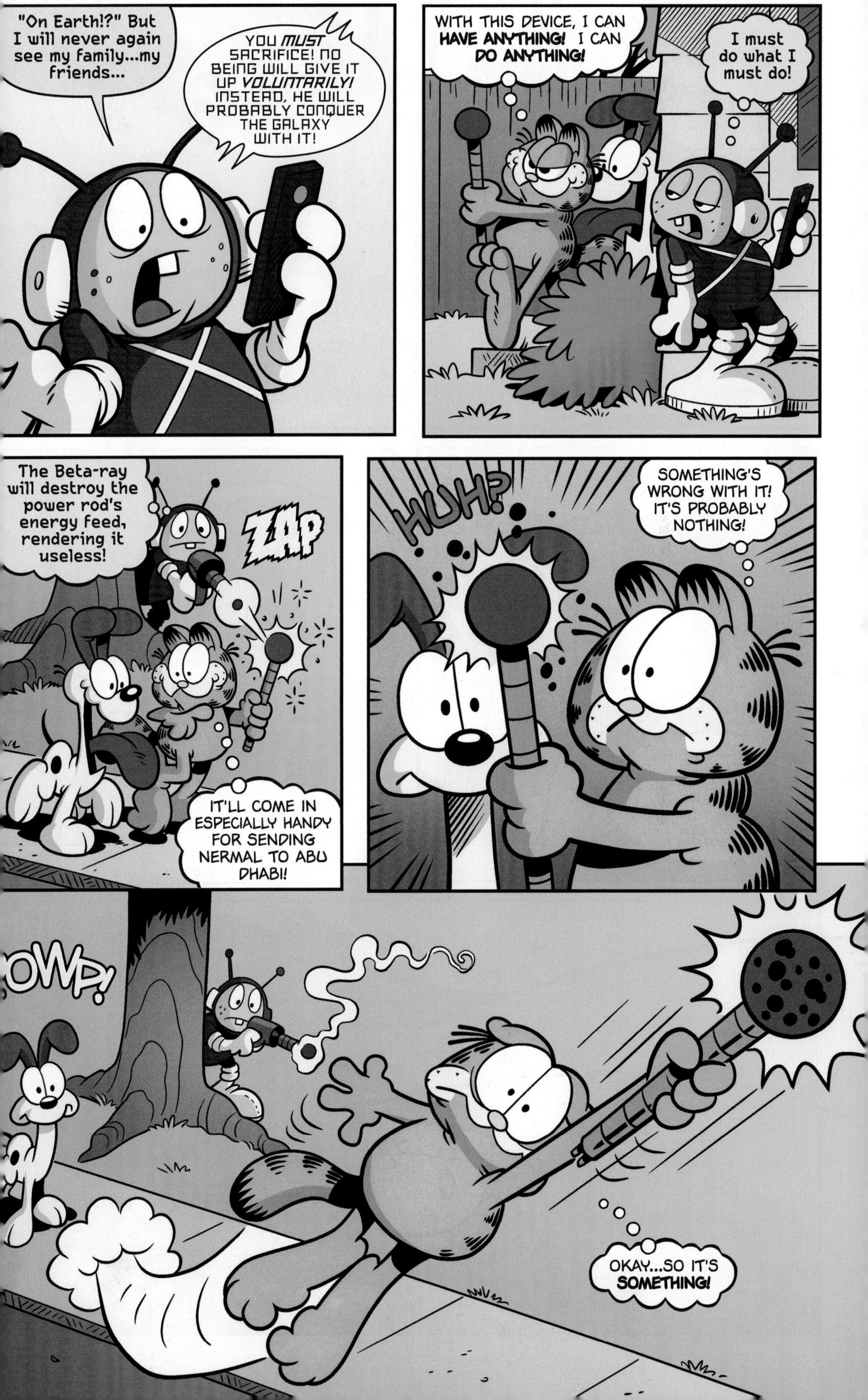
"On Earth!?" But I will never again see my family...my friends...
YOU MUST SACRIFICE! NO BEING WILL GIVE IT UP VOLUNTARILY! INSTEAD, HE WILL PROBABLY CONQUER THE GALAXY WITH IT!
WITH THIS DEVICE, I CAN HAVE ANYTHING! I CAN DO ANYTHING!
I must do what I must do!
The Beta-ray will destroy the power rod's energy feed, rendering it useless!
ZAP
IT'LL COME IN ESPECIALLY HANDY FOR SENDING NERMAL TO ABU DHABI!
HUH?
SOMETHING'S WRONG WITH IT! IT'S PROBABLY NOTHING!
OWP!
OKAY...SO IT'S SOMETHING!

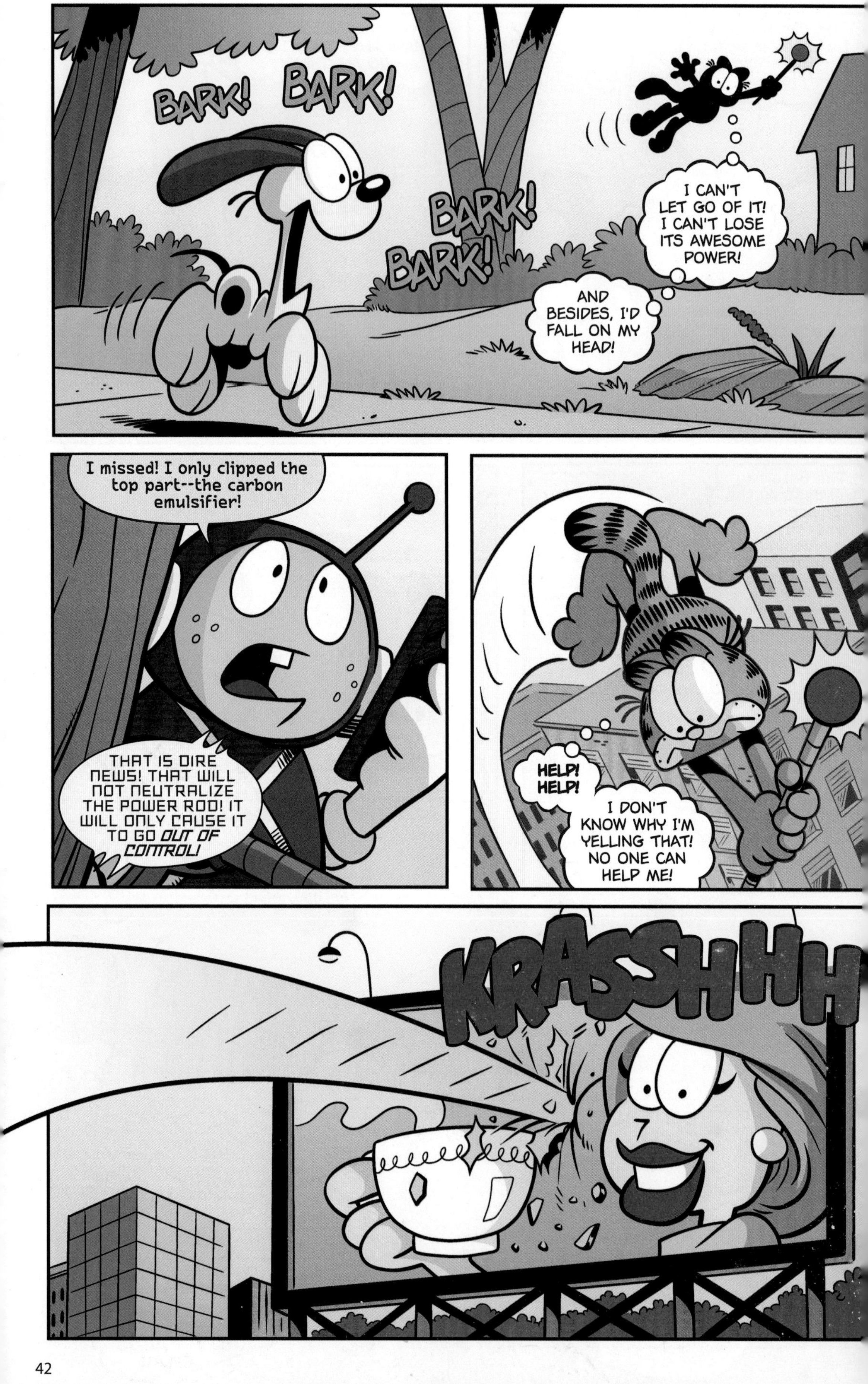
BARK! BARK!
BARK!
BARK!
I CAN'T LET GO OF IT! I CAN'T LOSE ITS AWESOME POWER!
AND BESIDES, I'D FALL ON MY HEAD!
I missed! I only clipped the top part--the carbon emulsifier!
THAT IS DIRE NEWS! THAT WILL NOT NEUTRALIZE THE POWER ROD! IT WILL ONLY CAUSE IT TO GO *OUT OF CONTROL!*
HELP! HELP!
I DON'T KNOW WHY I'M YELLING THAT! NO ONE CAN HELP ME!
KRASSHHH

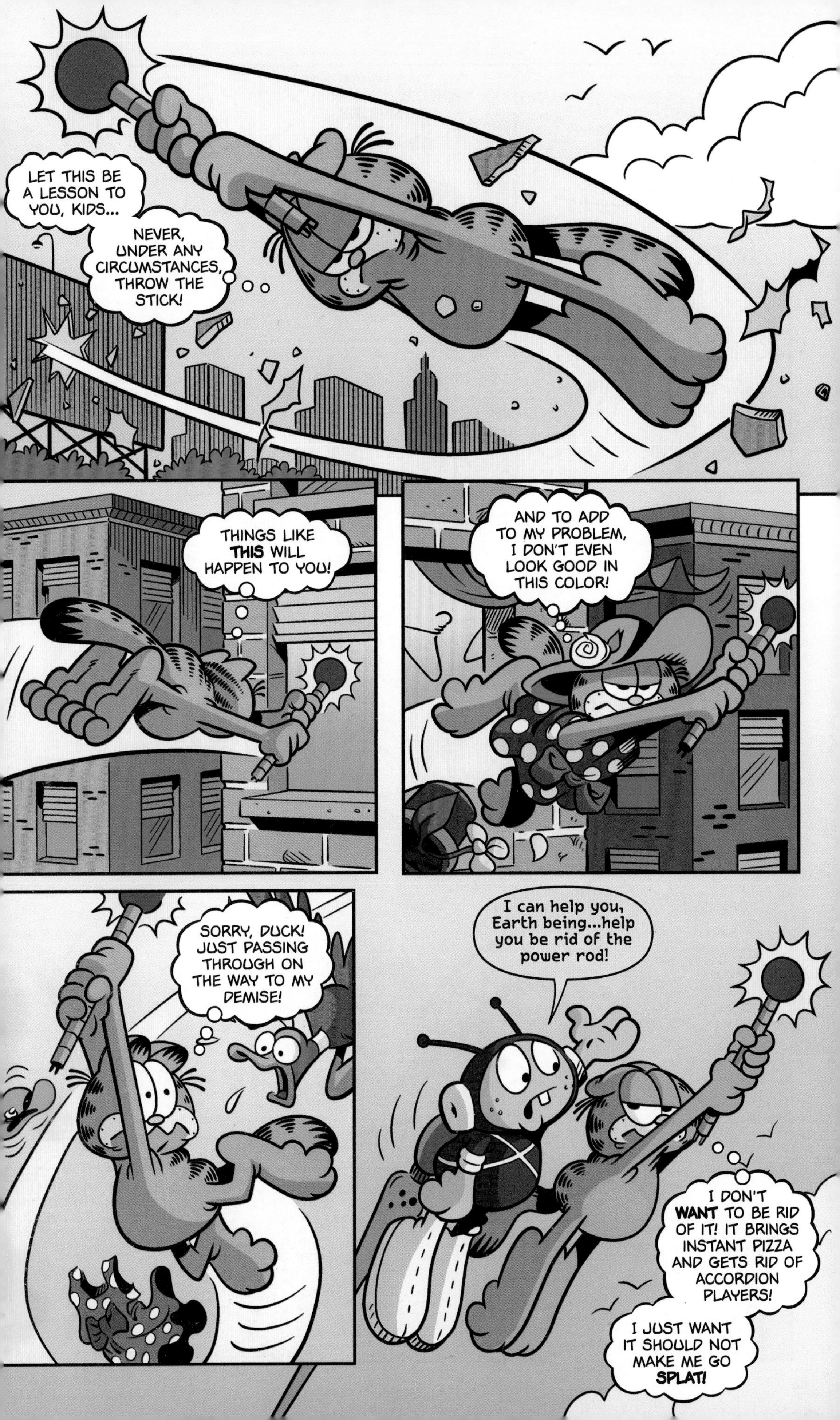

LET THIS BE A LESSON TO YOU, KIDS...
NEVER, UNDER ANY CIRCUMSTANCES, THROW THE STICK!
THINGS LIKE **THIS** WILL HAPPEN TO YOU!
AND TO ADD TO MY PROBLEM, I DON'T EVEN LOOK GOOD IN THIS COLOR!
SORRY, DUCK! JUST PASSING THROUGH ON THE WAY TO MY DEMISE!
I can help you, Earth being...help you be rid of the power rod!
I DON'T **WANT** TO BE RID OF IT! IT BRINGS INSTANT PIZZA AND GETS RID OF ACCORDION PLAYERS!
I JUST WANT IT SHOULD NOT MAKE ME GO **SPLAT!**

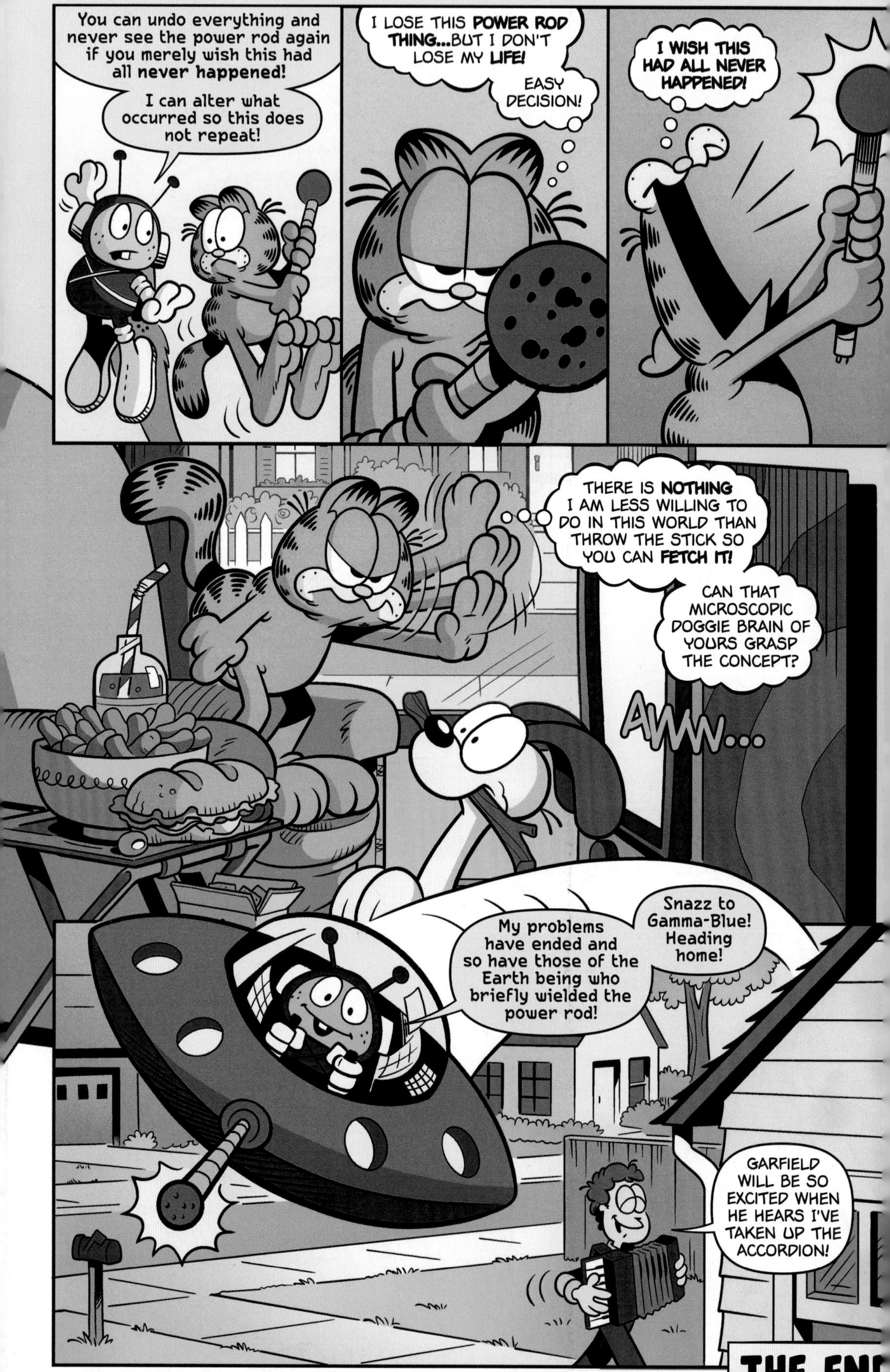
You can undo everything and never see the power rod again if you merely wish this had all **never happened**!
I can alter what occurred so this does not repeat!
I LOSE THIS **POWER ROD THING...**BUT I DON'T LOSE MY **LIFE!**
EASY DECISION!
I WISH THIS HAD ALL NEVER HAPPENED!
THERE IS **NOTHING** I AM LESS WILLING TO DO IN THIS WORLD THAN THROW THE STICK SO YOU CAN **FETCH IT!**
CAN THAT MICROSCOPIC DOGGIE BRAIN OF YOURS GRASP THE CONCEPT?
AWW...
My problems have ended and so have those of the Earth being who briefly wielded the power rod!
Snazz to Gamma-Blue! Heading home!
GARFIELD WILL BE SO EXCITED WHEN HE HEARS I'VE TAKEN UP THE ACCORDION!
THE END

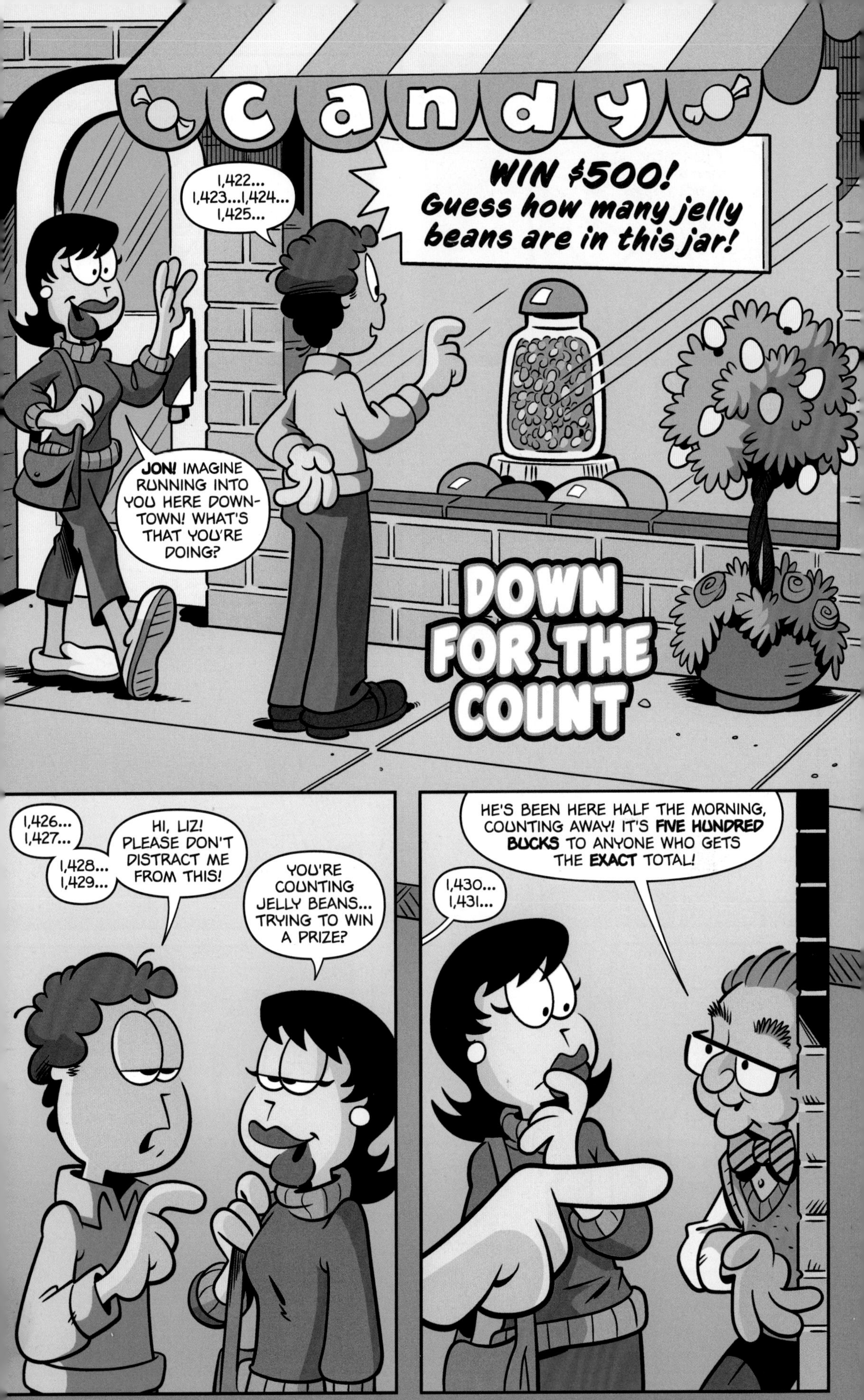
Candy
WIN $500! Guess how many jelly beans are in this jar!
1,422... 1,423...1,424... 1,425...
JON! IMAGINE RUNNING INTO YOU HERE DOWN-TOWN! WHAT'S THAT YOU'RE DOING?
DOWN FOR THE COUNT
1,426... 1,427...
1,428... 1,429...
HI, LIZ! PLEASE DON'T DISTRACT ME FROM THIS!
YOU'RE COUNTING JELLY BEANS... TRYING TO WIN A PRIZE?
1,430... 1,431...
HE'S BEEN HERE HALF THE MORNING, COUNTING AWAY! IT'S FIVE HUNDRED BUCKS TO ANYONE WHO GETS THE EXACT TOTAL!

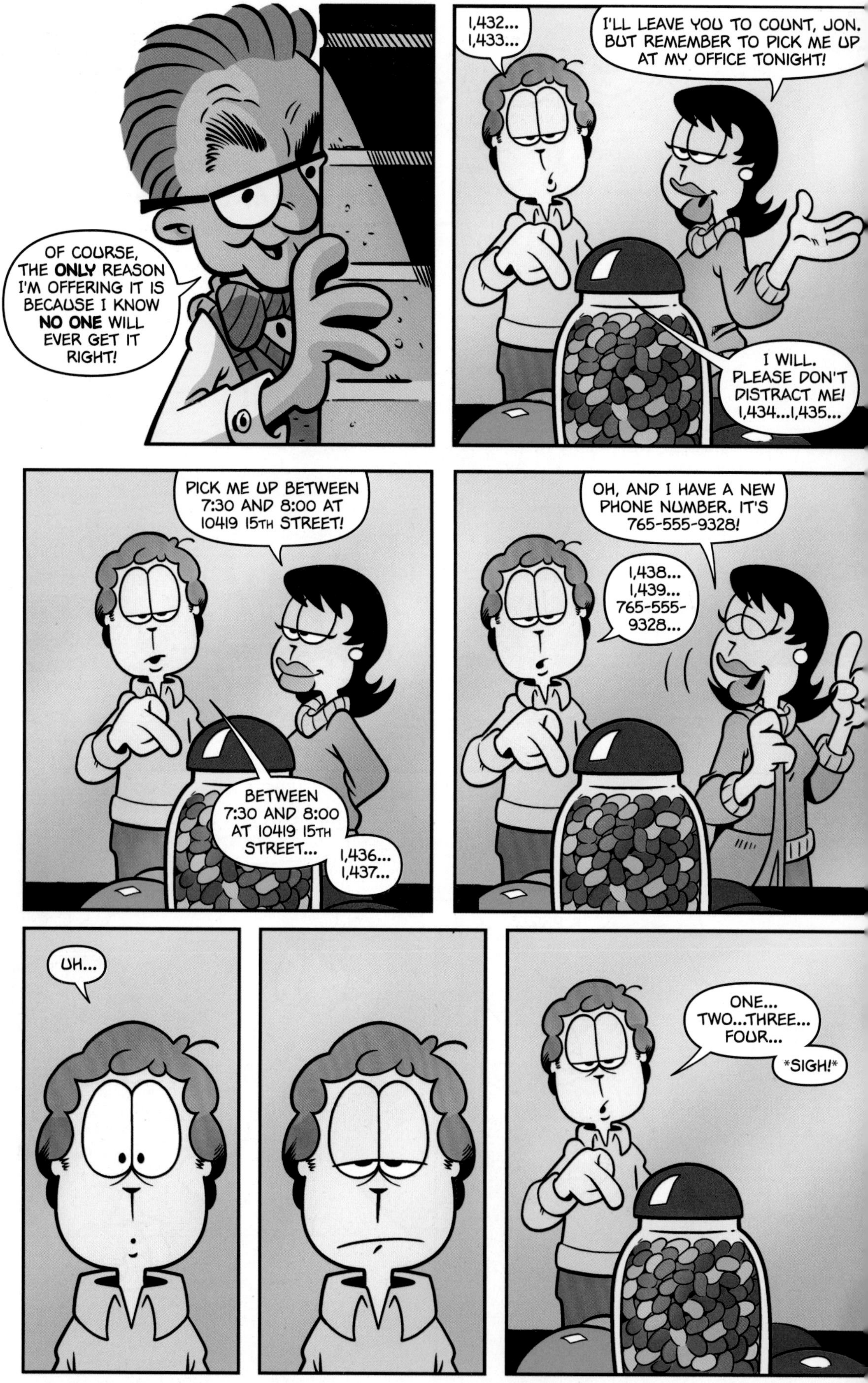
OF COURSE, THE **ONLY** REASON I'M OFFERING IT IS BECAUSE I KNOW **NO ONE** WILL EVER GET IT RIGHT!
1,432... 1,433...
I'LL LEAVE YOU TO COUNT, JON. BUT REMEMBER TO PICK ME UP AT MY OFFICE TONIGHT!
I WILL. PLEASE DON'T DISTRACT ME! 1,434...1,435...
PICK ME UP BETWEEN 7:30 AND 8:00 AT 10419 15TH STREET!
BETWEEN 7:30 AND 8:00 AT 10419 15TH STREET...
1,436... 1,437...
OH, AND I HAVE A NEW PHONE NUMBER. IT'S 765-555-9328!
1,438... 1,439... 765-555-9328...
UH...
ONE... TWO...THREE... FOUR...
SIGH!

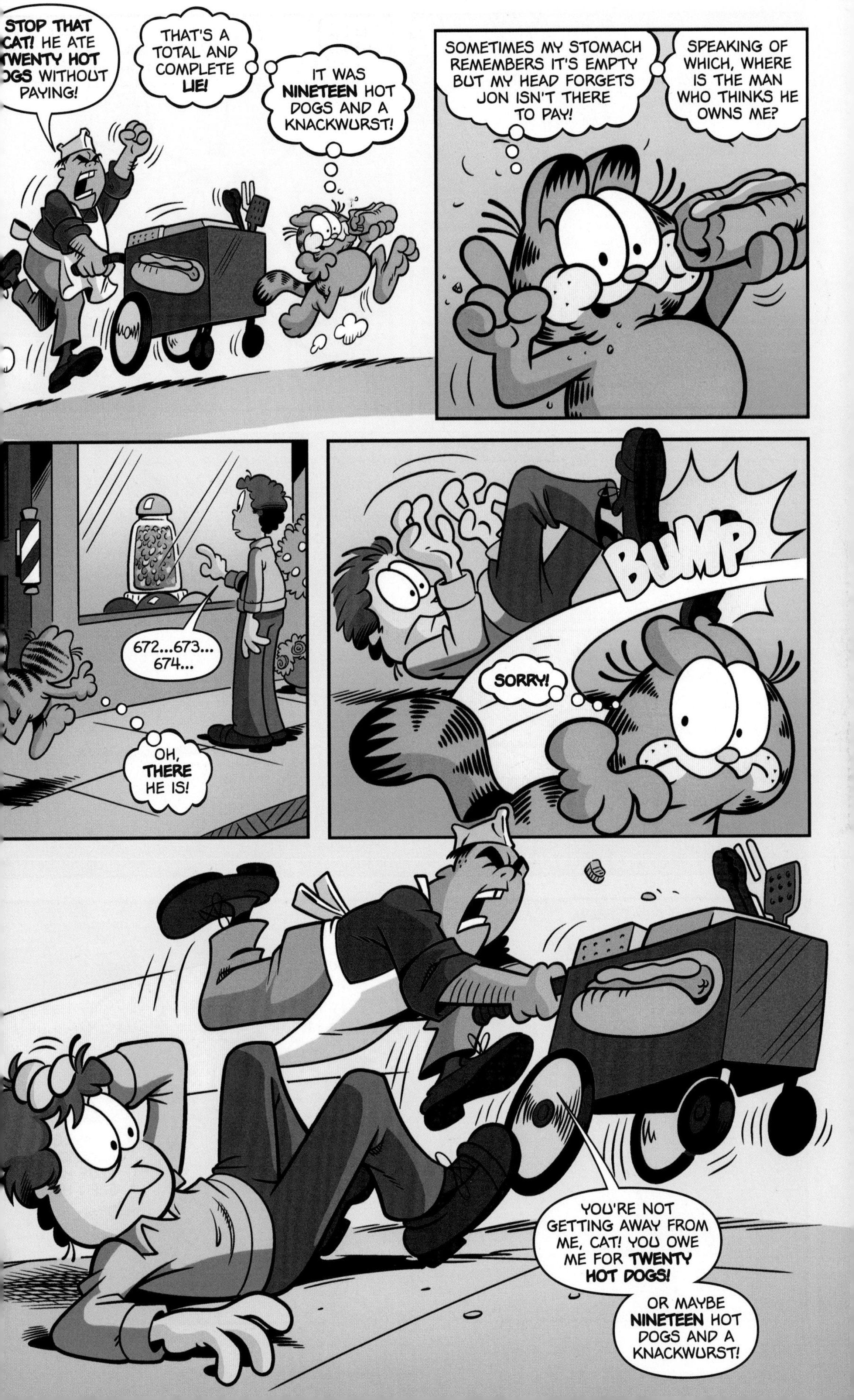
STOP THAT CAT! HE ATE TWENTY HOT DOGS WITHOUT PAYING!
THAT'S A TOTAL AND COMPLETE LIE!
IT WAS NINETEEN HOT DOGS AND A KNACKWURST!
WOW
SOMETIMES MY STOMACH REMEMBERS IT'S EMPTY BUT MY HEAD FORGETS JON ISN'T THERE TO PAY!
SPEAKING OF WHICH, WHERE IS THE MAN WHO THINKS HE OWNS ME?
672...673... 674...
OH, THERE HE IS!
BUMP
SORRY!
YOU'RE NOT GETTING AWAY FROM ME, CAT! YOU OWE ME FOR TWENTY HOT DOGS!
OR MAYBE NINETEEN HOT DOGS AND A KNACKWURST!

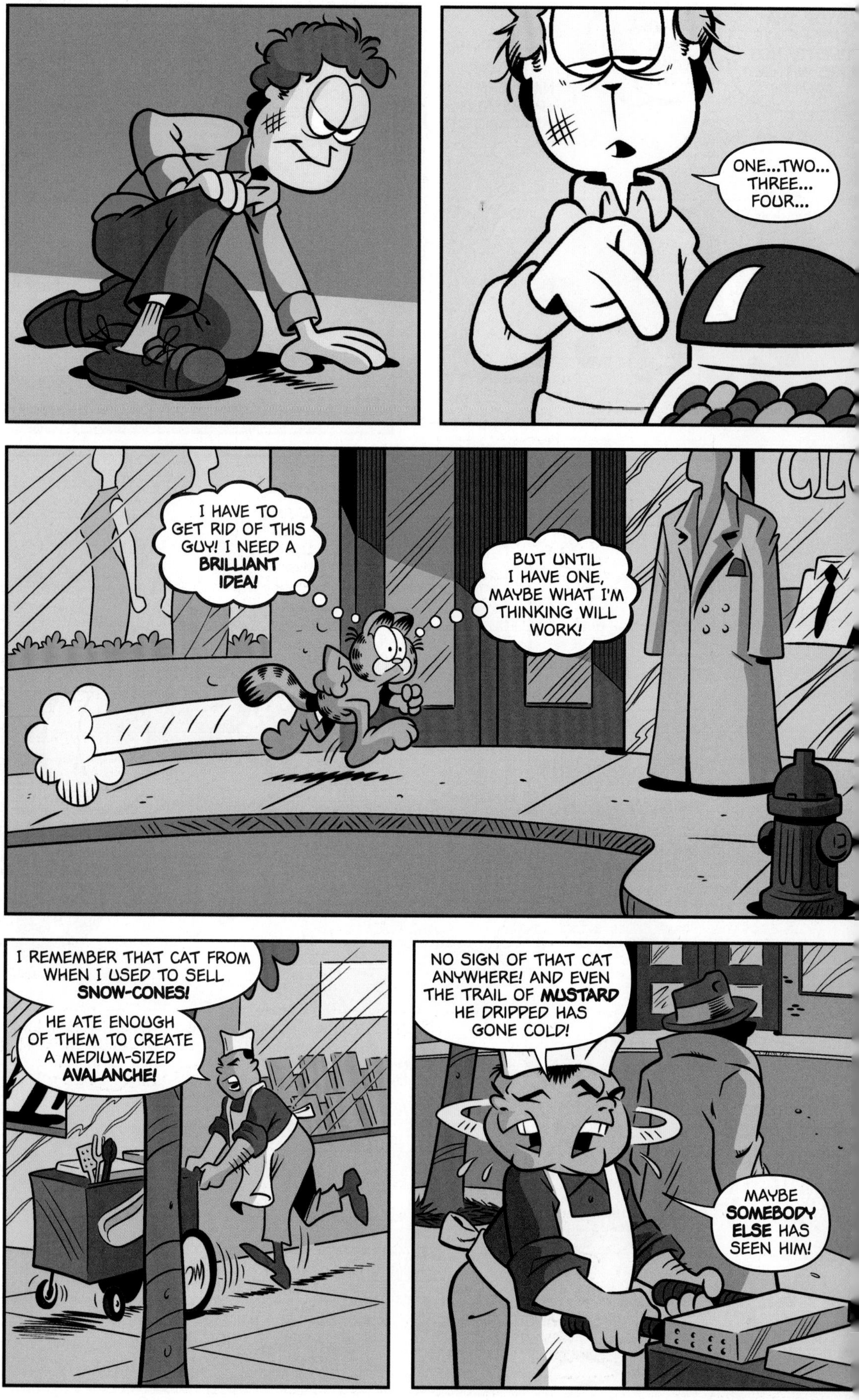
ONE...TWO... THREE... FOUR...
I HAVE TO GET RID OF THIS GUY! I NEED A **BRILLIANT IDEA!**
BUT UNTIL I HAVE ONE, MAYBE WHAT I'M THINKING WILL WORK!
I REMEMBER THAT CAT FROM WHEN I USED TO SELL **SNOW-CONES!**
HE ATE ENOUGH OF THEM TO CREATE A MEDIUM-SIZED **AVALANCHE!**
NO SIGN OF THAT CAT ANYWHERE! AND EVEN THE TRAIL OF **MUSTARD** HE DRIPPED HAS GONE COLD!
MAYBE **SOMEBODY ELSE** HAS SEEN HIM!

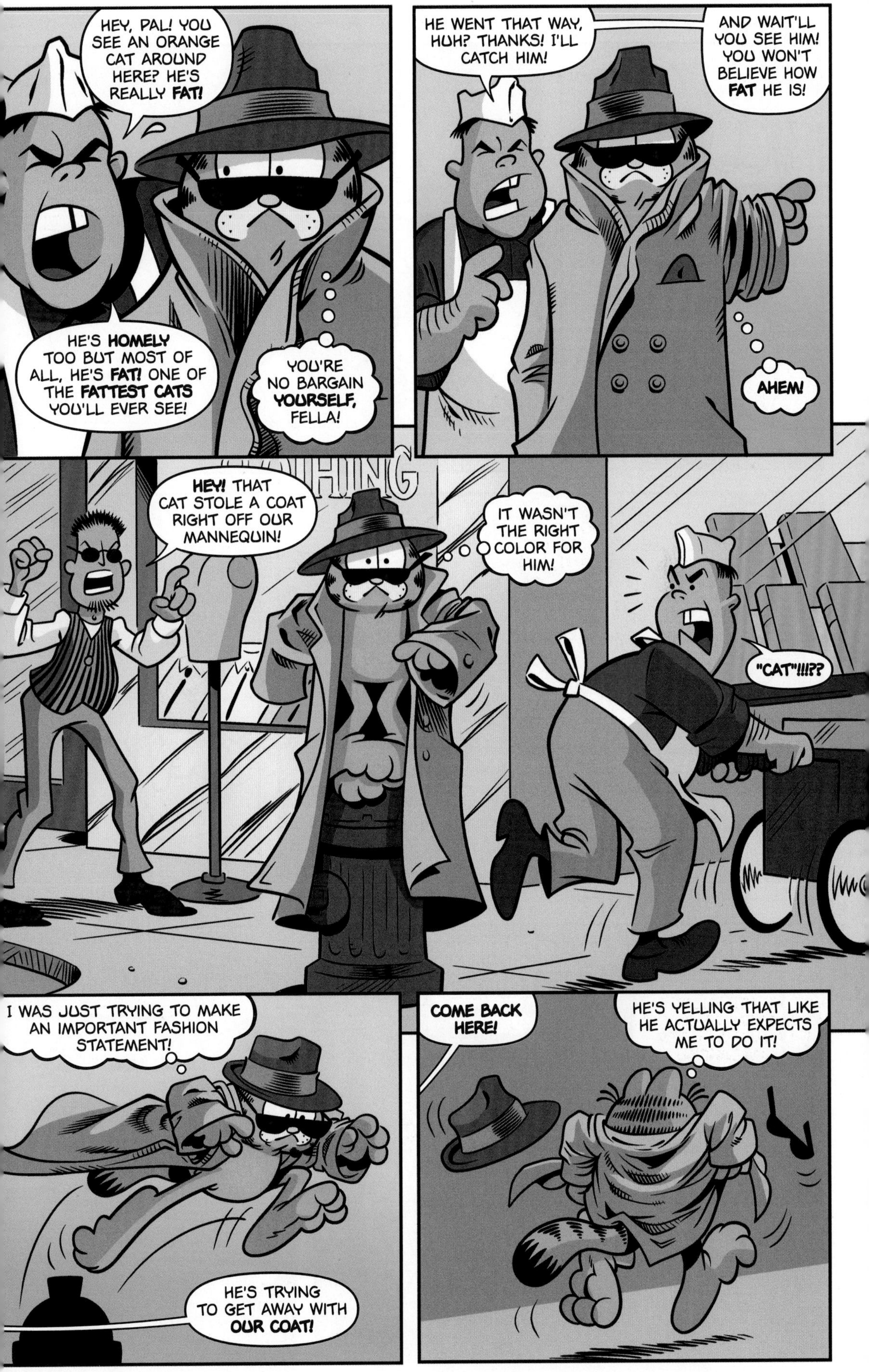

HEY, PAL! YOU SEE AN ORANGE CAT AROUND HERE? HE'S REALLY **FAT!**
HE'S **HOMELY** TOO BUT MOST OF ALL, HE'S **FAT!** ONE OF THE **FATTEST CATS** YOU'LL EVER SEE!
YOU'RE NO BARGAIN **YOURSELF,** FELLA!
HE WENT THAT WAY, HUH? THANKS! I'LL CATCH HIM!
AND WAIT'LL YOU SEE HIM! YOU WON'T BELIEVE HOW **FAT** HE IS!
AHEM!
HEY! THAT CAT STOLE A COAT RIGHT OFF OUR MANNEQUIN!
IT WASN'T THE RIGHT COLOR FOR HIM!
"CAT"!!!??
I WAS JUST TRYING TO MAKE AN IMPORTANT FASHION STATEMENT!
HE'S TRYING TO GET AWAY WITH **OUR COAT!**
COME BACK HERE!
HE'S YELLING THAT LIKE HE ACTUALLY EXPECTS ME TO DO IT!

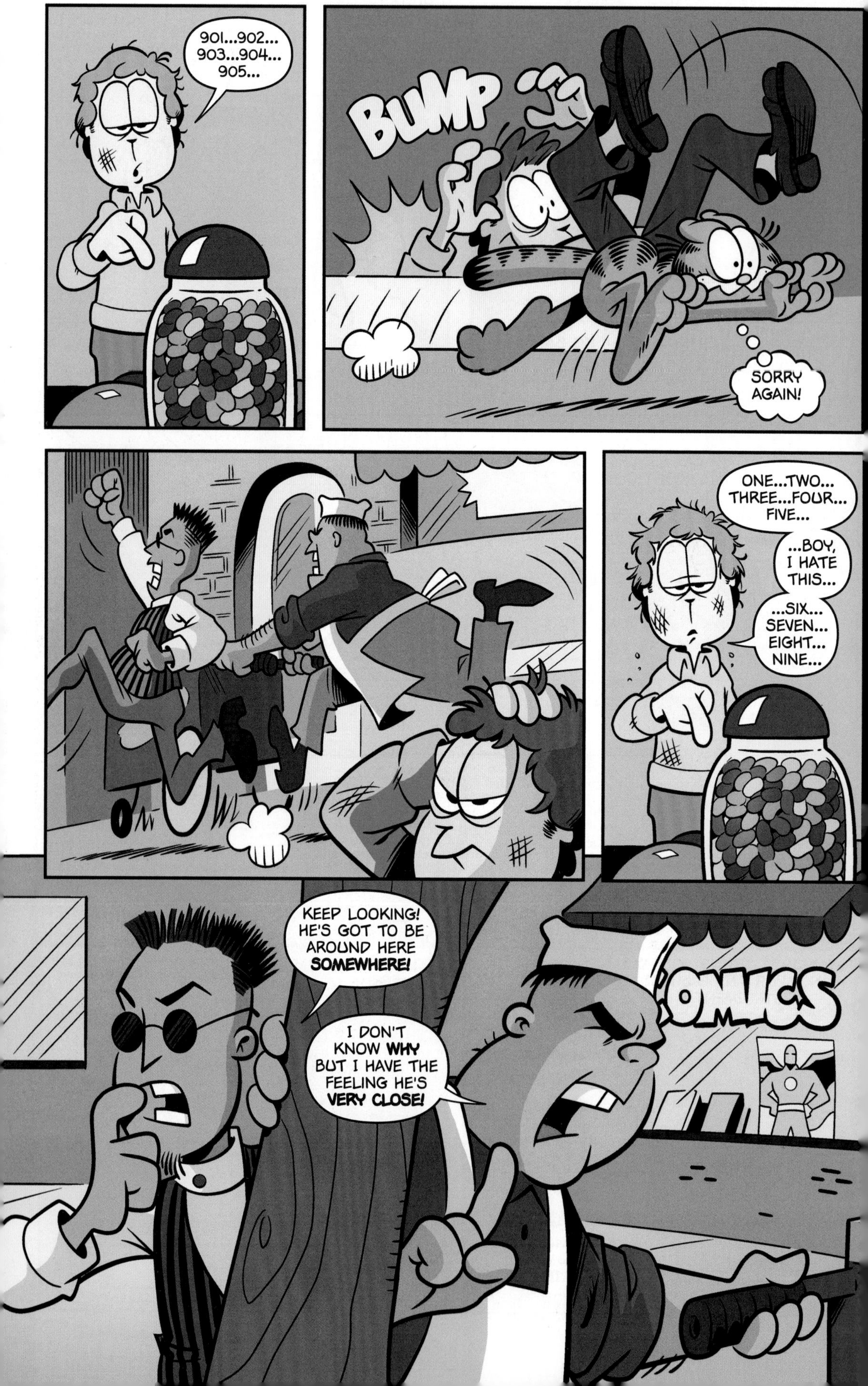

901...902...
903...904...
905...
BUMP
SORRY AGAIN!
ONE...TWO...
THREE...FOUR...
FIVE...
...BOY,
I HATE
THIS...
...SIX...
SEVEN...
EIGHT...
NINE...
KEEP LOOKING! HE'S GOT TO BE AROUND HERE **SOMEWHERE!**
I DON'T KNOW **WHY** BUT I HAVE THE FEELING HE'S **VERY CLOSE!**
OMICS

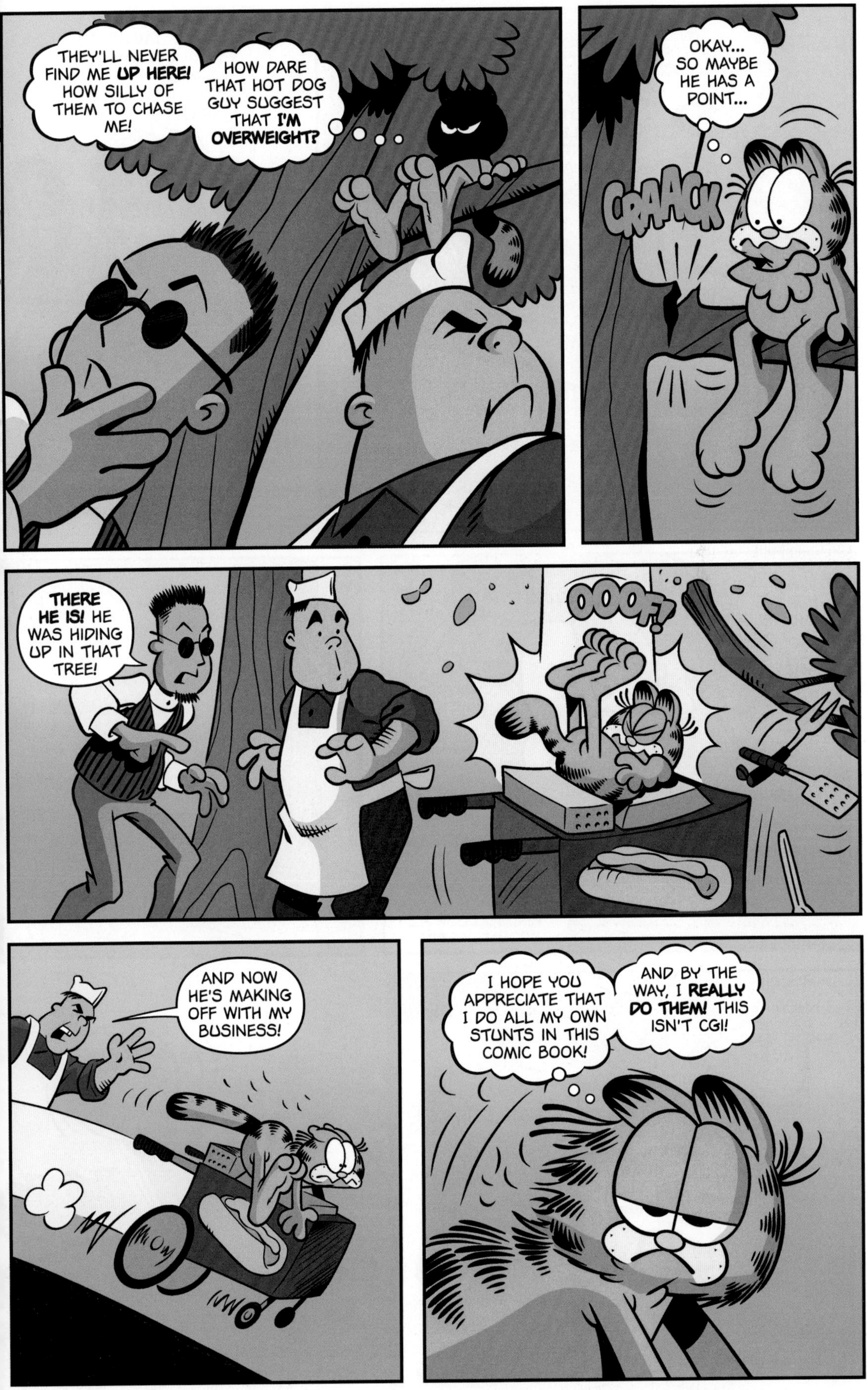

THEY'LL NEVER FIND ME **UP HERE!** HOW SILLY OF THEM TO CHASE ME!
HOW DARE THAT HOT DOG GUY SUGGEST THAT **I'M OVERWEIGHT?**
OKAY... SO MAYBE HE HAS A POINT...
CRAACK
THERE HE IS! HE WAS HIDING UP IN THAT TREE!
OOOF!
AND NOW HE'S MAKING OFF WITH MY BUSINESS!
I HOPE YOU APPRECIATE THAT I DO ALL MY OWN STUNTS IN THIS COMIC BOOK!
AND BY THE WAY, I **REALLY DO THEM!** THIS ISN'T CGI!

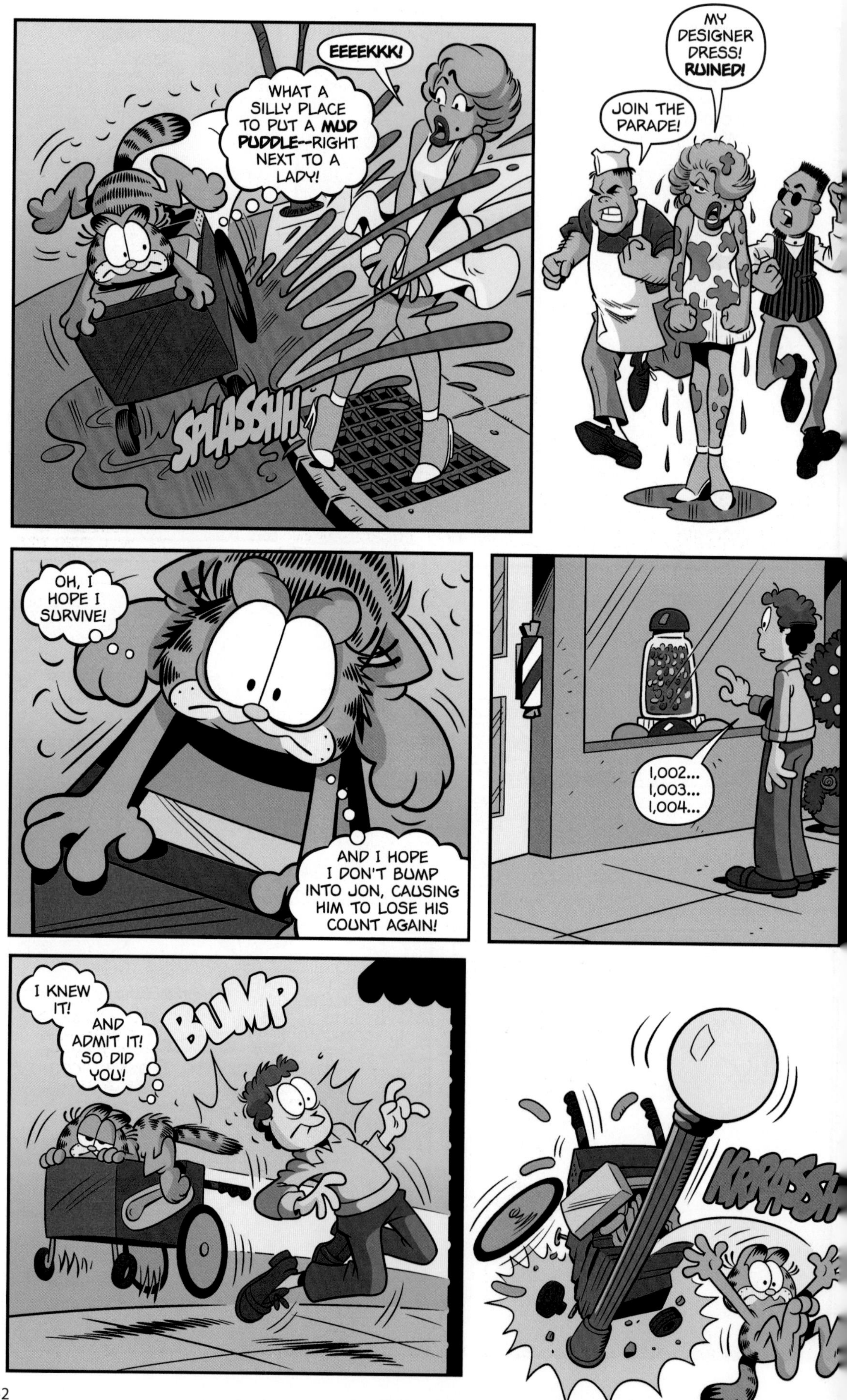
EEEEKKK!
WHAT A SILLY PLACE TO PUT A MUD PUDDLE--RIGHT NEXT TO A LADY!
SPLASSHH
MY DESIGNER DRESS! RUINED!
JOIN THE PARADE!
OH, I HOPE I SURVIVE!
AND I HOPE I DON'T BUMP INTO JON, CAUSING HIM TO LOSE HIS COUNT AGAIN!
1,002... 1,003... 1,004...
I KNEW IT!
AND ADMIT IT! SO DID YOU!
BUMP
KRRASSH

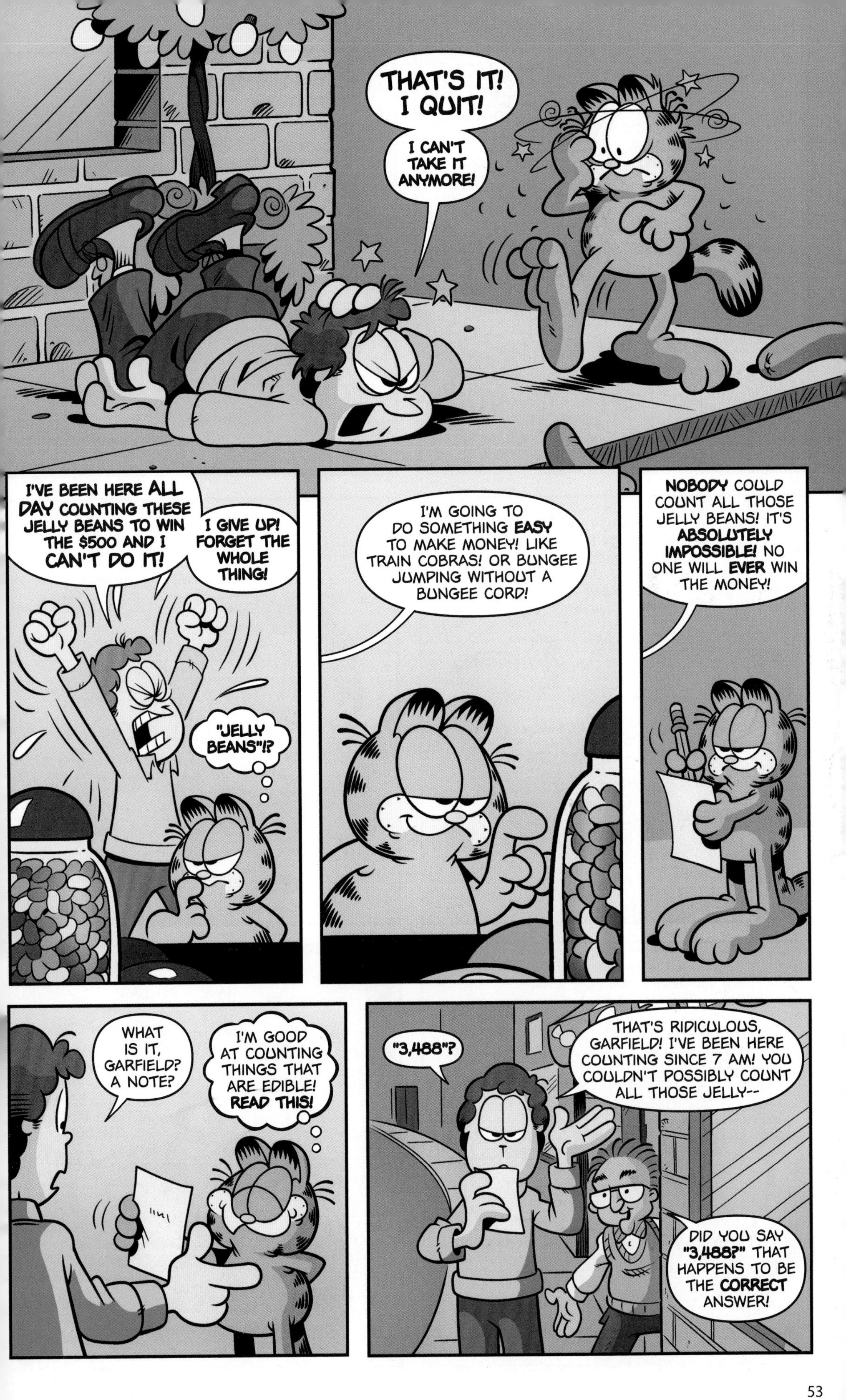
THAT'S IT! I QUIT!
I CAN'T TAKE IT ANYMORE!
I'VE BEEN HERE ALL DAY COUNTING THESE JELLY BEANS TO WIN THE $500 AND I CAN'T DO IT!
I GIVE UP! FORGET THE WHOLE THING!
"JELLY BEANS"!?
I'M GOING TO DO SOMETHING EASY TO MAKE MONEY! LIKE TRAIN COBRAS! OR BUNGEE JUMPING WITHOUT A BUNGEE CORD!
NOBODY COULD COUNT ALL THOSE JELLY BEANS! IT'S ABSOLUTELY IMPOSSIBLE! NO ONE WILL EVER WIN THE MONEY!
WHAT IS IT, GARFIELD? A NOTE?
I'M GOOD AT COUNTING THINGS THAT ARE EDIBLE! READ THIS!
"3,488"?
THAT'S RIDICULOUS, GARFIELD! I'VE BEEN HERE COUNTING SINCE 7 AM! YOU COULDN'T POSSIBLY COUNT ALL THOSE JELLY--
DID YOU SAY "3,488?" THAT HAPPENS TO BE THE CORRECT ANSWER!

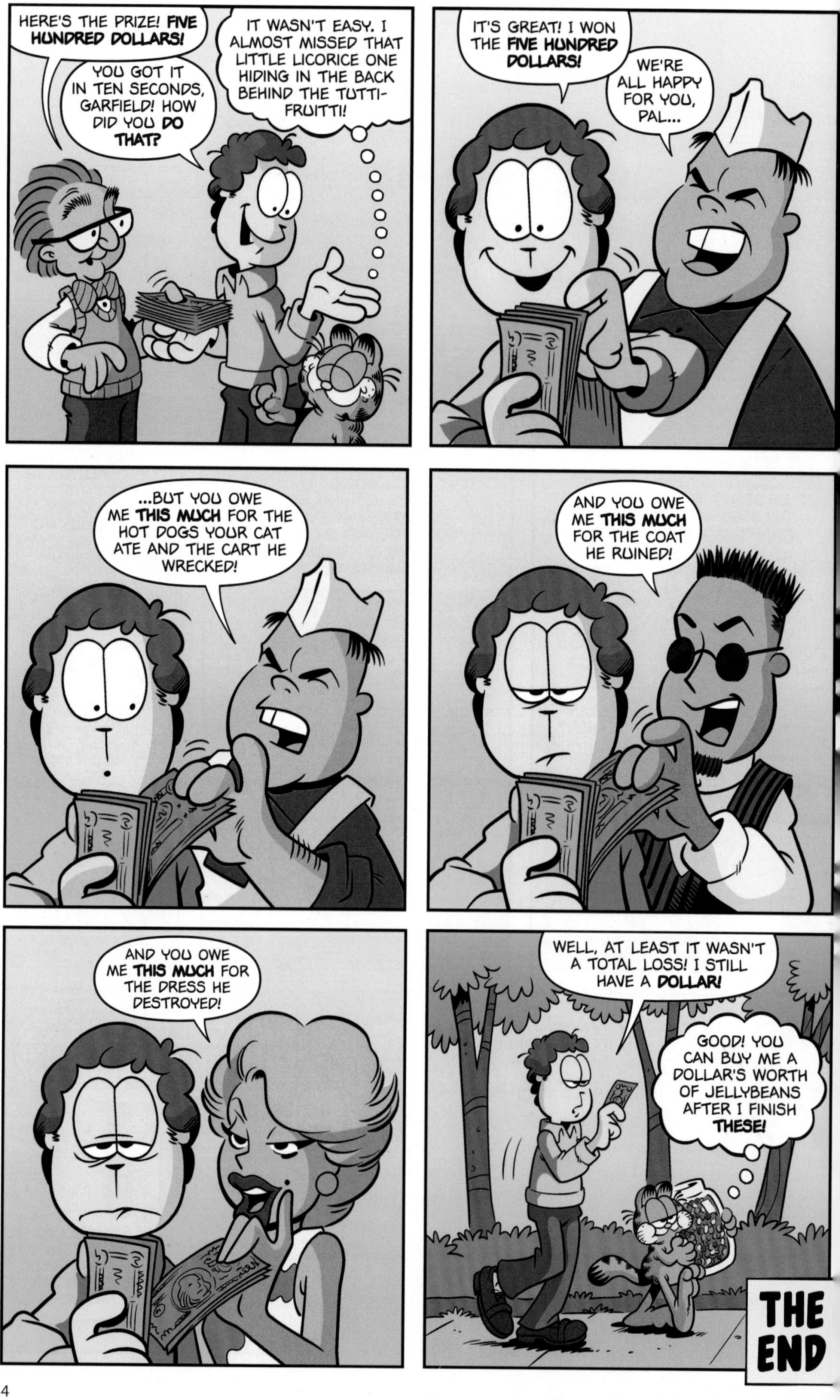
HERE'S THE PRIZE! FIVE HUNDRED DOLLARS!
YOU GOT IT IN TEN SECONDS, GARFIELD! HOW DID YOU DO THAT?
IT WASN'T EASY. I ALMOST MISSED THAT LITTLE LICORICE ONE HIDING IN THE BACK BEHIND THE TUTTI-FRUITTI!
IT'S GREAT! I WON THE FIVE HUNDRED DOLLARS!
WE'RE ALL HAPPY FOR YOU, PAL...
...BUT YOU OWE ME THIS MUCH FOR THE HOT DOGS YOUR CAT ATE AND THE CART HE WRECKED!
AND YOU OWE ME THIS MUCH FOR THE COAT HE RUINED!
AND YOU OWE ME THIS MUCH FOR THE DRESS HE DESTROYED!
WELL, AT LEAST IT WASN'T A TOTAL LOSS! I STILL HAVE A DOLLAR!
GOOD! YOU CAN BUY ME A DOLLAR'S WORTH OF JELLYBEANS AFTER I FINISH THESE!
THE END

CHAPTER THREE

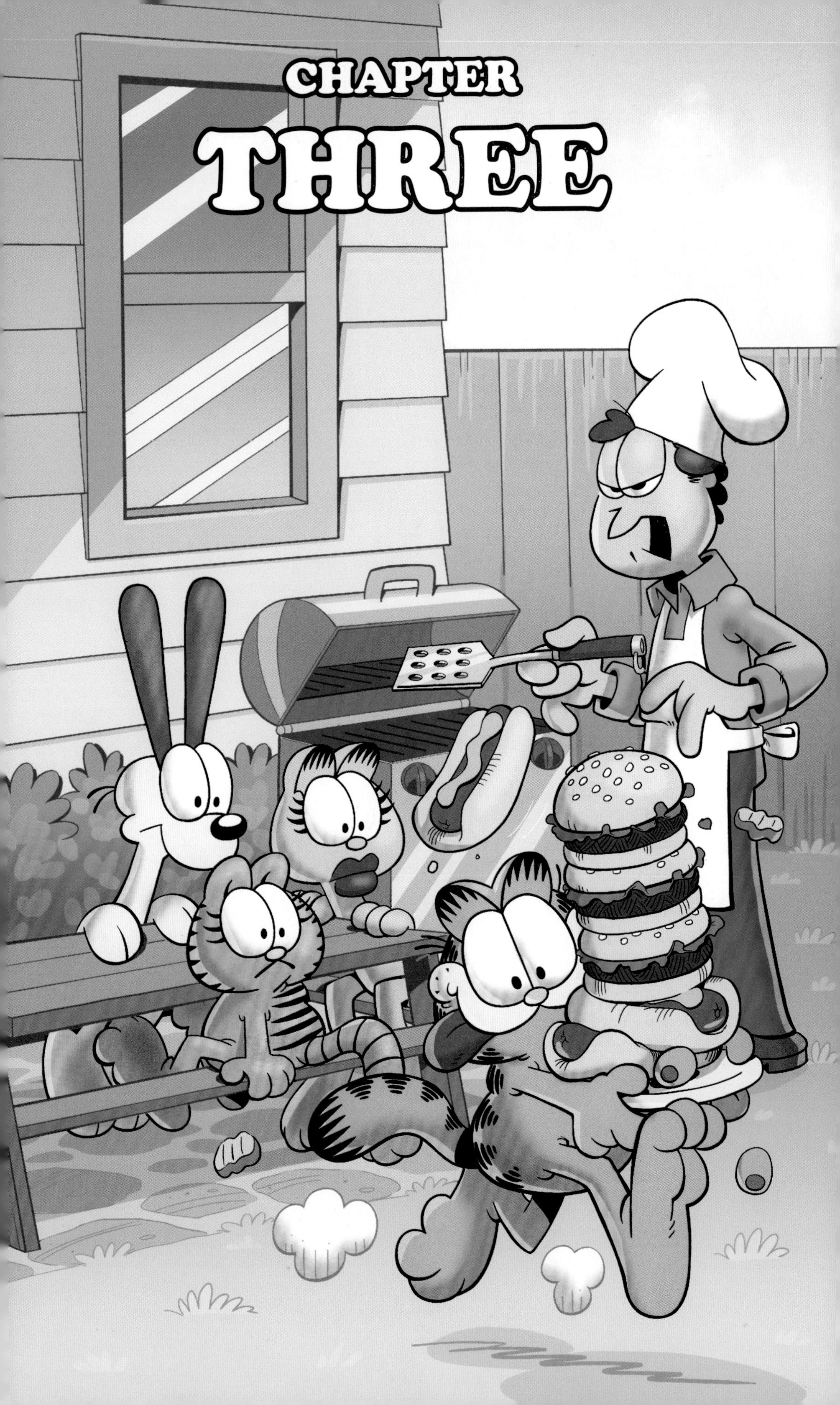

THE GREAT PIZZA NIGHTMARE
THE WONDERFUL WISHBONE

Written by
MARK EVANIER

Art by
GARY BARKER
AND **DAN DAVIS**

Colors by
LISA MOORE

Chapter Break Art by
GARY BARKER
WITH **BRADEN LAMB**

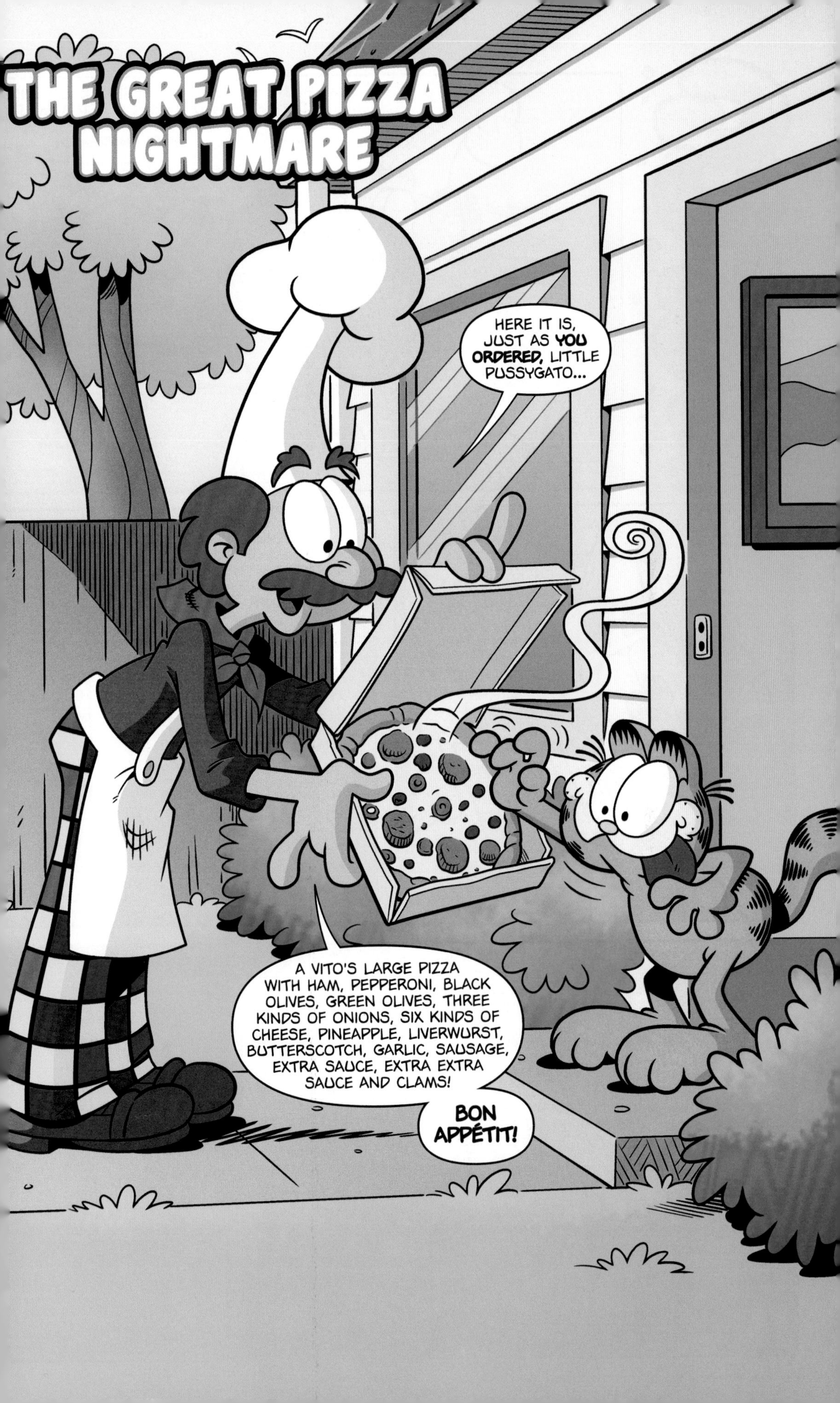
THE GREAT PIZZA NIGHTMARE
HERE IT IS, JUST AS YOU ORDERED, LITTLE PUSSYGATO...
A VITO'S LARGE PIZZA WITH HAM, PEPPERONI, BLACK OLIVES, GREEN OLIVES, THREE KINDS OF ONIONS, SIX KINDS OF CHEESE, PINEAPPLE, LIVERWURST, BUTTERSCOTCH, GARLIC, SAUSAGE, EXTRA SAUCE, EXTRA EXTRA SAUCE AND CLAMS!
BON APPÉTIT!

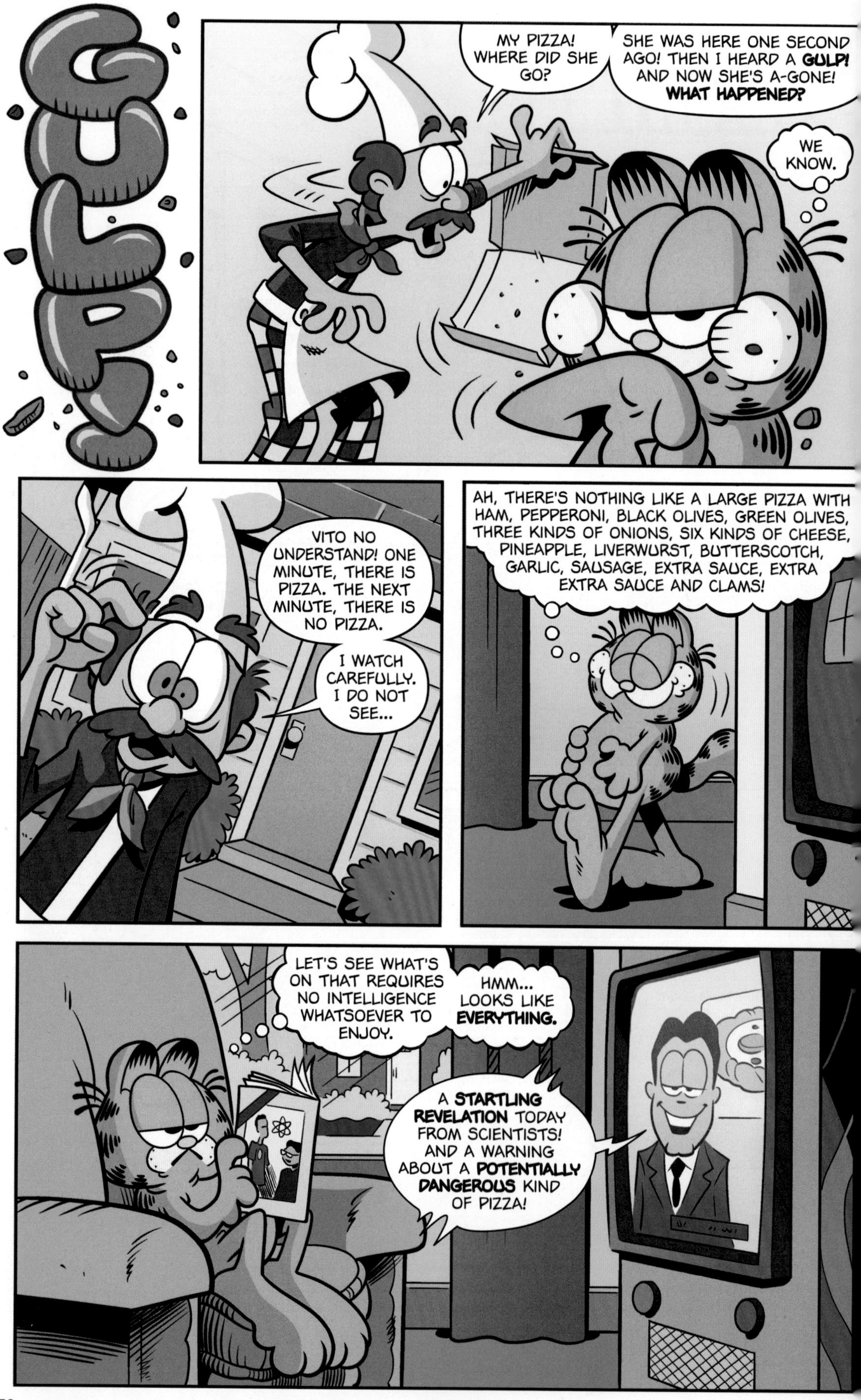
GULP
MY PIZZA! WHERE DID SHE GO?
SHE WAS HERE ONE SECOND AGO! THEN I HEARD A GULP! AND NOW SHE'S A-GONE! WHAT HAPPENED?
WE KNOW.
VITO NO UNDERSTAND! ONE MINUTE, THERE IS PIZZA. THE NEXT MINUTE, THERE IS NO PIZZA.
I WATCH CAREFULLY. I DO NOT SEE...
AH, THERE'S NOTHING LIKE A LARGE PIZZA WITH HAM, PEPPERONI, BLACK OLIVES, GREEN OLIVES, THREE KINDS OF ONIONS, SIX KINDS OF CHEESE, PINEAPPLE, LIVERWURST, BUTTERSCOTCH, GARLIC, SAUSAGE, EXTRA SAUCE, EXTRA EXTRA SAUCE AND CLAMS!
LET'S SEE WHAT'S ON THAT REQUIRES NO INTELLIGENCE WHATSOEVER TO ENJOY.
HMM... LOOKS LIKE EVERYTHING.
A STARTLING REVELATION TODAY FROM SCIENTISTS! AND A WARNING ABOUT A POTENTIALLY DANGEROUS KIND OF PIZZA!

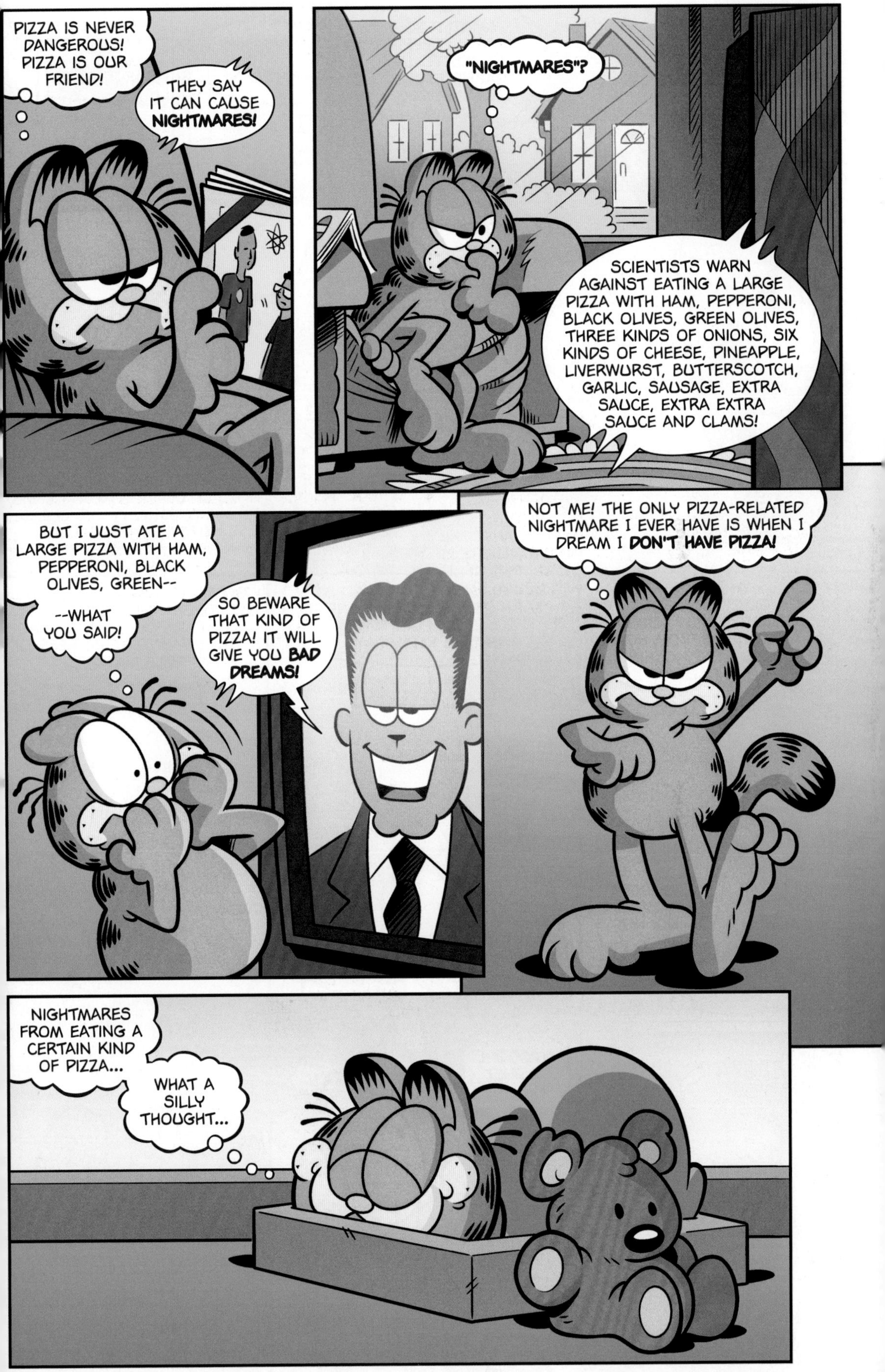
PIZZA IS NEVER DANGEROUS! PIZZA IS OUR FRIEND!
THEY SAY IT CAN CAUSE NIGHTMARES!
"NIGHTMARES"?
SCIENTISTS WARN AGAINST EATING A LARGE PIZZA WITH HAM, PEPPERONI, BLACK OLIVES, GREEN OLIVES, THREE KINDS OF ONIONS, SIX KINDS OF CHEESE, PINEAPPLE, LIVERWURST, BUTTERSCOTCH, GARLIC, SAUSAGE, EXTRA SAUCE, EXTRA EXTRA SAUCE AND CLAMS!
BUT I JUST ATE A LARGE PIZZA WITH HAM, PEPPERONI, BLACK OLIVES, GREEN--
--WHAT YOU SAID!
SO BEWARE THAT KIND OF PIZZA! IT WILL GIVE YOU BAD DREAMS!
NOT ME! THE ONLY PIZZA-RELATED NIGHTMARE I EVER HAVE IS WHEN I DREAM I DON'T HAVE PIZZA!
NIGHTMARES FROM EATING A CERTAIN KIND OF PIZZA...
WHAT A SILLY THOUGHT...

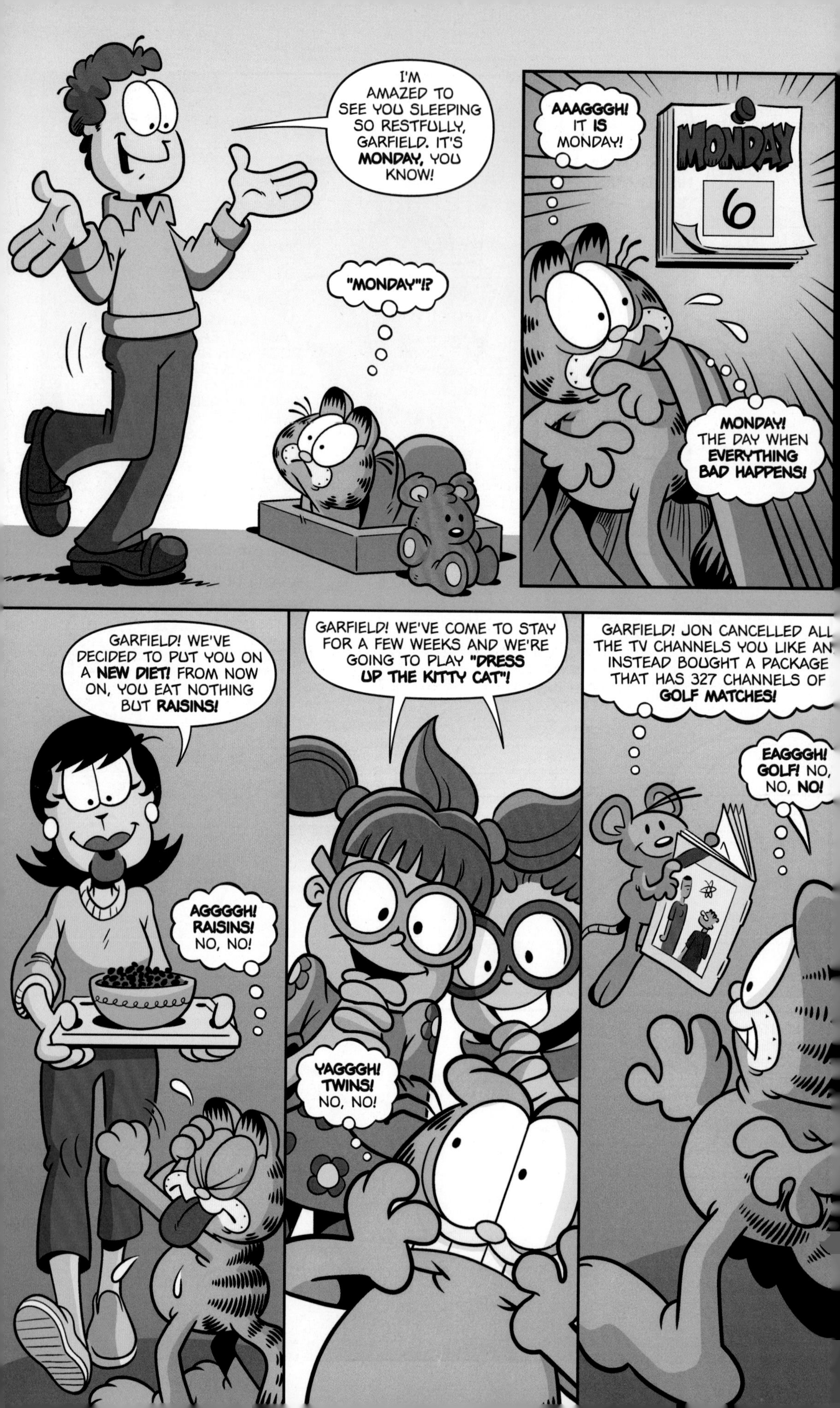

I'M AMAZED TO SEE YOU SLEEPING SO RESTFULLY, GARFIELD. IT'S MONDAY, YOU KNOW!
"MONDAY"!?
AAAGGGH! IT IS MONDAY!
MONDAY
6
MONDAY! THE DAY WHEN EVERYTHING BAD HAPPENS!
GARFIELD! WE'VE DECIDED TO PUT YOU ON A NEW DIET! FROM NOW ON, YOU EAT NOTHING BUT RAISINS!
AGGGGH! RAISINS! NO, NO!
GARFIELD! WE'VE COME TO STAY FOR A FEW WEEKS AND WE'RE GOING TO PLAY "DRESS UP THE KITTY CAT"!
YAGGGH! TWINS! NO, NO!
GARFIELD! JON CANCELLED ALL THE TV CHANNELS YOU LIKE AN INSTEAD BOUGHT A PACKAGE THAT HAS 327 CHANNELS OF GOLF MATCHES!
EAGGGH! GOLF! NO, NO, NO!

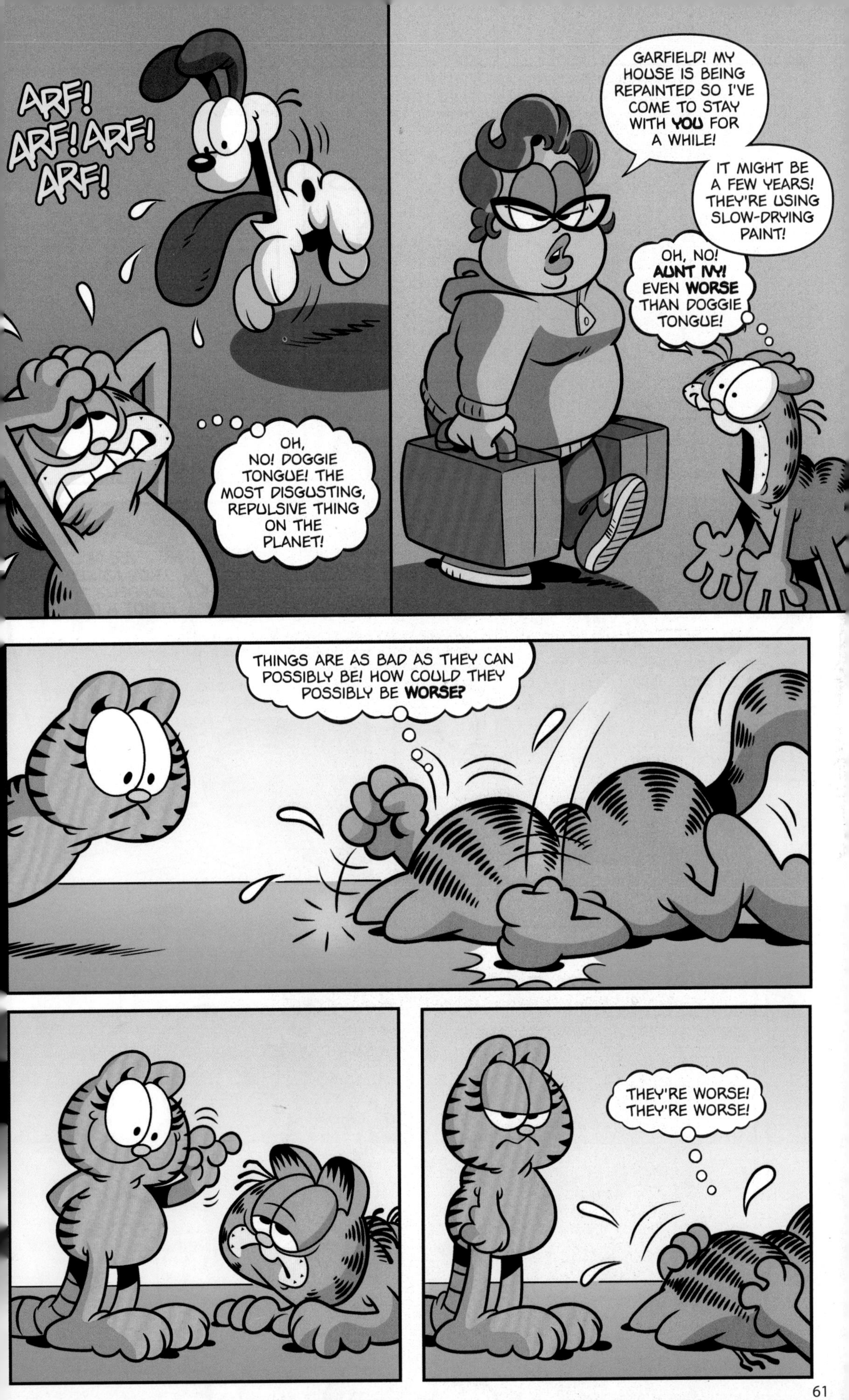
ARF! ARF! ARF! ARF!
OH, NO! DOGGIE TONGUE! THE MOST DISGUSTING, REPULSIVE THING ON THE PLANET!
GARFIELD! MY HOUSE IS BEING REPAINTED SO I'VE COME TO STAY WITH YOU FOR A WHILE!
IT MIGHT BE A FEW YEARS! THEY'RE USING SLOW-DRYING PAINT!
OH, NO! AUNT IVY! EVEN WORSE THAN DOGGIE TONGUE!
THINGS ARE AS BAD AS THEY CAN POSSIBLY BE! HOW COULD THEY POSSIBLY BE WORSE?
THEY'RE WORSE! THEY'RE WORSE!

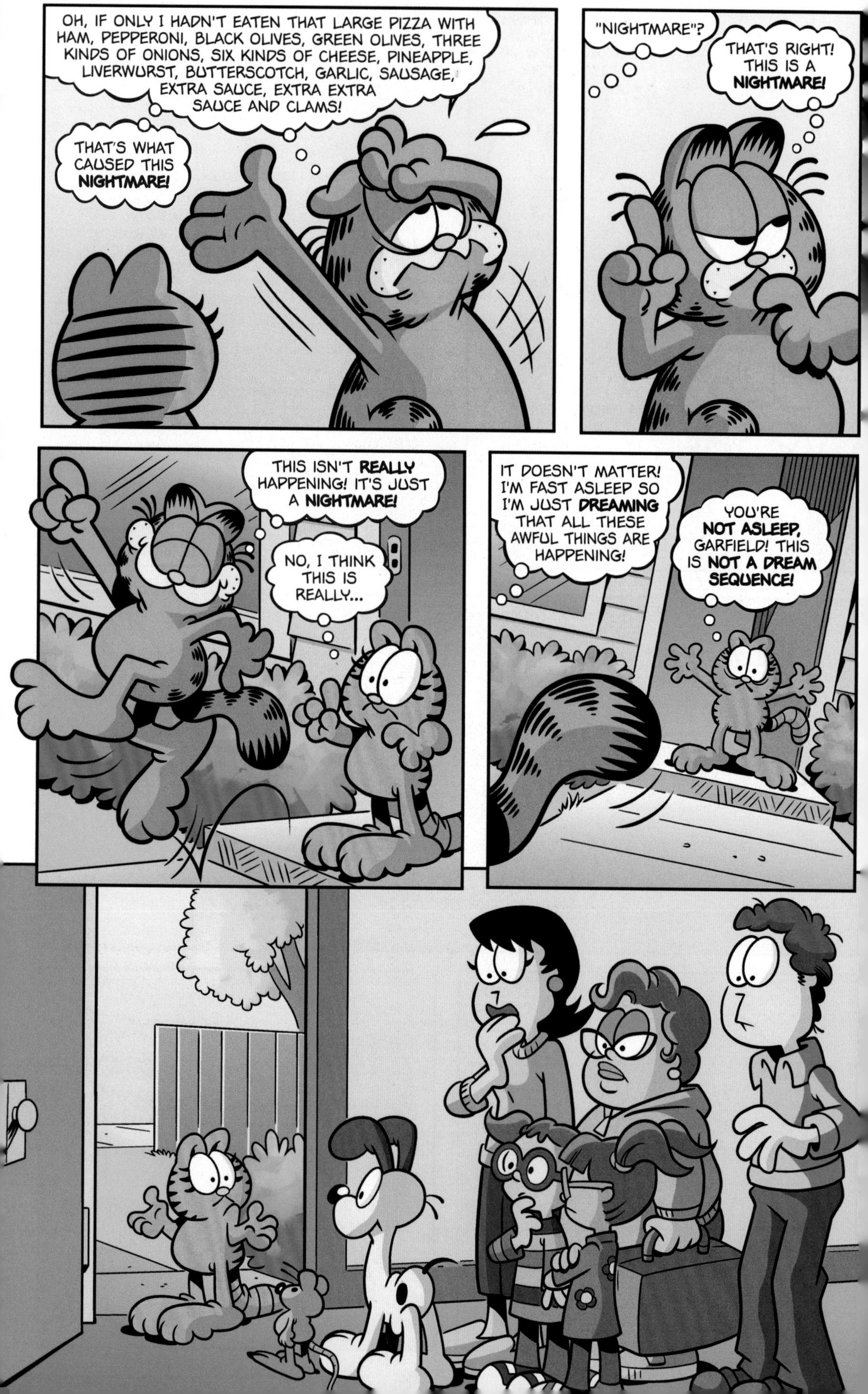

OH, IF ONLY I HADN'T EATEN THAT LARGE PIZZA WITH HAM, PEPPERONI, BLACK OLIVES, GREEN OLIVES, THREE KINDS OF ONIONS, SIX KINDS OF CHEESE, PINEAPPLE, LIVERWURST, BUTTERSCOTCH, GARLIC, SAUSAGE, EXTRA SAUCE, EXTRA EXTRA SAUCE AND CLAMS!
THAT'S WHAT CAUSED THIS **NIGHTMARE!**
"NIGHTMARE"?
THAT'S RIGHT! THIS IS A **NIGHTMARE!**
THIS ISN'T **REALLY** HAPPENING! IT'S JUST A **NIGHTMARE!**
NO, I THINK THIS IS REALLY...
IT DOESN'T MATTER! I'M FAST ASLEEP SO I'M JUST **DREAMING** THAT ALL THESE AWFUL THINGS ARE HAPPENING!
YOU'RE **NOT ASLEEP,** GARFIELD! THIS IS **NOT A DREAM SEQUENCE!**

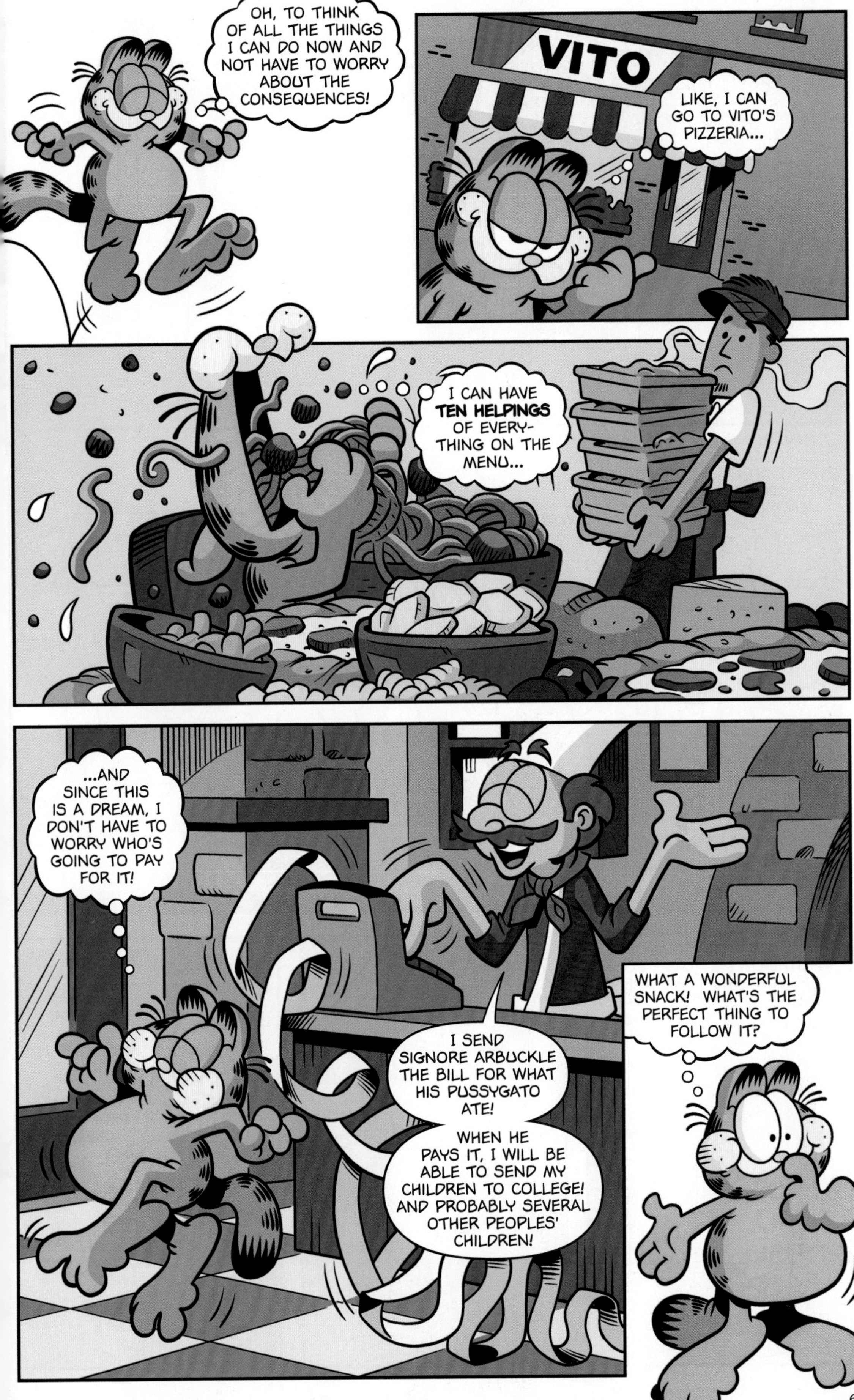
OH, TO THINK OF ALL THE THINGS I CAN DO NOW AND NOT HAVE TO WORRY ABOUT THE CONSEQUENCES!
VITO
LIKE, I CAN GO TO VITO'S PIZZERIA...
I CAN HAVE **TEN HELPINGS** OF EVERY-THING ON THE MENU...
...AND SINCE THIS IS A DREAM, I DON'T HAVE TO WORRY WHO'S GOING TO PAY FOR IT!
I SEND SIGNORE ARBUCKLE THE BILL FOR WHAT HIS PUSSYGATO ATE!
WHEN HE PAYS IT, I WILL BE ABLE TO SEND MY CHILDREN TO COLLEGE! AND PROBABLY SEVERAL OTHER PEOPLES' CHILDREN!
WHAT A WONDERFUL SNACK! WHAT'S THE PERFECT THING TO FOLLOW IT?

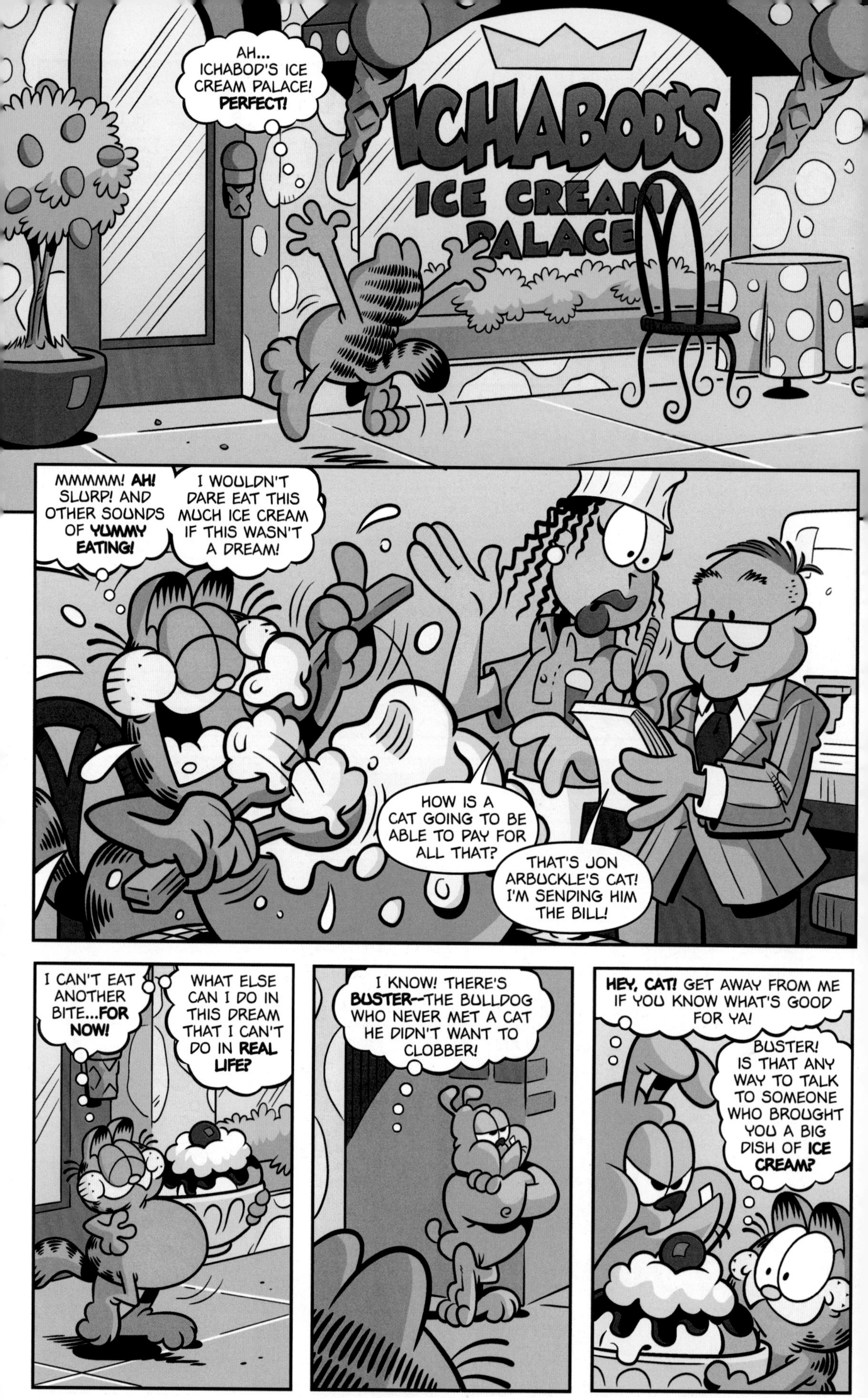
AH... ICHABOD'S ICE CREAM PALACE! **PERFECT!**
ICHABOD'S ICE CREAM PALACE
MMMMM! **AH!** SLURP! AND OTHER SOUNDS OF **YUMMY EATING!**
I WOULDN'T DARE EAT THIS MUCH ICE CREAM IF THIS WASN'T A DREAM!
HOW IS A CAT GOING TO BE ABLE TO PAY FOR ALL THAT?
THAT'S JON ARBUCKLE'S CAT! I'M SENDING HIM THE BILL!
I CAN'T EAT ANOTHER BITE...**FOR NOW!**
WHAT ELSE CAN I DO IN THIS DREAM THAT I CAN'T DO IN **REAL LIFE?**
I KNOW! THERE'S **BUSTER**--THE BULLDOG WHO NEVER MET A CAT HE DIDN'T WANT TO CLOBBER!
HEY, CAT! GET AWAY FROM ME IF YOU KNOW WHAT'S GOOD FOR YA!
BUSTER! IS THAT ANY WAY TO TALK TO SOMEONE WHO BROUGHT YOU A BIG DISH OF **ICE CREAM?**

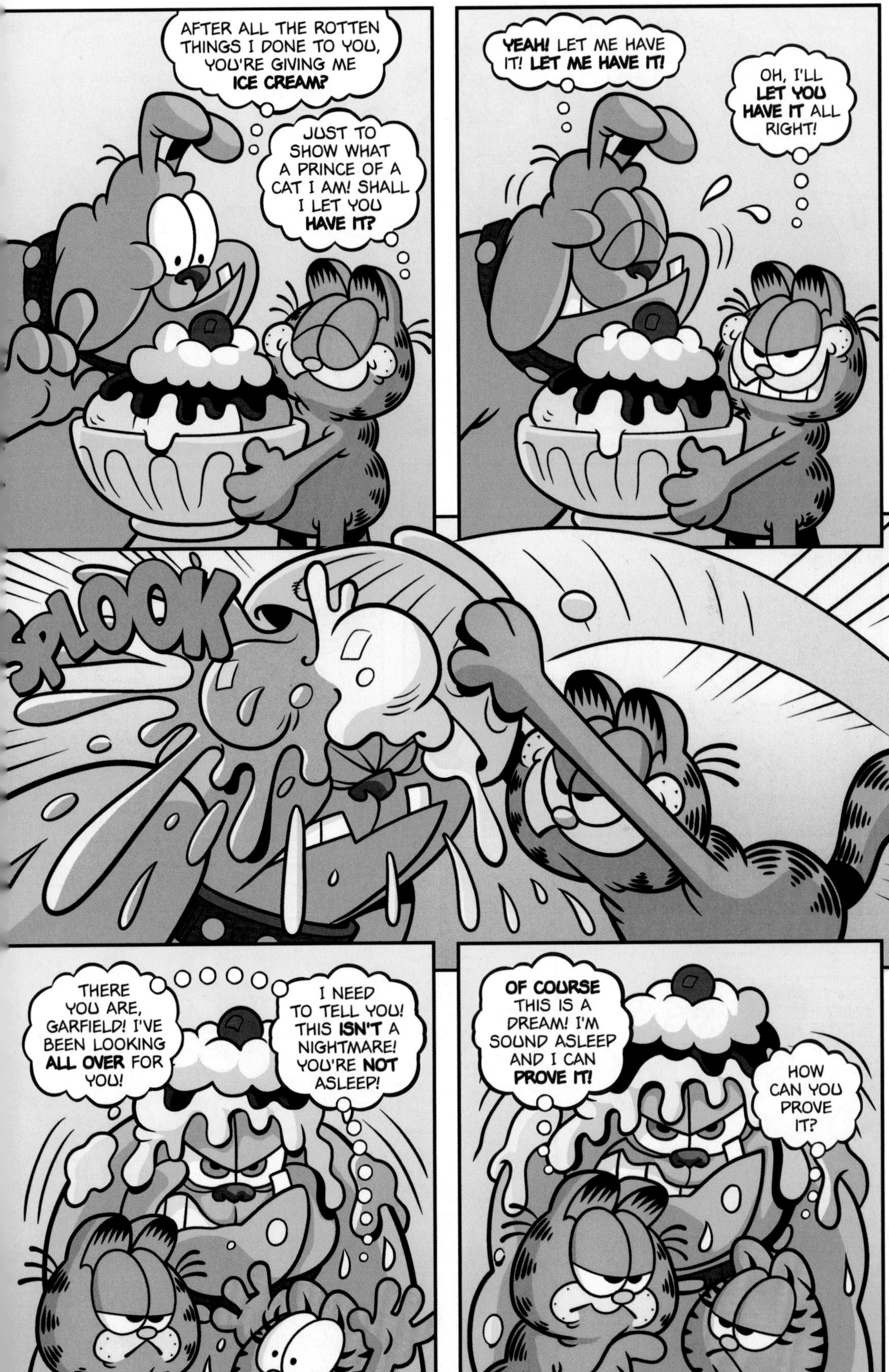

AFTER ALL THE ROTTEN THINGS I DONE TO YOU, YOU'RE GIVING ME **ICE CREAM?**
JUST TO SHOW WHAT A PRINCE OF A CAT I AM! SHALL I LET YOU **HAVE IT?**
YEAH! LET ME HAVE IT! **LET ME HAVE IT!**
OH, I'LL **LET YOU HAVE IT** ALL RIGHT!
SPLOOK
THERE YOU ARE, GARFIELD! I'VE BEEN LOOKING **ALL OVER** FOR YOU!
I NEED TO TELL YOU! THIS **ISN'T** A NIGHTMARE! YOU'RE **NOT** ASLEEP!
OF COURSE THIS IS A DREAM! I'M SOUND ASLEEP AND I CAN **PROVE IT!**
HOW CAN YOU PROVE IT?

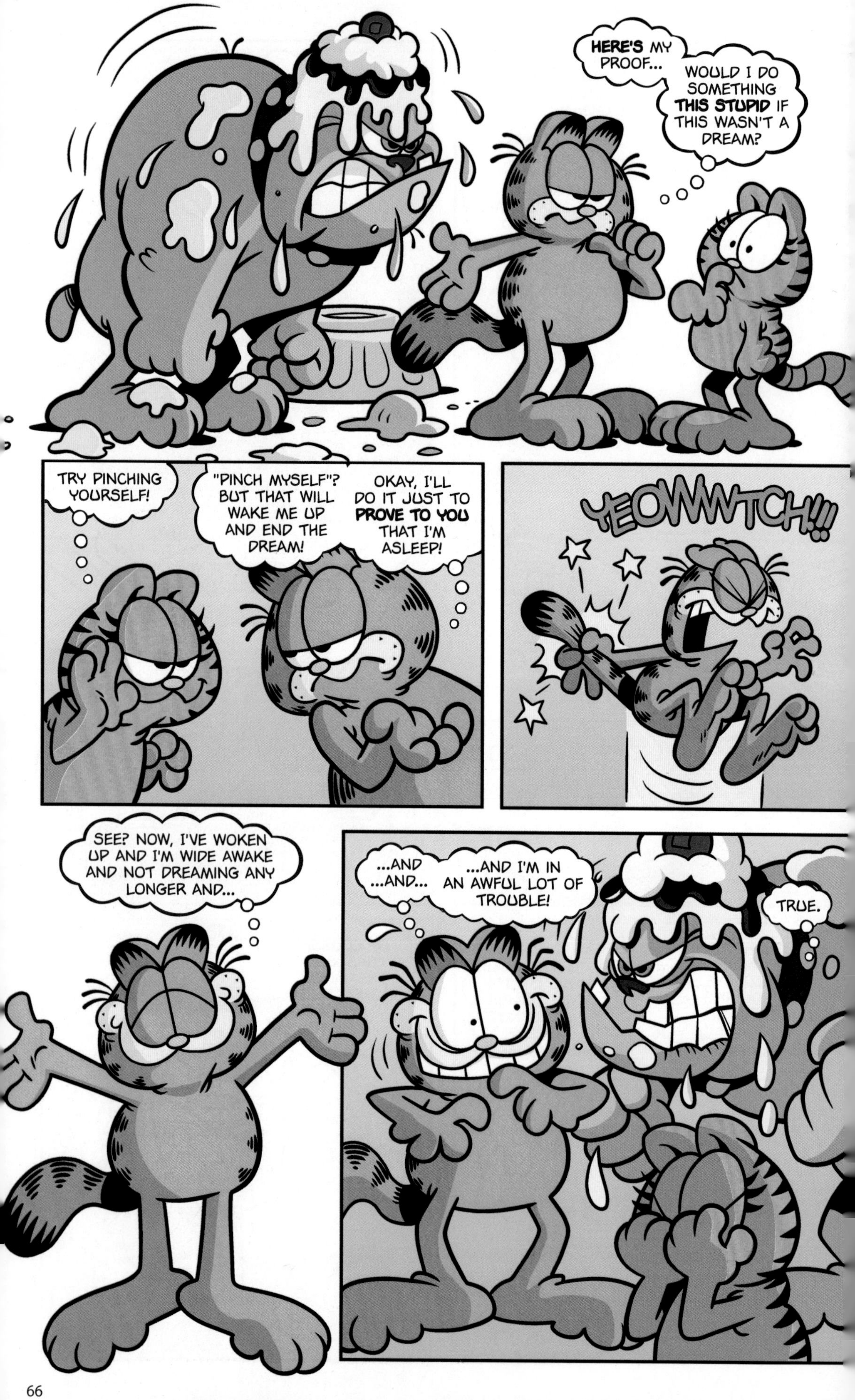
HERE'S MY PROOF...
WOULD I DO SOMETHING THIS STUPID IF THIS WASN'T A DREAM?
TRY PINCHING YOURSELF!
"PINCH MYSELF"? BUT THAT WILL WAKE ME UP AND END THE DREAM!
OKAY, I'LL DO IT JUST TO PROVE TO YOU THAT I'M ASLEEP!
YEOWWTCH!!!
SEE? NOW, I'VE WOKEN UP AND I'M WIDE AWAKE AND NOT DREAMING ANY LONGER AND...
...AND ...AND...
...AND I'M IN AN AWFUL LOT OF TROUBLE!
TRUE.

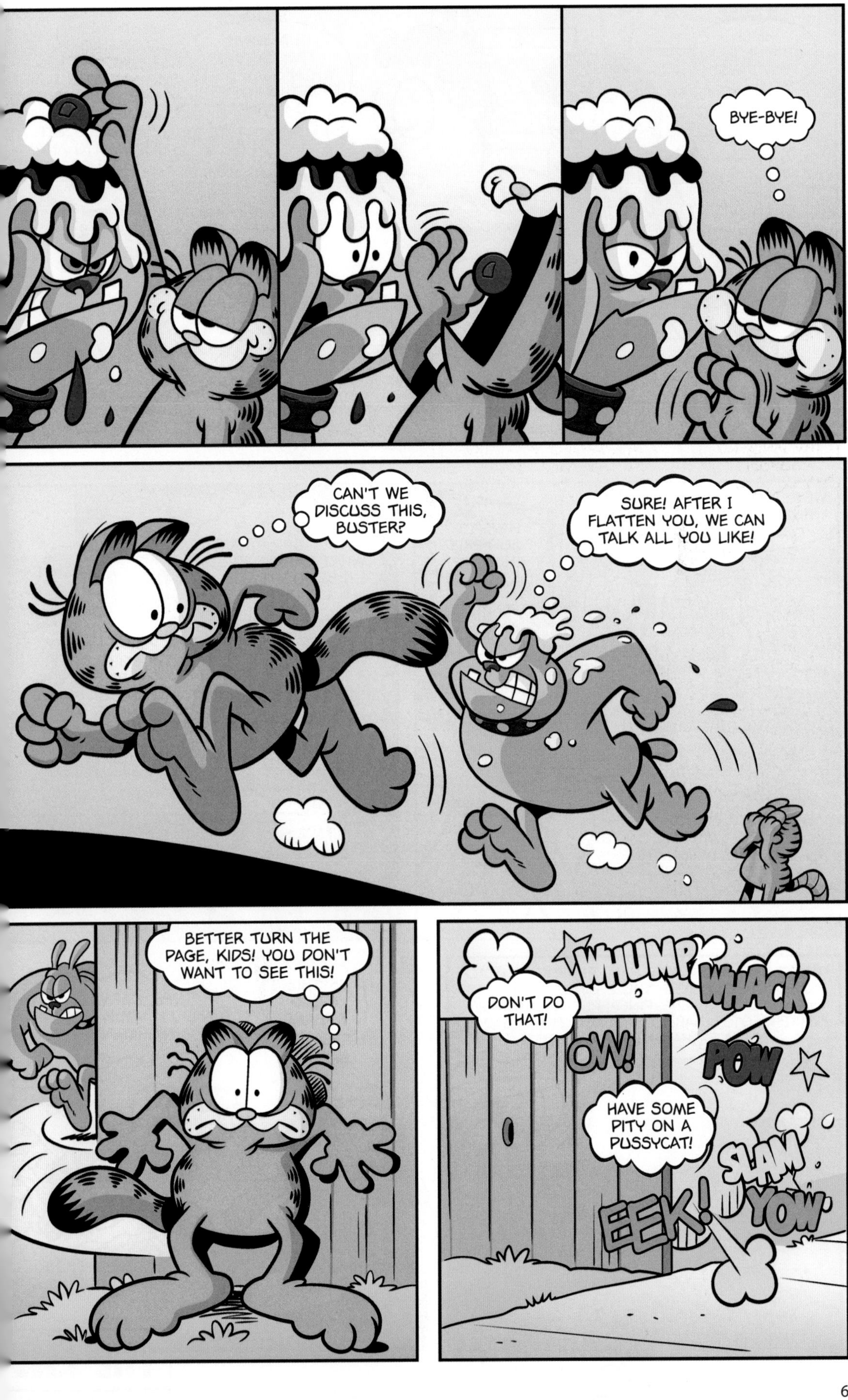
BYE-BYE!
CAN'T WE DISCUSS THIS, BUSTER?
SURE! AFTER I FLATTEN YOU, WE CAN TALK ALL YOU LIKE!
BETTER TURN THE PAGE, KIDS! YOU DON'T WANT TO SEE THIS!
WHUMP
WHACK
DON'T DO THAT!
OW!
POW
HAVE SOME PITY ON A PUSSYCAT!
SLAM
EEK!
YOW

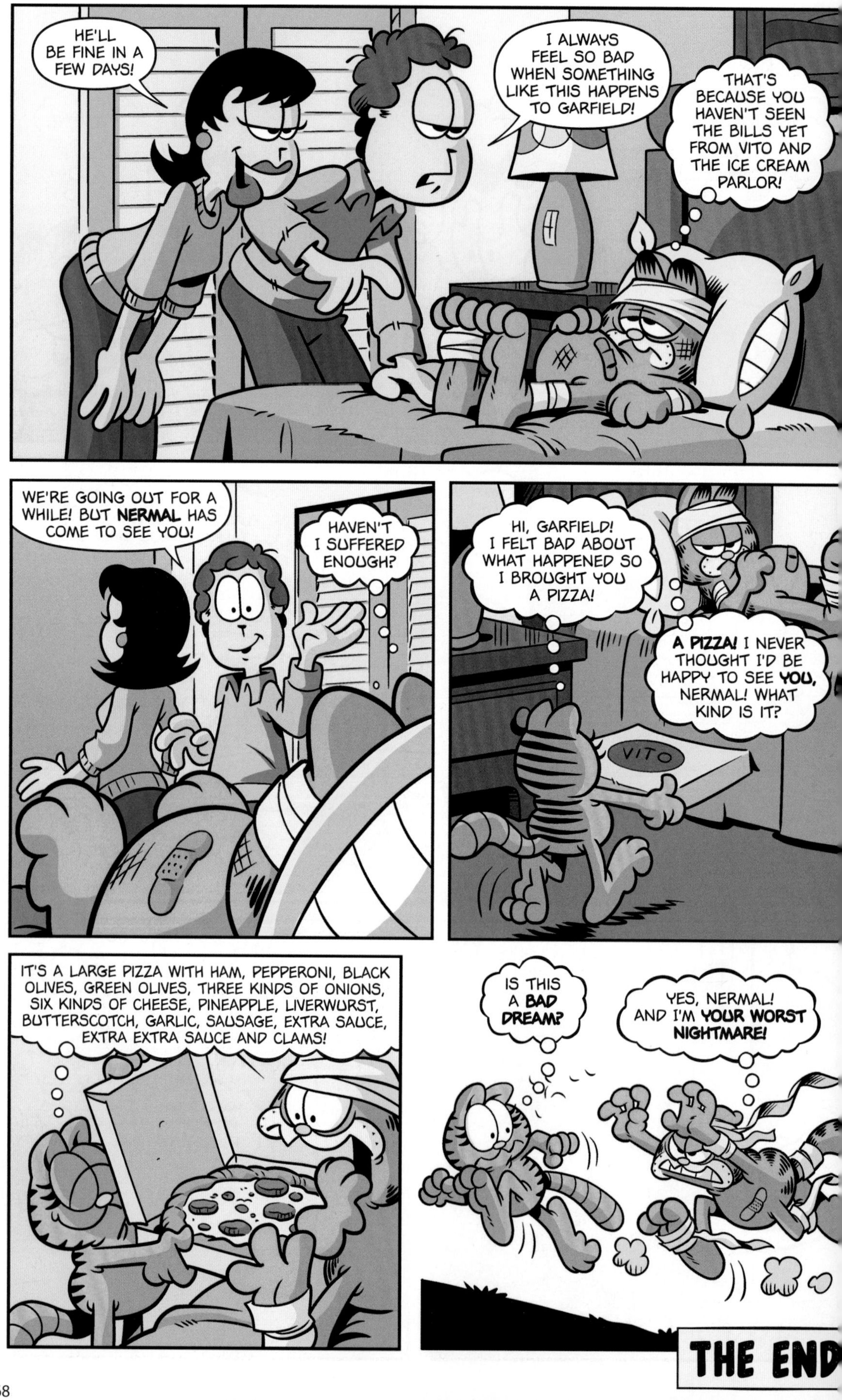
HE'LL BE FINE IN A FEW DAYS!
I ALWAYS FEEL SO BAD WHEN SOMETHING LIKE THIS HAPPENS TO GARFIELD!
THAT'S BECAUSE YOU HAVEN'T SEEN THE BILLS YET FROM VITO AND THE ICE CREAM PARLOR!
WE'RE GOING OUT FOR A WHILE! BUT NERMAL HAS COME TO SEE YOU!
HAVEN'T I SUFFERED ENOUGH?
HI, GARFIELD! I FELT BAD ABOUT WHAT HAPPENED SO I BROUGHT YOU A PIZZA!
VITO
A PIZZA! I NEVER THOUGHT I'D BE HAPPY TO SEE YOU, NERMAL! WHAT KIND IS IT?
IT'S A LARGE PIZZA WITH HAM, PEPPERONI, BLACK OLIVES, GREEN OLIVES, THREE KINDS OF ONIONS, SIX KINDS OF CHEESE, PINEAPPLE, LIVERWURST, BUTTERSCOTCH, GARLIC, SAUSAGE, EXTRA SAUCE, EXTRA EXTRA SAUCE AND CLAMS!
IS THIS A BAD DREAM?
YES, NERMAL! AND I'M YOUR WORST NIGHTMARE!
THE END

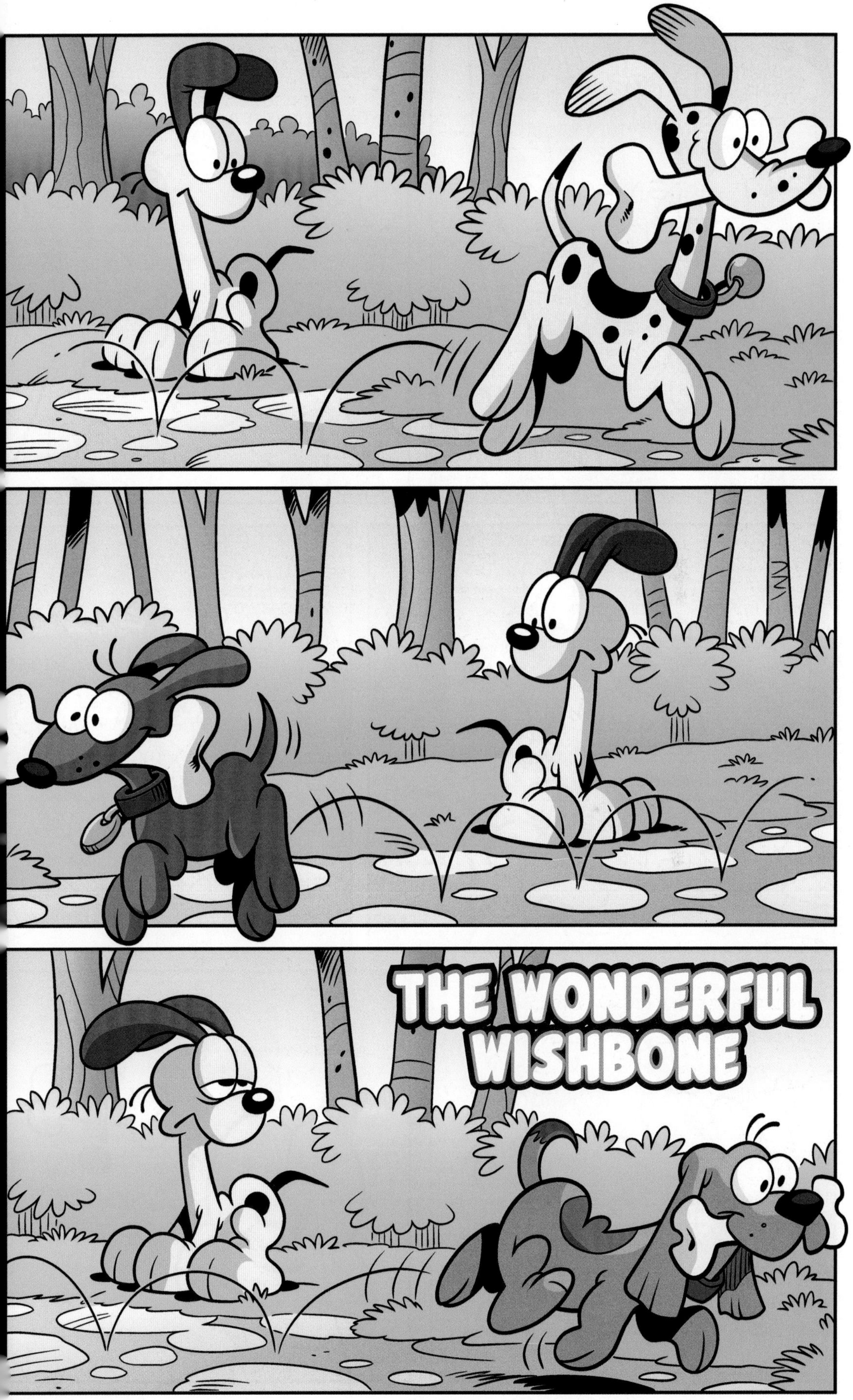
THE WONDERFUL WISHBONE

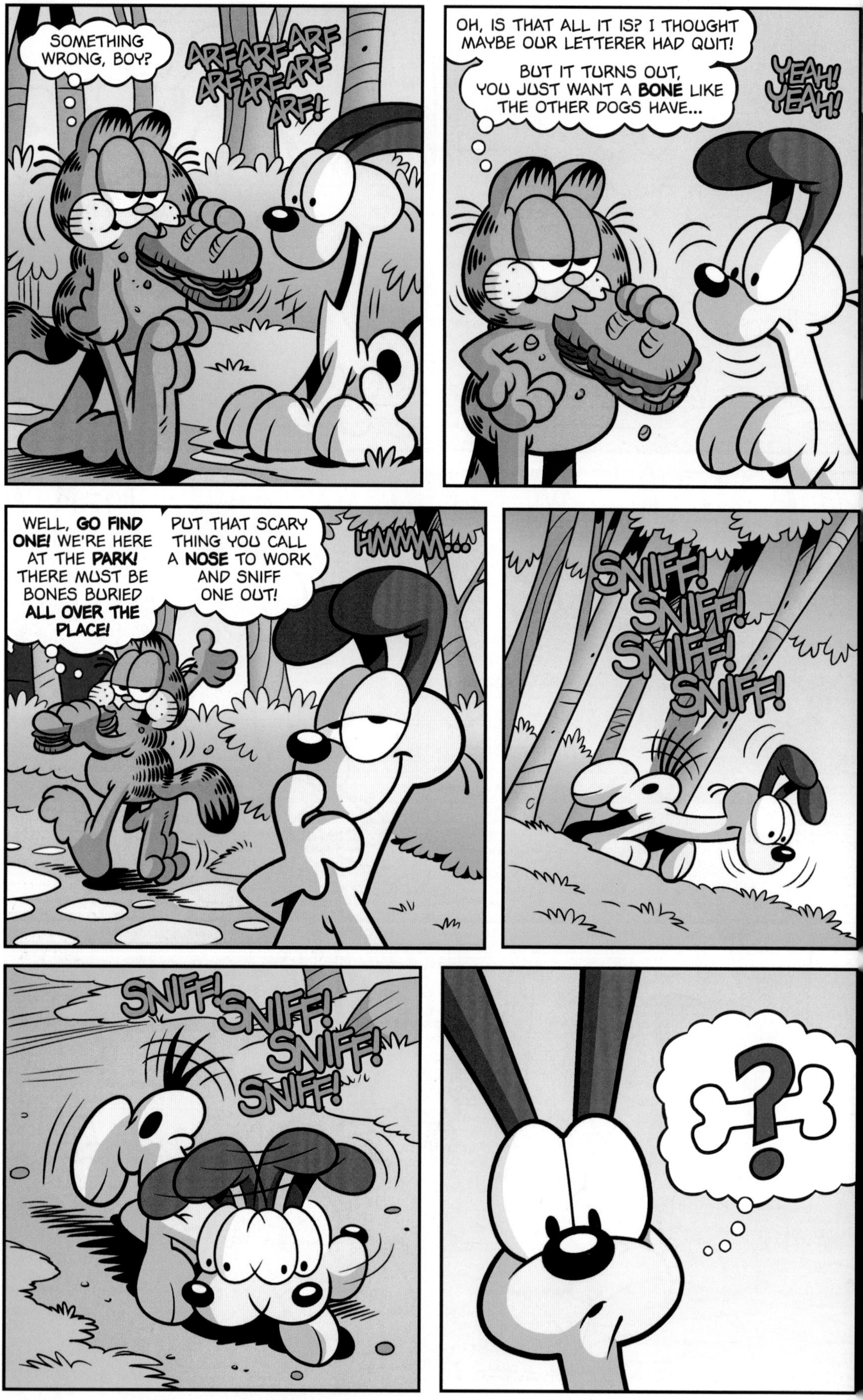
SOMETHING WRONG, BOY?
ARFARFARF ARFARFARF ARF!
OH, IS THAT ALL IT IS? I THOUGHT MAYBE OUR LETTERER HAD QUIT!
BUT IT TURNS OUT, YOU JUST WANT A **BONE** LIKE THE OTHER DOGS HAVE...
YEAH! YEAH!
WELL, **GO FIND ONE!** WE'RE HERE AT THE **PARK!** THERE MUST BE BONES BURIED **ALL OVER THE PLACE!**
PUT THAT SCARY THING YOU CALL A **NOSE** TO WORK AND SNIFF ONE OUT!
HMMM...
SNIFF! SNIFF! SNIFF! SNIFF!
SNIFF! SNIFF! SNIFF! SNIFF!
?

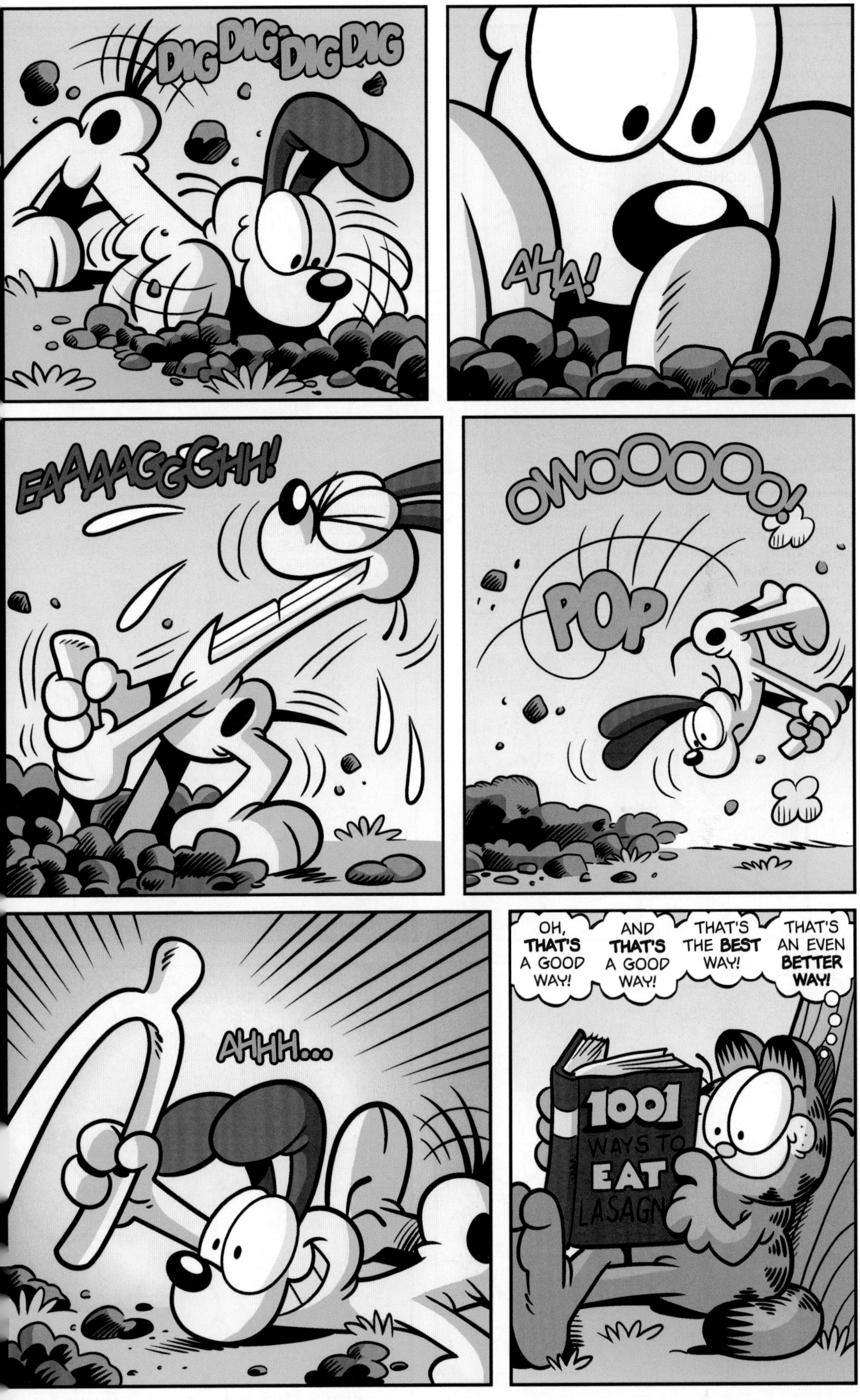
DIG DIG DIG DIG
AHA!
EAAAAGGGHH!
OWOOOOOO!
POP
AHHH...
OH, THAT'S A GOOD WAY!
AND THAT'S A GOOD WAY!
THAT'S THE BEST WAY!
THAT'S AN EVEN BETTER WAY!
1001 WAYS TO EAT LASAGN

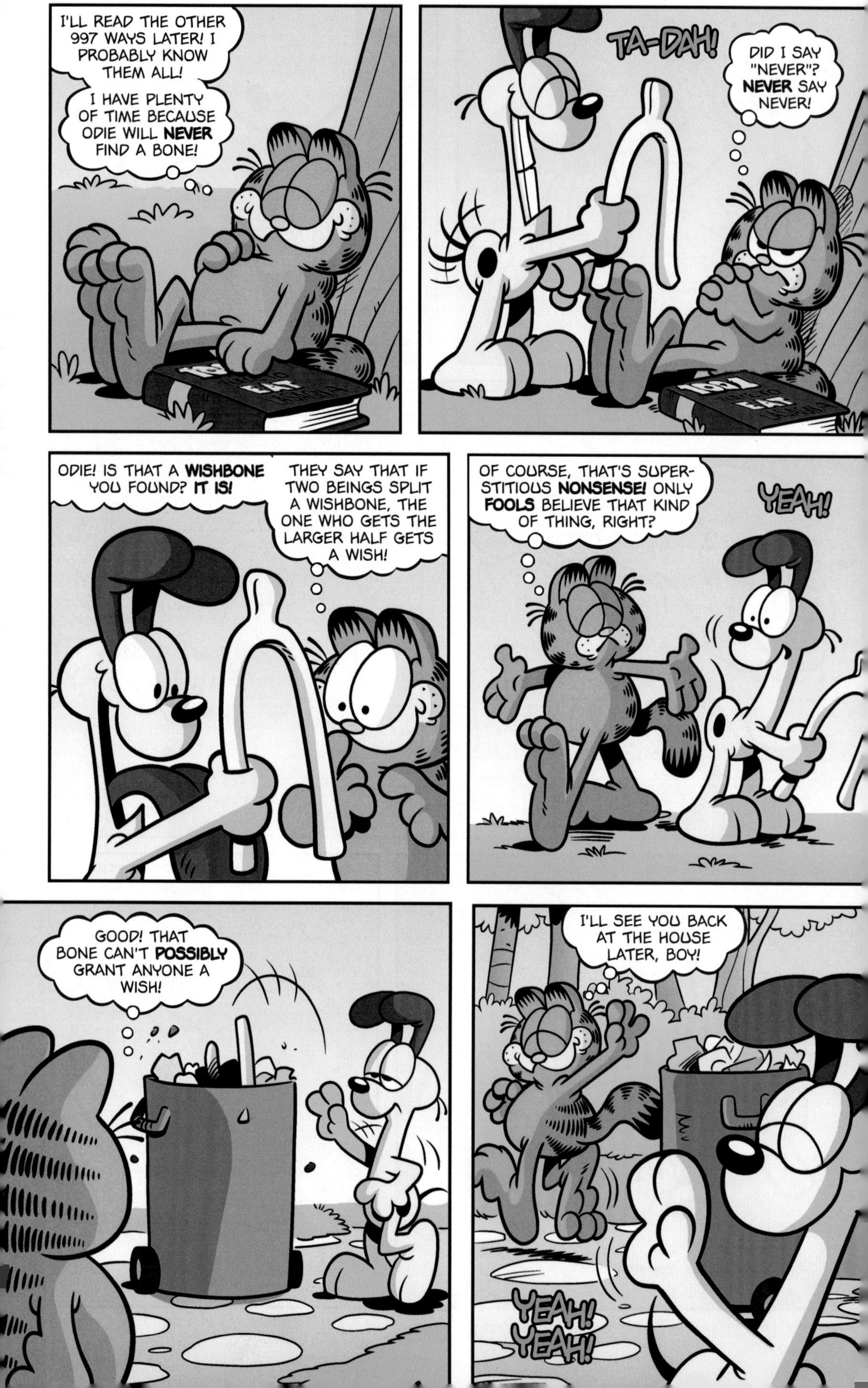

I'LL READ THE OTHER 997 WAYS LATER! I PROBABLY KNOW THEM ALL!
I HAVE PLENTY OF TIME BECAUSE ODIE WILL **NEVER** FIND A BONE!
TA-DAH!
DID I SAY "NEVER"? **NEVER** SAY NEVER!
ODIE! IS THAT A **WISHBONE** YOU FOUND? **IT IS!**
THEY SAY THAT IF TWO BEINGS SPLIT A WISHBONE, THE ONE WHO GETS THE LARGER HALF GETS A WISH!
OF COURSE, THAT'S SUPER-STITIOUS **NONSENSE!** ONLY **FOOLS** BELIEVE THAT KIND OF THING, RIGHT?
YEAH!
GOOD! THAT BONE CAN'T **POSSIBLY** GRANT ANYONE A WISH!
I'LL SEE YOU BACK AT THE HOUSE LATER, BOY!
YEAH! YEAH!

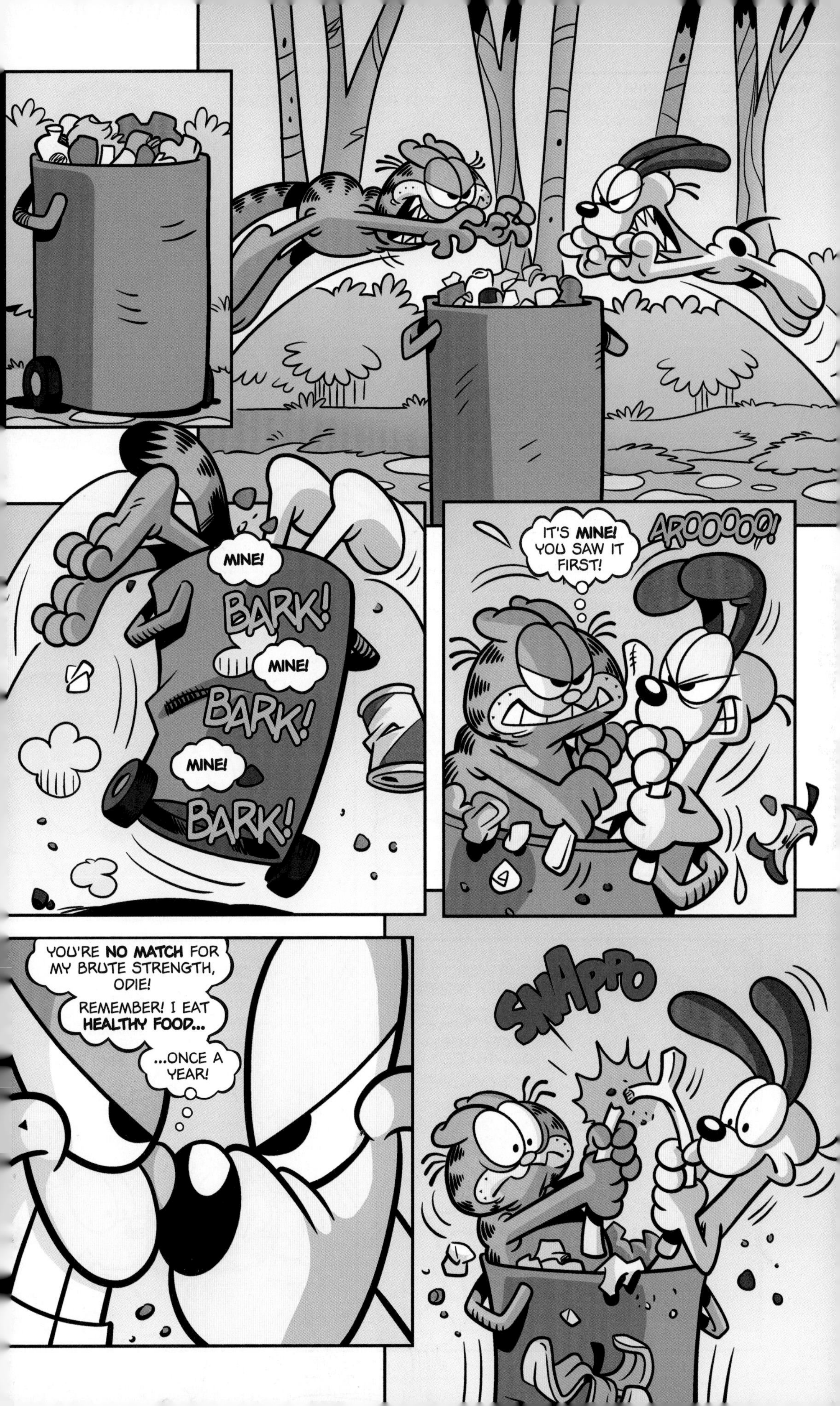
MINE!
BARK!
MINE!
BARK!
MINE!
BARK!
IT'S MINE! YOU SAW IT FIRST!
AROOOOO!
YOU'RE NO MATCH FOR MY BRUTE STRENGTH, ODIE!
REMEMBER! I EAT HEALTHY FOOD...
...ONCE A YEAR!
SNAPPO

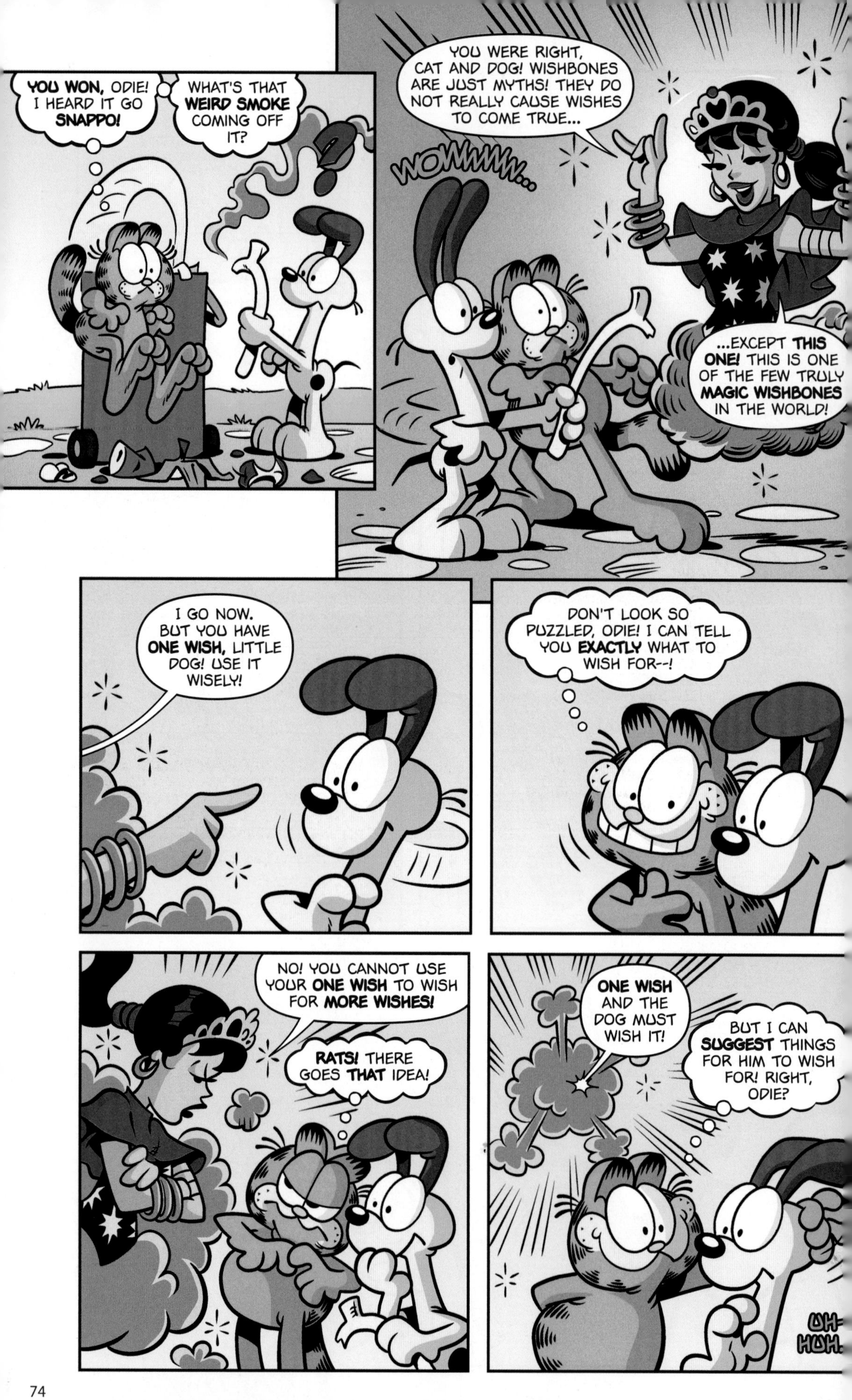
YOU WON, ODIE! I HEARD IT GO SNAPPO!
WHAT'S THAT WEIRD SMOKE COMING OFF IT?
YOU WERE RIGHT, CAT AND DOG! WISHBONES ARE JUST MYTHS! THEY DO NOT REALLY CAUSE WISHES TO COME TRUE...
WOWWWW...
...EXCEPT THIS ONE! THIS IS ONE OF THE FEW TRULY MAGIC WISHBONES IN THE WORLD!
I GO NOW. BUT YOU HAVE ONE WISH, LITTLE DOG! USE IT WISELY!
DON'T LOOK SO PUZZLED, ODIE! I CAN TELL YOU EXACTLY WHAT TO WISH FOR--!
NO! YOU CANNOT USE YOUR ONE WISH TO WISH FOR MORE WISHES!
RATS! THERE GOES THAT IDEA!
ONE WISH AND THE DOG MUST WISH IT!
BUT I CAN SUGGEST THINGS FOR HIM TO WISH FOR! RIGHT, ODIE?
UH-HUH.

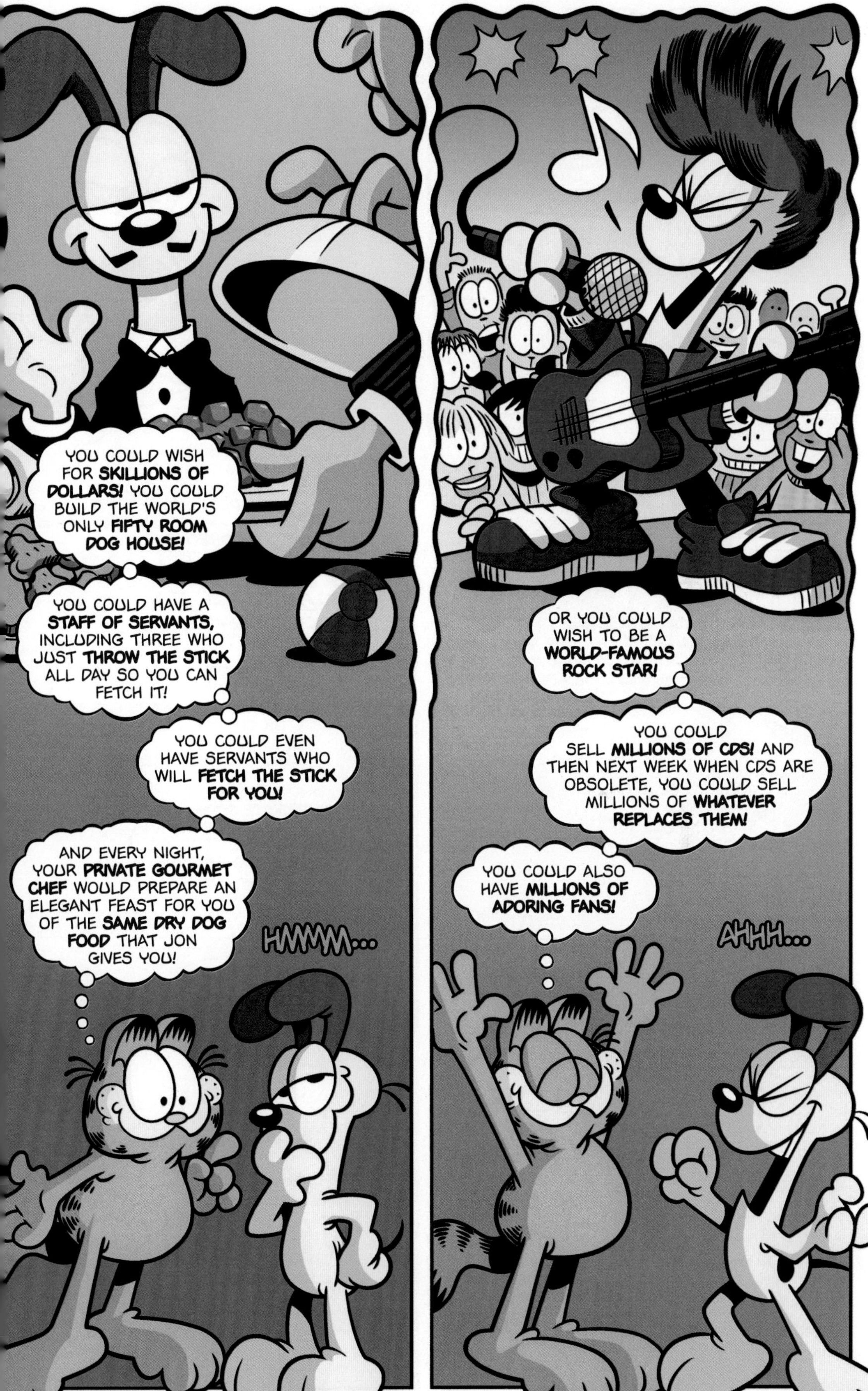

YOU COULD WISH FOR SKILLIONS OF DOLLARS! YOU COULD BUILD THE WORLD'S ONLY FIFTY ROOM DOG HOUSE!
YOU COULD HAVE A STAFF OF SERVANTS, INCLUDING THREE WHO JUST THROW THE STICK ALL DAY SO YOU CAN FETCH IT!
YOU COULD EVEN HAVE SERVANTS WHO WILL FETCH THE STICK FOR YOU!
AND EVERY NIGHT, YOUR PRIVATE GOURMET CHEF WOULD PREPARE AN ELEGANT FEAST FOR YOU OF THE SAME DRY DOG FOOD THAT JON GIVES YOU!
HMMM...
OR YOU COULD WISH TO BE A WORLD-FAMOUS ROCK STAR!
YOU COULD SELL MILLIONS OF CDS! AND THEN NEXT WEEK WHEN CDS ARE OBSOLETE, YOU COULD SELL MILLIONS OF WHATEVER REPLACES THEM!
YOU COULD ALSO HAVE MILLIONS OF ADORING FANS!
AHHH...

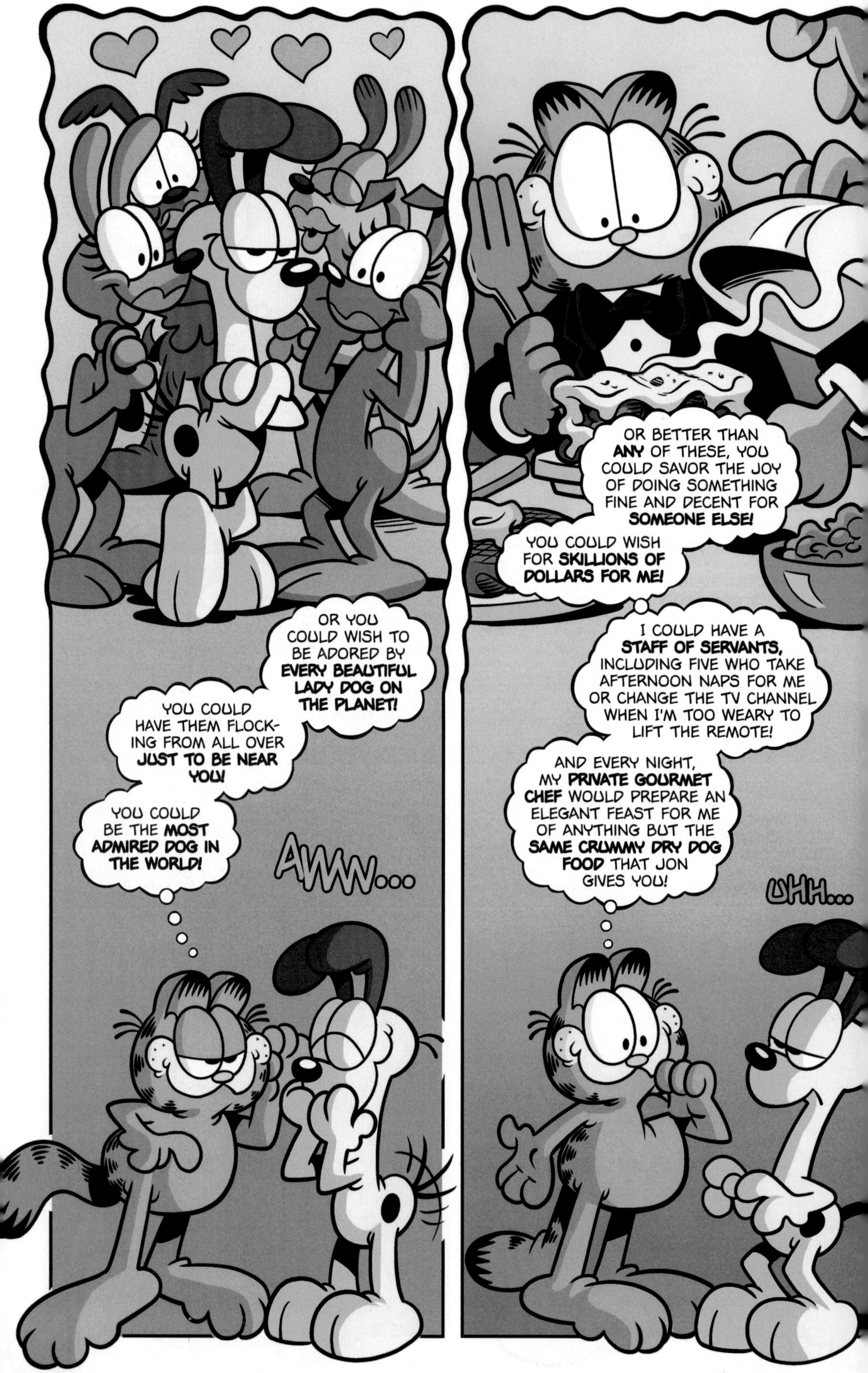

YOU COULD BE THE MOST ADMIRED DOG IN THE WORLD!
YOU COULD HAVE THEM FLOCKING FROM ALL OVER JUST TO BE NEAR YOU!
OR YOU COULD WISH TO BE ADORED BY EVERY BEAUTIFUL LADY DOG ON THE PLANET!
AWWW...
AND EVERY NIGHT, MY PRIVATE GOURMET CHEF WOULD PREPARE AN ELEGANT FEAST FOR ME OF ANYTHING BUT THE SAME CRUMMY DRY DOG FOOD THAT JON GIVES YOU!
I COULD HAVE A STAFF OF SERVANTS, INCLUDING FIVE WHO TAKE AFTERNOON NAPS FOR ME OR CHANGE THE TV CHANNEL WHEN I'M TOO WEARY TO LIFT THE REMOTE!
YOU COULD WISH FOR SKILLIONS OF DOLLARS FOR ME!
OR BETTER THAN ANY OF THESE, YOU COULD SAVOR THE JOY OF DOING SOMETHING FINE AND DECENT FOR SOMEONE ELSE!
UHH...

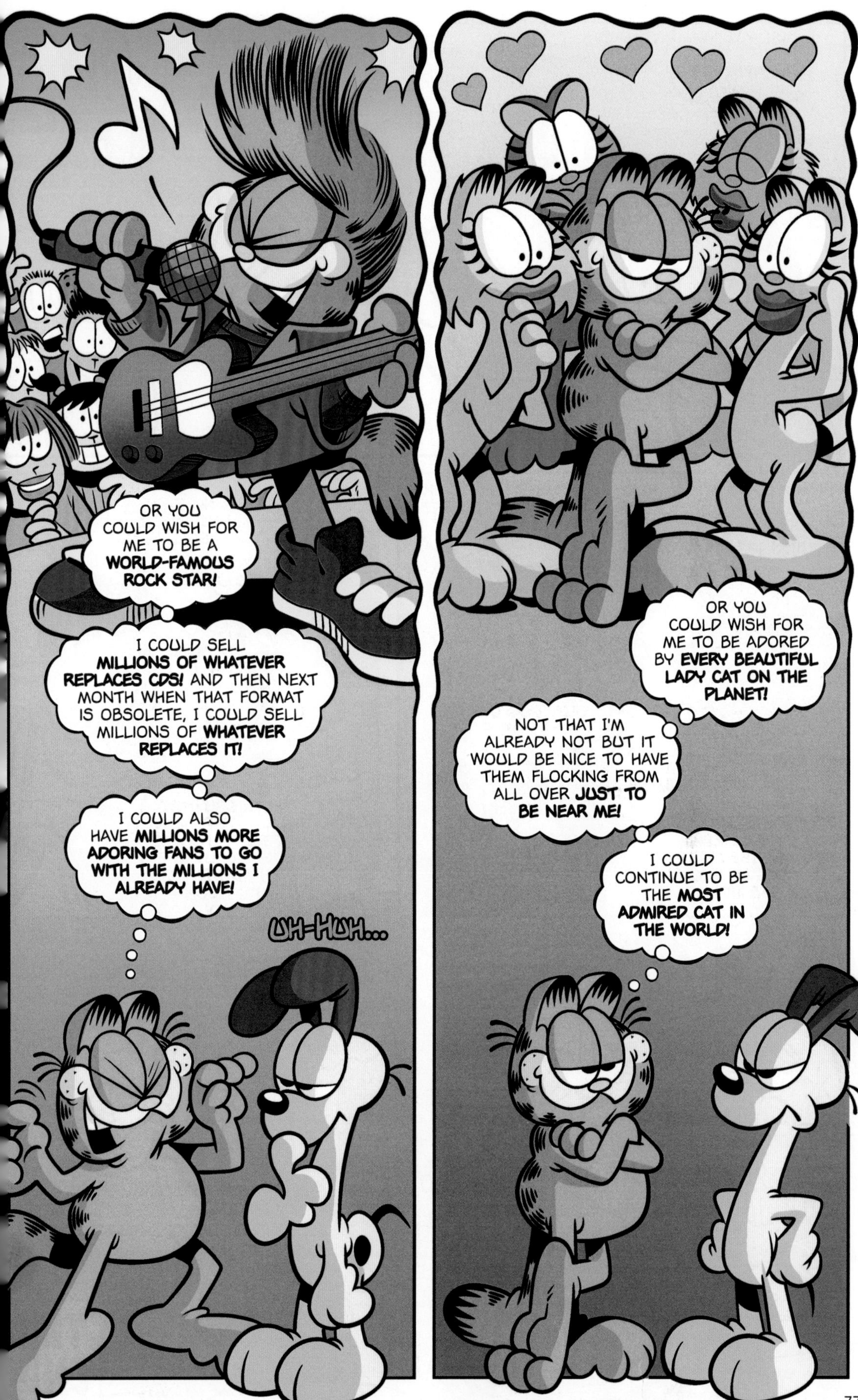

OR YOU COULD WISH FOR ME TO BE A WORLD-FAMOUS ROCK STAR!
I COULD SELL MILLIONS OF WHATEVER REPLACES CDS! AND THEN NEXT MONTH WHEN THAT FORMAT IS OBSOLETE, I COULD SELL MILLIONS OF WHATEVER REPLACES IT!
I COULD ALSO HAVE MILLIONS MORE ADORING FANS TO GO WITH THE MILLIONS I ALREADY HAVE!
UH-HUH...
OR YOU COULD WISH FOR ME TO BE ADORED BY EVERY BEAUTIFUL LADY CAT ON THE PLANET!
NOT THAT I'M ALREADY NOT BUT IT WOULD BE NICE TO HAVE THEM FLOCKING FROM ALL OVER JUST TO BE NEAR ME!
I COULD CONTINUE TO BE THE MOST ADMIRED CAT IN THE WORLD!

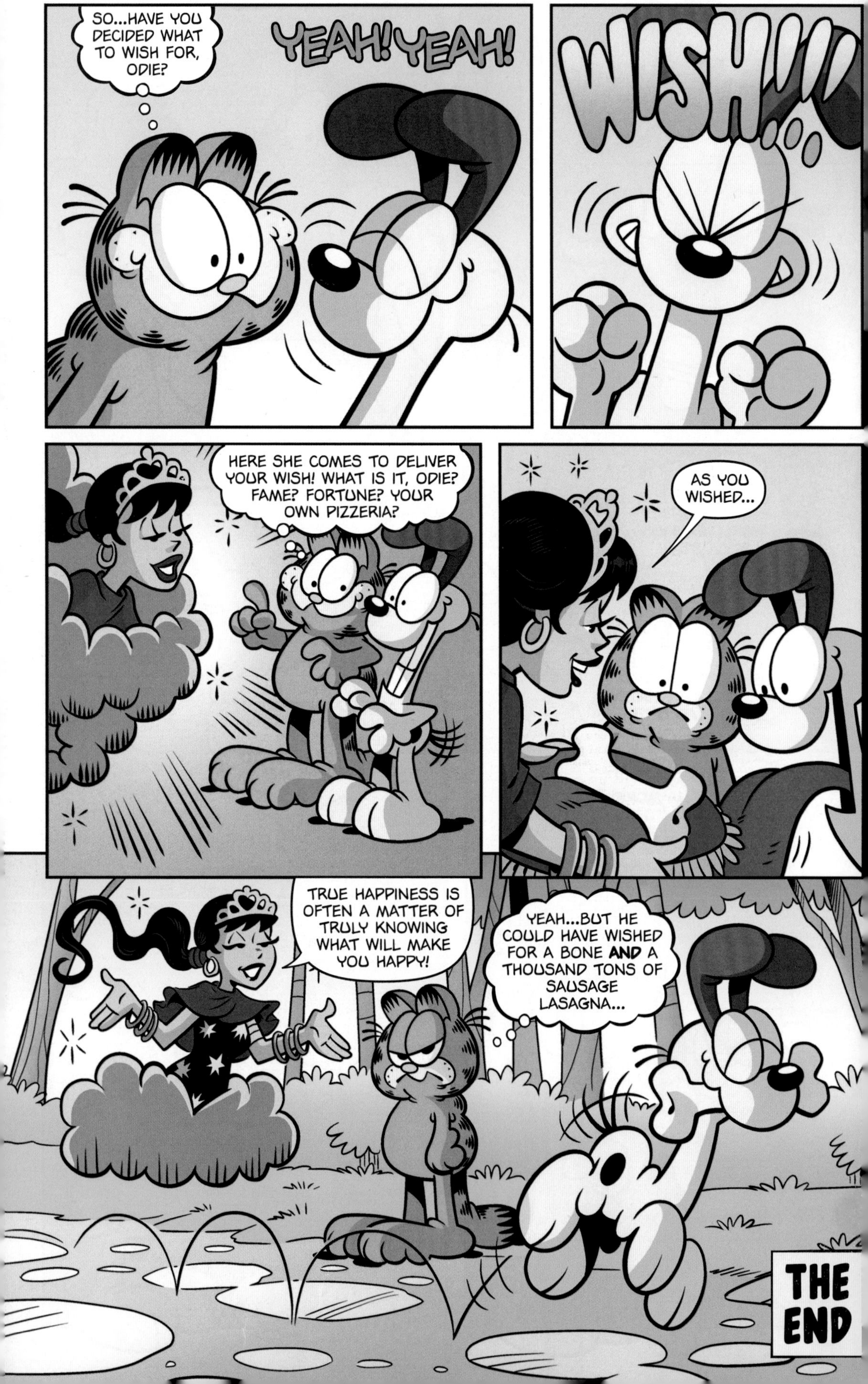
SO...HAVE YOU DECIDED WHAT TO WISH FOR, ODIE?
YEAH! YEAH!
WISH!!!
HERE SHE COMES TO DELIVER YOUR WISH! WHAT IS IT, ODIE? FAME? FORTUNE? YOUR OWN PIZZERIA?
AS YOU WISHED...
TRUE HAPPINESS IS OFTEN A MATTER OF TRULY KNOWING WHAT WILL MAKE YOU HAPPY!
YEAH...BUT HE COULD HAVE WISHED FOR A BONE **AND** A THOUSAND TONS OF SAUSAGE LASAGNA...
THE END

CHAPTER FOUR

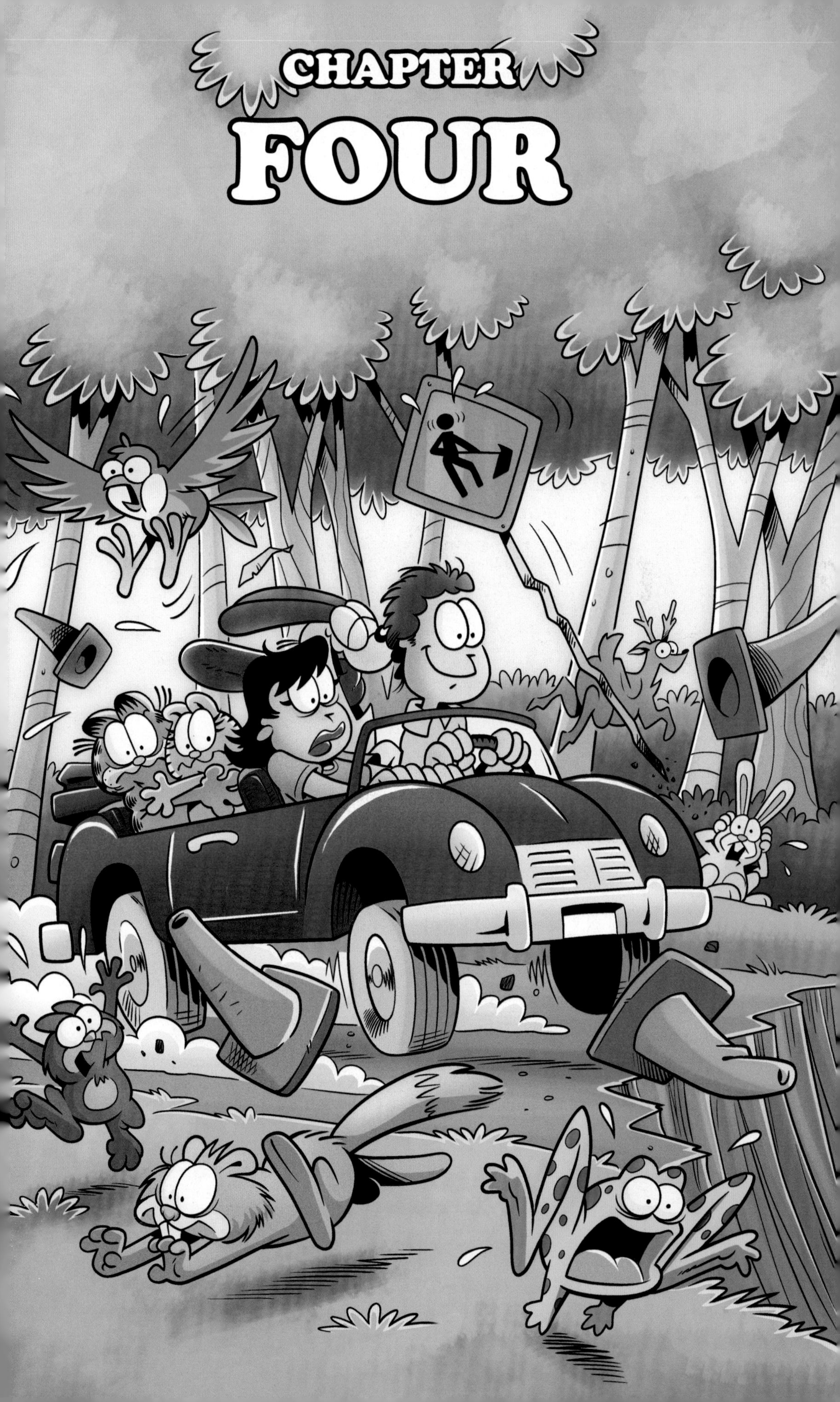

JON OF THE JUNGLE
THE VERY SMART LITTLE GIRL

Written by
MARK EVANIER

Art by
GARY BARKER
AND DAN DAVIS
(Pages 81-92)
MIKE DeCARLO
(Pages 93-102)

Colors by
LISA MOORE

Chapter Break Art by
GARY BARKER
WITH ## LISA MOORE

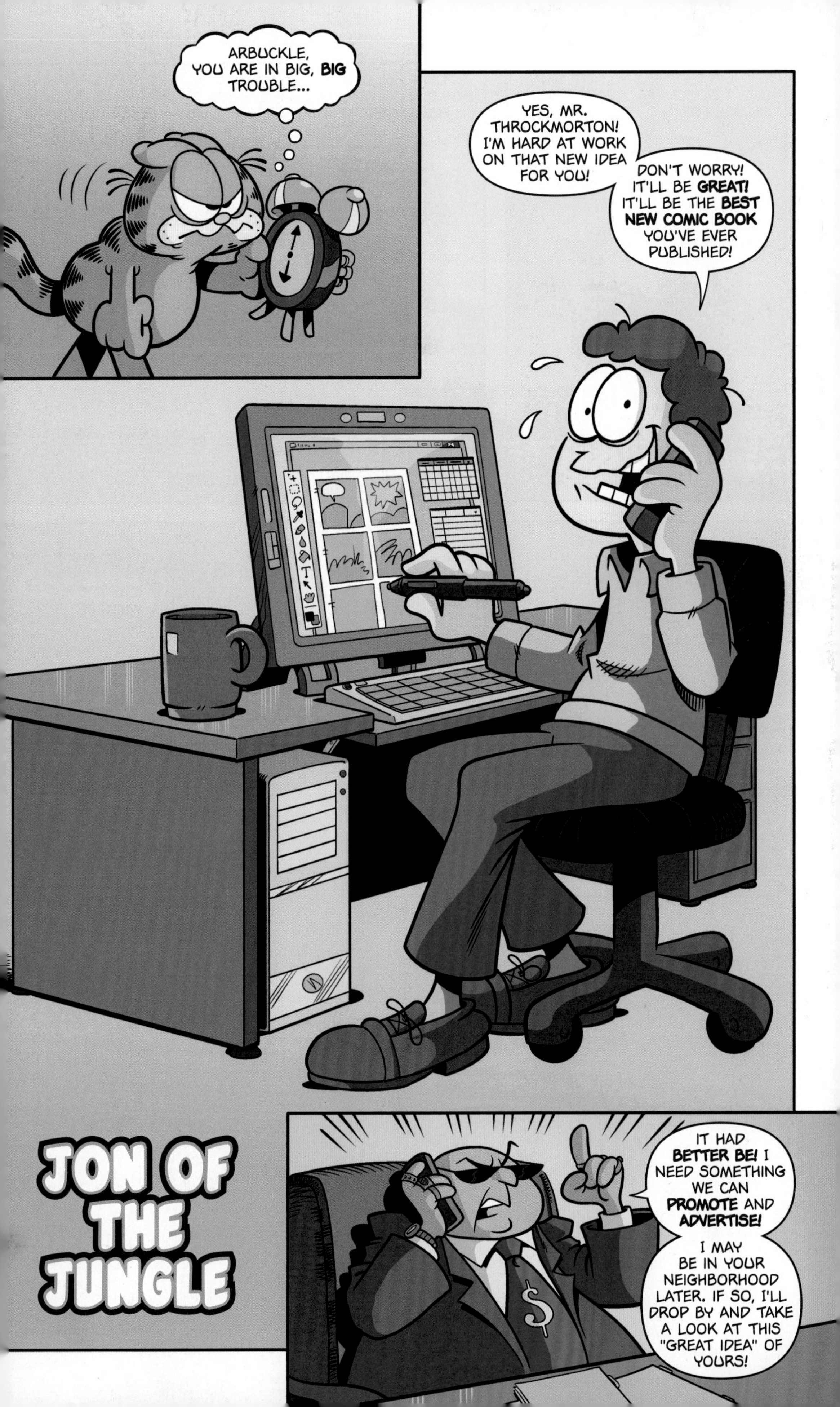
ARBUCKLE, YOU ARE IN BIG, **BIG** TROUBLE...
YES, MR. THROCKMORTON! I'M HARD AT WORK ON THAT NEW IDEA FOR YOU!
DON'T WORRY! IT'LL BE **GREAT!** IT'LL BE THE **BEST NEW COMIC BOOK** YOU'VE EVER PUBLISHED!
JON OF THE JUNGLE
IT HAD **BETTER BE!** I NEED SOMETHING WE CAN **PROMOTE** AND **ADVERTISE!**
I MAY BE IN YOUR NEIGHBORHOOD LATER. IF SO, I'LL DROP BY AND TAKE A LOOK AT THIS "GREAT IDEA" OF YOURS!

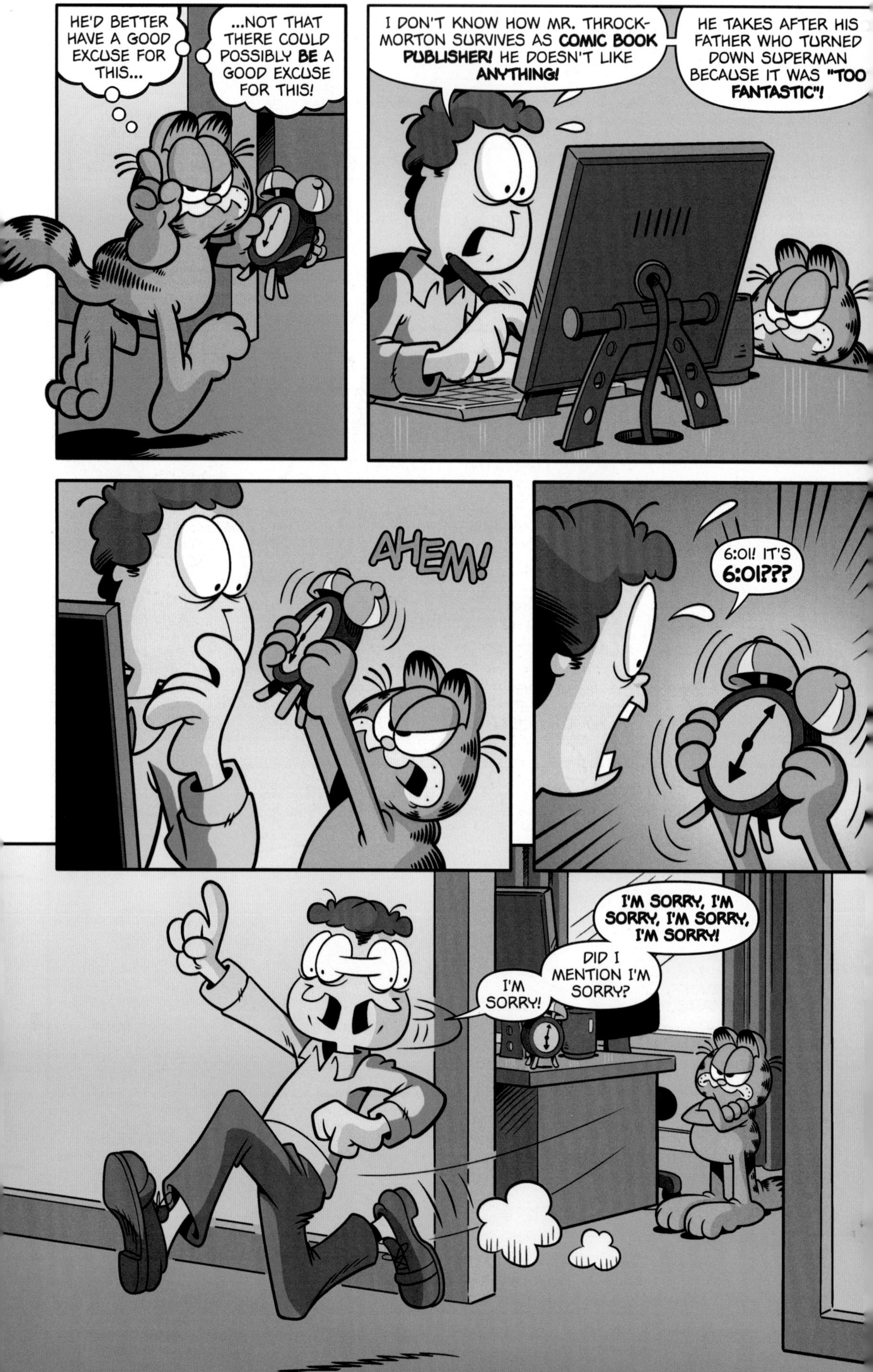
HE'D BETTER HAVE A GOOD EXCUSE FOR THIS...
...NOT THAT THERE COULD POSSIBLY **BE** A GOOD EXCUSE FOR THIS!
I DON'T KNOW HOW MR. THROCKMORTON SURVIVES AS **COMIC BOOK PUBLISHER!** HE DOESN'T LIKE **ANYTHING!**
HE TAKES AFTER HIS FATHER WHO TURNED DOWN SUPERMAN BECAUSE IT WAS **"TOO FANTASTIC"!**
AHEM!
6:01! IT'S **6:01???**
I'M SORRY!
DID I MENTION I'M SORRY?
I'M SORRY, I'M SORRY, I'M SORRY, I'M SORRY!

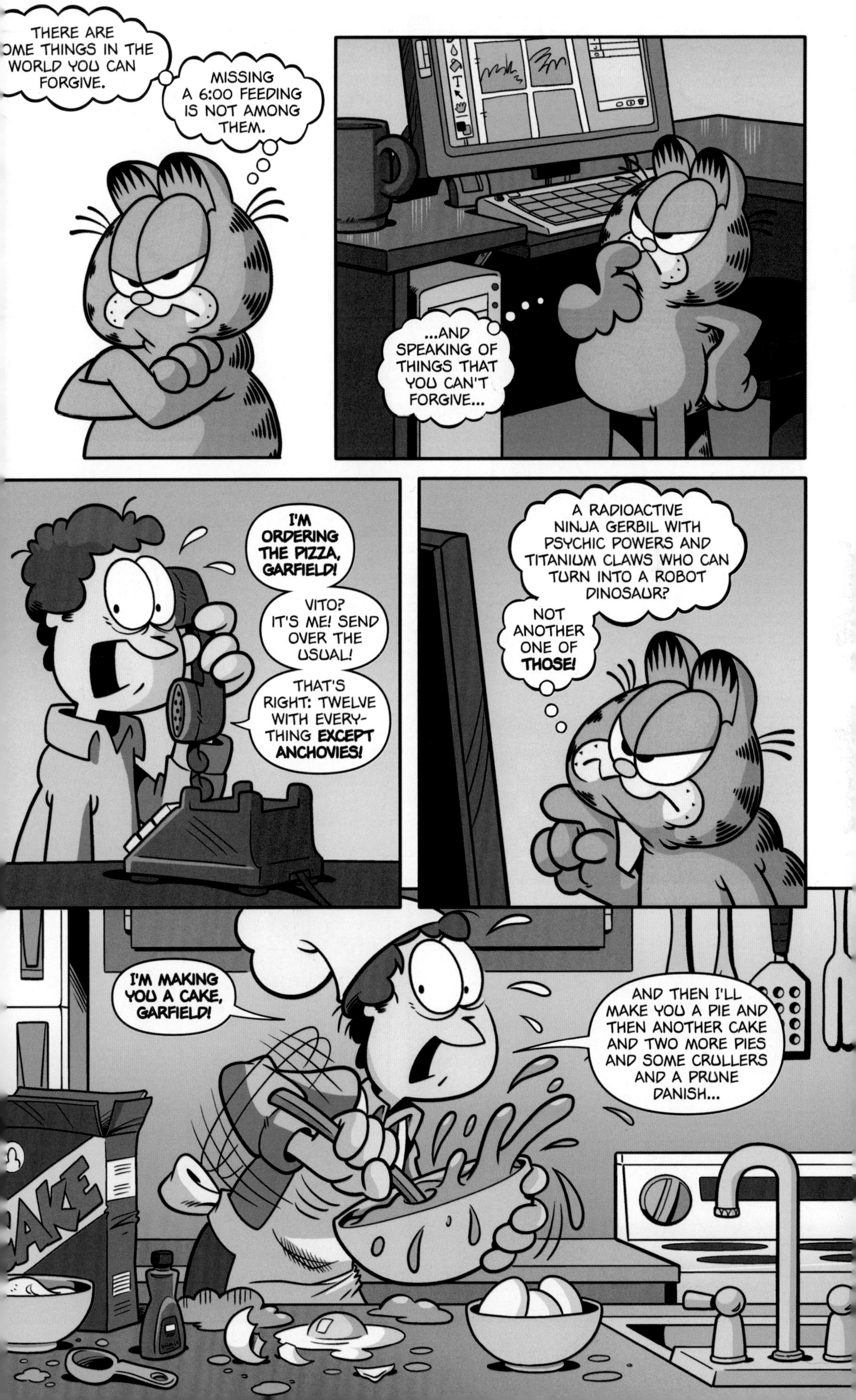
THERE ARE
OME THINGS IN THE
WORLD YOU CAN
FORGIVE.
MISSING A 6:00 FEEDING IS NOT AMONG THEM.
...AND SPEAKING OF THINGS THAT YOU CAN'T FORGIVE...
I'M ORDERING THE PIZZA, GARFIELD!
VITO? IT'S ME! SEND OVER THE USUAL!
THAT'S RIGHT: TWELVE WITH EVERY-THING EXCEPT ANCHOVIES!
A RADIOACTIVE NINJA GERBIL WITH PSYCHIC POWERS AND TITANIUM CLAWS WHO CAN TURN INTO A ROBOT DINOSAUR?
NOT ANOTHER ONE OF THOSE!
I'M MAKING YOU A CAKE, GARFIELD!
AND THEN I'LL MAKE YOU A PIE AND THEN ANOTHER CAKE AND TWO MORE PIES AND SOME CRULLERS AND A PRUNE DANISH...
CAKE

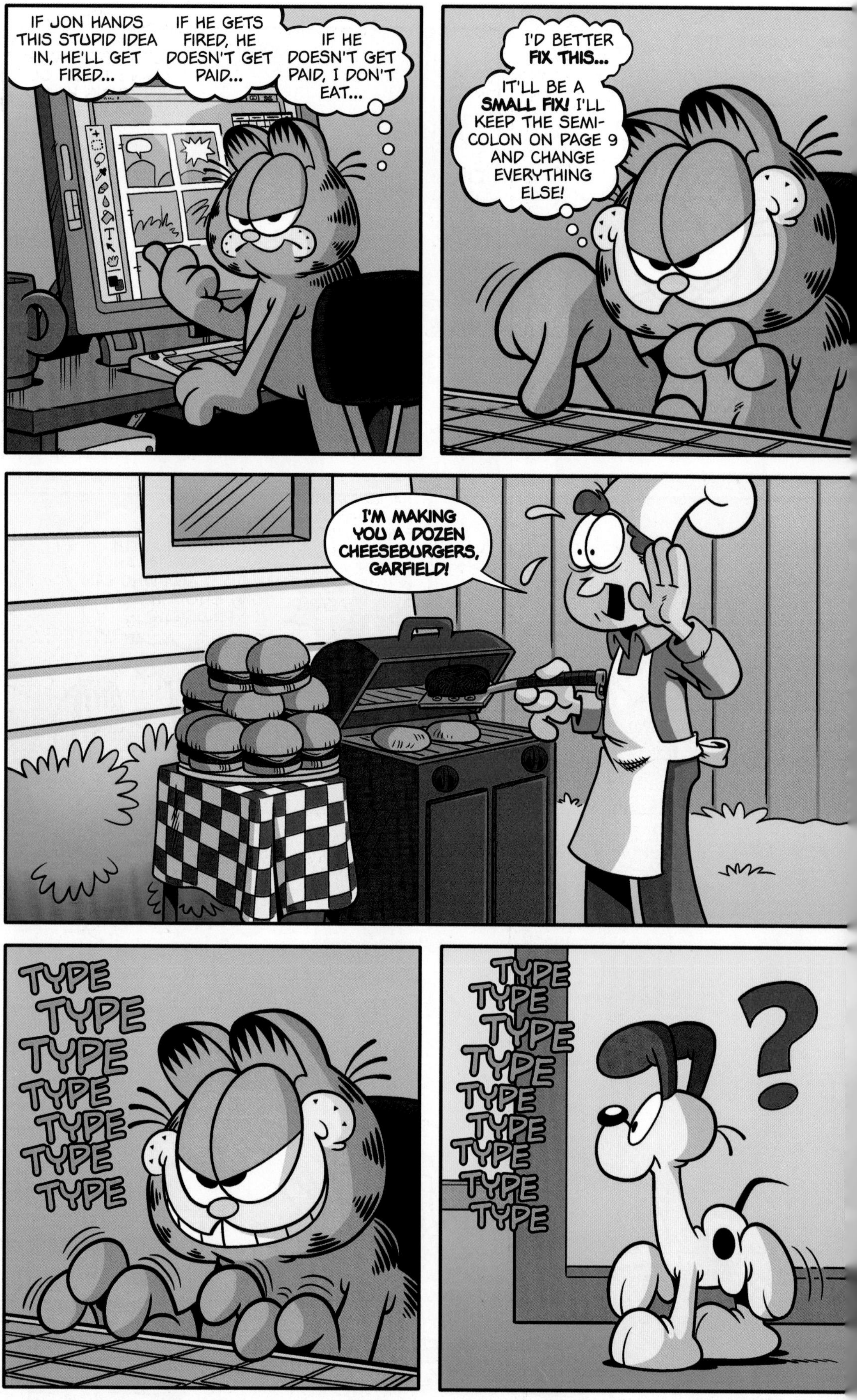

IF JON HANDS THIS STUPID IDEA IN, HE'LL GET FIRED...
IF HE GETS FIRED, HE DOESN'T GET PAID...
IF HE DOESN'T GET PAID, I DON'T EAT...
I'D BETTER FIX THIS...
IT'LL BE A SMALL FIX! I'LL KEEP THE SEMI-COLON ON PAGE 9 AND CHANGE EVERYTHING ELSE!
I'M MAKING YOU A DOZEN CHEESEBURGERS, GARFIELD!
TYPE TYPE TYPE TYPE TYPE TYPE TYPE
TYPE TYPE TYPE TYPE TYPE TYPE TYPE TYPE TYPE
?

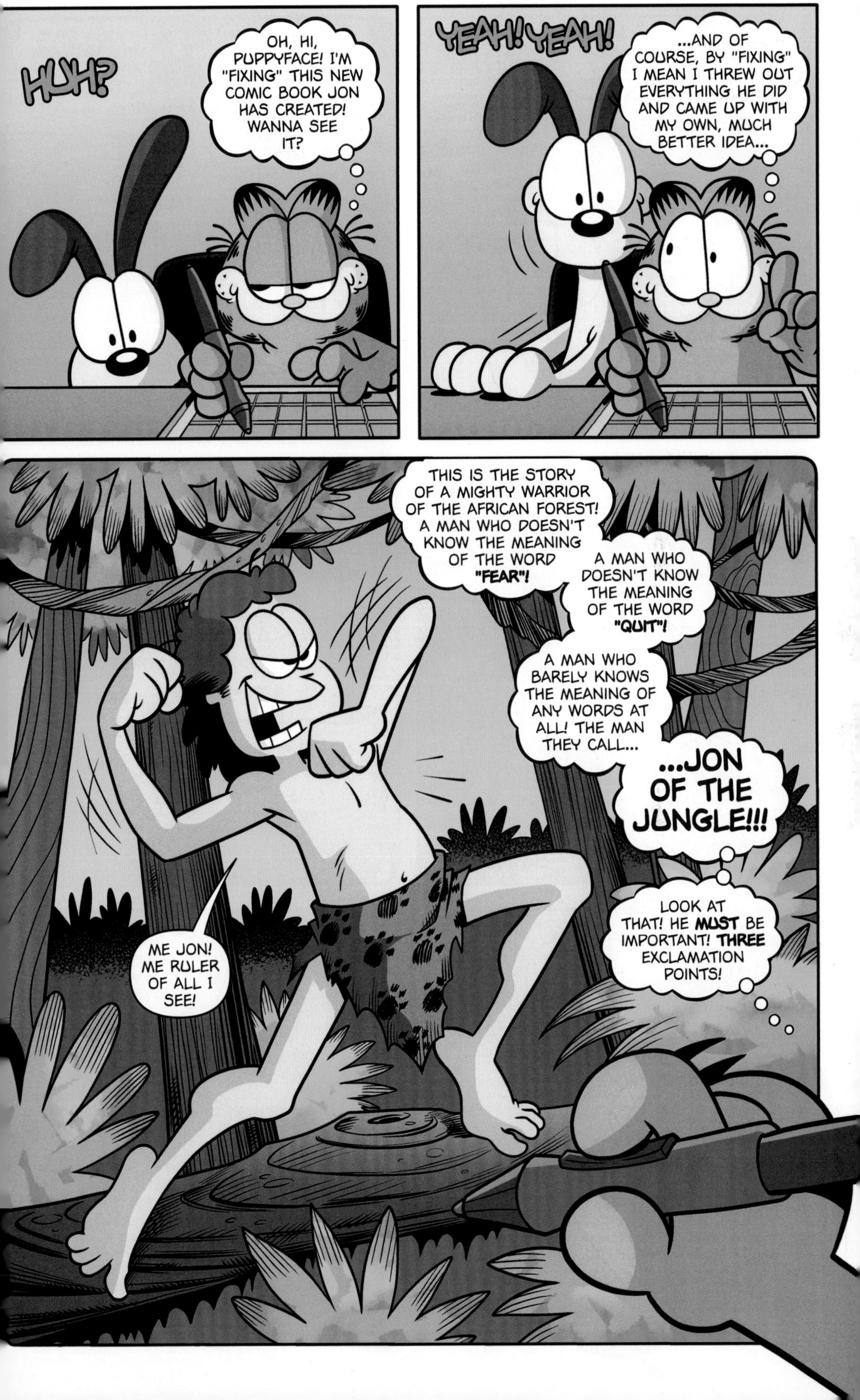
HUH?
OH, HI, PUPPYFACE! I'M "FIXING" THIS NEW COMIC BOOK JON HAS CREATED! WANNA SEE IT?
YEAH! YEAH!
...AND OF COURSE, BY "FIXING" I MEAN I THREW OUT EVERYTHING HE DID AND CAME UP WITH MY OWN, MUCH BETTER IDEA...
THIS IS THE STORY OF A MIGHTY WARRIOR OF THE AFRICAN FOREST! A MAN WHO DOESN'T KNOW THE MEANING OF THE WORD **"FEAR"**!
A MAN WHO DOESN'T KNOW THE MEANING OF THE WORD **"QUIT"**!
A MAN WHO BARELY KNOWS THE MEANING OF ANY WORDS AT ALL! THE MAN THEY CALL...
...JON OF THE JUNGLE!!!
ME JON! ME RULER OF ALL I SEE!
LOOK AT THAT! HE **MUST** BE IMPORTANT! **THREE** EXCLAMATION POINTS!

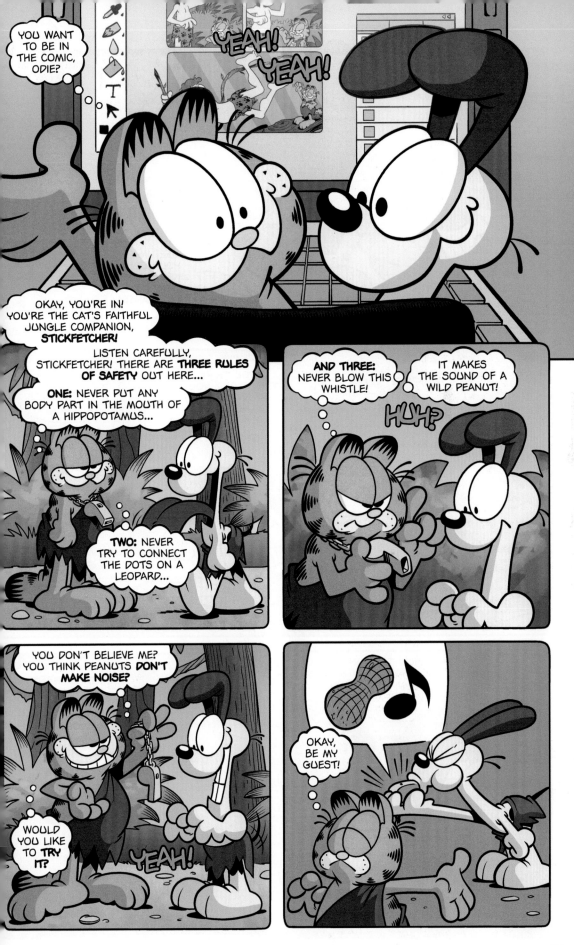

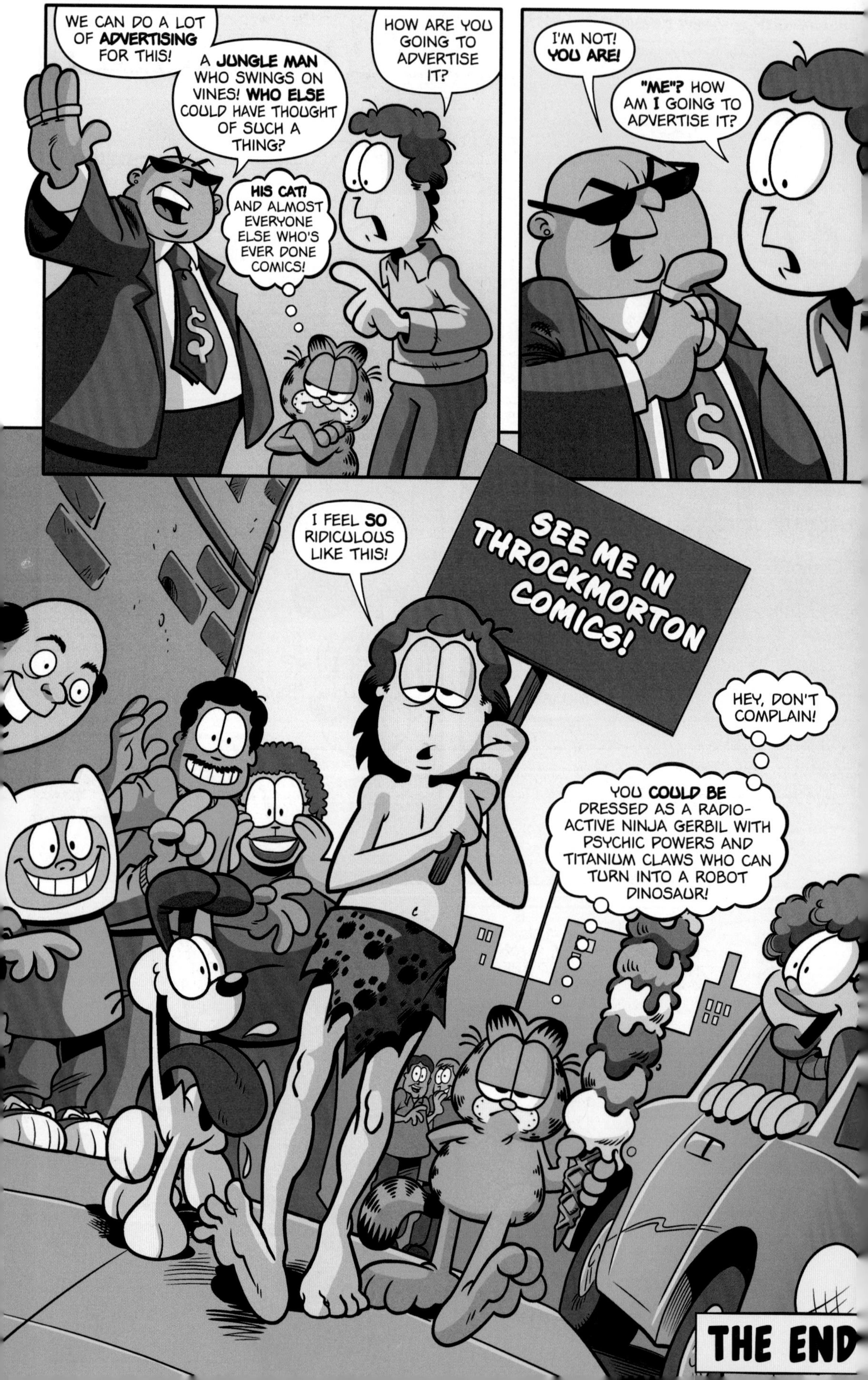

WE CAN DO A LOT OF **ADVERTISING** FOR THIS!
A **JUNGLE MAN** WHO SWINGS ON VINES! **WHO ELSE** COULD HAVE THOUGHT OF SUCH A THING?
HOW ARE YOU GOING TO ADVERTISE IT?
HIS CAT! AND ALMOST EVERYONE ELSE WHO'S EVER DONE COMICS!
I'M NOT! **YOU ARE!**
"ME"? HOW AM **I** GOING TO ADVERTISE IT?
I FEEL **SO** RIDICULOUS LIKE THIS!
SEE ME IN THROCKMORTON COMICS!
HEY, DON'T COMPLAIN!
YOU **COULD BE** DRESSED AS A RADIO-ACTIVE NINJA GERBIL WITH PSYCHIC POWERS AND TITANIUM CLAWS WHO CAN TURN INTO A ROBOT DINOSAUR!
THE END

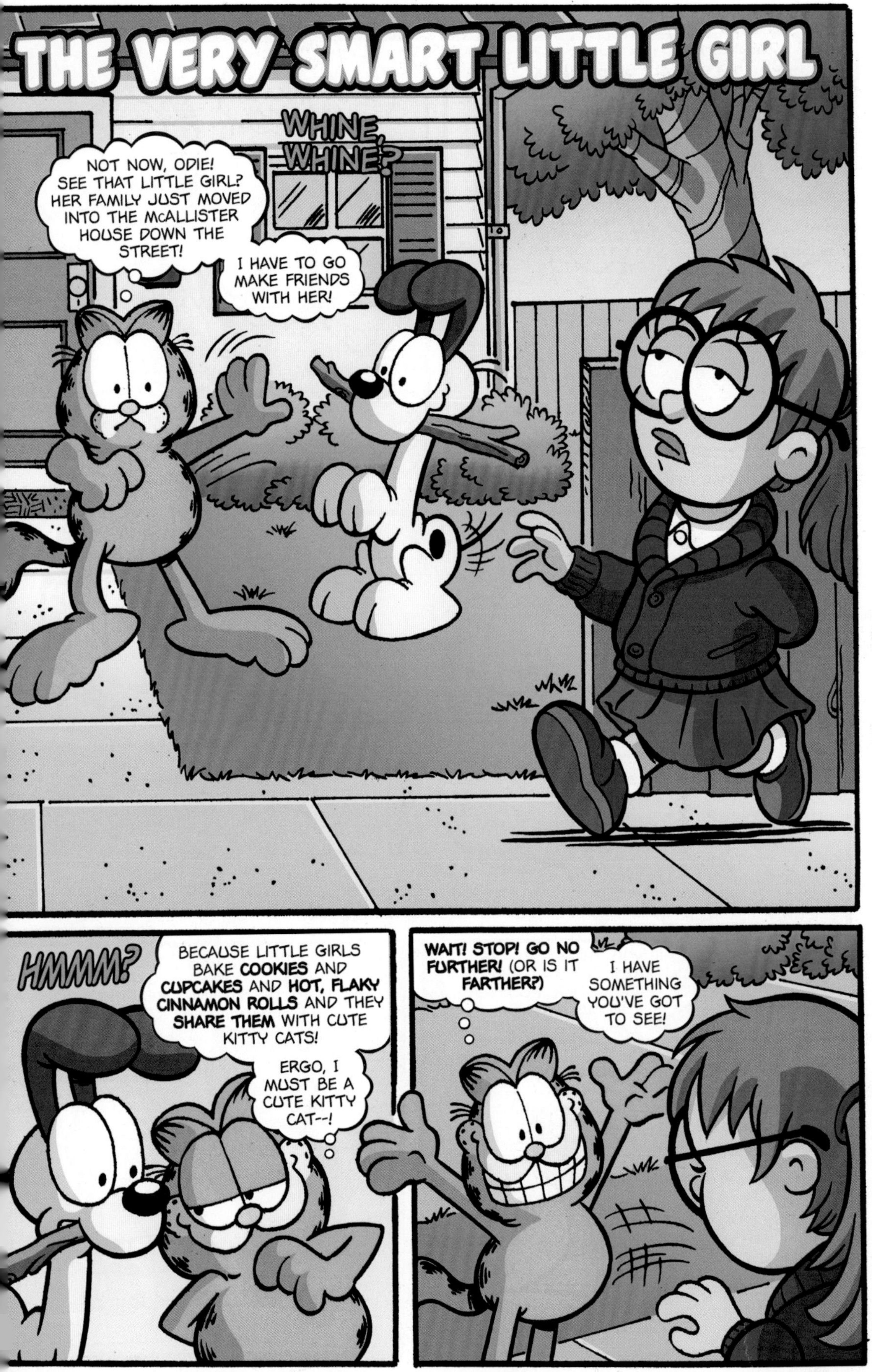
THE VERY SMART LITTLE GIRL
WHINE, WHINE?
NOT NOW, ODIE! SEE THAT LITTLE GIRL? HER FAMILY JUST MOVED INTO THE McALLISTER HOUSE DOWN THE STREET!
I HAVE TO GO MAKE FRIENDS WITH HER!
HMMM?
BECAUSE LITTLE GIRLS BAKE **COOKIES** AND **CUPCAKES** AND **HOT, FLAKY CINNAMON ROLLS** AND THEY **SHARE THEM** WITH CUTE KITTY CATS!
ERGO, I MUST BE A CUTE KITTY CAT--!
WAIT! STOP! GO NO FURTHER! (OR IS IT **FARTHER?**)
I HAVE SOMETHING YOU'VE GOT TO SEE!

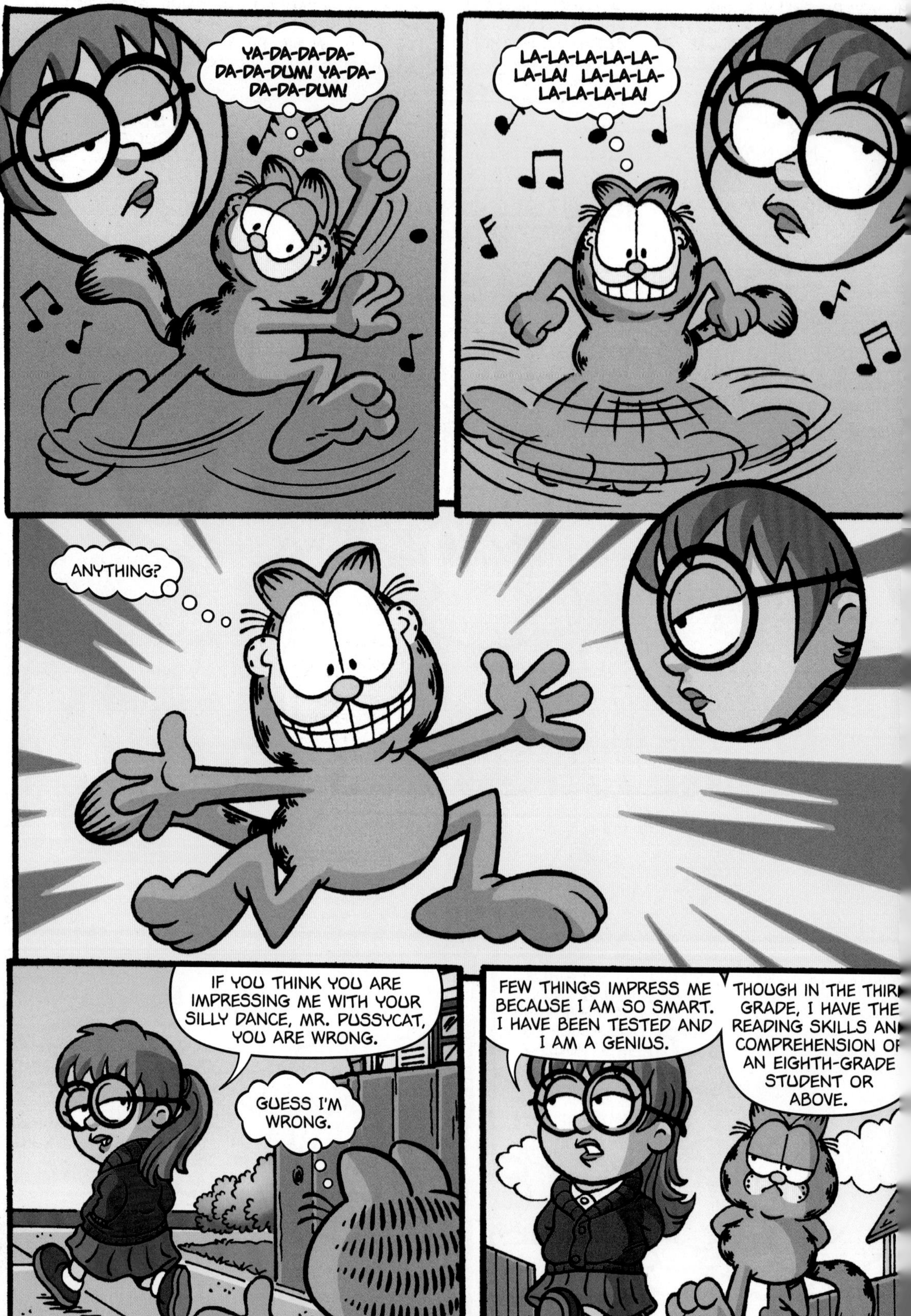

YA-DA-DA-DA-DA-DA-DUM! YA-DA-DA-DA-DUM!
LA-LA-LA-LA-LA-LA-LA! LA-LA-LA-LA-LA-LA-LA!
ANYTHING?
IF YOU THINK YOU ARE IMPRESSING ME WITH YOUR SILLY DANCE, MR. PUSSYCAT, YOU ARE WRONG.
GUESS I'M WRONG.
FEW THINGS IMPRESS ME BECAUSE I AM SO SMART. I HAVE BEEN TESTED AND I AM A GENIUS.
THOUGH IN THE THIR GRADE, I HAVE THE READING SKILLS AN COMPREHENSION OF AN EIGHTH-GRADE STUDENT OR ABOVE.

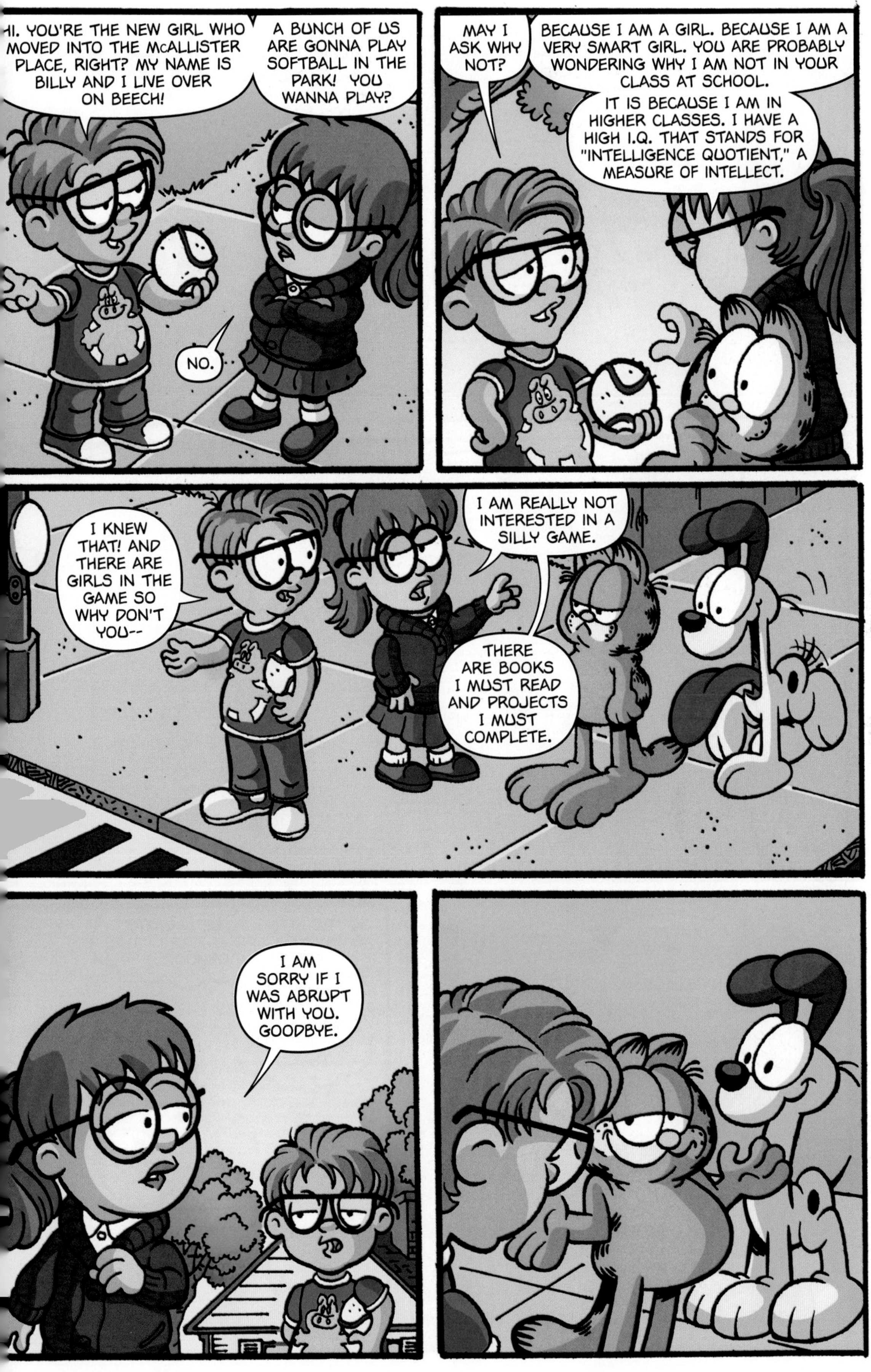
HI. YOU'RE THE NEW GIRL WHO MOVED INTO THE McALLISTER PLACE, RIGHT? MY NAME IS BILLY AND I LIVE OVER ON BEECH!
A BUNCH OF US ARE GONNA PLAY SOFTBALL IN THE PARK! YOU WANNA PLAY?
NO.
MAY I ASK WHY NOT?
BECAUSE I AM A GIRL. BECAUSE I AM A VERY SMART GIRL. YOU ARE PROBABLY WONDERING WHY I AM NOT IN YOUR CLASS AT SCHOOL.
IT IS BECAUSE I AM IN HIGHER CLASSES. I HAVE A HIGH I.Q. THAT STANDS FOR "INTELLIGENCE QUOTIENT," A MEASURE OF INTELLECT.
I KNEW THAT! AND THERE ARE GIRLS IN THE GAME SO WHY DON'T YOU--
I AM REALLY NOT INTERESTED IN A SILLY GAME.
THERE ARE BOOKS I MUST READ AND PROJECTS I MUST COMPLETE.
I AM SORRY IF I WAS ABRUPT WITH YOU. GOODBYE.

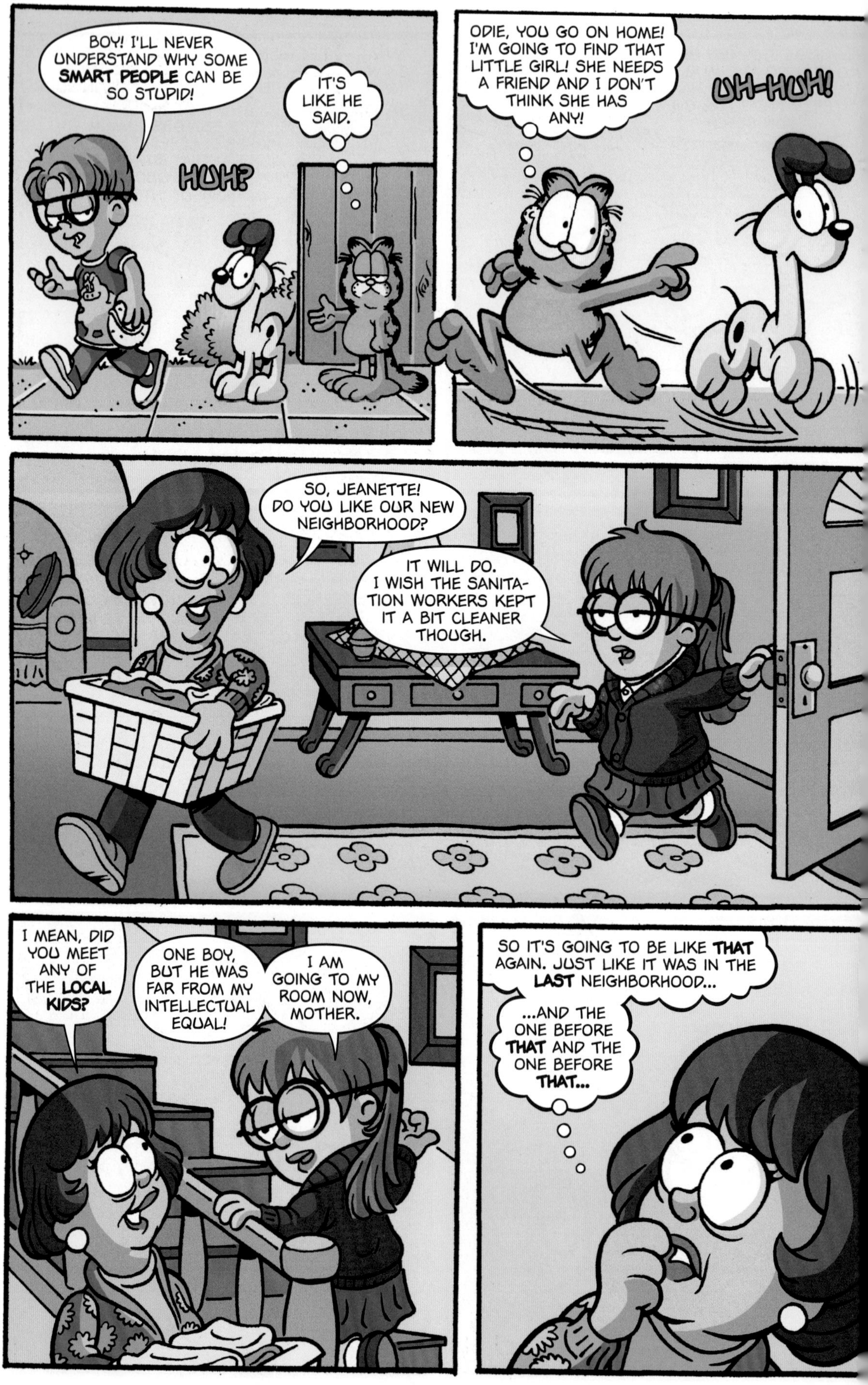

BOY! I'LL NEVER UNDERSTAND WHY SOME **SMART PEOPLE** CAN BE SO STUPID!
HUH?
IT'S LIKE HE SAID.
ODIE, YOU GO ON HOME! I'M GOING TO FIND THAT LITTLE GIRL! SHE NEEDS A FRIEND AND I DON'T THINK SHE HAS ANY!
UH-HUH!
SO, JEANETTE! DO YOU LIKE OUR NEW NEIGHBORHOOD?
IT WILL DO. I WISH THE SANITATION WORKERS KEPT IT A BIT CLEANER THOUGH.
I MEAN, DID YOU MEET ANY OF THE **LOCAL KIDS?**
ONE BOY, BUT HE WAS FAR FROM MY INTELLECTUAL EQUAL!
I AM GOING TO MY ROOM NOW, MOTHER.
SO IT'S GOING TO BE LIKE **THAT** AGAIN. JUST LIKE IT WAS IN THE **LAST** NEIGHBORHOOD...
...AND THE ONE BEFORE **THAT** AND THE ONE BEFORE **THAT...**

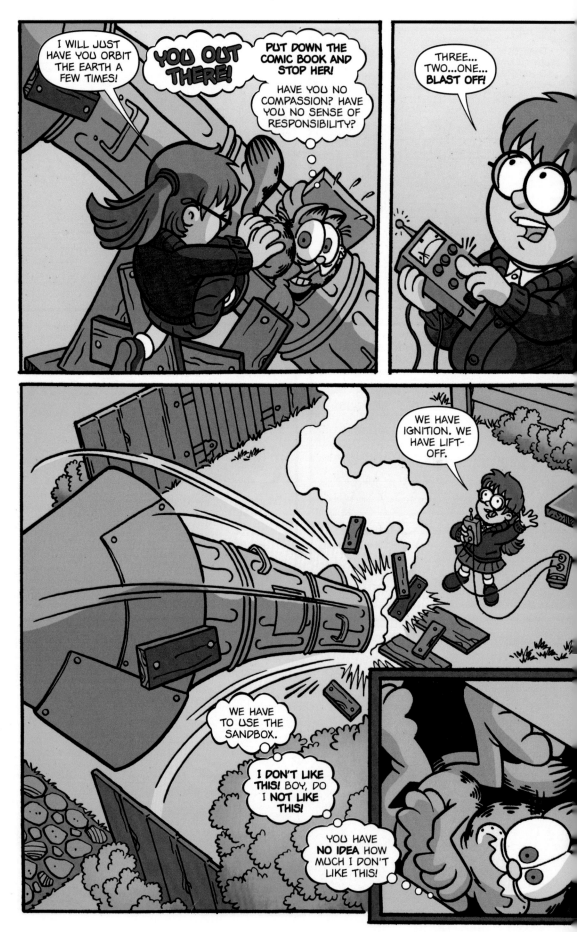

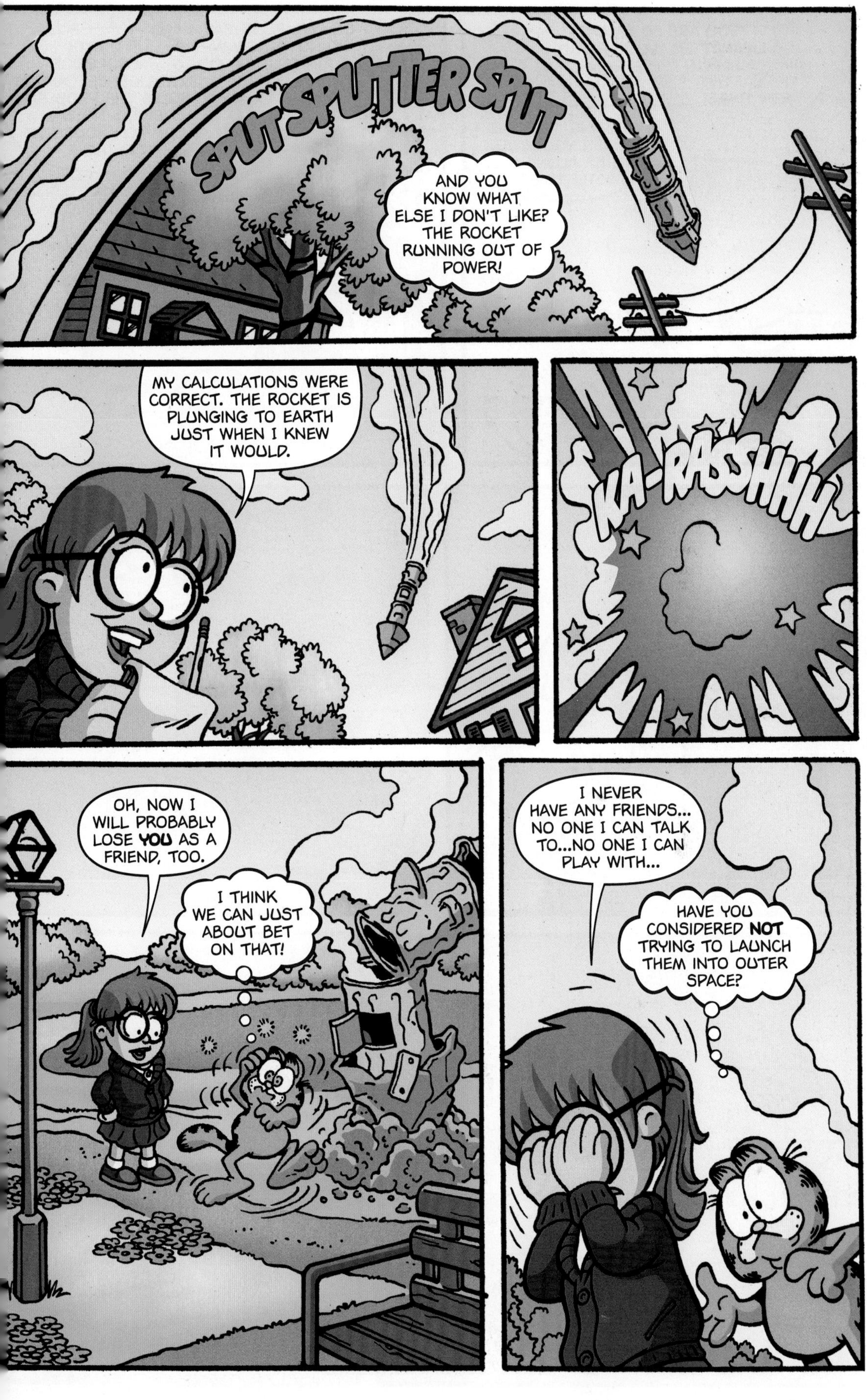
SPUT SPUTTER SPUT
AND YOU KNOW WHAT ELSE I DON'T LIKE? THE ROCKET RUNNING OUT OF POWER!
MY CALCULATIONS WERE CORRECT. THE ROCKET IS PLUNGING TO EARTH JUST WHEN I KNEW IT WOULD.
KA-RASSHHH
OH, NOW I WILL PROBABLY LOSE YOU AS A FRIEND, TOO.
I THINK WE CAN JUST ABOUT BET ON THAT!
I NEVER HAVE ANY FRIENDS... NO ONE I CAN TALK TO...NO ONE I CAN PLAY WITH...
HAVE YOU CONSIDERED NOT TRYING TO LAUNCH THEM INTO OUTER SPACE?

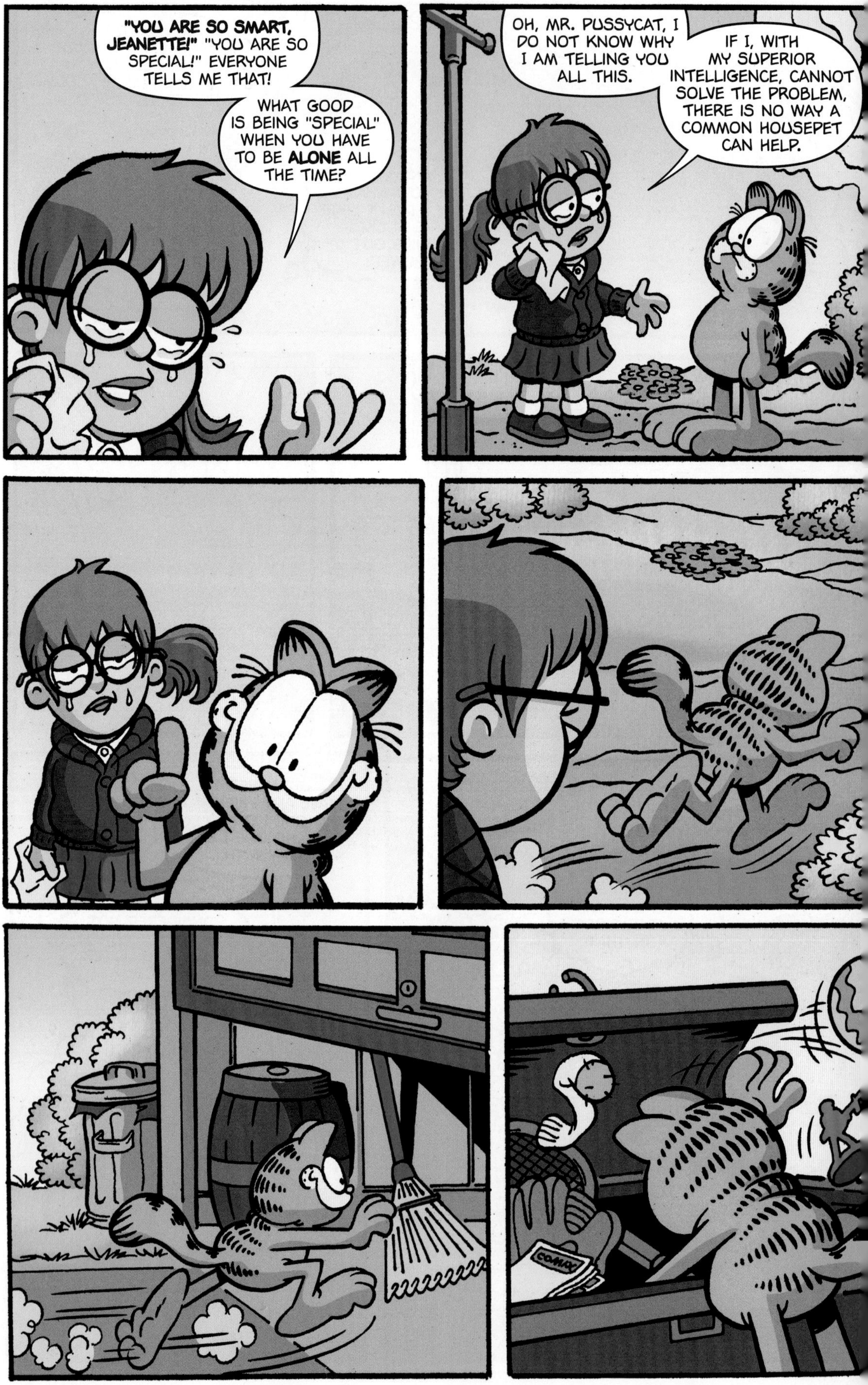
"YOU ARE SO SMART, JEANETTE!" "YOU ARE SO SPECIAL!" EVERYONE TELLS ME THAT!
WHAT GOOD IS BEING "SPECIAL" WHEN YOU HAVE TO BE ALONE ALL THE TIME?
OH, MR. PUSSYCAT, I DO NOT KNOW WHY I AM TELLING YOU ALL THIS.
IF I, WITH MY SUPERIOR INTELLIGENCE, CANNOT SOLVE THE PROBLEM, THERE IS NO WAY A COMMON HOUSEPET CAN HELP.
COMIC

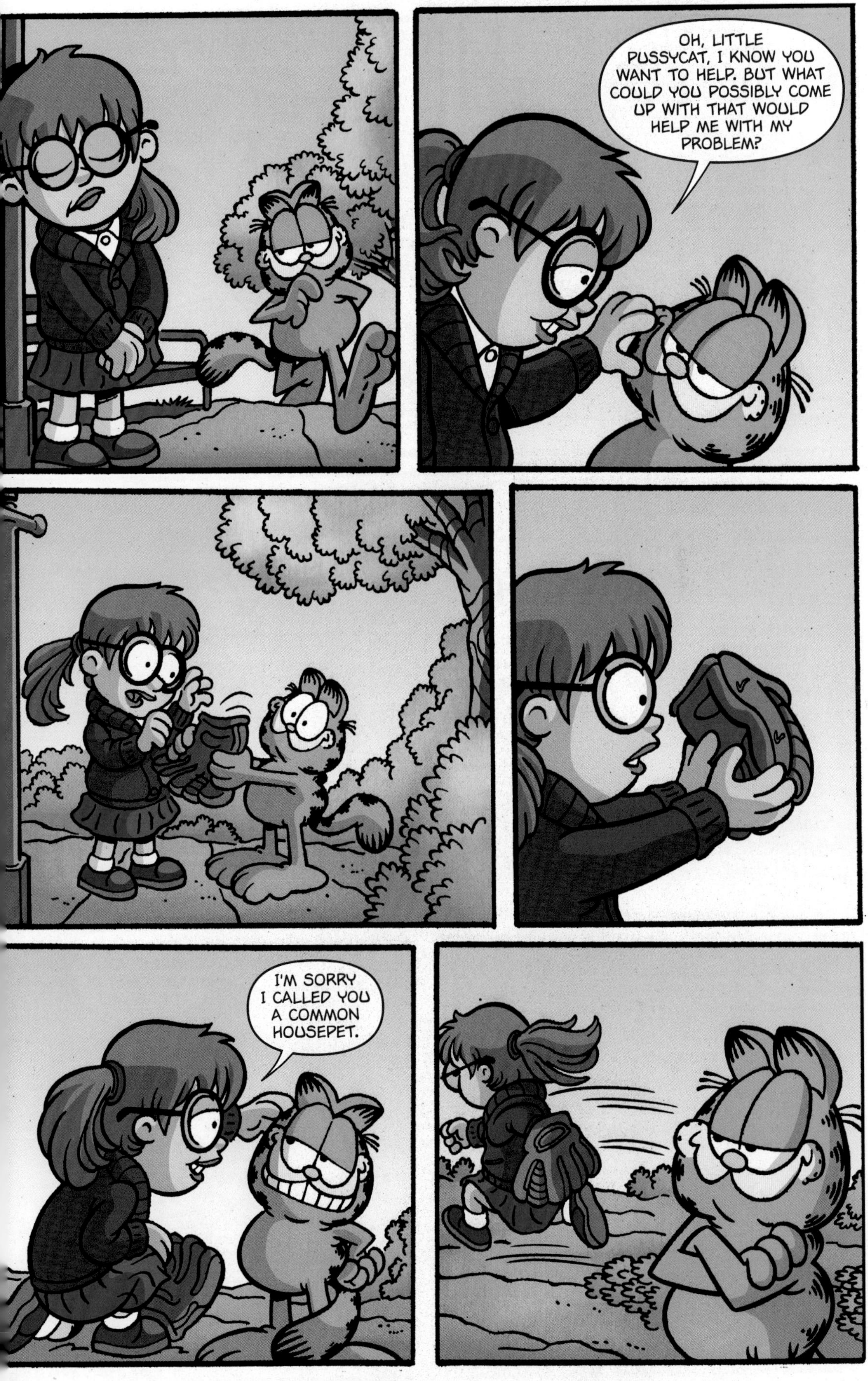
OH, LITTLE PUSSYCAT, I KNOW YOU WANT TO HELP. BUT WHAT COULD YOU POSSIBLY COME UP WITH THAT WOULD HELP ME WITH MY PROBLEM?
I'M SORRY I CALLED YOU A COMMON HOUSEPET.

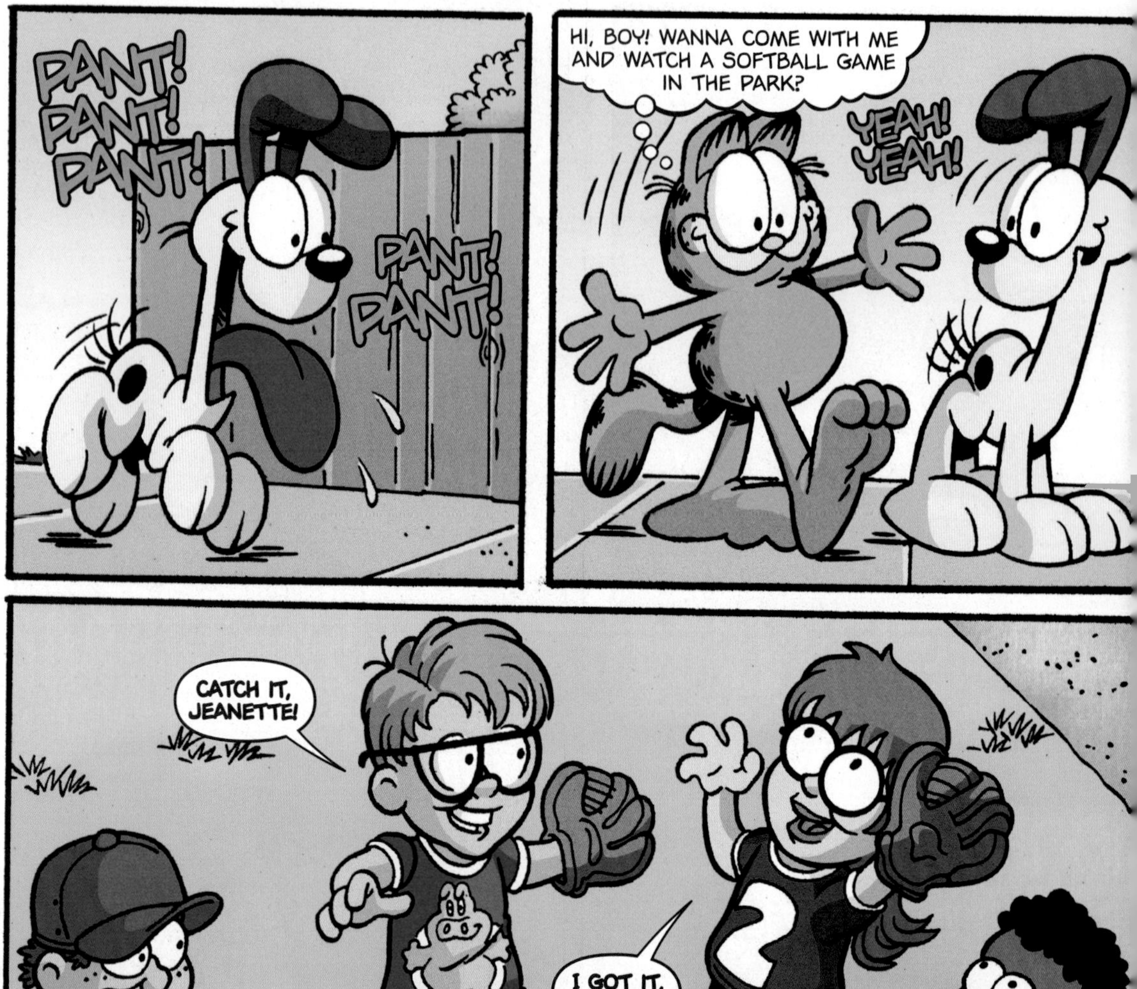
PANT! PANT! PANT!
PANT! PANT!
HI, BOY! WANNA COME WITH ME AND WATCH A SOFTBALL GAME IN THE PARK?
YEAH! YEAH!
CATCH IT, JEANETTE!
I GOT IT, I GOT IT!
HMMM...
ONE OF THE MOST IMPORTANT THINGS YOU HAVE TO LEARN IN THIS WORLD, ODIE...
...YOU CAN'T WIN IF YOU DON'T GET IN THE GAME!
THE END

CHAPTER FIVE

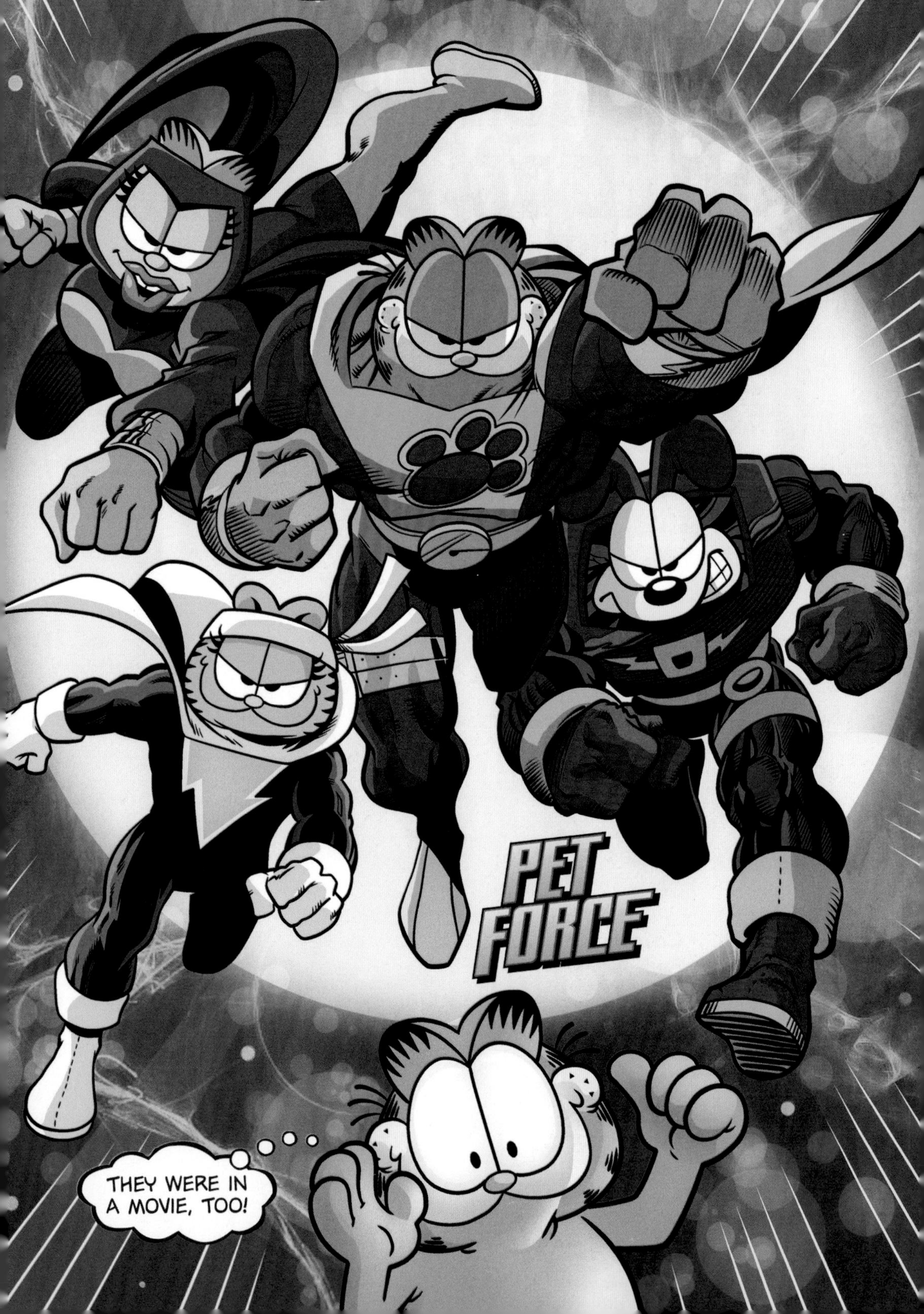
PET FORCE
THEY WERE IN A MOVIE, TOO!

THE MOUSE WHO WANTED TO BE A CAT
THE MOUSE WHO WANTED TO BE A DOG
PET FORCE: THE CREATURE STALKS!

Written by
MARK EVANIER

Art by
MIKE DeCARLO
(Pages 105-116)
GARY BARKER
AND **DAN DAVIS**
(Pages 117-126)

Colors by
LISA MOORE

Chapter Break Art by
GARY BARKER
AND **DAN DAVIS**
WITH **LISA MOORE**

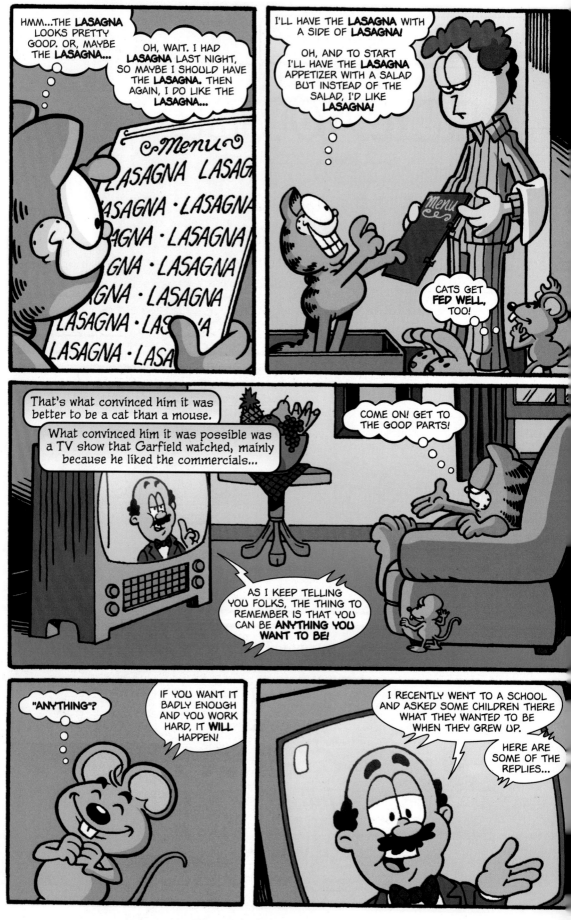

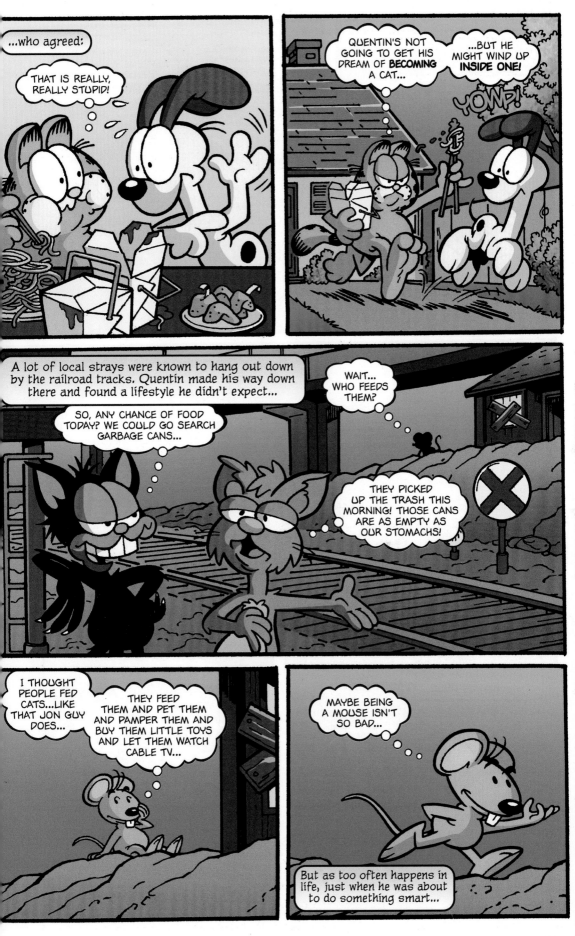

...who agreed:

THAT IS REALLY, REALLY STUPID!

QUENTIN'S NOT GOING TO GET HIS DREAM OF **BECOMING** A CAT...

...BUT HE MIGHT WIND UP **INSIDE ONE!**

YOWP!

A lot of local strays were known to hang out down by the railroad tracks. Quentin made his way down there and found a lifestyle he didn't expect...

SO, ANY CHANCE OF FOOD TODAY? WE COULD GO SEARCH GARBAGE CANS...

WAIT... WHO FEEDS THEM?

THEY PICKED UP THE TRASH THIS MORNING! THOSE CANS ARE AS EMPTY AS OUR STOMACHS!

I THOUGHT PEOPLE FED CATS...LIKE THAT JON GUY DOES...

THEY FEED THEM AND PET THEM AND PAMPER THEM AND BUY THEM LITTLE TOYS AND LET THEM WATCH CABLE TV...

MAYBE BEING A MOUSE ISN'T SO BAD...

But as too often happens in life, just when he was about to do something smart...

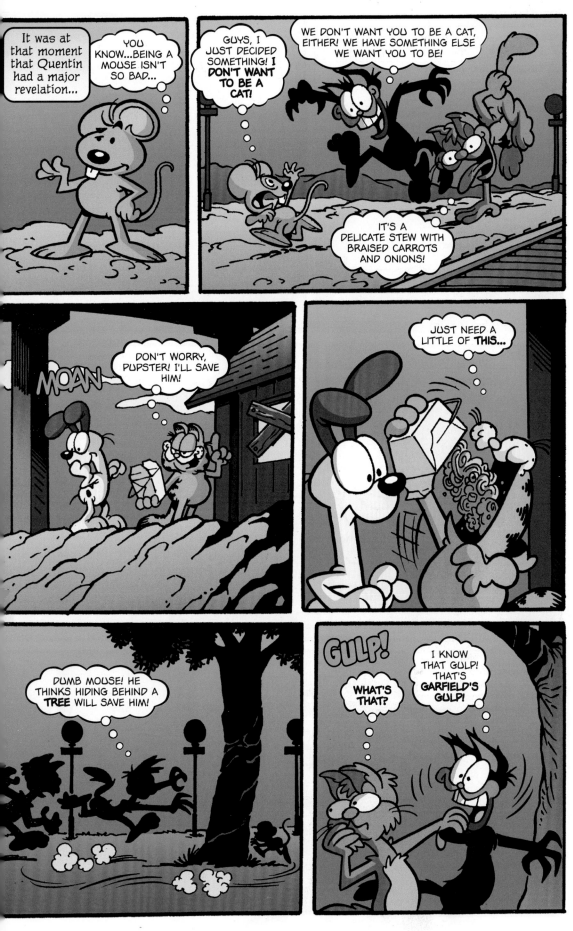

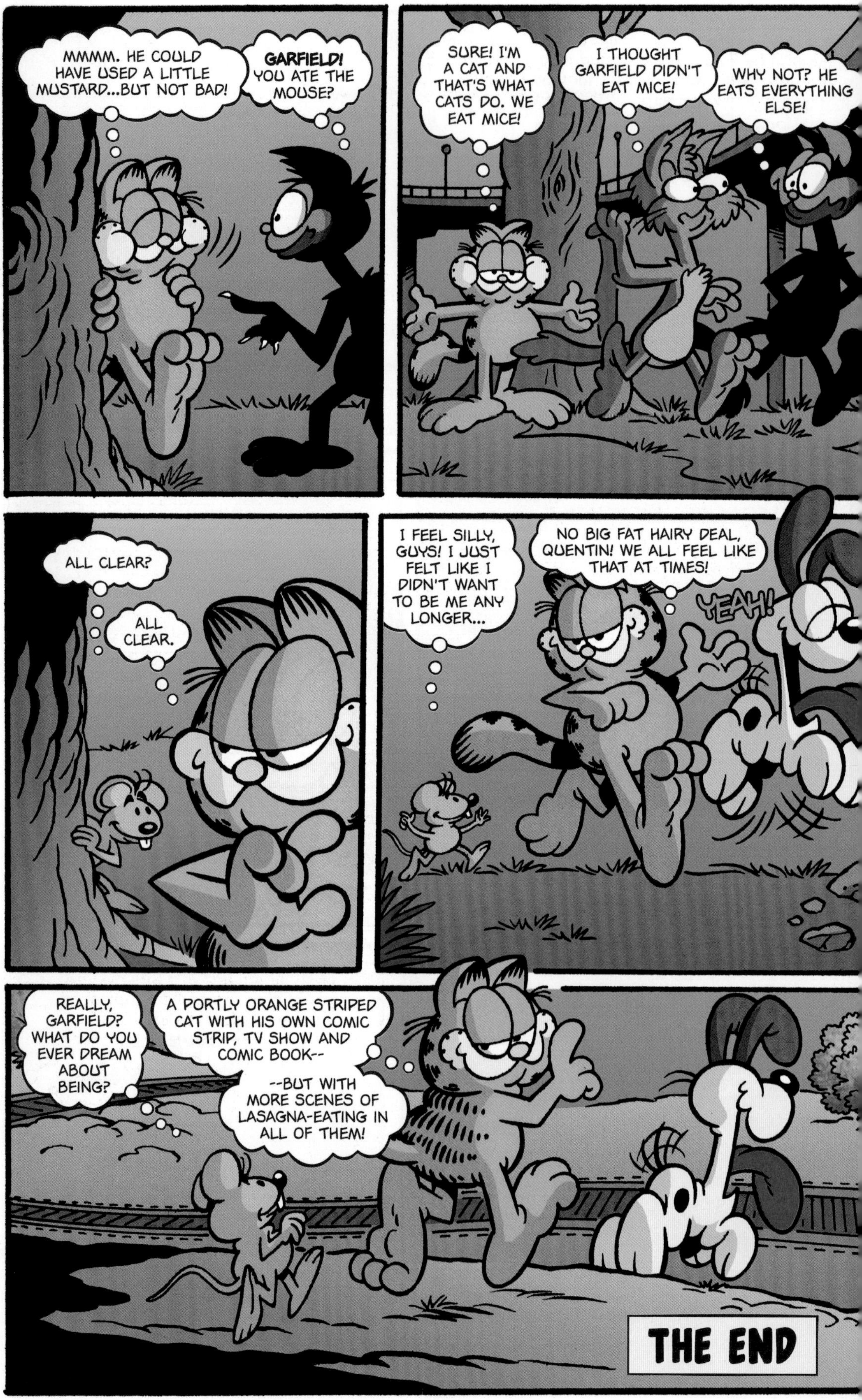
MMMM. HE COULD HAVE USED A LITTLE MUSTARD...BUT NOT BAD!
GARFIELD! YOU ATE THE MOUSE?
SURE! I'M A CAT AND THAT'S WHAT CATS DO. WE EAT MICE!
I THOUGHT GARFIELD DIDN'T EAT MICE!
WHY NOT? HE EATS EVERYTHING ELSE!
ALL CLEAR?
ALL CLEAR.
I FEEL SILLY, GUYS! I JUST FELT LIKE I DIDN'T WANT TO BE ME ANY LONGER...
NO BIG FAT HAIRY DEAL, QUENTIN! WE ALL FEEL LIKE THAT AT TIMES!
YEAH!
REALLY, GARFIELD? WHAT DO YOU EVER DREAM ABOUT BEING?
A PORTLY ORANGE STRIPED CAT WITH HIS OWN COMIC STRIP, TV SHOW AND COMIC BOOK--
--BUT WITH MORE SCENES OF LASAGNA-EATING IN ALL OF THEM!
THE END

PET FORCE: THE CREATURE STALKS!

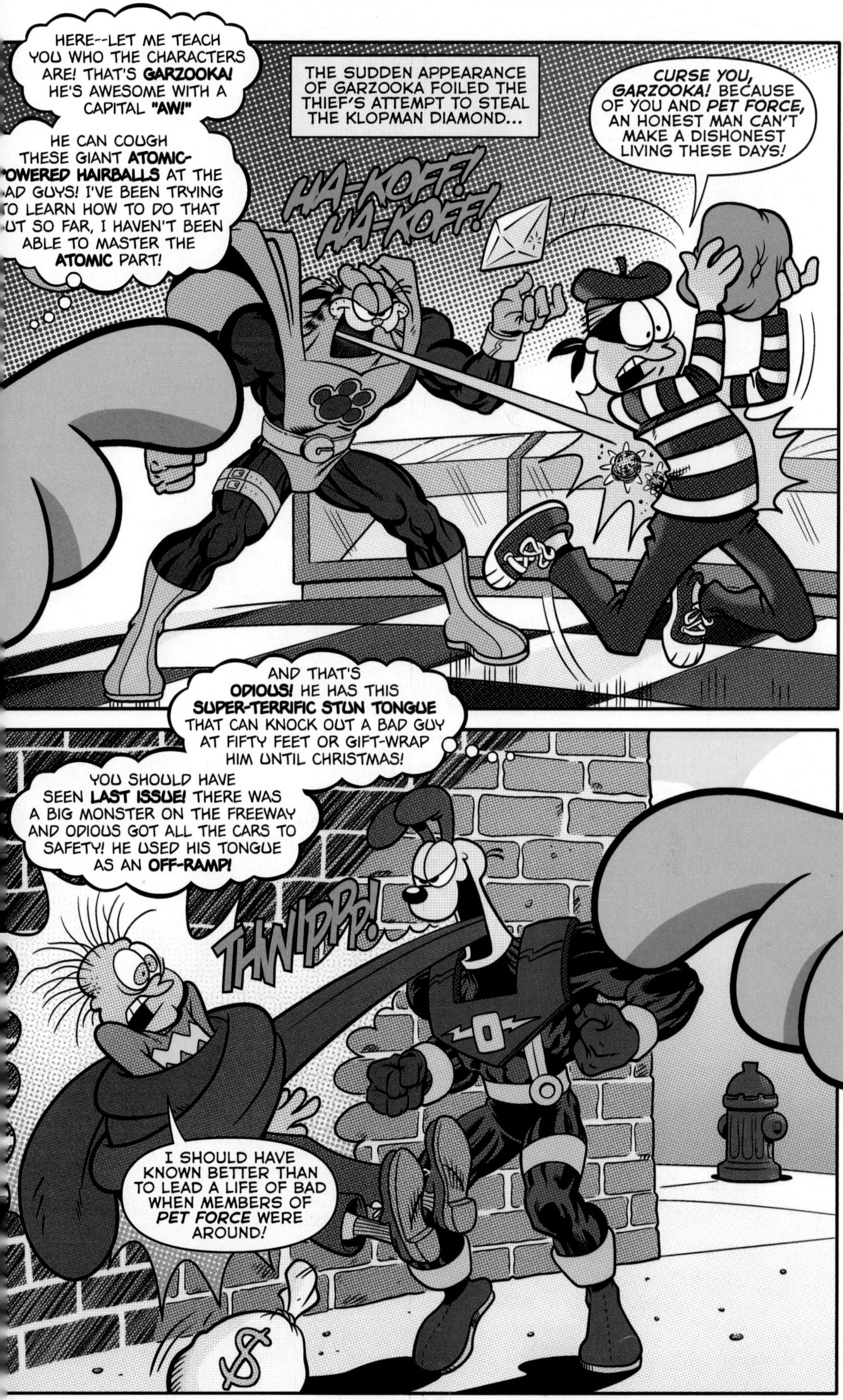

HERE--LET ME TEACH YOU WHO THE CHARACTERS ARE! THAT'S GARZOOKA! HE'S AWESOME WITH A CAPITAL "AW!"
HE CAN COUGH THESE GIANT ATOMIC-OWERED HAIRBALLS AT THE AD GUYS! I'VE BEEN TRYING O LEARN HOW TO DO THAT UT SO FAR, I HAVEN'T BEEN ABLE TO MASTER THE ATOMIC PART!
THE SUDDEN APPEARANCE OF GARZOOKA FOILED THE THIEF'S ATTEMPT TO STEAL THE KLOPMAN DIAMOND...
CURSE YOU, GARZOOKA! BECAUSE OF YOU AND PET FORCE, AN HONEST MAN CAN'T MAKE A DISHONEST LIVING THESE DAYS!
HA-KOFF! HA-KOFF!
AND THAT'S ODIOUS! HE HAS THIS SUPER-TERRIFIC STUN TONGUE THAT CAN KNOCK OUT A BAD GUY AT FIFTY FEET OR GIFT-WRAP HIM UNTIL CHRISTMAS!
YOU SHOULD HAVE SEEN LAST ISSUE! THERE WAS A BIG MONSTER ON THE FREEWAY AND ODIOUS GOT ALL THE CARS TO SAFETY! HE USED HIS TONGUE AS AN OFF-RAMP!
THWIPPP!
I SHOULD HAVE KNOWN BETTER THAN TO LEAD A LIFE OF BAD WHEN MEMBERS OF PET FORCE WERE AROUND!

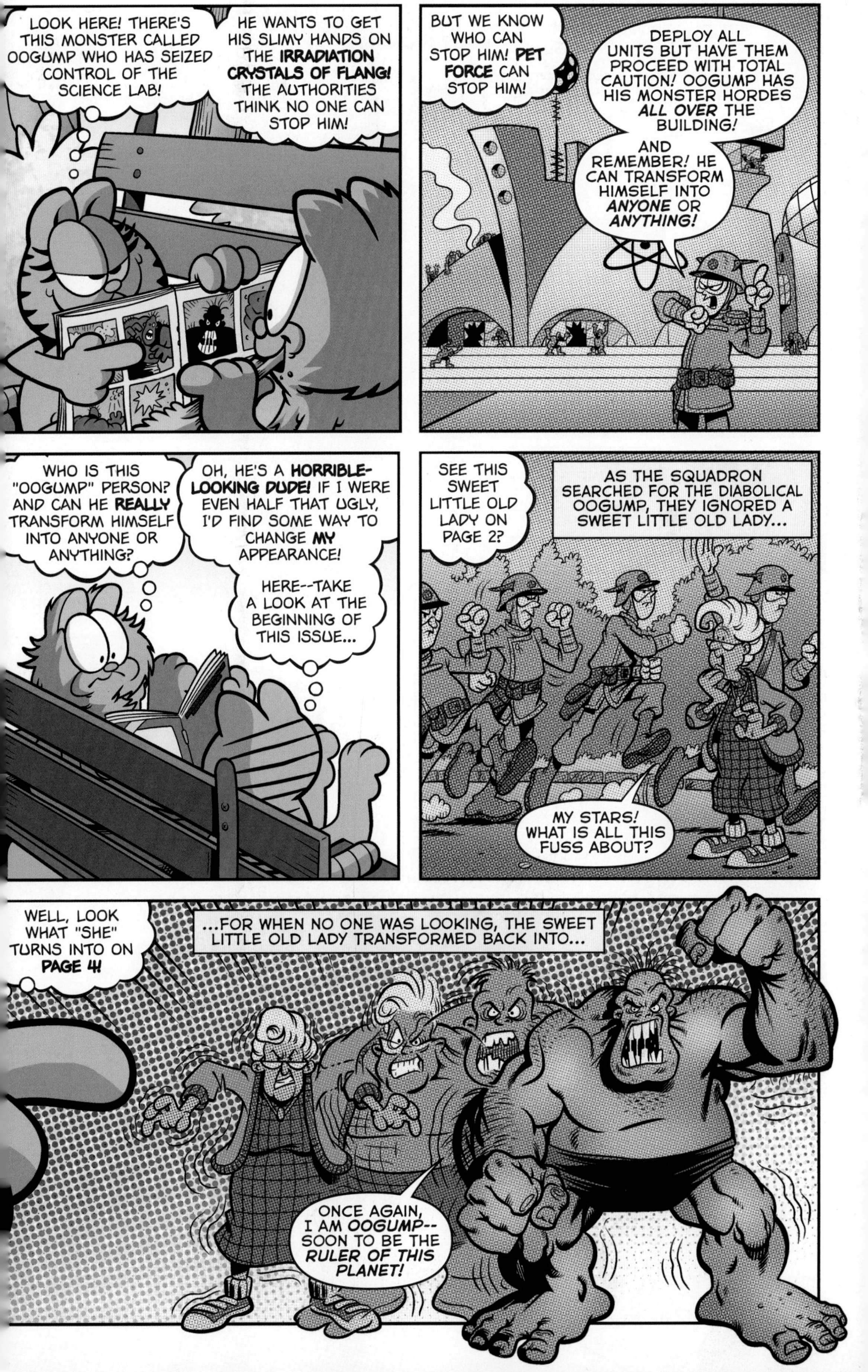
LOOK HERE! THERE'S THIS MONSTER CALLED OOGUMP WHO HAS SEIZED CONTROL OF THE SCIENCE LAB!
HE WANTS TO GET HIS SLIMY HANDS ON THE **IRRADIATION CRYSTALS OF FLANG!** THE AUTHORITIES THINK NO ONE CAN STOP HIM!
BUT WE KNOW WHO CAN STOP HIM! **PET FORCE** CAN STOP HIM!
DEPLOY ALL UNITS BUT HAVE THEM PROCEED WITH TOTAL CAUTION! OOGUMP HAS HIS MONSTER HORDES ***ALL OVER*** THE BUILDING!
AND REMEMBER! HE CAN TRANSFORM HIMSELF INTO ***ANYONE*** OR ***ANYTHING!***
WHO IS THIS "OOGUMP" PERSON? AND CAN HE **REALLY** TRANSFORM HIMSELF INTO ANYONE OR ANYTHING?
OH, HE'S A **HORRIBLE-LOOKING DUDE!** IF I WERE EVEN HALF THAT UGLY, I'D FIND SOME WAY TO CHANGE **MY** APPEARANCE!
HERE--TAKE A LOOK AT THE BEGINNING OF THIS ISSUE...
SEE THIS SWEET LITTLE OLD LADY ON PAGE 2?
AS THE SQUADRON SEARCHED FOR THE DIABOLICAL OOGUMP, THEY IGNORED A SWEET LITTLE OLD LADY...
MY STARS! WHAT IS ALL THIS FUSS ABOUT?
WELL, LOOK WHAT "SHE" TURNS INTO ON **PAGE 4!**
...FOR WHEN NO ONE WAS LOOKING, THE SWEET LITTLE OLD LADY TRANSFORMED BACK INTO...
ONCE AGAIN, I AM ***OOGUMP***-- SOON TO BE THE ***RULER OF THIS PLANET!***

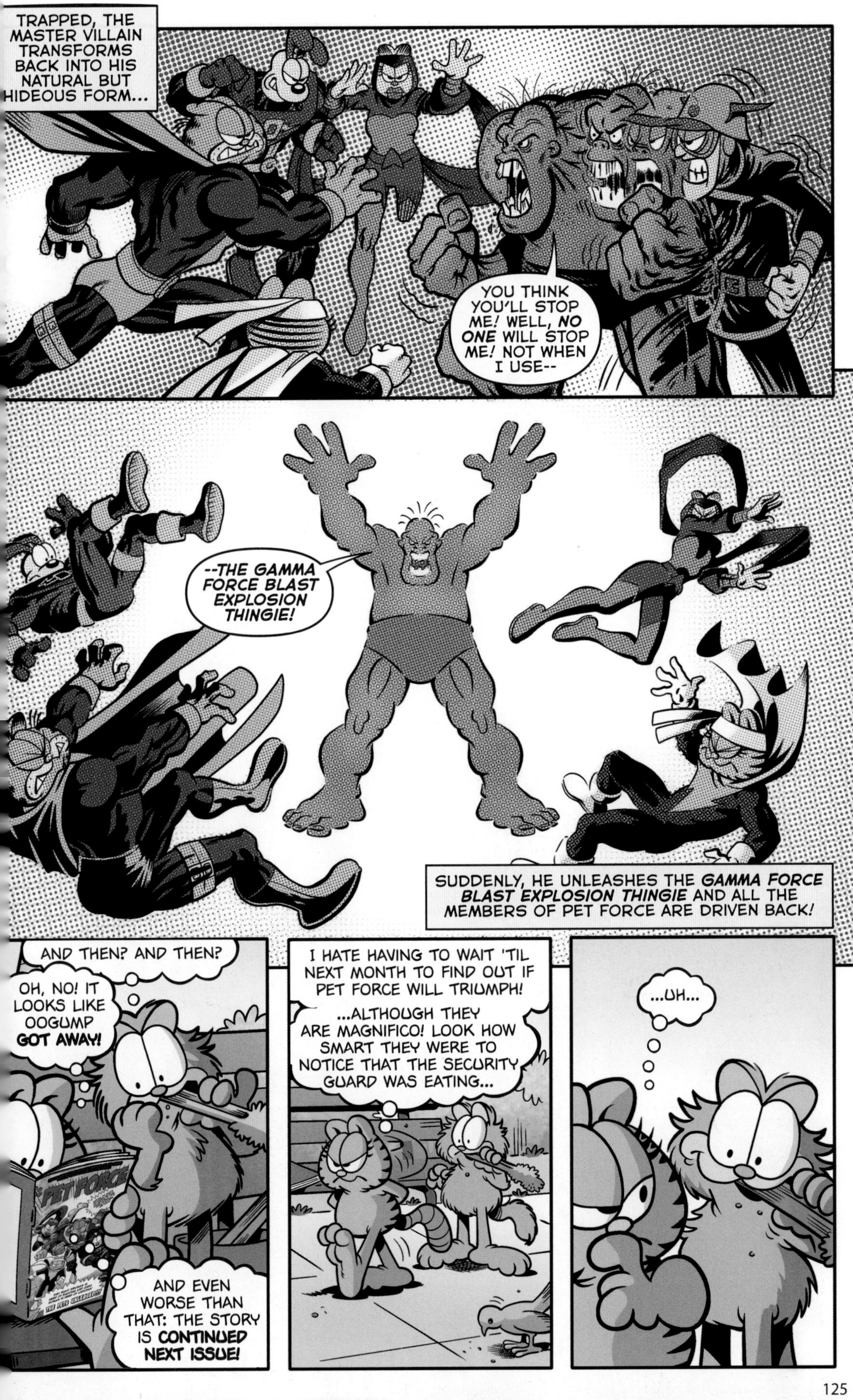
TRAPPED, THE MASTER VILLAIN TRANSFORMS BACK INTO HIS NATURAL BUT HIDEOUS FORM...
YOU THINK YOU'LL STOP ME! WELL, NO ONE WILL STOP ME! NOT WHEN I USE--
--THE GAMMA FORCE BLAST EXPLOSION THINGIE!
SUDDENLY, HE UNLEASHES THE GAMMA FORCE BLAST EXPLOSION THINGIE AND ALL THE MEMBERS OF PET FORCE ARE DRIVEN BACK!
AND THEN? AND THEN?
OH, NO! IT LOOKS LIKE OOGUMP GOT AWAY!
PET FORCE
AND EVEN WORSE THAN THAT: THE STORY IS CONTINUED NEXT ISSUE!
I HATE HAVING TO WAIT 'TIL NEXT MONTH TO FIND OUT IF PET FORCE WILL TRIUMPH!
...ALTHOUGH THEY ARE MAGNIFICO! LOOK HOW SMART THEY WERE TO NOTICE THAT THE SECURITY GUARD WAS EATING...
...UH...

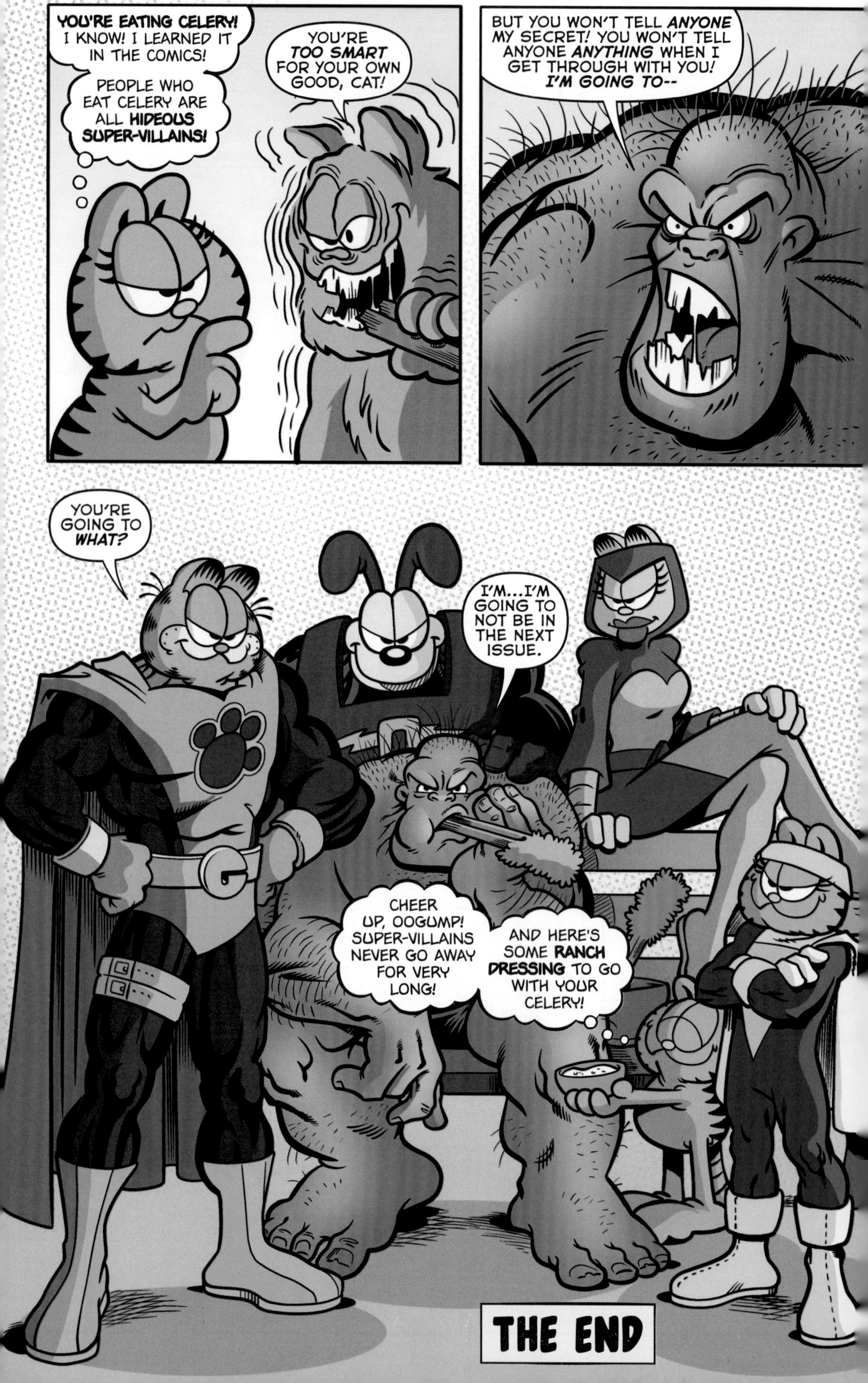
YOU'RE EATING CELERY! I KNOW! I LEARNED IT IN THE COMICS!
PEOPLE WHO EAT CELERY ARE ALL HIDEOUS SUPER-VILLAINS!
YOU'RE TOO SMART FOR YOUR OWN GOOD, CAT!
BUT YOU WON'T TELL ANYONE MY SECRET! YOU WON'T TELL ANYONE ANYTHING WHEN I GET THROUGH WITH YOU! I'M GOING TO--
YOU'RE GOING TO WHAT?
I'M...I'M GOING TO NOT BE IN THE NEXT ISSUE.
CHEER UP, OOGUMP! SUPER-VILLAINS NEVER GO AWAY FOR VERY LONG!
AND HERE'S SOME RANCH DRESSING TO GO WITH YOUR CELERY!
THE END

CHAPTER SIX

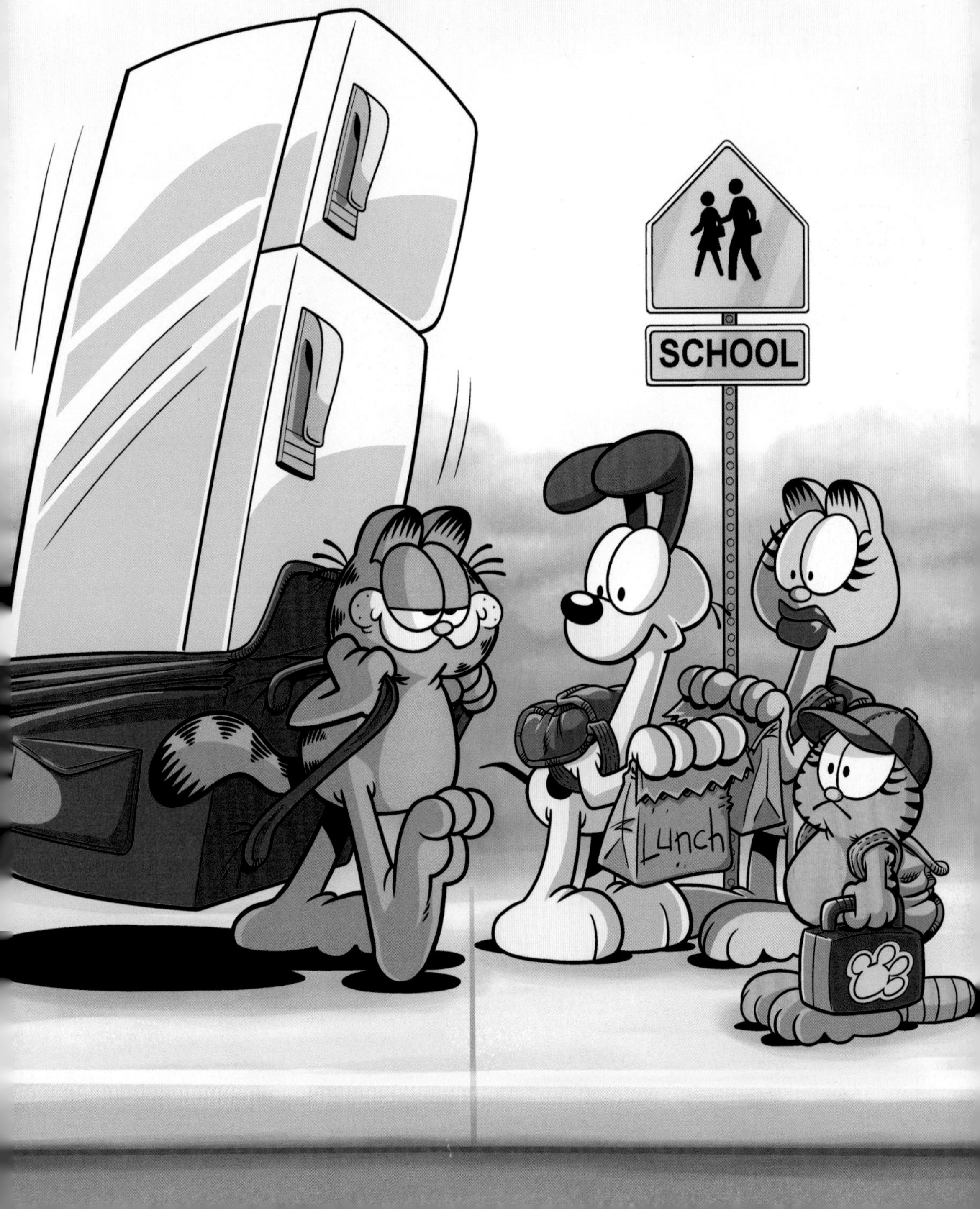
SCHOOL
Lunch

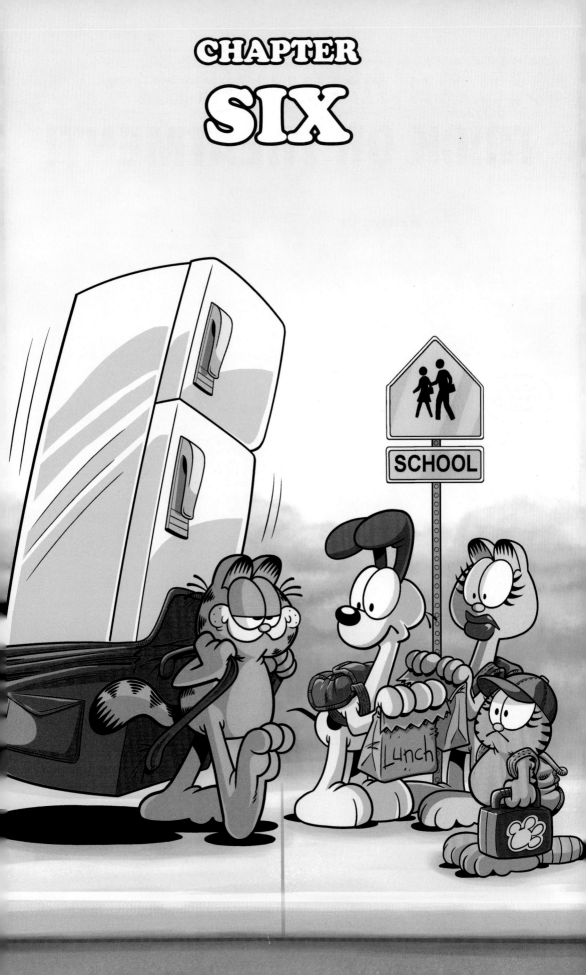

THE PHARAOH'S PET
TRICK OR TREATMENT!

Written by
MARK EVANIER

Art by
MIKE DeCARLO
(Pages 129-140)
GARY BARKER
AND DAN DAVIS
(Pages 141-150)

Colors by
LISA MOORE

Chapter Break Art by
GARY BARKER
AND DAN DAVIS
WITH LISA MOORE

THE PHARAOH'S PET

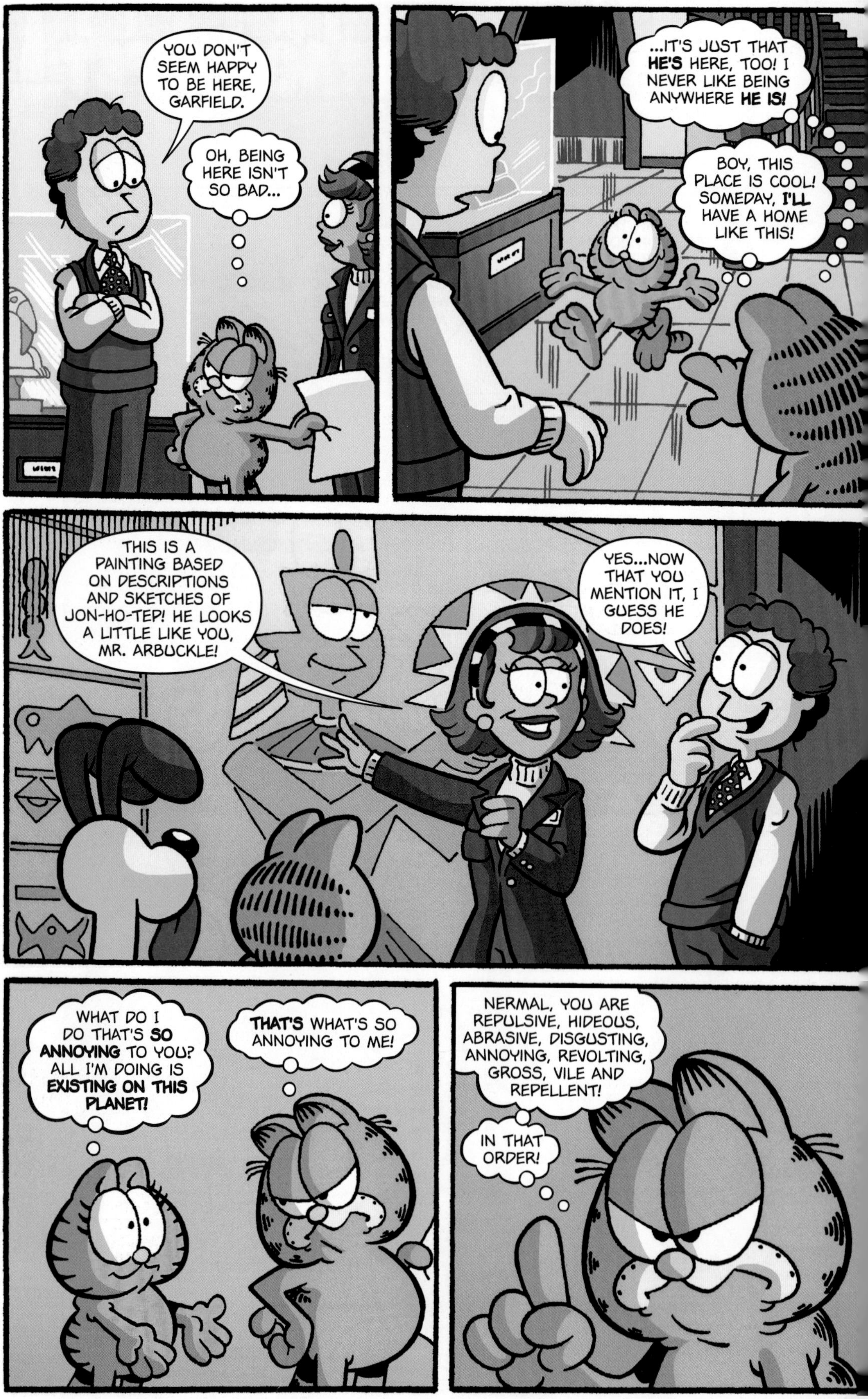

YOU DON'T SEEM HAPPY TO BE HERE, GARFIELD.
OH, BEING HERE ISN'T SO BAD...
...IT'S JUST THAT **HE'S** HERE, TOO! I NEVER LIKE BEING ANYWHERE **HE IS!**
BOY, THIS PLACE IS COOL! SOMEDAY, **I'LL** HAVE A HOME LIKE THIS!
THIS IS A PAINTING BASED ON DESCRIPTIONS AND SKETCHES OF JON-HO-TEP! HE LOOKS A LITTLE LIKE YOU, MR. ARBUCKLE!
YES...NOW THAT YOU MENTION IT, I GUESS HE DOES!
WHAT DO I DO THAT'S **SO ANNOYING** TO YOU? ALL I'M DOING IS **EXISTING ON THIS PLANET!**
THAT'S WHAT'S SO ANNOYING TO ME!
NERMAL, YOU ARE REPULSIVE, HIDEOUS, ABRASIVE, DISGUSTING, ANNOYING, REVOLTING, GROSS, VILE AND REPELLENT!
IN THAT ORDER!

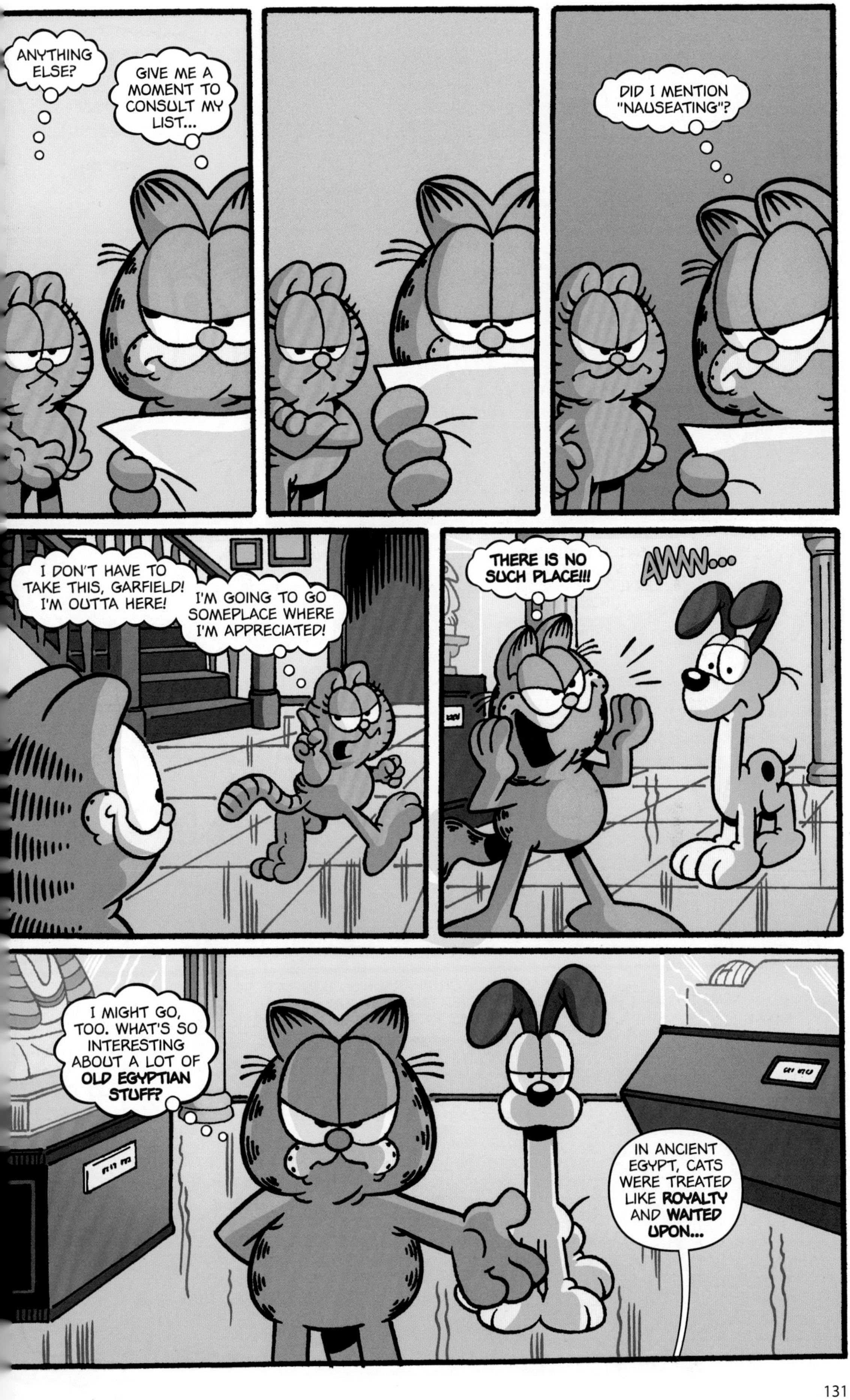

ANYTHING ELSE?
GIVE ME A MOMENT TO CONSULT MY LIST...
DID I MENTION "NAUSEATING"?
I DON'T HAVE TO TAKE THIS, GARFIELD! I'M OUTTA HERE!
I'M GOING TO GO SOMEPLACE WHERE I'M APPRECIATED!
THERE IS NO SUCH PLACE!!!
AWWW...
I MIGHT GO, TOO. WHAT'S SO INTERESTING ABOUT A LOT OF **OLD EGYPTIAN STUFF?**
IN ANCIENT EGYPT, CATS WERE TREATED LIKE **ROYALTY** AND **WAITED UPON...**

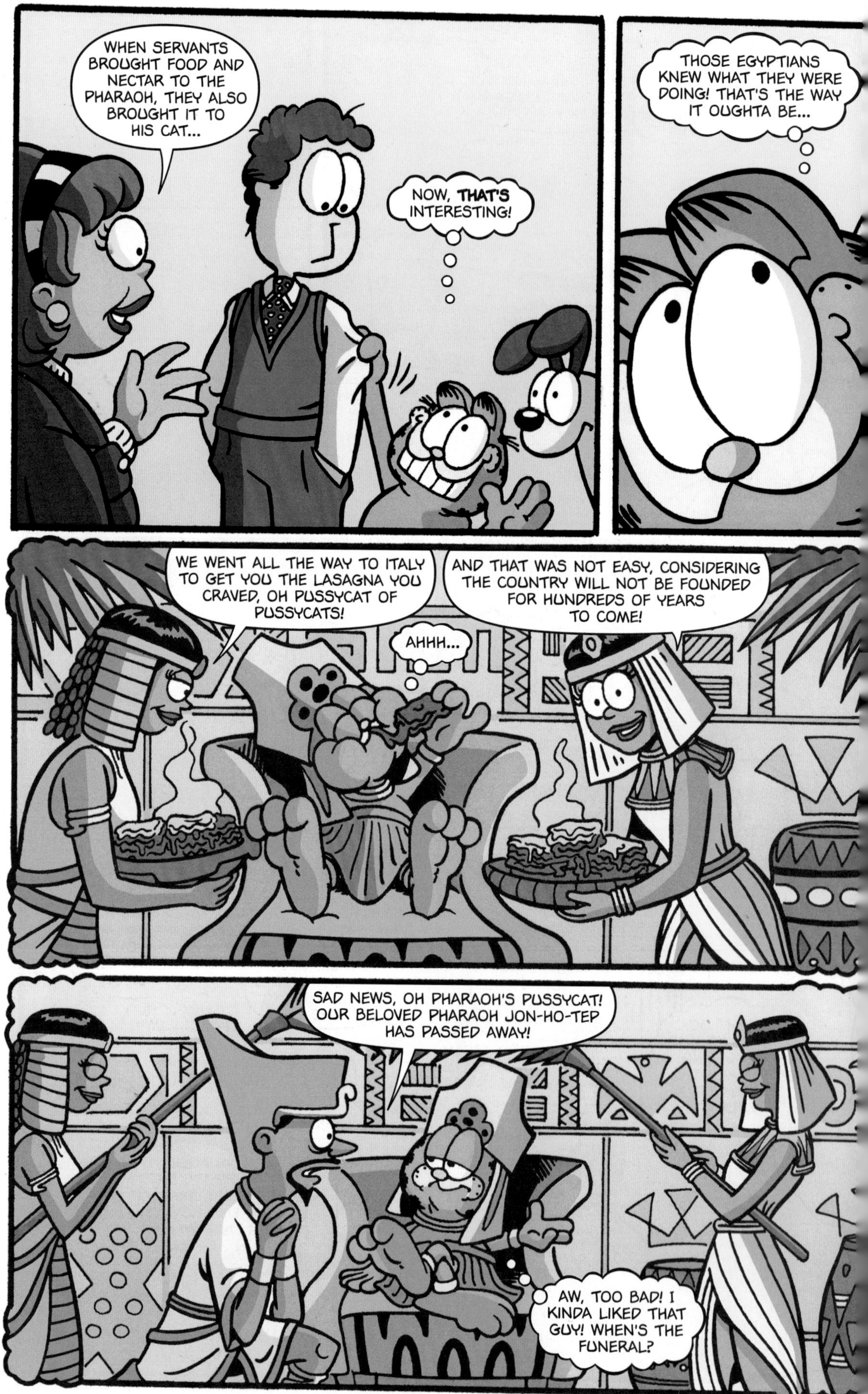
WHEN SERVANTS BROUGHT FOOD AND NECTAR TO THE PHARAOH, THEY ALSO BROUGHT IT TO HIS CAT...
NOW, **THAT'S** INTERESTING!
THOSE EGYPTIANS KNEW WHAT THEY WERE DOING! THAT'S THE WAY IT OUGHTA BE...
WE WENT ALL THE WAY TO ITALY TO GET YOU THE LASAGNA YOU CRAVED, OH PUSSYCAT OF PUSSYCATS!
AND THAT WAS NOT EASY, CONSIDERING THE COUNTRY WILL NOT BE FOUNDED FOR HUNDREDS OF YEARS TO COME!
AHHH...
SAD NEWS, OH PHARAOH'S PUSSYCAT! OUR BELOVED PHARAOH JON-HO-TEP HAS PASSED AWAY!
AW, TOO BAD! I KINDA LIKED THAT GUY! WHEN'S THE FUNERAL?

133

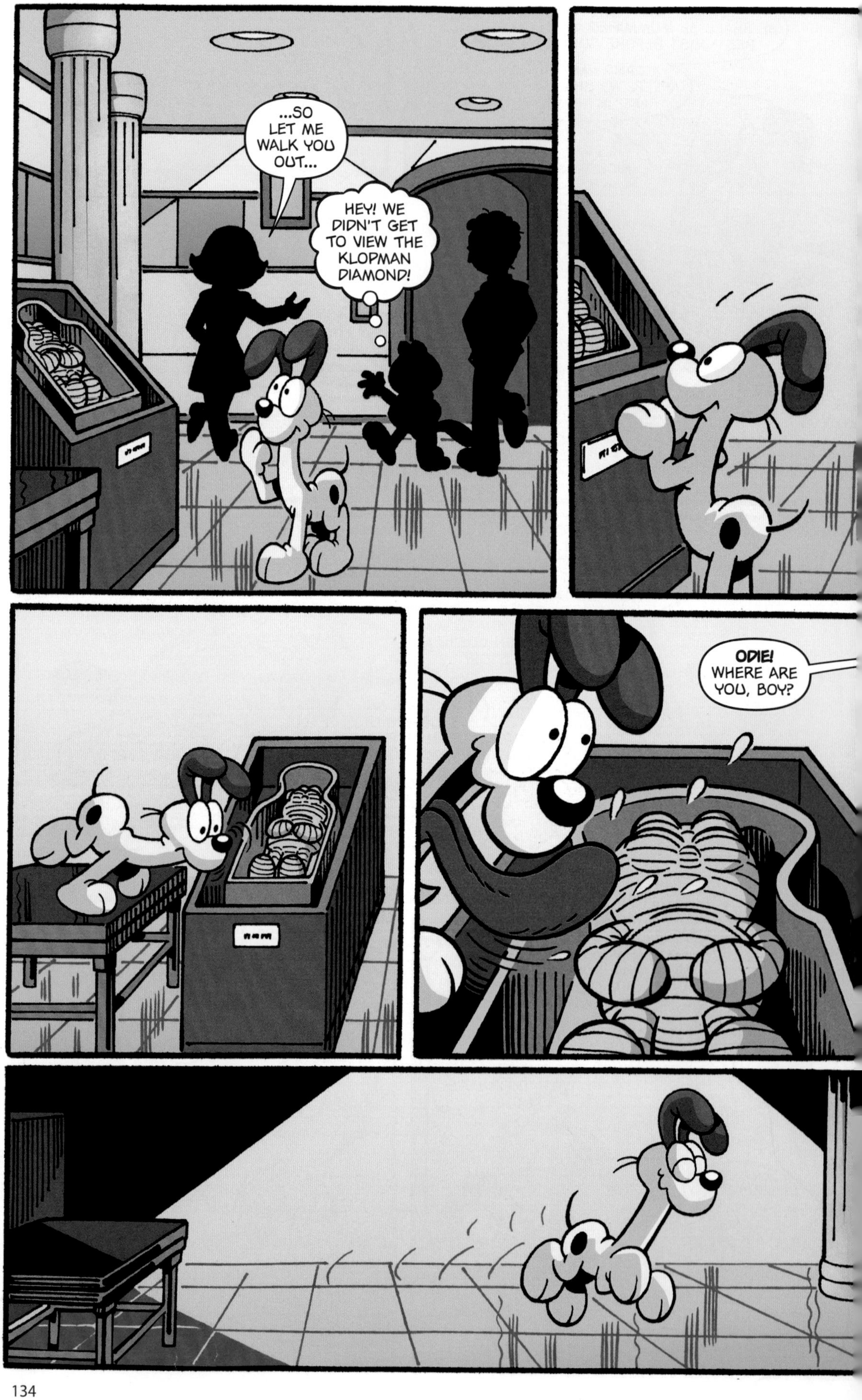
...SO LET ME WALK YOU OUT...
HEY! WE DIDN'T GET TO VIEW THE KLOPMAN DIAMOND!
ODIE! WHERE ARE YOU, BOY?

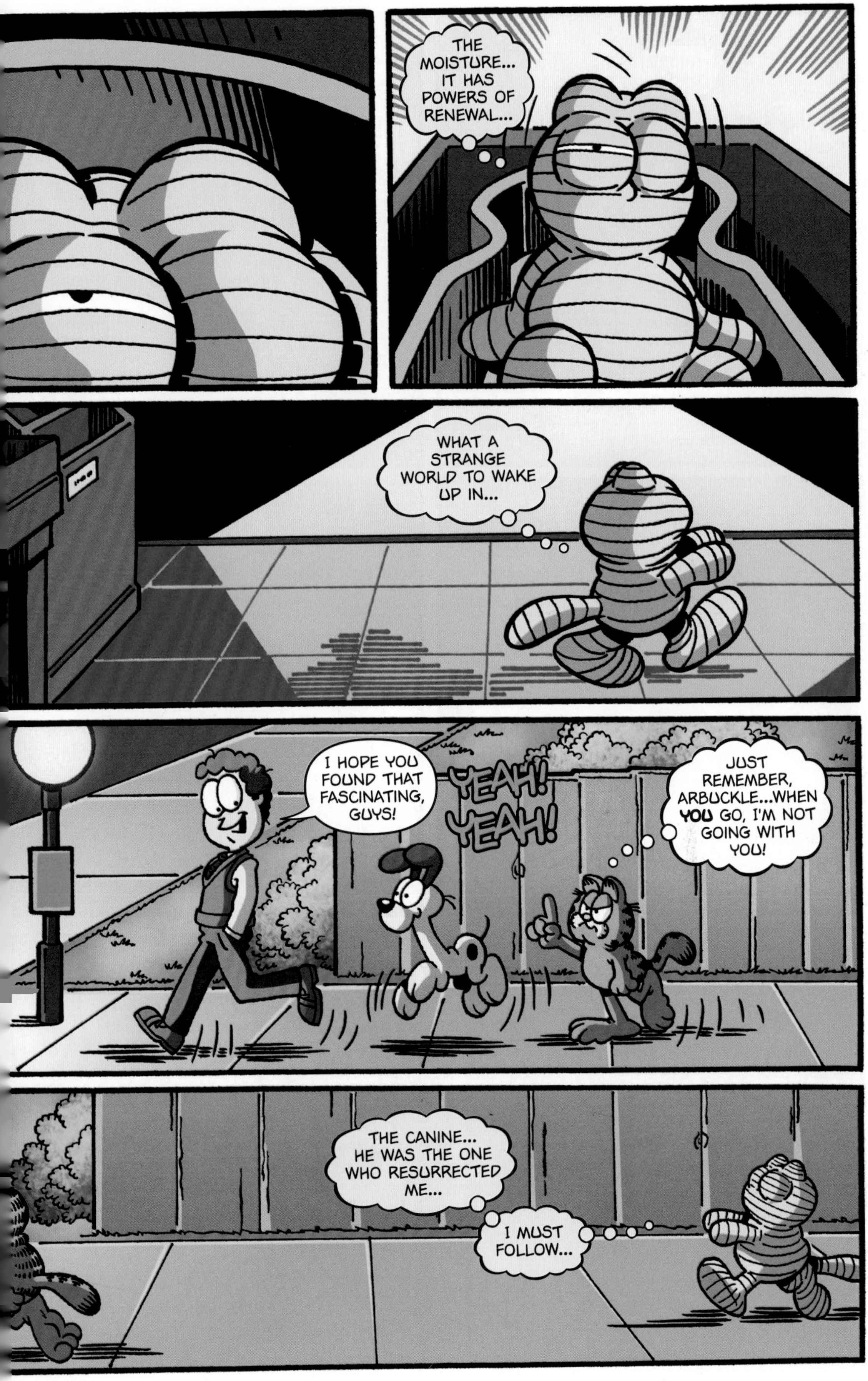

THE MOISTURE... IT HAS POWERS OF RENEWAL...
WHAT A STRANGE WORLD TO WAKE UP IN...
I HOPE YOU FOUND THAT FASCINATING, GUYS!
YEAH! YEAH!
JUST REMEMBER, ARBUCKLE...WHEN YOU GO, I'M NOT GOING WITH YOU!
THE CANINE... HE WAS THE ONE WHO RESURRECTED ME...
I MUST FOLLOW...

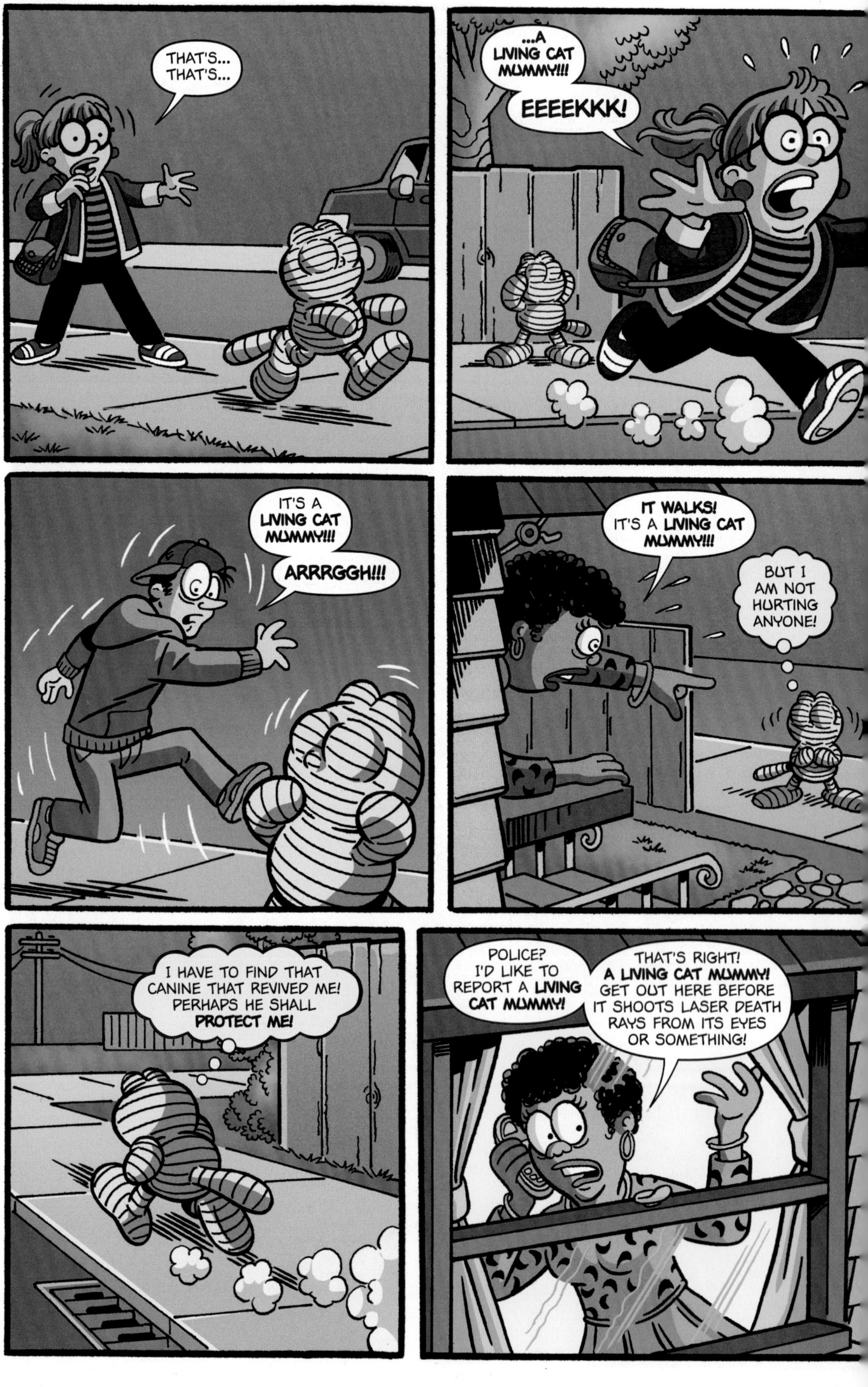
THAT'S... THAT'S...
...A LIVING CAT MUMMY!!!
EEEEKKK!
IT'S A LIVING CAT MUMMY!!!
ARRRGGH!!!
IT WALKS! IT'S A LIVING CAT MUMMY!!!
BUT I AM NOT HURTING ANYONE!
I HAVE TO FIND THAT CANINE THAT REVIVED ME! PERHAPS HE SHALL PROTECT ME!
POLICE? I'D LIKE TO REPORT A LIVING CAT MUMMY!
THAT'S RIGHT! A LIVING CAT MUMMY! GET OUT HERE BEFORE IT SHOOTS LASER DEATH RAYS FROM ITS EYES OR SOMETHING!

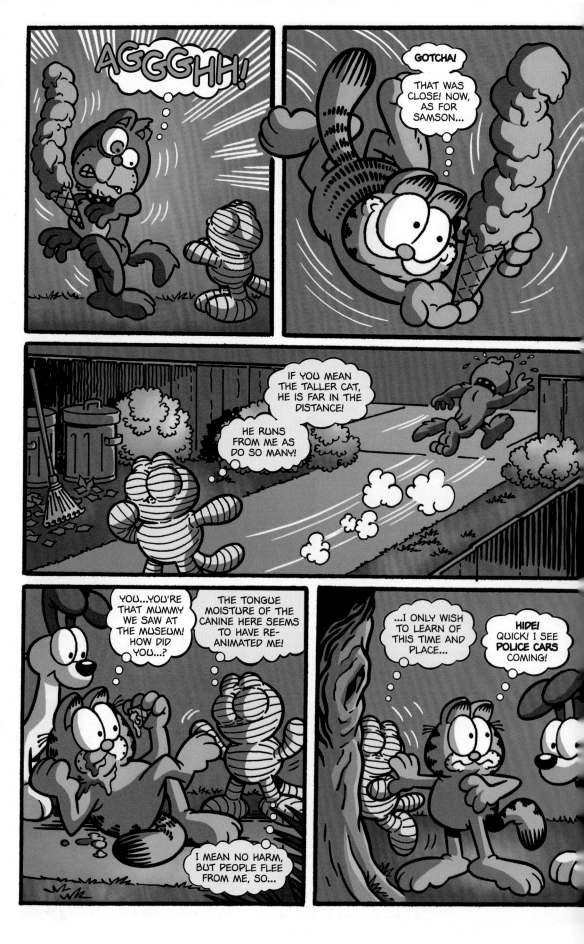

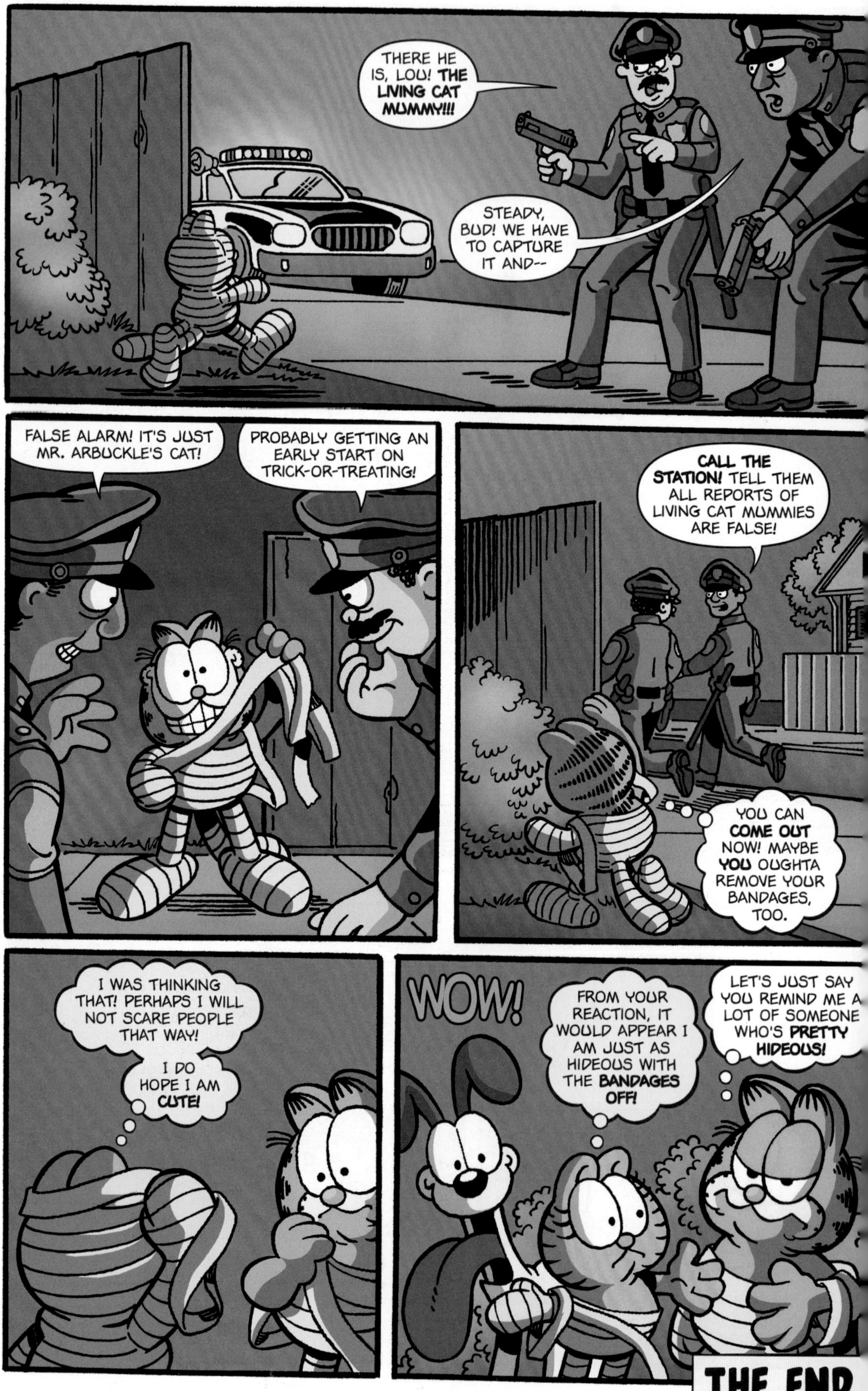

THERE HE IS, LOU! THE LIVING CAT MUMMY!!!
STEADY, BUD! WE HAVE TO CAPTURE IT AND--
FALSE ALARM! IT'S JUST MR. ARBUCKLE'S CAT!
PROBABLY GETTING AN EARLY START ON TRICK-OR-TREATING!
CALL THE STATION! TELL THEM ALL REPORTS OF LIVING CAT MUMMIES ARE FALSE!
YOU CAN COME OUT NOW! MAYBE YOU OUGHTA REMOVE YOUR BANDAGES, TOO.
I WAS THINKING THAT! PERHAPS I WILL NOT SCARE PEOPLE THAT WAY!
I DO HOPE I AM CUTE!
WOW!
FROM YOUR REACTION, IT WOULD APPEAR I AM JUST AS HIDEOUS WITH THE BANDAGES OFF!
LET'S JUST SAY YOU REMIND ME A LOT OF SOMEONE WHO'S PRETTY HIDEOUS!
THE END

TRICK OR TREATMENT!

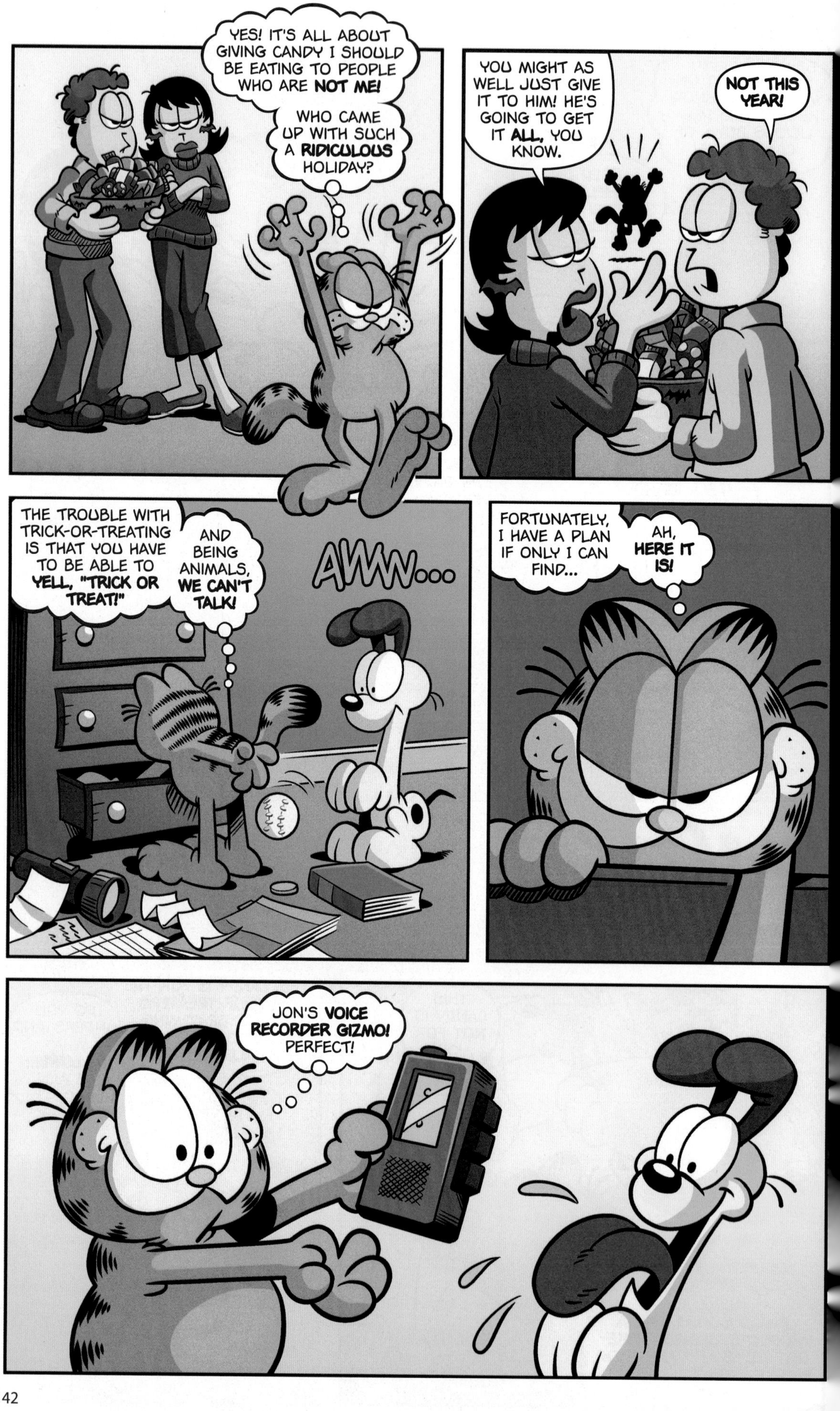

YES! IT'S ALL ABOUT GIVING CANDY I SHOULD BE EATING TO PEOPLE WHO ARE **NOT ME!**
WHO CAME UP WITH SUCH A **RIDICULOUS** HOLIDAY?
YOU MIGHT AS WELL JUST GIVE IT TO HIM! HE'S GOING TO GET IT **ALL**, YOU KNOW.
NOT THIS YEAR!
THE TROUBLE WITH TRICK-OR-TREATING IS THAT YOU HAVE TO BE ABLE TO **YELL, "TRICK OR TREAT!"**
AND BEING ANIMALS, **WE CAN'T TALK!**
AWW...
FORTUNATELY, I HAVE A PLAN IF ONLY I CAN FIND...
AH, **HERE IT IS!**
JON'S **VOICE RECORDER GIZMO!** PERFECT!

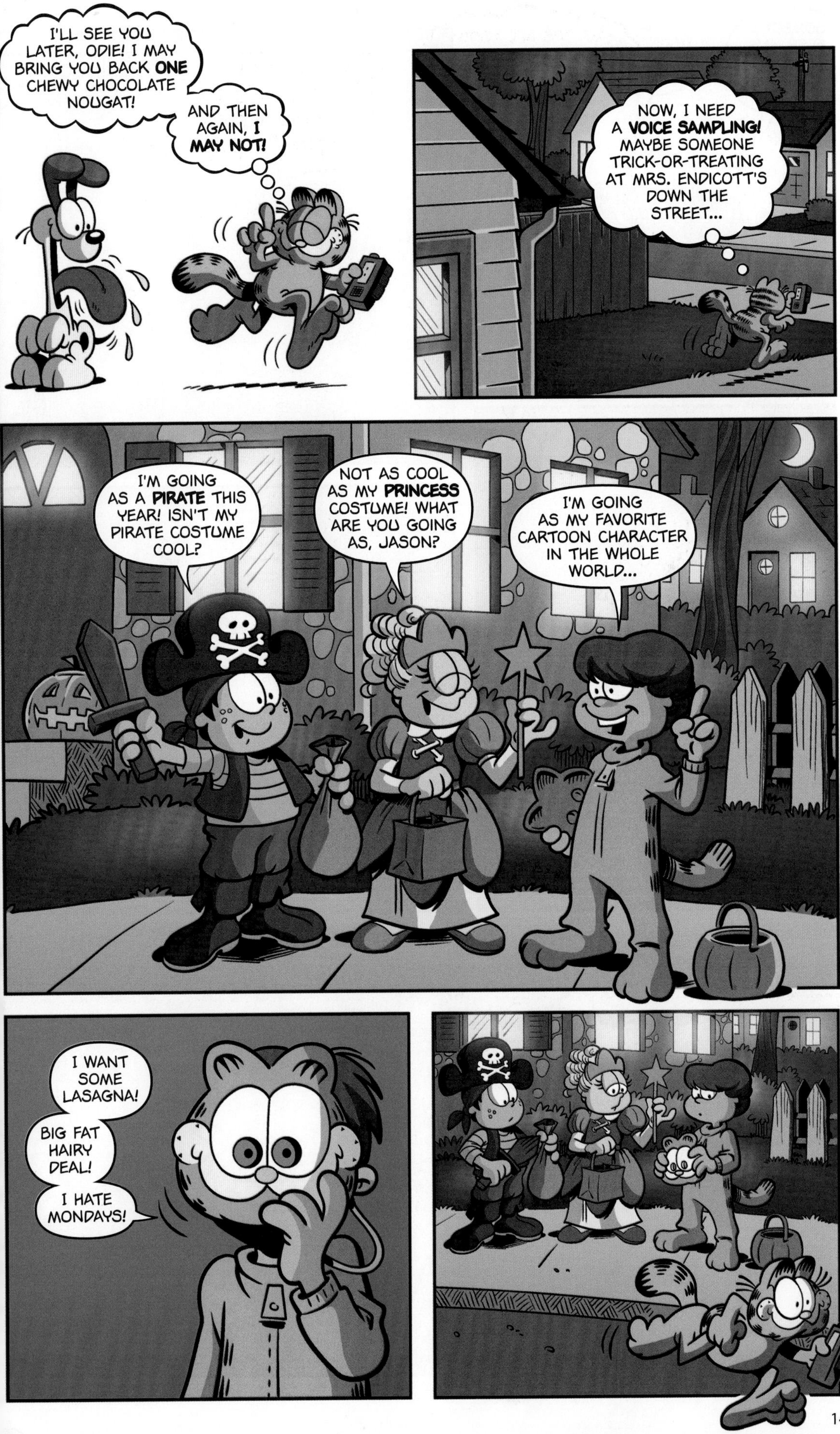

I'LL SEE YOU LATER, ODIE! I MAY BRING YOU BACK **ONE** CHEWY CHOCOLATE NOUGAT!
AND THEN AGAIN, **I MAY NOT!**
NOW, I NEED A **VOICE SAMPLING!** MAYBE SOMEONE TRICK-OR-TREATING AT MRS. ENDICOTT'S DOWN THE STREET...
I'M GOING AS A **PIRATE** THIS YEAR! ISN'T MY PIRATE COSTUME COOL?
NOT AS COOL AS MY **PRINCESS** COSTUME! WHAT ARE YOU GOING AS, JASON?
I'M GOING AS MY FAVORITE CARTOON CHARACTER IN THE WHOLE WORLD...
I WANT SOME LASAGNA!
BIG FAT HAIRY DEAL!
I HATE MONDAYS!

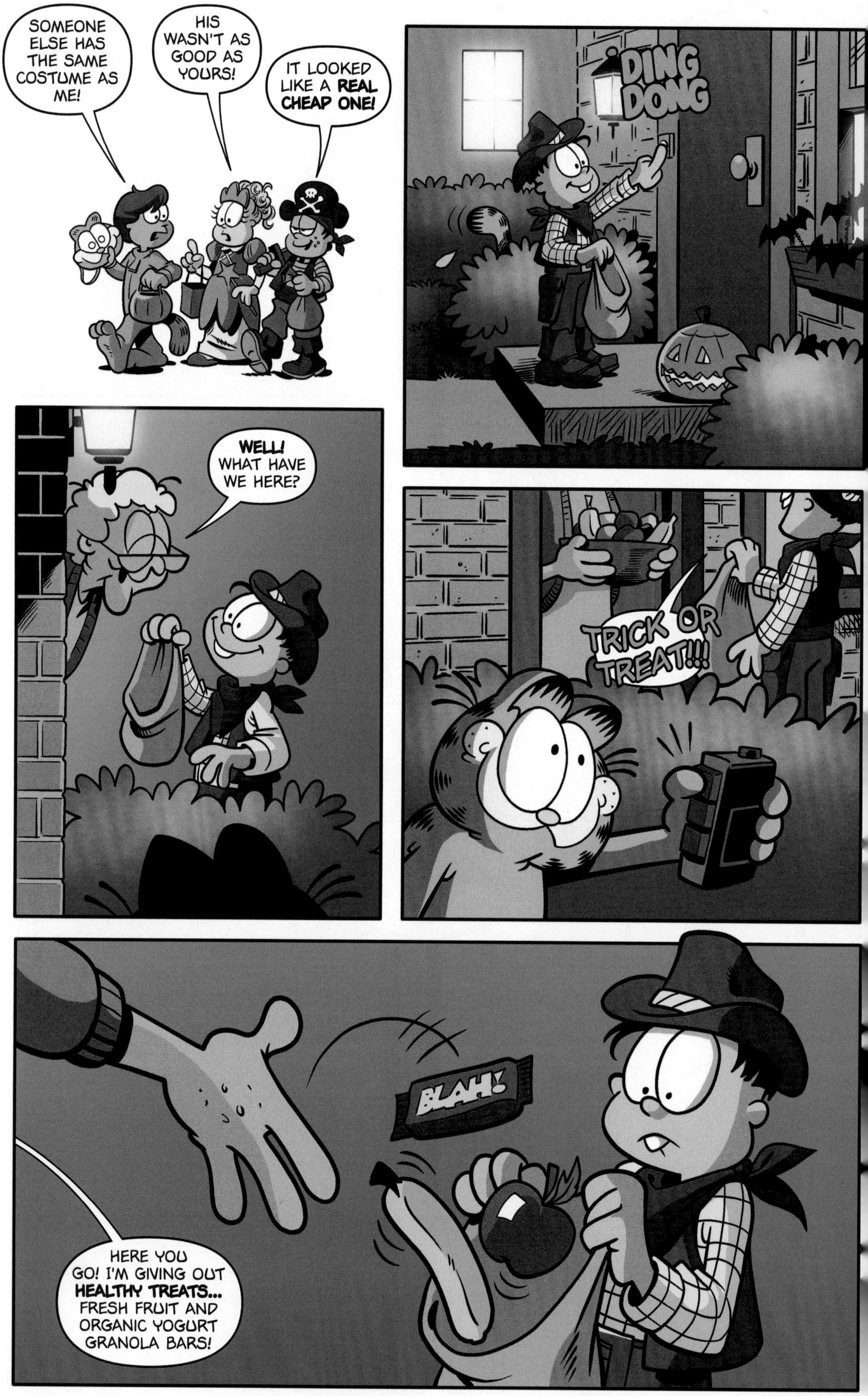
SOMEONE ELSE HAS THE SAME COSTUME AS ME!
HIS WASN'T AS GOOD AS YOURS!
IT LOOKED LIKE A **REAL CHEAP ONE!**
DING DONG
WELL! WHAT HAVE WE HERE?
TRICK OR TREAT!!!
BLAH!
HERE YOU GO! I'M GIVING OUT **HEALTHY TREATS...** FRESH FRUIT AND ORGANIC YOGURT GRANOLA BARS!

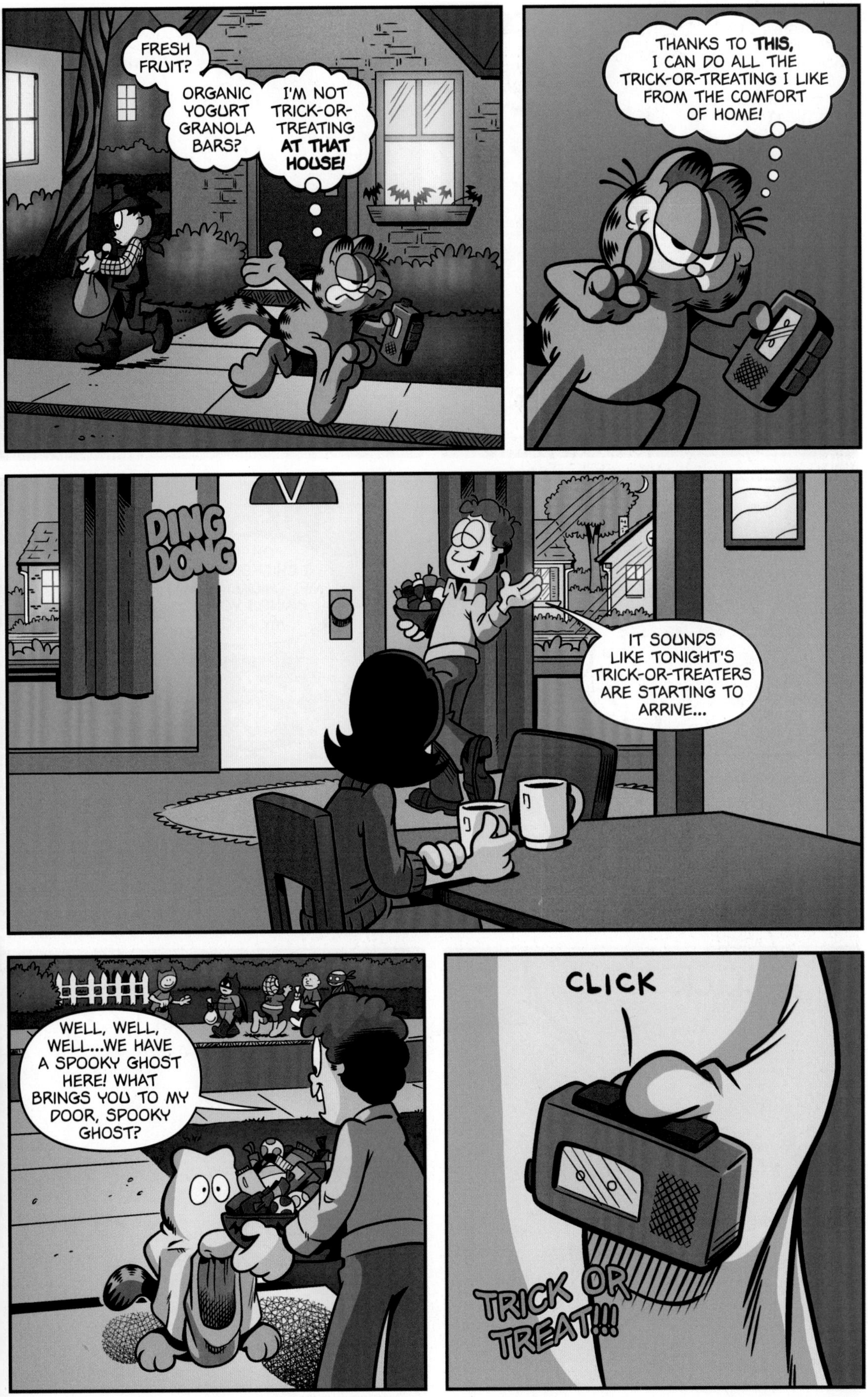
FRESH FRUIT?
ORGANIC YOGURT GRANOLA BARS?
I'M NOT TRICK-OR-TREATING **AT THAT HOUSE!**
THANKS TO **THIS,** I CAN DO ALL THE TRICK-OR-TREATING I LIKE FROM THE COMFORT OF HOME!
DING DONG
IT SOUNDS LIKE TONIGHT'S TRICK-OR-TREATERS ARE STARTING TO ARRIVE...
WELL, WELL, WELL...WE HAVE A SPOOKY GHOST HERE! WHAT BRINGS YOU TO MY DOOR, SPOOKY GHOST?
CLICK
TRICK OR TREAT!!!

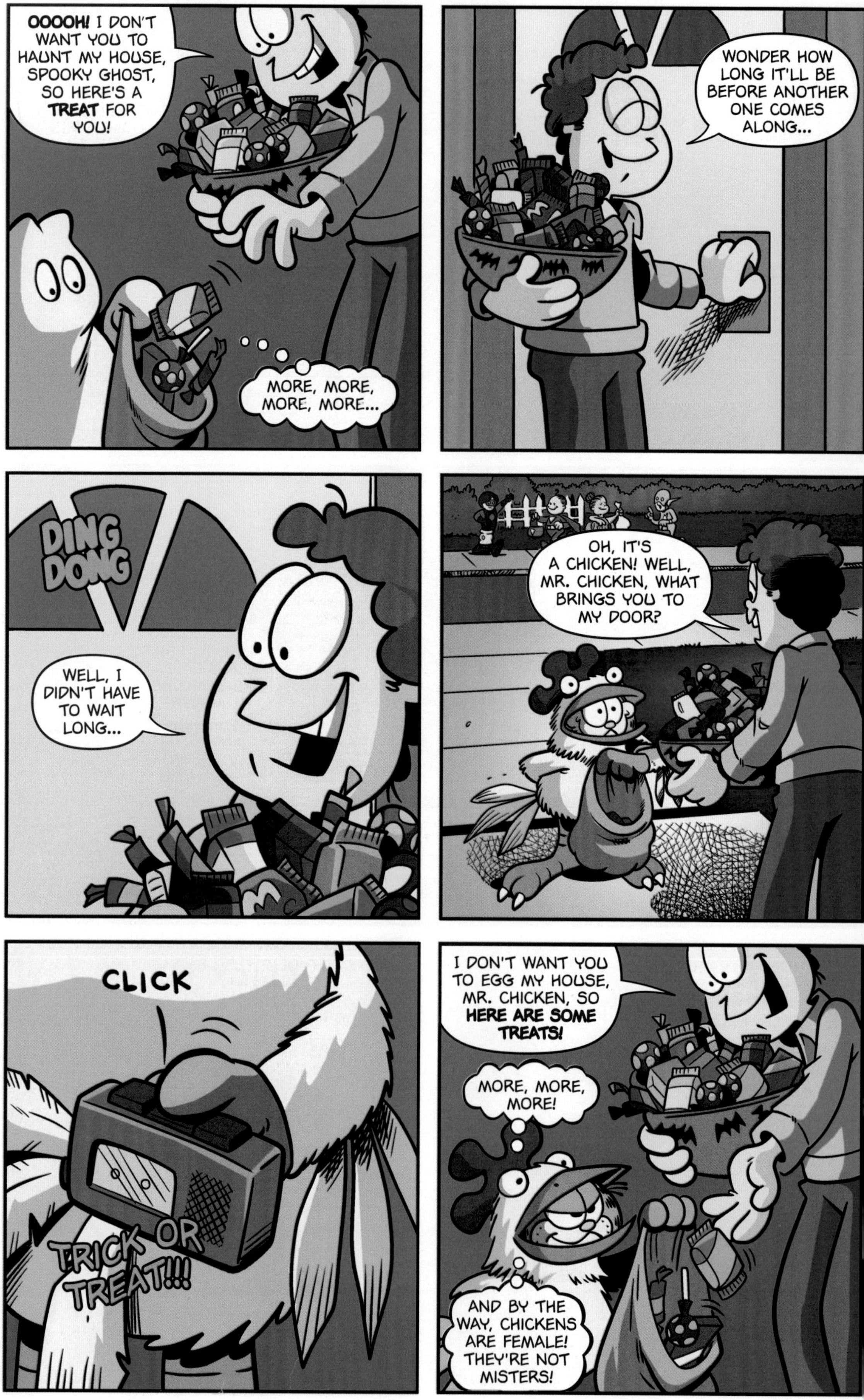
OOOOH! I DON'T WANT YOU TO HAUNT MY HOUSE, SPOOKY GHOST, SO HERE'S A TREAT FOR YOU!
MORE, MORE, MORE, MORE...
WONDER HOW LONG IT'LL BE BEFORE ANOTHER ONE COMES ALONG...
DING DONG
WELL, I DIDN'T HAVE TO WAIT LONG...
OH, IT'S A CHICKEN! WELL, MR. CHICKEN, WHAT BRINGS YOU TO MY DOOR?
CLICK
TRICK OR TREAT!!!
I DON'T WANT YOU TO EGG MY HOUSE, MR. CHICKEN, SO HERE ARE SOME TREATS!
MORE, MORE, MORE!
AND BY THE WAY, CHICKENS ARE FEMALE! THEY'RE NOT MISTERS!

147

149

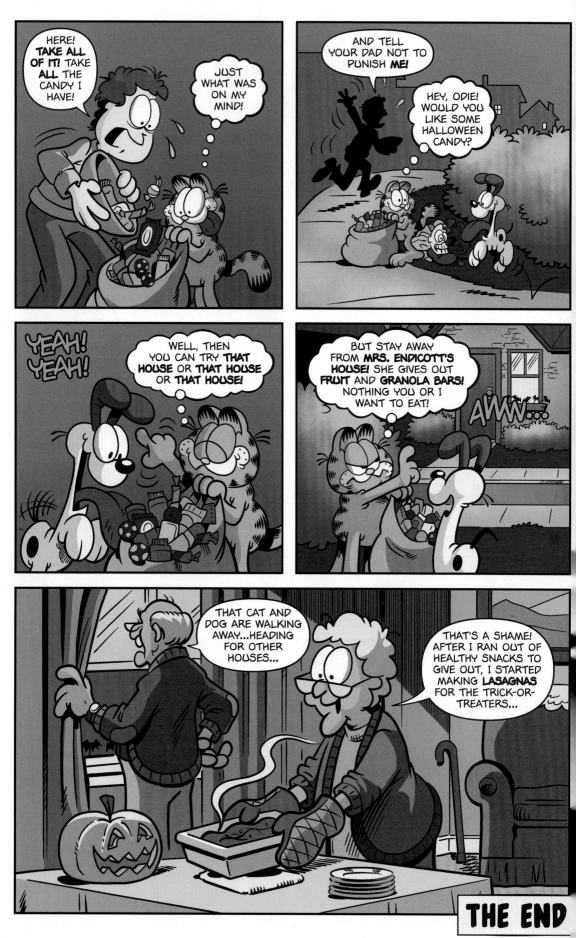

CHAPTER SEVEN

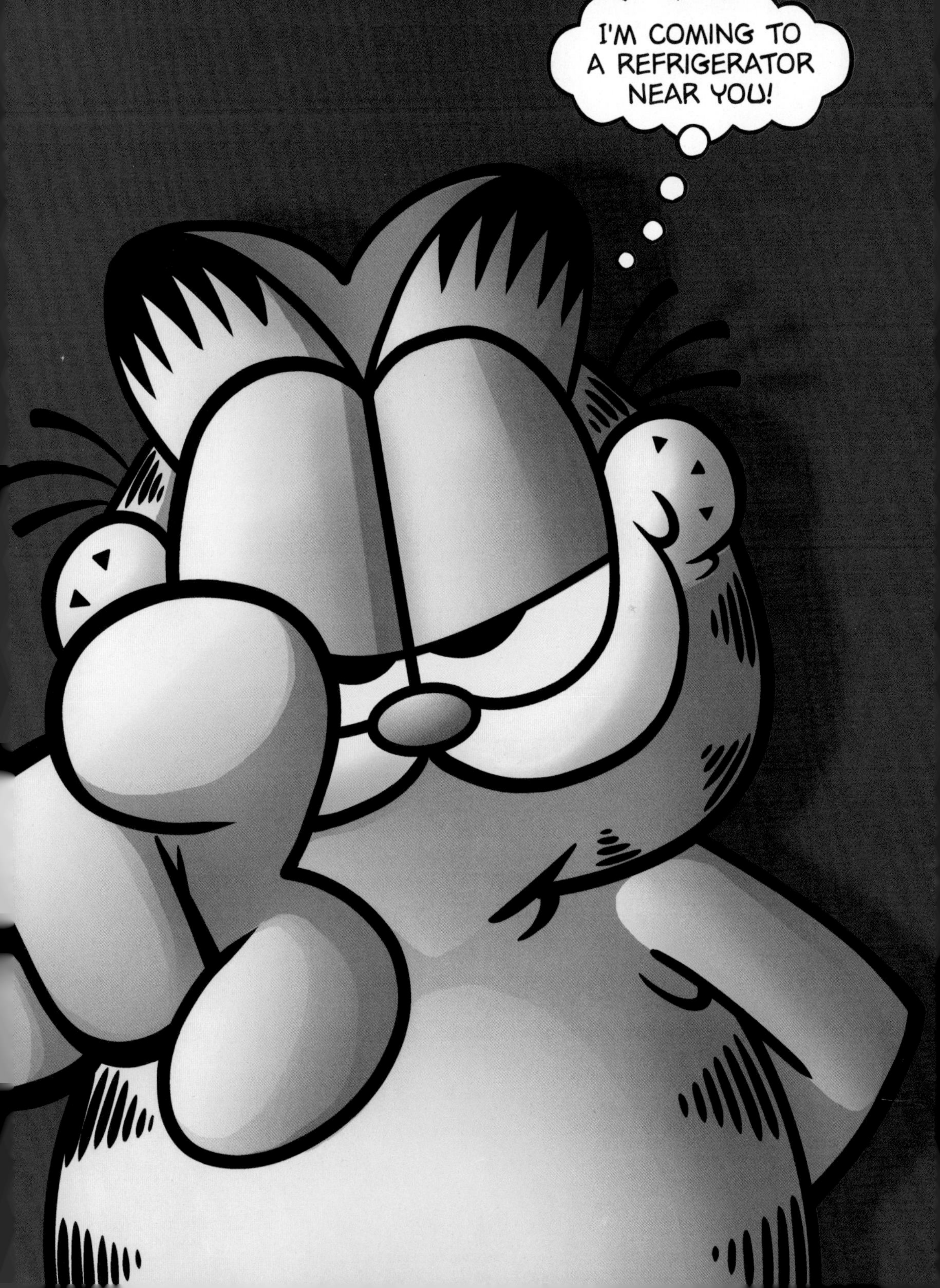

THE CAT WITH NO NAME
THANKSGIVING DAZE

Written by
MARK EVANIER

Art by
ANDY HIRSCH
AND DAN DAVIS
WITH MARK
AND STEPHANIE HEIKE
(Pages 153-164)
MIKE DeCARLO
(Pages 165-174)

Colors by
LISA MOORE

Chapter Break Art by
GARY BARKER
AND DAN DAVIS
WITH LISA MOORE

154

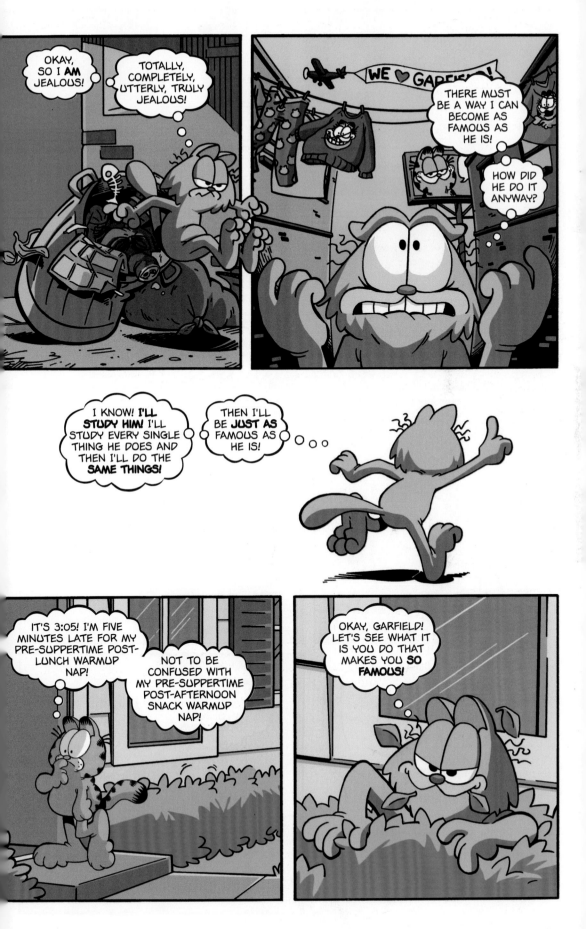

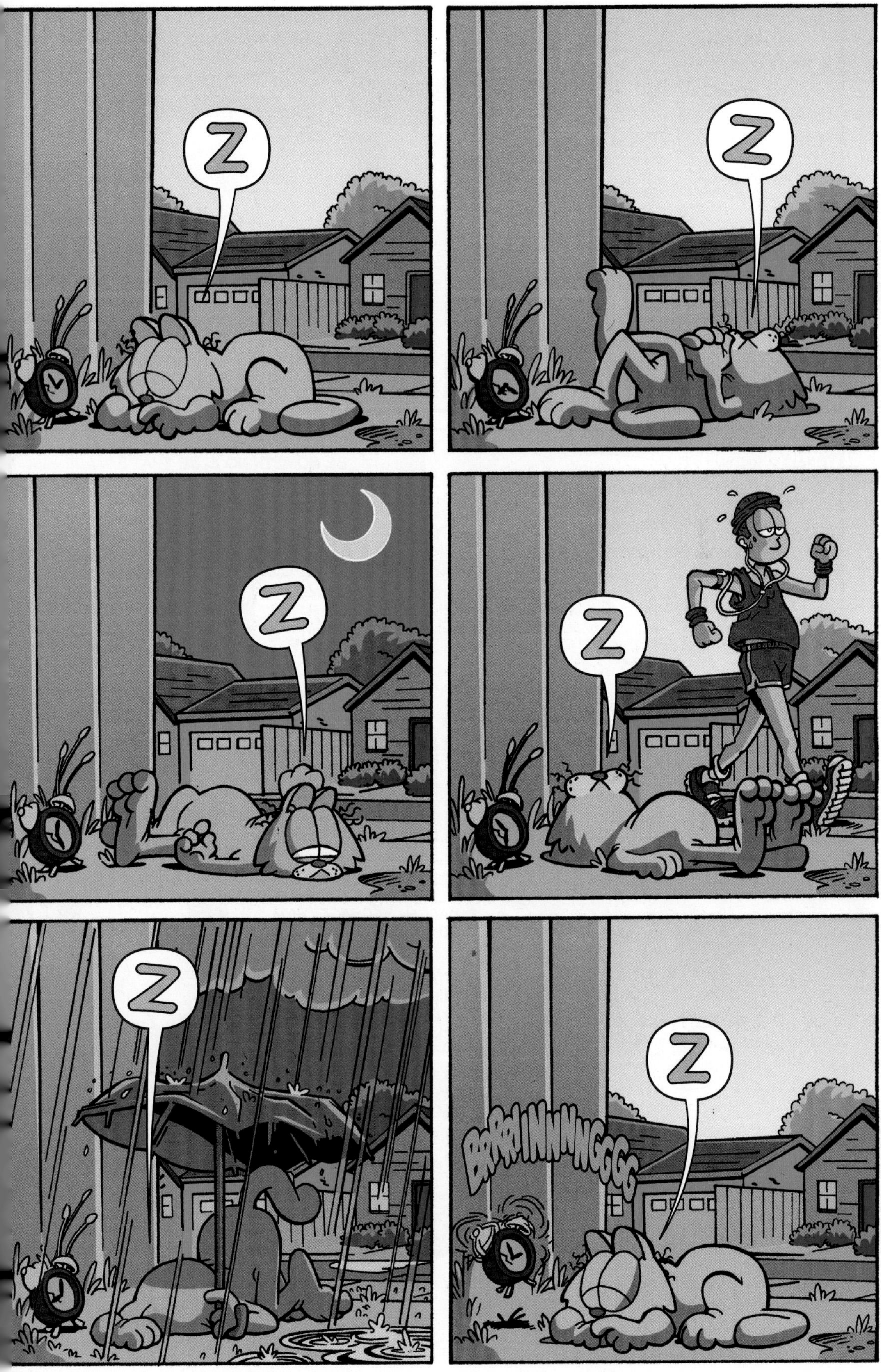
Z
Z
Z
Z
Z
Z
BRRRINNNNGGGG

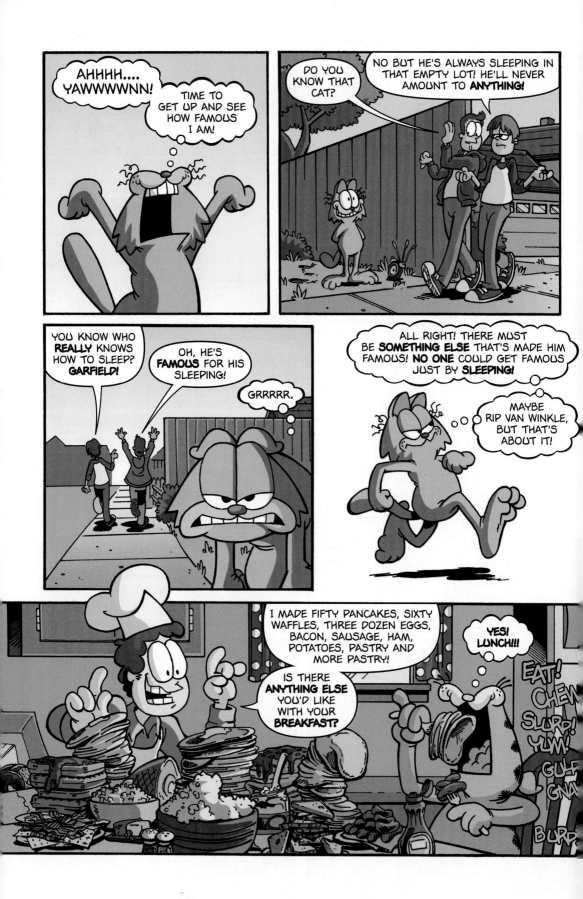

163

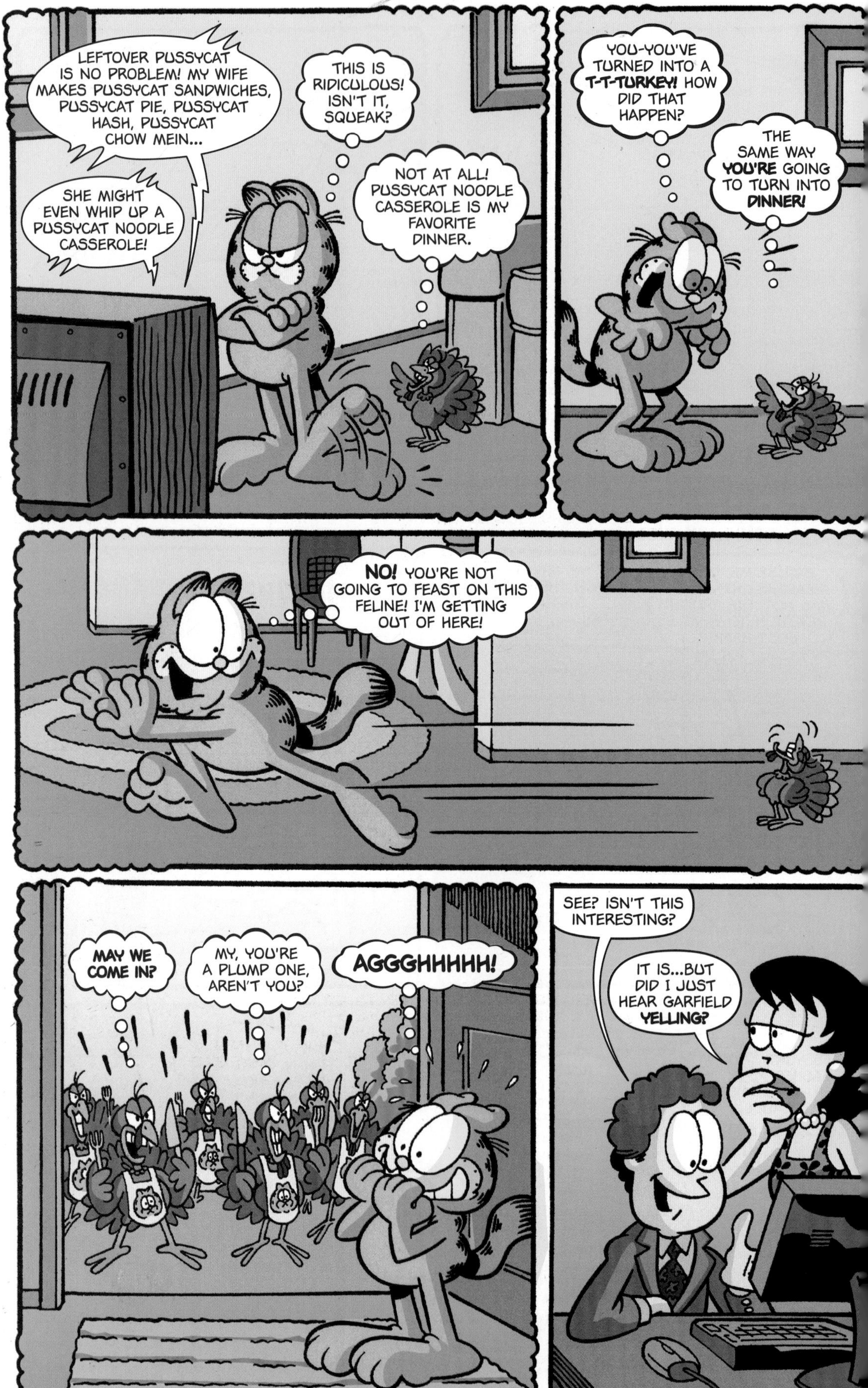
LEFTOVER PUSSYCAT IS NO PROBLEM! MY WIFE MAKES PUSSYCAT SANDWICHES, PUSSYCAT PIE, PUSSYCAT HASH, PUSSYCAT CHOW MEIN...
SHE MIGHT EVEN WHIP UP A PUSSYCAT NOODLE CASSEROLE!
THIS IS RIDICULOUS! ISN'T IT, SQUEAK?
NOT AT ALL! PUSSYCAT NOODLE CASSEROLE IS MY FAVORITE DINNER.
YOU-YOU'VE TURNED INTO A T-T-TURKEY! HOW DID THAT HAPPEN?
THE SAME WAY YOU'RE GOING TO TURN INTO DINNER!
NO! YOU'RE NOT GOING TO FEAST ON THIS FELINE! I'M GETTING OUT OF HERE!
MAY WE COME IN?
MY, YOU'RE A PLUMP ONE, AREN'T YOU?
AGGGHHHHH!
SEE? ISN'T THIS INTERESTING?
IT IS...BUT DID I JUST HEAR GARFIELD YELLING?

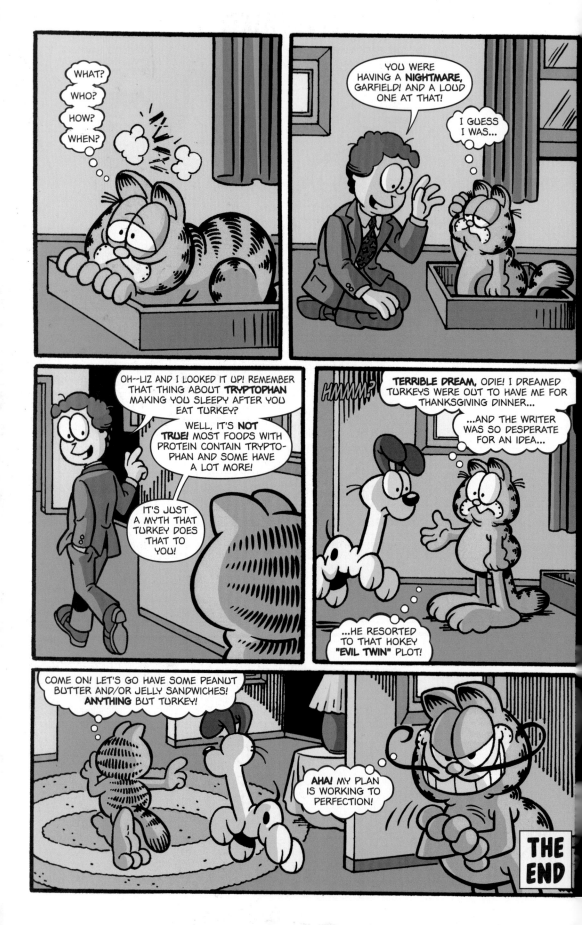

CHAPTER EIGHT

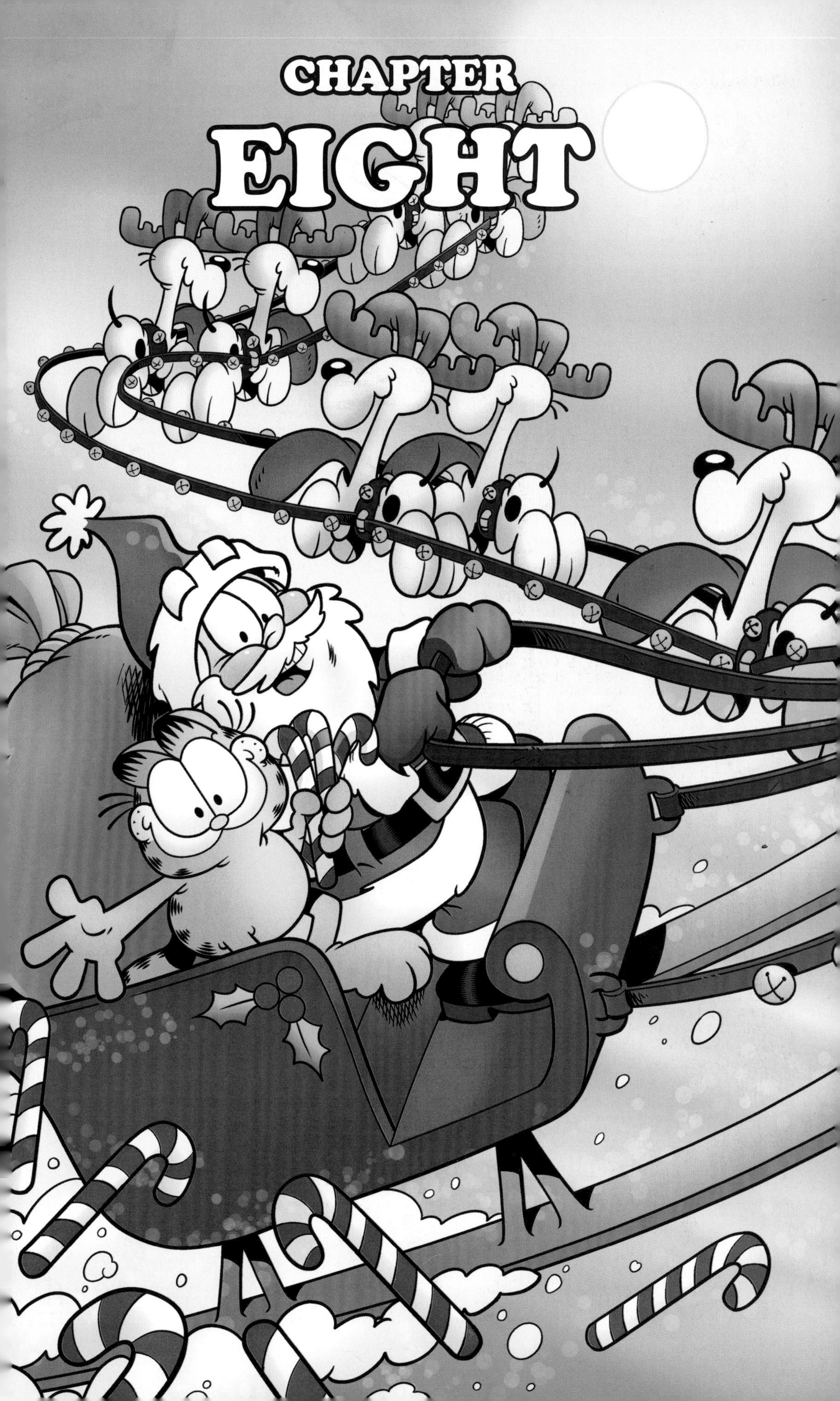

THE NEVER-ENDING TALE OF SANTA MOUSE
SNOW PROBLEM

Written by
MARK EVANIER
(Pages 177-188)
SCOTT NICKEL
(Pages 189-198)

Art by
ANDY HIRSCH
WITH MARK
AND STEPHANIE HEIKE
(Pages 177-188)
MIKE DeCARLO
(Pages 189-198)

Colors by
LISA MOORE

Chapter Break Art by
GARY BARKER
AND DAN DAVIS
WITH LISA MOORE

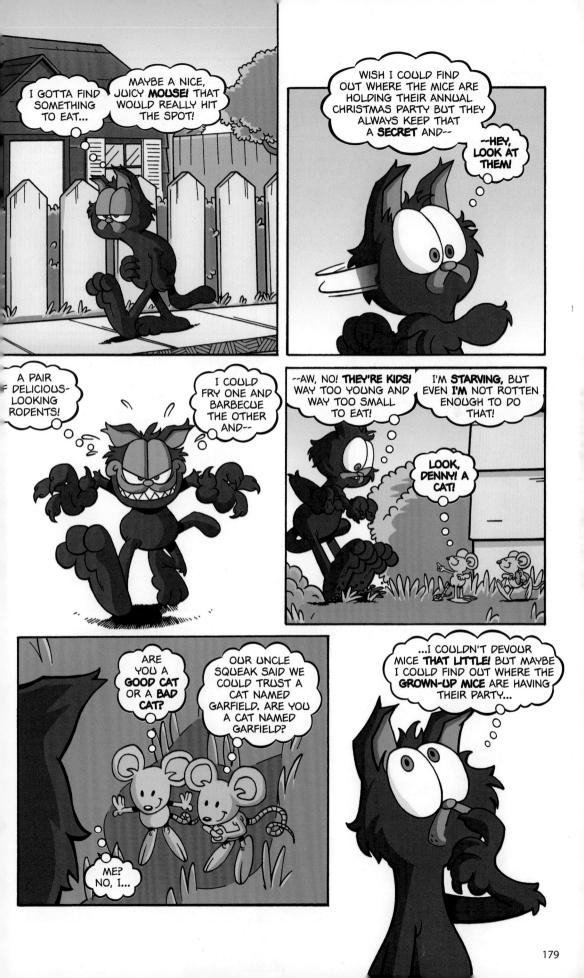

179

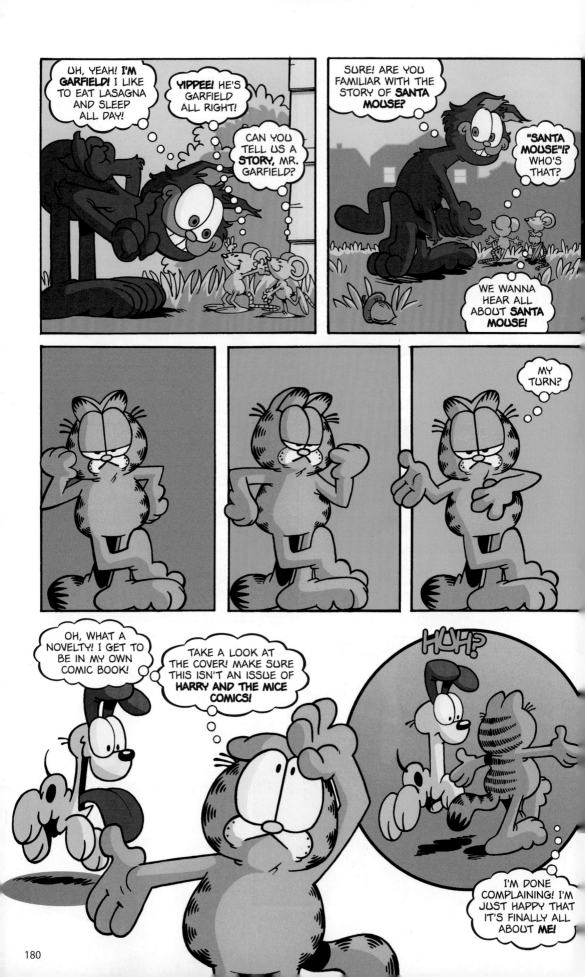

THE END

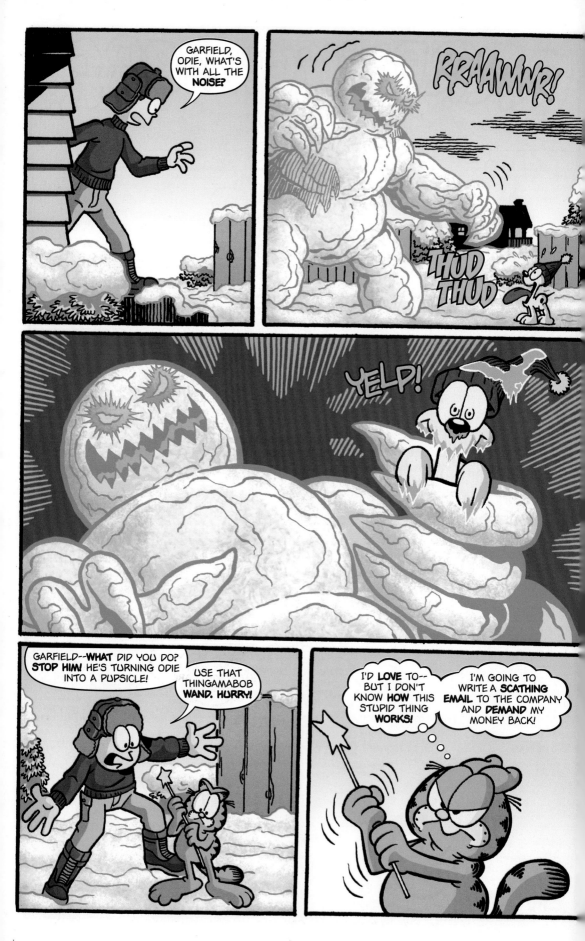

COVER GALLERY

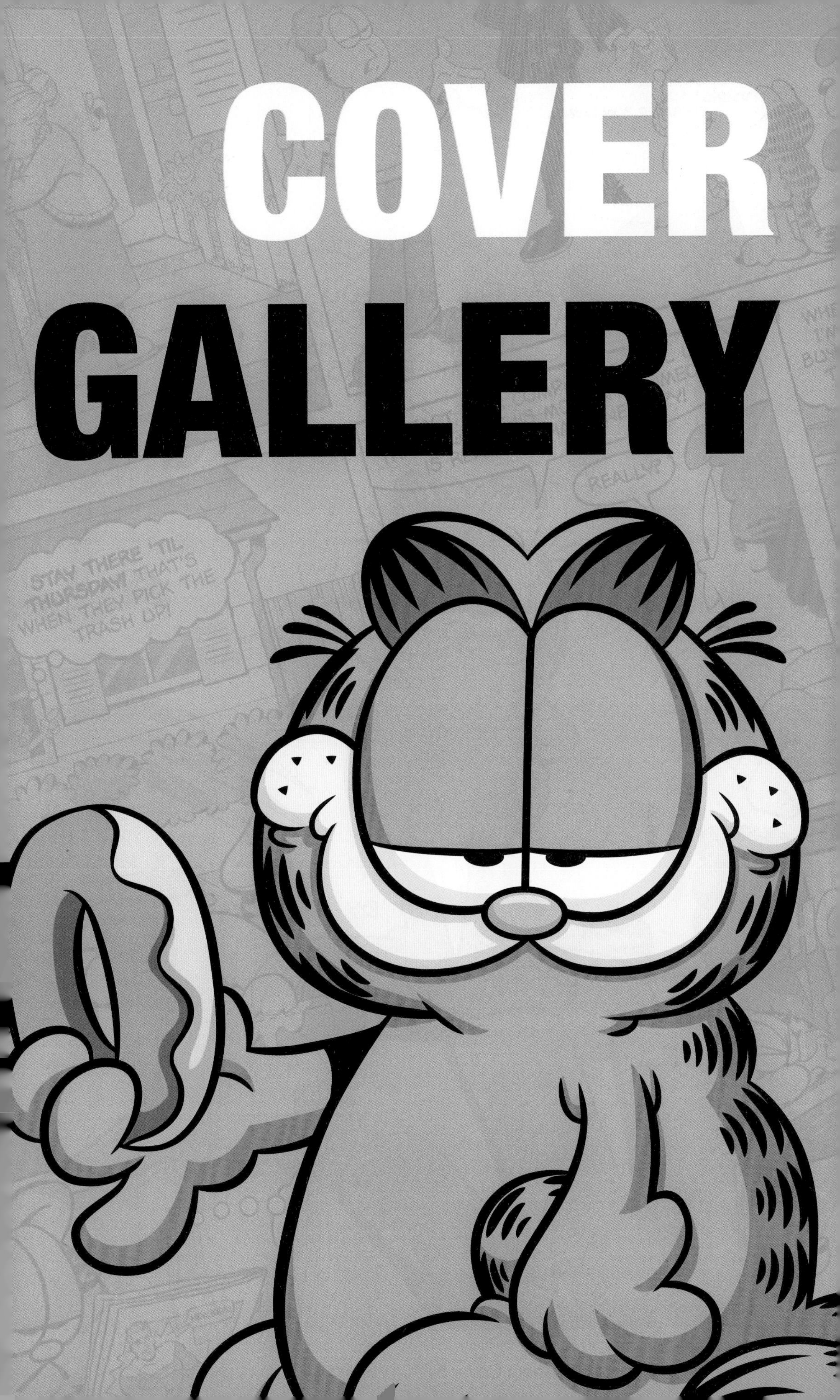
STAY THERE 'TIL THURSDAY! THAT'S WHEN THEY PICK THE TRASH UP!
REALLY?

Garfield #1 Variant Cover by **GARY BARKER** with **BRADEN LAMB**

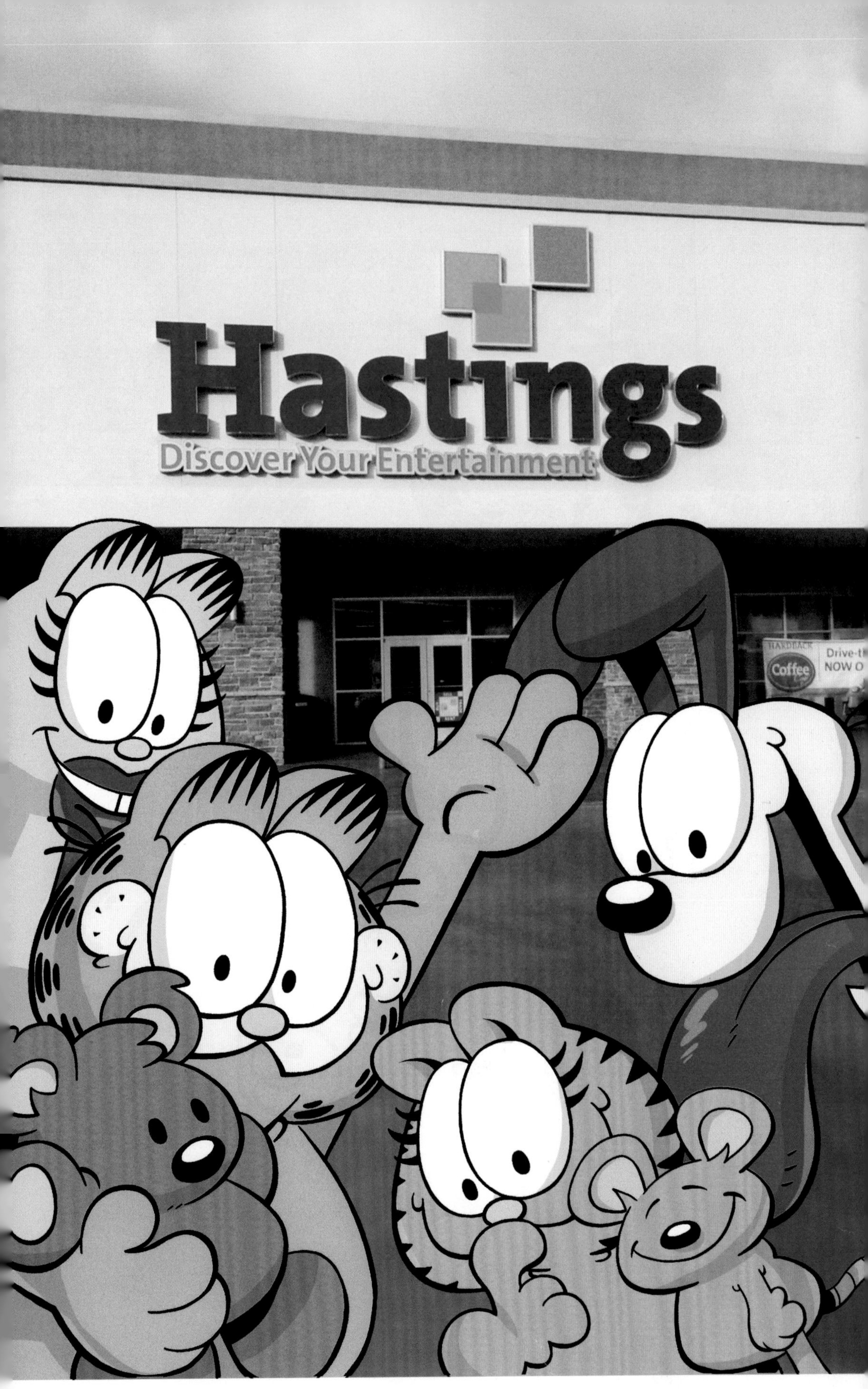
Hastings
Discover Your Entertainment
Coffee
Drive-th
NOW O

Garfield #1 Hastings Exclusive Variant Cover by **GARY BARKER**

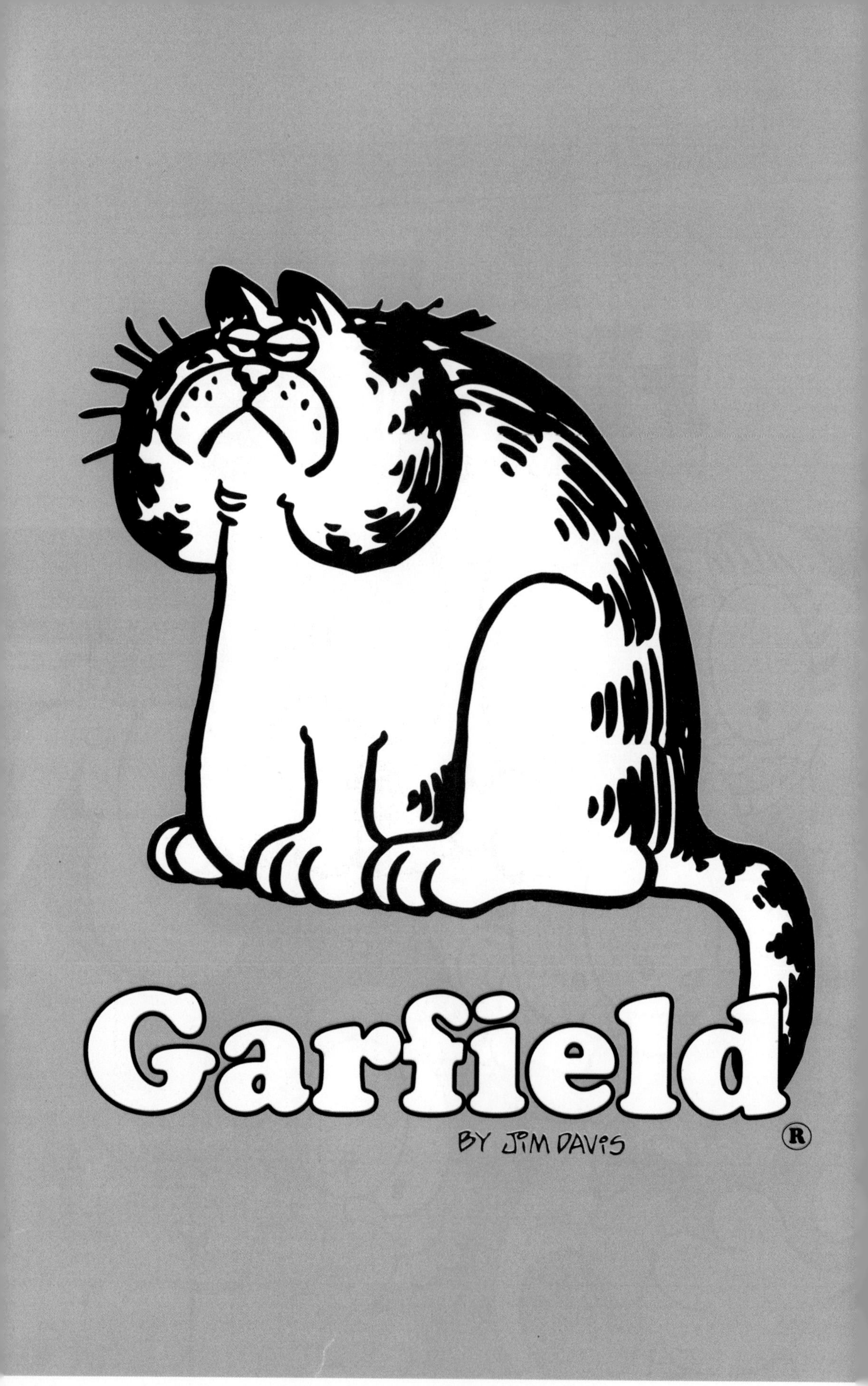
Garfield
BY JIM DAVIS
®

Garfield #1 Variant Cover by **JIM DAVIS**

Garfield #2 Variant Cover by **JIM DAVIS**

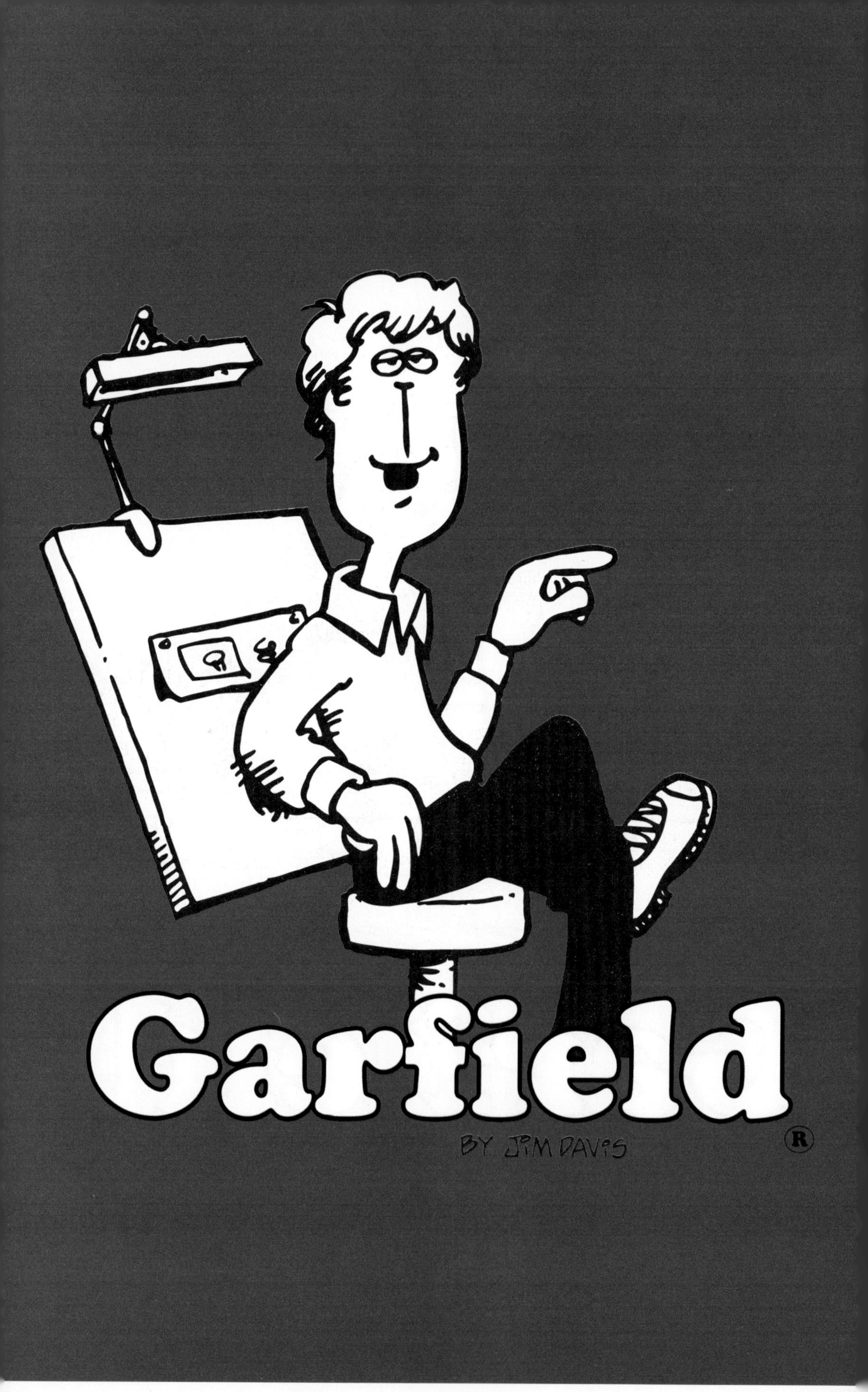
Garfield
BY JIM DAVIS
®

Garfield #3 Variant Cover by **JIM DAVIS**

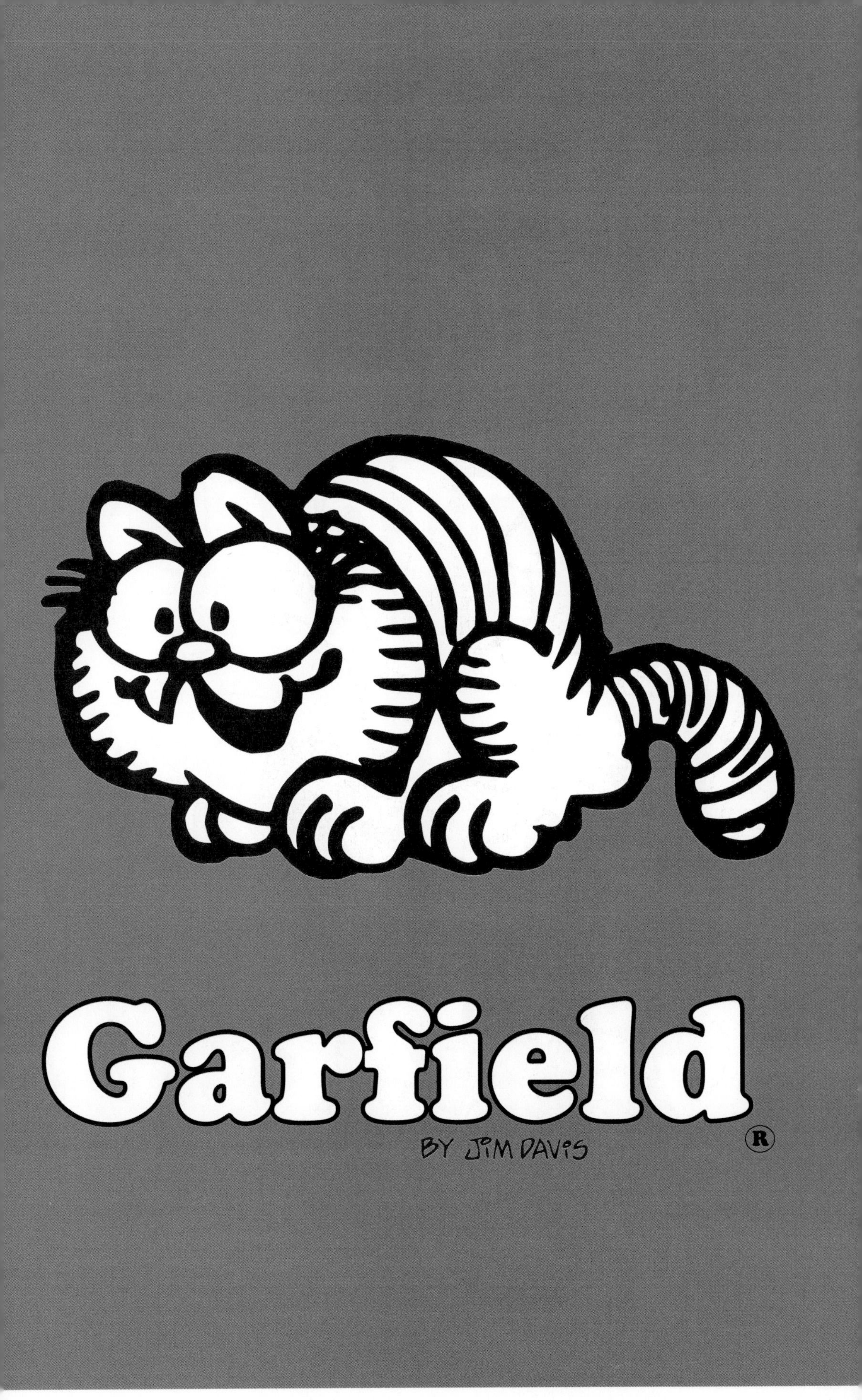
Garfield
BY JIM DAVIS
®

Garfield #4 Variant Cover by **JIM DAVIS**

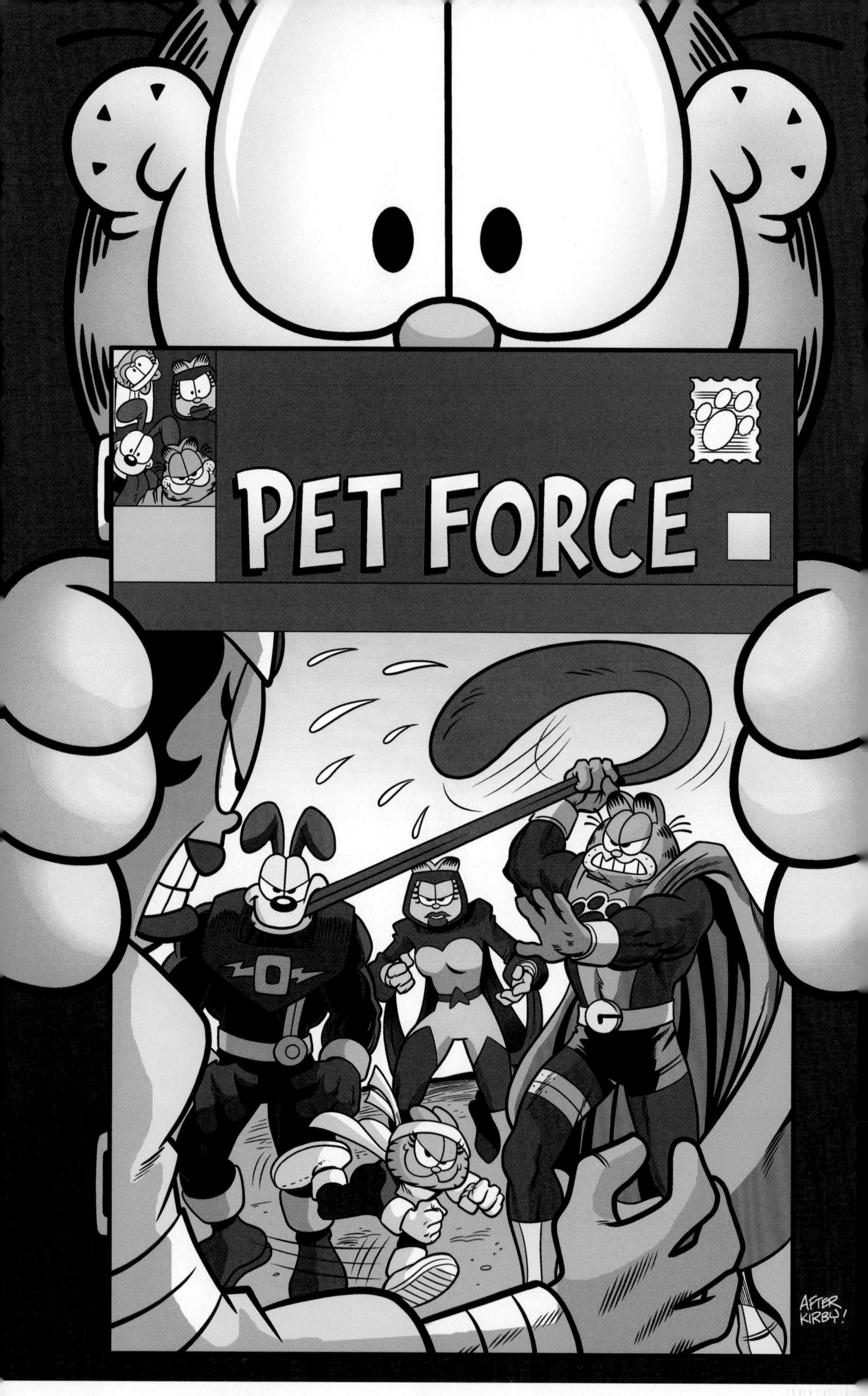
PET FORCE
AFTER KIRBY!

Garfield #5 Variant Cover by **GARY BARKER** and **DAN DAVIS** with **LISA MOORE**

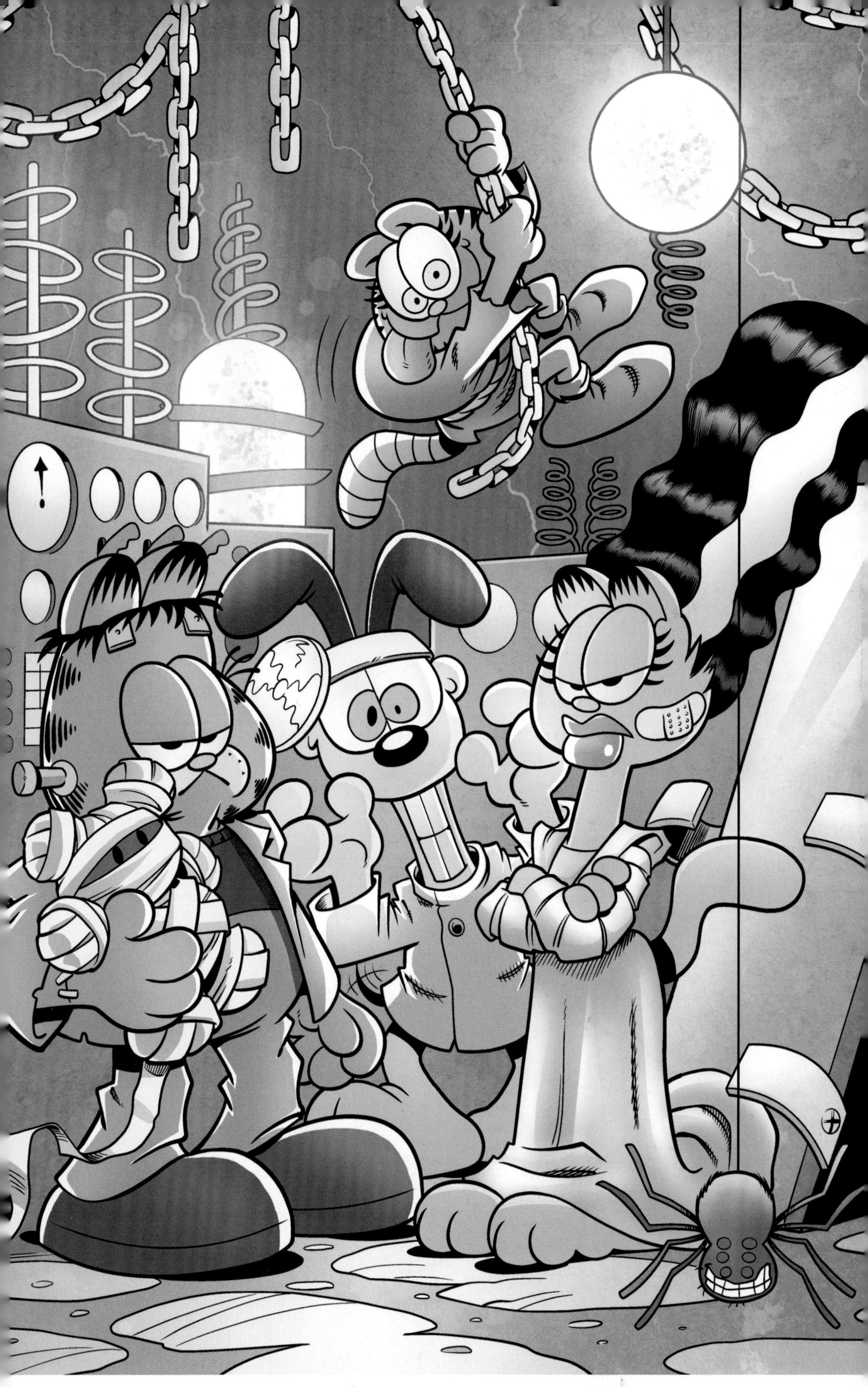

Garfield #6 Variant Cover by **GARY BARKER** and **DAN DAVIS** with **LISA MOORE**

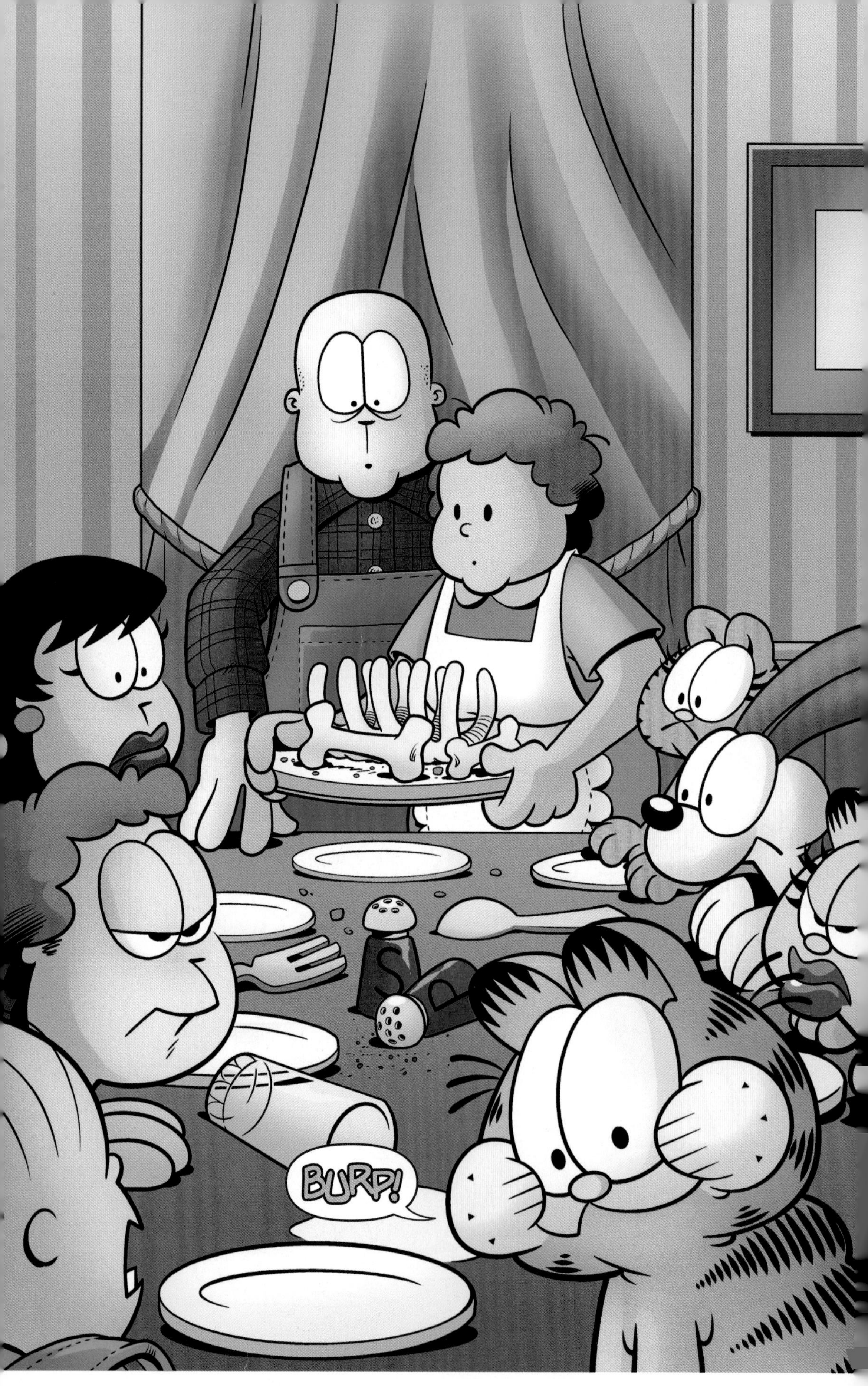
S
P
BURP!

Garfield #7 Variant Cover by **GARY BARKER** and **DAN DAVIS** with **LISA MOORE**

Garfield #8 Variant Cover by **GARY BARKER** and **DAN DAVIS** with **LISA MOORE**

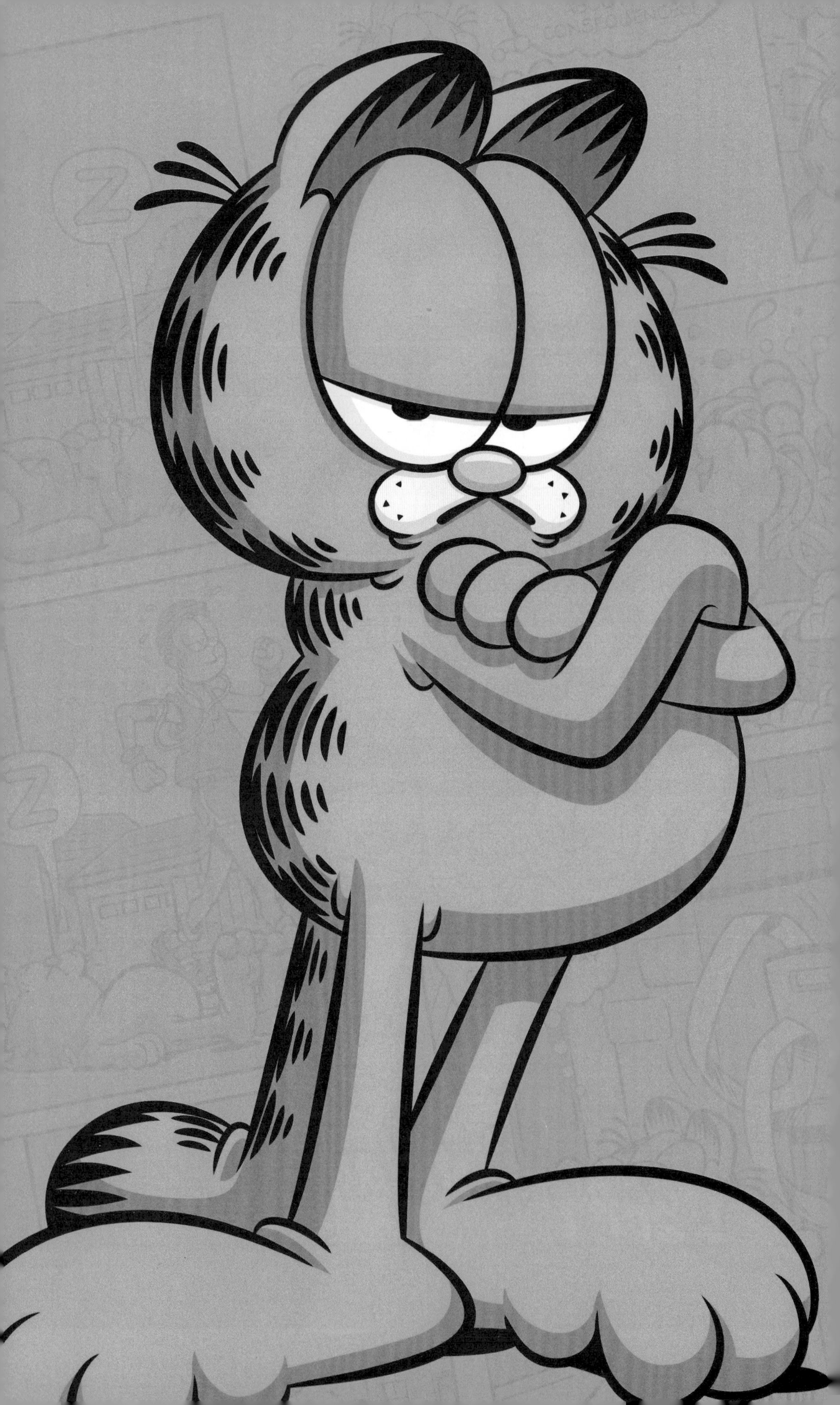

Garfield & Jon
First appearance
June 19, 1978

Odie
First appearance
August 8, 1978

Nermal
First appearance
September 3, 1979

45TH GARFIELD™

IT'S A CAT'S LIFE

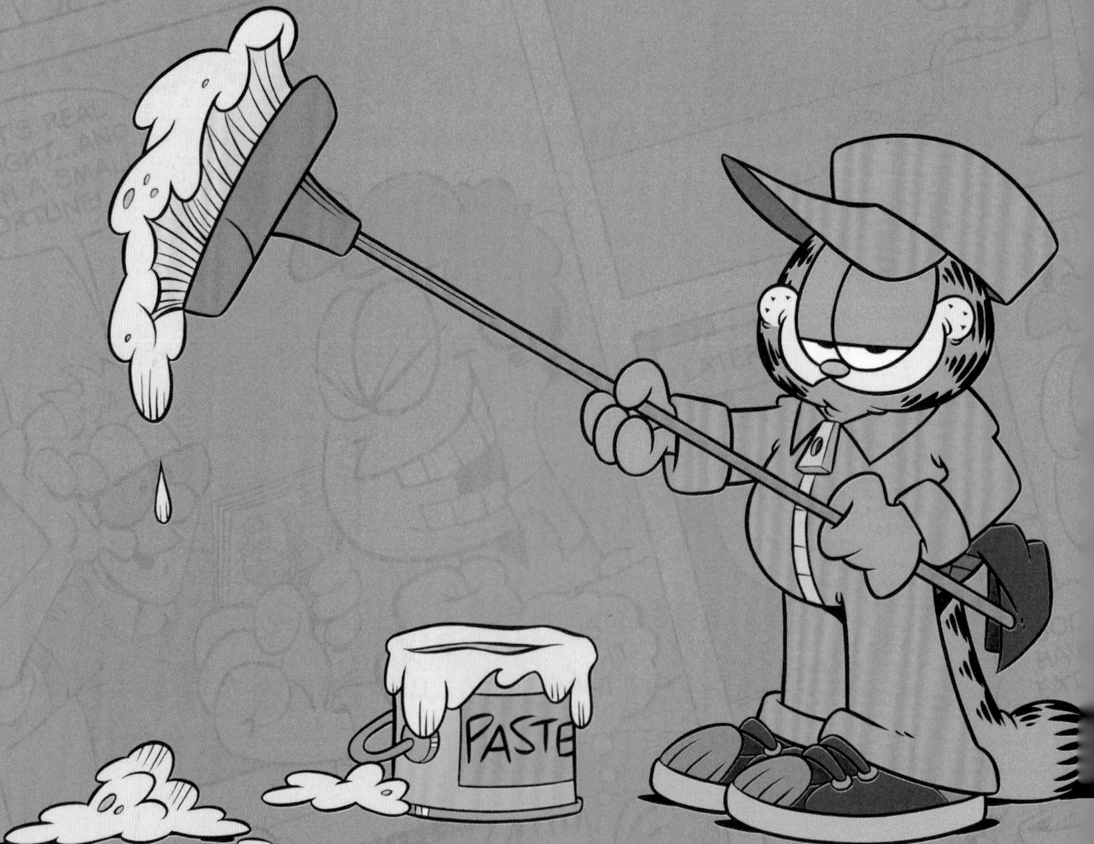
PASTE

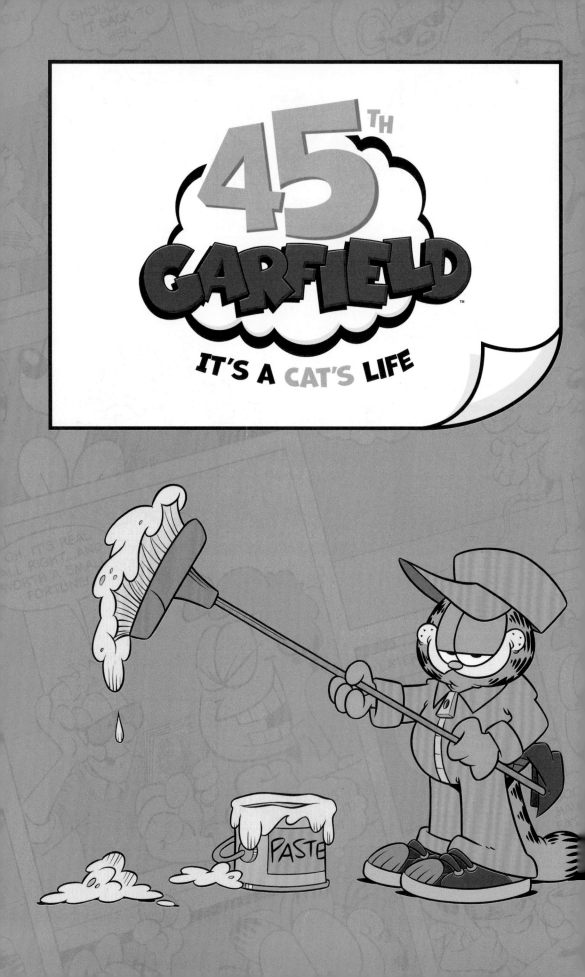

1978

1980

1994

1998

2007

2010

2017

2023

Full Course

Coming Next:

Garfield: Full Course Volume 2

kaboom! **DISCOVER** YOURS

ISBN 978-1-60886-150-7 | $16.99
Available in March 2024!

GARFIELD Copyright © 2023 by Paws, Inc. All Rights Reserved. "GARFIELD" and the GARFIELD characters are trademarks of Paws, Inc.
Based on the Garfield® characters created by Jim Davis. Nickelodeon is a Trademark of Viacom International Inc.

RUGRATS

RUGRATS: VOLUME ONE

AVAILABLE JULY 2024

Everyone's favorite imaginative tikes are back for another adventure. **Tommy, Chuckie, Phil, & Lil** have noticed something—they are being watched. Somehow their parents can see every little thing they can do. They're going to have to find a way to have fun while avoiding the electronic eyes of the babycam! And diapers are flying everywhere after **Grandpa Lou** reads a crazy conspiracy story line that leads **Tommy** to believe that everyone is being replaced by giant lizard people. It's up to the gang to get to the bottom of it all.

Collects the previously published *Rugrats Volume 1* and *Rugrats Volume 2*.

ISBN 978-1-60886-242-9 | $16.99

RUGRATS: VOLUME TWO

AVAILABLE DECEMBER 2024

Collects *Rugrats The Last Token* Graphic Novel, *Rugrats C is for Chanukah*, and *Rugrats R is for Reptar*.

It's a Rugrats family vacation to the mountains, complete with **Grandpa Lou** and **Boris** arguing over which holiday is better—Chanukah or Christmas. **Boris** is determined to win and starts giving **Tommy** and the babies a history lesson on the Golem which sets imaginations ablaze.

Tommy, Chuckie, Phil & Lil now feel that they have to save Chanukah from the Golem before it can steal the holiday away for good! Back at the Pickles house, babies and adults come together to share their favorite **Reptar** stories when the power goes out! **Stu and Drew** take the babies to the local arcade for a relaxing day of pizza and games. But the arcade's token stock goes down to one and a frenzy breaks loose upon the arcade floor. When **Tommy** gets his hands on the only remaining token left in the building, the noble fellowship of babies take on an epic quest to save the day.

kaboom! **DISCOVER** YOURS

nickelodeon ©2023 Viacom International Inc. All Rights Reserved.

🐦 /boomstudios   f /BOOMStudioscomics   📷 /boom_studios
▶ /BOOMStudiosInc   ♪ /boomstudios

WWW.BOOM-STUDIOS.COM

EVERY DAY IS A DANGEROUS DAY WHEN YOU'RE ROCKO THE WALLABY...

ROCKO'S MODERN LIFE ™

ROCKO'S MODERN LIFE...AND AFTER LIFE

Unemployed, Rocko has to resort to desperate measures just to pay the bills, working odd jobs, and even taking in a hard-partying sloth as a roommate. Rocko and the gang will need to navigate the modern dating life, and Spunky's rise to internet stardom. But his troubles don't just stop there—will Rocko survive the zombie outbreak that's taken over his hometown?!

Collects *Rocko's Modern Life* #1-#8 and *Rocko's Modern Afterlife* #1-#4.

AVAILABLE AUGUST 2024!
ISBN 978-1-60886-471-3 | $18.99

kaboom! **DISCOVER** YOURS

nickelodeon
©2023 Viacom International Inc. All Rights Reserved.

🐦 /boomstudios   f /BOOMStudioscomics   📷 /boom_stu
▶ /BOOMStudiosInc   ♪ /boomst

WWW.BOOM-STUDIOS.CO